Bloo

1.00

TOPS BESTSELLER LISTS
ACROSS THE NATION!

The New York Times   The Los Angeles Times
The Washington Post   The Minneapolis Tribune
The Pittsburgh Press The Milwaukee Journal
The Chicago Tribune   Publishers Weekly
        American Library Assn.
        Newsday

When the daughter
of one of the world's richest men
inherits his multi-billion-dollar business,
she inherits his position
at the top of the company
and at the top of the victim's list
of his murderer!

SIDNEY SHELDON'S NEWEST NOVEL—
AND HIS GREATEST.

The Incomparable Sidney Sheldon

Best known today for his exciting, blockbuster novels, Sidney Sheldon is the author of *The Other Side of Midnight, A Stranger in the Mirror, Bloodline, Rage of Angels, Master of the Game, If Tomorrow Comes,* and *Windmills of the Gods.* All have been number one international bestsellers. His first and only other book, *The Naked Face,* was acclaimed by the *New York Times* as "the best first mystery of the year." Most of his novels have become major feature films or TV mini-series, and there are 100 million copies of his books in print throughout the world. However, before he ever authored a book, Sidney Sheldon had won a Tony Award for Broadway's *Redhead* and an Academy Award for *The Bachelor and the Bobby Soxer.* He wrote the screenplays for twenty-three motion pictures including *Easter Parade* (with Judy Garland) and *Annie Get Your Gun.* In addition, he penned six other Broadway hits and created four long-running television series including "Hart to Hart" and "I Dream of Jeannie," which he also produced and directed. A writer who has delighted millions with his award-winning plays, movies, novels, and television shows, Sidney Sheldon reigns as one of the most popular storytellers of all time.

SIDNEY SHELDON

Bloodline

WARNER BOOKS

A Warner Communications Company

A Warner Communications Company

Printed in the United States of America

First Warner Books Printing: February, 1979

Reissued: January, 1986

45   44   43   42

For Natalie
with love

Acknowledgments

While this is a work of fiction, the backgrounds are authentic, and I wish to express my gratitude to those who so generously contributed to my research. If, in adapting their information to the requirements of a novel, I have found it necessary to expand or contract certain time elements, I take full responsibility. My deepest appreciation goes to

Dr. Margaret M. McCarron
Associate Medical Director
Los Angeles County,
  University of Southern California

Dean Brady, USC Pharmacy School

Dr. Gregory A. Thompson
Director, Drug Information Center
Los Angeles County,
  University of Southern California

Dr. Bernd W. Schulze
Drug Information Center
Los Angeles County,
  University of Southern California

Dr. Judy Flesh

Urs Jäggi, Hoffmann-La Roche & Co., A. G., Basel

Dr. Gunter Siebel, Schering A. G., Berlin

The Criminal Investigation Divisions
  of Scotland Yard, Zurich and Berlin

Charles Walford, Sotheby Parke Bernet, London

And to Jorja, who makes all things possible.

"The physician will carefully prepare a mixture of crocodile dung, lizard flesh, bat's blood and camel's spit . . ."

—from a papyrus listing 811 prescriptions used by the Egyptians in 1550 B.C.

BOOK
ONE

CHAPTER

1

Istanbul.
Saturday, September 5.
Ten p.m.

He was seated in the dark, alone, behind the desk of Hajib Kafir, staring unseeingly out of the dusty office window at the timeless minarets of Istanbul. He was a man who was at home in a dozen capitals of the world, but Istanbul was one of his favorite cities. Not the tourist Istanbul of Beyoglu Street, or the gaudy Lalezab Bar of the Hilton, but the out-of-the-way places that only the Moslems knew: the *yalis*, and the small markets beyond the *souks*, and the Telli Baba, the cemetery where only one person was buried, and the people came to pray to him.

His waiting had the patience of a hunter, the quiet stillness of a man in control of his body and his emotions. He was Welsh, with the dark, stormy good looks of his ancestors. He had black hair and a strong face, and quick intelligent eyes that were a deep blue. He was over six feet tall, with the lean muscular body of a man who kept himself in good physical condition. The office was filled with the odors of Hajib Kafir, his sickly sweet tobacco, his acrid Turkish coffee, his fat, oily body. Rhys Williams was unaware of them. He was thinking about the telephone call he had received from Chamonix an hour earlier.

". . . A terrible accident! Believe me, Mr. Williams, we are all devastated. It happened so quickly that there was no chance to save him. Mr. Roffe was killed instantly . . ."

Sam Roffe, president of Roffe and Sons, the second largest pharmaceutical company in the world, a multibillion-dollar dynasty that girdled the globe. It was impossible to think of Sam Roffe as being dead. He had always been so vital, so full of life and energy, a man on the move, living in airplanes that raced him to company factories and offices all over the world, where he solved problems others could not deal with, created new concepts, pushed everyone to do more, to do better. Even though he had married, and fathered a child, his only real interest had been the business. Sam Roffe had been a brilliant and extraordinary man. Who could replace him? Who was capable of running the enormous empire he had left? Sam Roffe had not chosen an heir apparent. But then, he had not planned to die at fifty-two. He had thought there would be plenty of time.

And now his time had run out.

The lights in the office suddenly flashed on and Rhys Williams looked toward the doorway, momentarily blinded.

"Mr. Williams! I did not know anyone was here."

It was Sophie, one of the company secretaries, who was assigned to Rhys Williams whenever he was in Istanbul. She was Turkish, in her middle twenties, with an attractive face and a lithe, sensuous body, rich with promise. She had let Rhys know in subtle, ancient ways that she was available to bring him whatever pleasures he wished, whenever he desired them, but Rhys was not interested.

Now she said, "I returned to finish some letters for Mr. Kafir." She added softly, "Perhaps there is something I can do for you?"

As she moved closer to the desk, Rhys could sense the musky smell of a wild animal in season.

"Where is Mr. Kafir?"

Sophie shook her head regretfully. "He has left for the day." She smoothed the front of her dress with the palms of soft, clever hands. "Can I help you in some way?" Her eyes were dark and moist.

"Yes," Rhys said. "Find him."

She frowned. "I have no idea where he could—"

"Try the Kervansaray, or the Mermara." It would probably be the former, where one of Hajib Kafir's mistresses worked as a belly dancer. Although you never knew with Kafir, Rhys thought. He might even be with his wife.

Sophie was apologetic. "I will try, but I am afraid I—"

"Explain to him that if he's not here in one hour, he no longer has a job."

The expression on her face changed. "I will see what I can do, Mr. Williams." She started toward the door.

"Turn out the lights."

Somehow, it was easier to sit in the dark with his thoughts. The image of Sam Roffe kept intruding. Mont Blanc should have been an easy climb this time of the year, early September. Sam had tried the climb before, but storms had kept him from reaching the peak.

"I'll plant the company flag up there this time," he had promised Rhys, jokingly.

And then the telephone call a short while ago as Rhys was checking out of the Pera Palace. He could hear the agitated voice on the telephone. ". . . They were doing a traverse over a glacier. . . . Mr. Roffe lost his footing and his rope broke. . . . He fell into a bottomless crevasse . . ."

Rhys could visualize Sam's body smashing against the unforgiving ice, hurtling downward into the crevasse. He forced his mind away from the scene. That was the past. There was the present to worry about now. The members of Sam Roffe's family had to be notified of his death, and they were scattered in various parts of the world. A press announcement had to be prepared. The news was going to travel through international financial circles like a shock wave. With the company in the midst of a financial crisis, it was vital that the impact of Sam Roffe's death be minimized as much as possible. That would be Rhys's job.

Rhys Williams had first met Sam Roffe nine years earlier. Rhys, then twenty-five, had been sales manager for a small drug firm. He was brilliant and innovative, and as the company had expanded, Rhys's reputation had quickly spread. He was offered a job at Roffe and Sons and when he turned it down, Sam Roffe bought the company Rhys worked for and sent for him. Even now he could recall the overwhelming power of Sam Roffe's presence at their first meeting.

"You belong here at Roffe and Sons," Sam Roffe

20

had informed him. "That's why I bought that horse-and-buggy outfit you were with."

Rhys had found himself flattered and irritated at the same time. "Suppose I don't want to stay?"

Sam Roffe had smiled and said confidently, "You'll want to stay. You and I have something in common, Rhys. We're both ambitious. We want to own the world. I'm going to show you how."

The words were magic, a promised feast for the fierce hunger that burned in the young man, for he knew something that Sam Roffe did not: There was no Rhys Williams. He was a myth that had been created out of desperation and poverty and despair.

He had been born near the coalfields of Gwent and Carmarthen, the red scarred valleys of Wales where layers of sandstone and saucer-shaped beds of limestone and coal puckered the green earth. He grew up in a fabled land where the very names were poetry: Brecon and Pen-y Fan and Penderyn and Glyncorrwg and Maesteg. It was a land of legend, where the coal buried deep in the ground had been created 280 million years before, where the landscape was once covered with so many trees that a squirrel could travel from Brecon Beacons to the sea without ever touching the ground. But the industrial revolution had come along and the beautiful green trees were chopped down by the charcoal burners to feed the insatiable fires of the iron industry.

The young boy grew up with the heroes of another time and another world. Robert Farrer, burned at the stake by the Roman Catholic Church because he would not take a vow of celibacy and abandon his wife; King Hywel the Good, who brought the law to Wales in the tenth century; the fierce warrior Brychen who sired twelve sons and twenty-four daughters and savagely put down all attacks on his kingdom. It was a land of glorious histories in which the lad had been raised. But it was not all glory. Rhys's ancestors were miners, every one of them, and the young boy used to listen to the tales of hell that his father and his uncles recounted. They talked of the terrible times when there was no work, when the rich coalfields of Gwent and Carmarthen had been closed in a bitter fight between the companies and the miners, and the miners were debased by a poverty that eroded ambition and pride, that sapped a man's spirit and strength and finally made him surrender.

When the mines were open, it was another kind of hell. Most of Rhys's family had died in the mines. Some had perished in the bowels of the earth, others had coughed their blackened lungs away. Few had lived past the age of thirty.

Rhys used to listen to his father and his aging young uncles discussing the past, the cave-ins and the cripplings and the strikes; talking of the good times and the bad, and to the young boy they seemed the same. All bad. The thought of spending his years in the darkness of the earth appalled Rhys. He knew he had to escape.

He ran away from home when he was twelve. He left the valleys of coal and went to the coast, to Sully Ranny Bay and Lavernock, where the rich tourists flocked, and the young boy fetched and carried and made himself useful, helping ladies down the steep cliffs to the beach, lugging heavy picnic baskets, driving a pony cart at Penarth, and working at the amusement park at Whitmore Bay.

He was only a few hours away from home, but the distance could not be measured. The people here were from another world. Rhys Williams had never imagined such beautiful people or such glorious finery. Each woman looked like a queen to him and the men were all elegant and splendid. This was the world where he belonged, and there was nothing he would not do to make it his.

By the time Rhys Williams was fourteen, he had saved enough money to pay for his passage to London. He spent the first three days simply walking around the huge city, staring at everything, hungrily drinking in the incredible sights and the sounds and the smells.

His first job was as a delivery boy at a draper's shop. There were two male clerks, superior beings both, and a female clerk, who made the young Welsh boy's heart sing every time he looked at her. The men treated Rhys as he was meant to be treated, like dirt. He was a curiosity. He dressed peculiarly, had abominable manners and spoke with an incomprehensible accent. They could not even pronounce his name. They called him Rice, and Rye, and Rise. "It's pronounced Reese," Rhys kept telling them.

The girl took pity on him. Her name was Gladys Simpkins and she shared a tiny flat in Tooting with three other girls. One day she allowed the young boy to walk her home after work and invited him in for a cup of tea. Young Rhys was overcome with nervousness. He had thought this was going to be his first sexual experience, but when he began to put his arm around Gladys, she stared at him a moment, then laughed. "I'm not giving none of that to you," she said. "But I'll give you some advice. If you

23

want to make somethin' of yourself, get yourself some proper clothes and a bit of education and learn yourself some manners." She studied the thin, passionate young face and looked into Rhys's deep blue eyes, and said softly, "You're gonna be a bit of all right when you grow up."

If you want to make somethin' of yourself . . . That was the moment when the fictitious Rhys Williams was born. The real Rhys Williams was an uneducated, ignorant boy with no background, no breeding, no past, no future. But he had imagination, intelligence and a fiery ambition. It was enough. He started with the image of what he wanted to be, who he intended to be. When he looked in his mirror, he did not see the clumsy, grubby little boy with a funny accent; his mirror image was polished and suave and successful. Little by little, Rhys began to match himself to the image in his mind. He attended night school, and he spent his weekends in art galleries. He haunted public libraries and went to the theater, sitting in the gallery, studying the fine clothes of the men seated in the stalls. He scrimped on food, so that once a month he could go to a good restaurant, where he carefully copied the table manners of others. He observed and learned and remembered. He was like a sponge, erasing the past, soaking up the future.

In one short year Rhys had learned enough to realize that Gladys Simpkins, his princess, was a cheap Cockney girl who was already beneath his tastes. He quit the draper's shop and went to work as a clerk at a chemist's shop that was part of a large chain. He was almost sixteen now, but he looked older. He had filled out and was taller. Women were beginning to pay attention to his dark Welsh good looks and his quick, flattering tongue. He was an instant success in the shop. Female customers would wait until Rhys was available to take care of them. He dressed well and spoke correctly, and he knew he had come a long way from Gwent and Carmarthen, but when he looked in the mirror, he was still not satisfied. The journey he intended to make was still ahead of him.

Within two years Rhys Williams was made manager of the shop where he worked. The district manager of the chain said to Rhys, "This is just the beginning, Williams. Work hard and one day you'll be the superintendent of half a dozen stores."

Rhys almost laughed aloud. To think that that could be the height of anyone's ambition! Rhys had never stopped going to school. He was studying business administration and marketing and commercial law. He wanted more. His image in the mirror was at the top of the ladder; Rhys felt he was still at the bottom. His opportunity to move up came when a drug salesman walked in one day, watched Rhys charm several ladies into buying products they had no use for, and said, "You're wasting your time here, lad. You should be working in a bigger pond."

"What did you have in mind?" Rhys asked.

"Let me talk to my boss about you."

Two weeks later Rhys was working as a salesman at the small drug firm. He was one of fifty salesmen, but when Rhys looked in his special mirror, he knew that that was not true. His only competition was himself. He was getting closer to his image now, closer to the fictitious character he was creating. A man who was intelligent, cultured, sophisticated and charming. What he was trying to do was impossible. Everyone knew that one had to be born with those qualities; they could not be created. But Rhys did it. He became the image he had envisioned.

He traveled around the country, selling the firm's products, talking and listening. He would return to London full of practical suggestions, and he quickly began to move up the ladder.

Three years after he had joined the company, Rhys was made general sales manager. Under his skillful guidance the company began to expand.

And four years later, Sam Roffe had come into his life. He had recognized the hunger in Rhys.

"You're like me," Sam Roffe had said. "We want to own the world. I'm going to show you how." And he had.

Sam Roffe had been a brilliant mentor. Over the next nine years under Sam Roffe's tutelage, Rhys Williams had become invaluable to the company. As time went on, he was given more and more responsibility, reorganizing various divisions, troubleshooting in whatever part of the world he was needed, coordinating the different branches of Roffe and Sons, creating new concepts. In the end Rhys knew more about running the company than anyone except Sam Roffe himself. Rhys Williams was the logical successor to the presidency. One morning, when Rhys and Sam Roffe were returning from Caracas in a company jet, a luxurious converted Boeing 707-320, one of a fleet of eight planes, Sam Roffe had complimented Rhys on a lucrative deal that he had concluded with the Venezuelan government.

"There'll be a fat bonus in this for you, Rhys."

Rhys had replied quietly, "I don't want a bonus, Sam. I'd prefer some stock and a place on your board of directors."

He had earned it, and both men were aware of it. But Sam had said, "I'm sorry. I can't change the rules, even for you. Roffe and Sons is a privately held company. No one outside of the family can sit on the board or hold stock."

Rhys had known that, of course. He attended all board meetings, but not as a member. He was an outsider. Sam Roffe was the last male in the Roffe bloodline. The other Roffes, Sam's cousins, were females. The men they had married sat on the board of the company. Walther Gassner, who had married Anna Roffe; Ivo Palazzi, married to Simonetta Roffe; Charles Martel, married to Hélène Roffe. And Sir Alec Nichols, whose mother had been a Roffe.

So Rhys had been forced to make a decision. He knew that he deserved to be on the board, that one day he should be running the company. Present circumstances prevented it, but circumstances had a way of changing. Rhys had decided to stay, to wait and see what happened. Sam had taught him patience. And now Sam was dead.

The office lights blazed on again, and Hajib Kafir stood in the doorway. Kafir was the Turkish sales manager for Roffe and Sons. He was a short, swarthy man who wore diamonds and his fat belly like proud ornaments. He had the disheveled air of a man who

27

had dressed hastily. So Sophie had not found him in a nightclub. Ah, well, Rhys thought. A side effect of Sam Roffe's death. Coitus interruptus.

"Rhys!" Kafir was exclaiming. "My dear fellow, forgive me! I had no idea you were still in Istanbul! You were on your way to catch a plane, and I had some urgent business to——"

"Sit down, Hajib. Listen carefully. I want you to send four cables in company code. They're going to different countries. I want them hand-delivered by our own messengers. Do you understand?"

"Of course," Kafir said, bewildered. "Perfectly."

Rhys glanced at the thin, gold Baume & Mercier watch on his wrist. "The New City Post Office will be closed. Send the cables from Yeni Posthane Cad. I want them on their way within thirty minutes." He handed Kafir a copy of the cable he had written out. "Anyone who discusses this will be instantly discharged."

Kafir glanced at the cable and his eyes widened. "My God!" he said. "Oh, my God!" He looked up at Rhys's dark face. "How——how did this terrible thing happen?"

"Sam Roffe died in an accident," Rhys said.

Now, for the first time, Rhys allowed his thoughts to go to what he had been pushing away from his consciousness, what he had been trying to avoid thinking about: Elizabeth Roffe, Sam's daughter. She was twenty-four now. When Rhys had first met her, she had been a fifteen-year-old girl with braces on her teeth, fiercely shy and overweight, a lonely rebel. Over the years Rhys had watched Elizabeth develop into a very special young woman, with her mother's beauty and her father's intelligence and spirit. She had become close to Sam. Rhys knew how deeply the news would affect her. He would have to tell her himself.

Two hours later, Rhys Williams was over the Mediterranean on a company jet, headed for New York.

CHAPTER

2

Berlin.
Monday, September 7.
Ten a.m.

Anna Roffe Gassner knew that she must not let herself scream again or Walther would return and kill her. She crouched in a corner of her bedroom, her body trembling uncontrollably, waiting for death. What had started out as a beautiful fairy tale had ended in terror, unspeakable horror. It had taken her too long to face the truth: the man she had married was a homicidal maniac.

Anna Roffe had never loved anyone before she met Walther Gassner, including her mother, her father and herself. Anna had been a frail, sickly child who suffered from fainting spells. She could not remember a time when she had been free of hospitals or nurses or specialists flown in from far-off places. Because her father was Anton Roffe, of Roffe and Sons, the top medical experts flew to Anna's bedside in Berlin. But when they had examined her and tested her and finally departed, they knew no more than they had known before. They could not diagnose her condition.

Anna was unable to go to school like other children, and in time she had become withdrawn, creating a world of her own, full of dreams and fantasies, where no one else was allowed to enter. She painted her own pictures of life, because the colors of reality were too harsh for her to accept. When Anna was eighteen, her dizziness and fainting spells disappeared as mysteriously as they had started. But they had marred her life. At an age when most girls were getting engaged or married, Anna had never even been kissed by a boy. She insisted to herself that she did not mind. She was content to live her own dream life, apart from everything and everyone. In her middle twenties suitors came calling, for Anna Roffe was an heiress who bore one of the most prestigious names in the world, and many men were eager to share her fortune. She received proposals from a Swedish count, an Italian poet and half a dozen princes from indigent countries. Anna refused them all. On his daughter's thirtieth birthday, Anton Roffe moaned, "I'm going to die without leaving any grandchildren."

On her thirty-fifth birthday Anna had gone to Kitzbühel, in Austria, and there she had met Walther Gassner, a ski instructor thirteen years younger than she.

The first time Anna had seen Walther, the sight of him had literally taken her breath away. He was skiing down the *Hahnenkamm*, the steep racing slope, and it was the most beautiful sight Anna had ever seen. She had moved closer to the bottom of the ski run to get a better look at him. He was like a young god, and Anna had been satisfied to do nothing but watch him. He had caught her staring at him.

"Aren't you skiing, *gnädiges Fräulein?*"

She had shaken her head, not trusting her voice, and he had smiled and said, "Then let me buy you lunch."

Anna had fled in a panic, like a schoolgirl. From then on, Walther Gassner had pursued her. Anna Roffe was not a fool. She was aware that she was neither pretty nor brilliant, that she was a plain woman, and that, aside from her name, she had seemingly very little to offer a man. But Anna knew that trapped within that ordinary facade was a beautiful, sensitive girl filled with love and poetry and music.

Perhaps because Anna was not beautiful, she had a deep reverence for beauty. She would go to the great museums and spend hours staring at the paintings and the statues. When she had seen Walther Gassner it was as though all the gods had come alive for her.

Anna was having breakfast on the terrace of the Tennerhof Hotel on the second day when Walther Gassner joined her. He did look like a young god. He had a regular, clean-cut profile, and his features were delicate, sensitive, strong. His face was deeply tanned and his teeth were white and even. He had blond hair and his eyes were a slate gray. Beneath his ski clothes Anna could see the movement of his biceps and thigh muscles, and she felt tremors going through her loins. She hid her hands in her lap so that he could not see the keratosis.

"I looked for you on the slopes yesterday afternoon," Walther said. Anna could not speak. "If you don't ski, I'd like to teach you." He smiled, and added, "No charge."

He had taken her to the *Hausberg*, the beginners slope, for her first lesson. It was immediately apparent to them both that Anna had no talent for skiing. She kept losing her balance and falling down, but she insisted on trying again and again because she was afraid that Walther would despise her if she failed. Instead, he had picked her up after her tenth fall and had said gently, "You were meant to do better things than this."

"What things?" Anna had asked, miserable.

"I'll tell you at dinner tonight."

They had dined that evening and breakfasted the next morning, and then had lunch and dinner again. Walther neglected his clients. He skipped skiing lessons in order to go into the village with Anna. He took her to the casino in Der Goldene Greif, and they went sleigh riding and shopping and hiking, and sat on the terrace of the hotel hour after hour, talking. For Anna, it was a time of magic.

Five days after they had met, Walther took her hands in his and said, "Anna, *liebchen*, I want to marry you."

He had spoiled it. He had taken her out of her wonderful fairyland and brought her back to the cruel reality of who and what she was. An unattractive, thirty-five-year-old virginal prize for fortune hunters.

She had tried to leave but Walther had stopped her. "We love each other, Anna. You can't run away from that."

She listened to him lying, listened to him saying, "I've never loved anyone before," and she made it easy for him because she wanted so desperately to believe him. She took him back to her room, and they sat there, talking, and as Walther told Anna the story of his life, she suddenly began to believe, thinking with wonder, *It is really the story of my own life.*

Like her, Walther had never had anyone to love. He had been alienated from the world by his birth as a bastard, as Anna had been alienated by her illness. Like her, Walther had been filled with the need to give love. He had been brought up in an orphanage, and when he was thirteen and his extraordinary good looks were already apparent, the women in the orphanage had begun to use him, bringing him to their rooms at night, taking him to bed with them, teaching him how to please them. As a reward the young boy was given extra food and pieces of meat, and desserts made with real sugar. He received everything but love.

When Walther was old enough to run away from the orphanage, he found that the world outside was no different. Women wanted to use his good looks, to wear him as a badge; but it never went any deeper than that. They gave him gifts of money and clothes and jewelry, but never of themselves.

Walther was her soul mate, Anna realized, her doppelgänger. They were married in a quiet ceremony at the town hall.

Anna had expected her father to be overjoyed. Instead, he had flown into a rage. "You're a silly, vain fool," Anton Roffe screamed at her. "You've married a no-good fortune hunter. I've had him checked out. All his life he's lived off women, but he's never found anyone stupid enough to marry him before."

"Stop it!" Anna cried. "You don't understand him."

But Anton Roffe knew that he understood Walther Gassner only too well. He asked his new son-in-law to come to his office.

Walther looked around approvingly at the dark paneling and the old paintings hanging on the walls. "I like this place," Walther said.

"Yes. I'm sure it's better than the orphanage."

Walther looked up at him sharply, his eyes suddenly wary. "I beg your pardon?"

Anton said, "Let's cut out the *Scheiss*. You've made a mistake. My daughter has no money."

Walther's gray eyes seemed to turn to stone. "What are you trying to tell me?"

"I'm not trying to tell you anything. I'm telling you. You won't get anything from Anna because she hasn't got anything. If you had done your homework more thoroughly, you would have learned that Roffe and Sons is a close-held corporation. That means that none of its stock can be sold. We live comfortably, but that's it. There is no big fortune to be milked here." He fumbled in his pocket, drew out an envelope and threw it on the desk in front of Walther. "This will reimburse you for your trouble. I will expect you to be out of Berlin by six o'clock. I don't want Anna ever to hear from you again."

Walther said quietly, "Did it ever cross your mind that I might have married Anna because I fell in love with her?"

"No," Anton said acidly. "Did it ever cross yours?"

Walther looked at him a moment. "Let's see what my market price is." He tore open the envelope and counted the money. He looked up at Anton Roffe again. "I value myself at much higher than twenty thousand marks."

"It's all you're getting. Count yourself lucky."

"I do," Walther said. "If you want to know the truth, I think I am very lucky. Thank you." He put the money in his pocket with a careless gesture and a moment later was walking out the door.

Anton Roffe was relieved. He experienced a slight sense of guilt and distaste for what he had done and yet he knew it had been the only solution. Anna would be unhappy at being deserted by her groom, but it was better to have it happen now than later. He would try to see to it that she met some eligible men her own age, who would at least respect her if not love her. Someone who would be interested in her and not her money or her name. Someone who would not be bought for twenty thousand marks.

When Anton Roffe arrived home, Anna ran up to greet him, tears in her eyes. He took her in his arms and hugged her, and said, "Anna, *liebchen,* it's going to be all right. You'll get over him—"

And Anton looked over her shoulder, and standing in the doorway was Walther Gassner. Anna was holding up her finger, saying, "Look what Walther bought me! Isn't it the most beautiful ring you've ever seen? It cost twenty thousand marks."

In the end, Anna's parents were forced to accept Walther Gassner. As a wedding gift they bought them a lovely Schinkel manor house in Wannsee, with French furniture, mixed with antiques, comfortable couches and easy chairs, a Roentgen desk in the library, and bookcases lining the walls. The upstairs was furnished with elegant eighteenth-century pieces from Denmark and Sweden.

"It's too much," Walther told Anna. "I don't want anything from them or from you. I want to be able to buy you beautiful things, *liebchen*." He gave her that boyish grin and said, "But I have no money."

"Of course you do," Anna replied. "Everything I have belongs to you."

Walther smiled at her sweetly and said, "Does it?"

At Anna's insistence—for Walther seemed reluctant to discuss money—she explained her financial situation to him. She had a trust fund that was enough for her to live on comfortably, but the bulk of her fortune was in shares of Roffe and Sons. The shares could not be sold without the unanimous approval of the board of directors.

"How much is your stock worth?" Walther asked.

Anna told him. Walther could not believe it. He made her repeat the sum.

"And you can't sell the stock?"

"No. My cousin Sam won't let it be sold. He holds the controlling shares. One day . . ."

Walther expressed an interest in working in the family business. Anton Roffe was against it.

"What can a ski bum contribute to Roffe and Sons?" he asked.

But in the end he gave in to his daughter, and Walther was given a job with the company in administration. He proved to be excellent at it and advanced rapidly. When Anna's father died two year's later, Walther Gassner was made a member of the board. Anna was so proud of him. He was the perfect husband and lover. He was always bringing her flowers and little gifts, and he seemed content to stay at home with her in the evening, just the two of them. Anna's happiness was almost too much for her to bear. *Ach, danke, lieber Gott*, she would say silently.

Anna learned to cook, so that she could make Walther's favorite dishes. She made *choucroute*, a bed of crunchy sauerkraut and creamy mashed potatoes heaped with a smoked pork chop, a frankfurter and a Nuremberg sausage. She prepared fillet of pork cooked in beer and flavored with cumin, and served it with a fat baked apple, cored and peeled, the center filled with *airelles*, the little red berries.

"You're the best cook in the world, *liebchen*," Walther would say, and Anna would blush with pride.

In the third year of their marriage, Anna became pregnant.

There was a great deal of pain during the first eight months of her pregnancy, but Anna bore that happily. It was something else that worried her.

It started one day after lunch. She had been knitting a sweater for Walther, daydreaming, and suddenly she heard Walther's voice, saying, "My God, Anna, what are you doing, sitting here in the dark?"

The afternoon had turned to dusk, and she looked down at the sweater in her lap and she had not touched it. Where had the day gone? Where had her mind been? After that, Anna had other similar experiences, and she began to wonder whether this sliding away into nothingness was a portent, an omen that she was going to die. She did not think she was afraid of death, but she could not bear the thought of leaving Walther.

Four weeks before the baby was due, Anna lapsed

into one of her daydreams, missed a step and fell down an entire flight of stairs.

She awakened in the hospital.

Walther was seated on the edge of the bed, holding her hand. "You gave me a terrible scare."

In a sudden panic she thought, The baby! I can't feel the baby. She reached down. Her stomach was flat. "Where is my baby?"

And Walther held her close and hugged her.

The doctor said, "You had twins, Mrs. Gassner."

Anna turned to Walther, and his eyes were filled with tears. "A boy and girl, *liebchen.*"

And she could have died right then of happiness. She felt a sudden, irresistible longing to have them in her arms. She had to see them, feel them, hold them.

"We'll talk about that when you're stronger," the doctor said. "Not until you're stronger."

They assured Anna that she was getting better every day, but she was becoming frightened. Something was happening to her that she did not understand. Walther would arrive and take her hand and say good-bye, and she would look at him in surprise and start to say, "But you just got here . . ." And then she would see the clock, and three or four hours would have passed.

She had no idea where they had gone.

She had a vague recollection that they had brought the children to her in the night and that she had fallen asleep. She could not remember too clearly, and she was afraid to ask. It did not matter. She would have them to herself when Walther took her home.

* * *

The wonderful day finally arrived. Anna left her hospital room in a wheelchair, even though she insisted she was strong enough to walk. She actually felt very weak, but she was so excited that nothing mattered except the fact that she was going to see her babies. Walther carried her into the house, and he started to take her upstairs to their bedroom.

"No, no!" she said. "Take me to the nursery."

"You must rest now, darling. You're not strong enough to—"

She did not listen to the rest of what he was saying. She slipped out of his arms and ran into the nursery.

The blinds were drawn and the room was dark and it took Anna's eyes a moment to adjust. She was filled with such excitement that it made her dizzy. She was afraid she was going to faint.

Walther had come in behind her. He was talking to her, trying to explain something, but whatever it was was unimportant.

For there they were. They were both asleep in their cribs, and Anna moved toward them softly, so as not to disturb them, and stood there, staring down at them. They were the most beautiful children she had ever seen. Even now, she could see that the boy would have Walther's handsome features and his thick blond hair. The girl was like an exquisite doll, with soft, golden hair and a small, triangular face.

Anna turned to Walther and said, her voice choked, "They're beautiful. I—I'm so happy."

"Come, Anna," Walther whispered. He put his arms around Anna, and held her close, and there was a fierce hunger in him, and she began to feel a stirring within her. They had not made love for such a long time. Walther was right. There would be plenty of time for the children later.

The boy she named Peter and the girl Birgitta. They were two beautiful miracles that she and Walther had made, and Anna would spend hour after hour in the nursery, playing with them, talking to them. Even though they could not understand her yet, she knew they could feel her love. Sometimes, in the middle of play, she would turn and Walther would be standing in the doorway, home from the office, and Anna would realize that somehow the whole day had slipped by.

"Come and join us," she would say. "We're playing a game."

"Have you fixed dinner yet?" Walther would ask, and she would suddenly feel guilty. She would resolve to pay more attention to Walther, and less to the children, but the next day the same thing would happen. The twins were like an irresistible magnet that drew her to them. Anna still loved Walther very much, and she tried to assuage her guilt by telling herself that the children were a part of him. Every night, as soon as Walther was asleep, Anna would slip out of bed and creep into the nursery, and sit and stare at the children until dawn started filtering into the room. Then she would turn and hurry back to bed before Walther awoke.

Once, in the middle of the night, Walther walked into the nursery and caught her. "What in God's name do you think you're doing?" he said.

"Nothing, darling. I was just—"

"Go back to bed!"

He had never spoken to her like that before.

At breakfast Walther said, "I think we should

take a vacation. It will be good for us to get away."

"But, Walther, the children are too young to travel."

"I'm talking about the two of us."

She shook her head. "I couldn't leave them."

He took her hand and said, "I want you to forget about the children."

"Forget about the children?" There was shock in her voice.

He looked into her eyes and said, "Anna, remember how wonderful it was between us before you were pregnant? What good times we had? How much joy it was to be together, just the two of us, with no one else around to interfere?"

It was then that she understood. Walther was jealous of the children.

The weeks and months passed swiftly. Walther never went near the children now. On their birthdays Anna bought them lovely presents. Walther always managed to be out of town on business. Anna could not go on deceiving herself forever. The truth was that Walther had no interest in the children at all. Anna felt that perhaps it was her fault, because she was *too* interested in them. *Obsessed* was the word Walther had used. He had asked her to consult a doctor about it, and she had gone only to please Walther. But the doctor was a fool. The moment he had started talking to her, Anna had shut him out, letting her mind drift, until she heard him say, "Our time is up, Mrs. Gassner. Will I see you next week?"

"Of course."

She never returned.

Anna felt that the problem was as much Walther's

as hers. If her fault lay in loving the children too much, then his fault lay in not loving them enough.

Anna learned not to mention the children in Walther's presence, but she could hardly wait for him to leave for the office, so she could hurry into the nursery to be with her babies. Except that they were no longer babies. They had had their third birthday, and already Anna could see what they would look like as adults. Peter was tall for his age and his body was strong and athletic, like his father's. Anna would hold him on her lap and croon, "Ah, Peter, what are you going to do to the poor fräuleins? Be gentle with them, my darling son. They won't have a chance."

And Peter would smile shyly and hug her.

Then Anna would turn to Birgitta. Birgitta grew prettier each day. She looked like neither Anna nor Walther. She had spun-golden hair and skin as delicate as porcelain. Peter had his father's fiery temper and sometimes it would be necessary for Anna to spank him gently, but Birgitta had the disposition of an angel. When Walther was not around, Anna played records or read to them. Their favorite book was *101 Märchens*. They would insist that Anna read them the tales of ogres and goblins and witches over and over again, and at night, Anna would put them to bed, singing them a lullaby:

> *Schlaf, Kindlein, schlaf,*
> *Der Vater hüt't die Schaf . . .*

Anna had prayed that time would soften Walther's attitude, that he would change. He did change, but for the worse. He hated the children. In the beginning Anna had told herself that it was because

Walther wanted all of her love for himself, that he was unwilling to share it with anyone else. But slowly she became aware that it had nothing to do with loving her. It had to do with hating her. Her father had been right. Walther had married her for her money. The children were a threat to him. He wanted to get rid of them. More and more he talked to Anna about selling the stock. "Sam has no right to stop us! We could take all that money and go away somewhere. Just the two of us."

She stared at him. "What about the children?"

His eyes were feverish. "No. Listen to me. For both our sakes we've got to get rid of them. We must."

It was then that Anna began to realize that he was insane. She was terrified. Walther had fired all the domestic help, and except for a cleaning woman who came in once a week, Anna and the children were alone with him, at his mercy. He needed help. Perhaps it was not too late to cure him. In the fifteenth century they gathered the insane and imprisoned them forever on houseboats, *Narrenschiffe*, the ships of fools, but today, with modern medicine, she felt there must be something they could do to help Walther.

Now, on this day in September, Anna sat huddled on the floor in her bedroom, where Walther had locked her, waiting for him to return. She knew what she had to do. For his sake, as well as hers and the children's. Anna rose unsteadily and walked over to the telephone. She hesitated for only an instant, then picked it up and began to dial 110, the police emergency number.

An alien voice in her ear said, "*Hallo. Hier ist der Notruf der Polizei. Kann ich ihnen helfen?*"

"*Ja, bitte!*" Her voice was choked. "*Ich—*"

A hand came out of nowhere and tore the receiver from her, and slammed it down into the cradle.

Anna backed away. "Oh, please," she whimpered, "don't hurt me."

Walther was moving toward her, his eyes bright, his voice so soft that she could hardly make out the words. "*Liebchen*, I'm not going to hurt you. I love you, don't you know that?" He touched her, and she could feel her flesh crawl. "It's just that we don't want the police coming here, do we?" She shook her head from side to side, too filled with terror to speak. "It's the children that are causing the trouble, Anna. We're going to get rid of them. I—"

Downstairs the front doorbell rang. Walther stood there, hesitating. It rang again.

"Stay here," he ordered. "I'll be back."

Anna watched, petrified, as he walked out the bedroom door. He slammed it behind him and she could hear the click of the key as he locked it.

I'll be back, he had said.

Walther Gassner hurried down the stairs, walked to the front door and opened it. A man in a gray messenger's uniform stood there, holding a sealed manila envelope.

"I have a special delivery for Mr. and Mrs. Walther Gassner."

"Yes," Walther said. "I will take it."

He closed the door, looked at the envelope in his hand, then ripped it open. Slowly, he read the message inside.

DEEPLY REGRET TO INFORM YOU THAT SAM
ROFFE WAS KILLED IN A CLIMBING
ACCIDENT. PLEASE BE IN ZURICH
FRIDAY NOON FOR AN EMERGENCY
MEETING OF THE BOARD OF DIRECTORS.

It was signed "Rhys Williams."

CHAPTER

3

Rome.
Monday, September 7.
Six p.m.

Ivo Palazzi stood in the middle of his bedroom, the blood streaming down his face. "*Mamma mia! Mi hai rovinato!*"

"I haven't begun to ruin you, you miserable *figlio di putana!*" Donatella screamed at him.

They were both naked in the large bedroom of their apartment in Via Montemignaio. Donatella had the most sensuous, exciting body Ivo Palazzi had ever seen, and even now, as his life's blood poured from his face, from the terrible scratches she had inflicted on him, he felt a familiar stirring in his loins. *Dio,* she was beautiful. There was an innocent decadence about her that drove him wild. She had the face of a leopard, high cheekbones and slant eyes, full ripe lips, lips that nibbled him and sucked him and—but he must not think of that now. He picked up a white cloth from a chair to stanch the flow of blood, and too late he realized that it was his shirt. Donatella was standing in the middle of their huge double bed, yelling at him. "I hope you bleed to death! When I've finished with you, you filthy whoremonger, there won't be enough left for a *gattino* to shit on!"

For the hundredth time Ivo Palazzi wondered how he had gotten himself into this impossible situation. He had always prided himself on being the happiest of men, and all his friends had agreed with him. His *friends? Everybody!* Because Ivo had no enemies. In his bachelor days he had been a happy-go-lucky Roman without a care in the world, a Don Giovanni who was the envy of half the males in Italy. His philosophy was summed up in the phrase *Farsi onore con una donna*—"Honor oneself with a woman." It kept Ivo very busy. He was a true romantic. He kept falling in love, and each time he used his new love to help him forget his old love. Ivo adored women, and to him they were all beautiful, from the *putane* who plied their ancient trade along the Via Appia, to the high-fashion models strutting along the Via Condotti. The only girls Ivo did not care for were the Americans. They were too independent for his taste. Besides, what could one expect of a nation whose language was so unromantic that they would translate the name of Giuseppe Verdi to Joe Green?

Ivo always managed to have a dozen girls in various states of preparation. There were five stages. In stage one were the girls he had just met. They received daily phone calls, flowers, slim volumes of erotic poetry. In stage two were those to whom he sent little gifts of Gucci scarves and porcelain boxes filled with Perugina chocolates. Those in stage three received jewelry and clothes and were taken to dinner at El Toula, or Taverna Flavia. Those in stage four shared Ivo's bed and enjoyed his formidable skills as a lover. An assignation with Ivo was a production. His beautifully decorated little apartment on the Via Margutta would be filled with flowers, *garofani* or *papaveri*, the music would be opera, classical or rock, according to the chosen girl's taste. Ivo was a superb cook, and one of his specialties, appropriately enough, was *pollo alla cacciatora*, chicken of the hunter. After dinner, a bottle of chilled champagne to drink in bed . . . Ah, yes, Ivo loved stage four.

But stage five was probably the most delicate of them all. It consisted of a heartbreaking farewell speech, a generous parting gift and a tearful *arrivederci*.

But all that was in the past. Now Ivo Palazzi took a quick glance at his bleeding, scratched face in the mirror over his bed and was horrified. He looked as though he had been attacked by a mad threshing machine.

"Look at what you've done to me!" he cried. *"Cara,* I know you didn't mean it."

He moved over to the bed to take Donatella in his arms. Her soft arms flew around him and as he started to hug her, she buried her long fingernails in his naked back and clawed him like a wild animal. Ivo yelled with pain.

"Scream!" Donatella shouted. "If I had a knife, I'd cut your *cazzo* and ram it down your miserable throat."

"Please!" Ivo begged. "The children will hear you."

"Let them!" she shrieked. "It's time they found out what kind of monster their father is."

He took a step toward her. *"Carissima—"*

"Don't you touch me! I'd give my body to the first drunken syphilitic sailor I met on the streets before I'd ever let you come near me again."

Ivo drew himself up, his pride offended. "That is not the way I expect the mother of my children to talk to me."

"You want me to talk nice to you? You want me to stop treating you like the vermin you are?" Donatella's voice rose to a scream. *"Then give me what I want!"*

Ivo looked nervously toward the door. *"Carissima*—I can't. I don't have it."

"Then get it for me!" she cried. "You promised!"

She was beginning to get hysterical again, and Ivo decided the best thing for him to do was to get out of there quickly before the neighbors called the carabinieri again.

"It will take time to get a million dollars," he said soothingly. "But I'll—I'll find a way."

He hastily donned his undershorts and pants, and socks and shoes, while Donatella stormed around the room, her magnificent, firm breasts waving in the air, and Ivo thought to himself, My God, what a woman! How I adore her! He reached for his bloodstained shirt. There was no help for it. He put it on, feeling the cold stickiness against his back and chest. He took a last look in the mirror. Small pools of blood were still oozing from the deep gashes where Donatella had raked her fingernails across his face.

"*Carissima*," Ivo moaned, "how am I ever going to explain this to my wife?"

Ivo Palazzi's wife was Simonetta Roffe, an heiress of the Italian branch of the Roffe family. Ivo had been a young architect when he had met Simonetta. His firm had sent him to supervise some changes in the Roffe villa at Porto Ercole. The instant Simonetta had set eyes on Ivo, his bachelor days were numbered. Ivo had gotten to the fourth stage with her on the first night, and found himself married to her a short time later. Simonetta was as determined as she was lovely, and she knew what she wanted: she wanted Ivo Palazzi. Thus it was that Ivo found himself transformed from a carefree bachelor to the husband of a beautiful young heiress. He gave up his architectural aspirations with no regrets and joined Roffe and Sons, with a magnificent office in EUR, the section of Rome started with such high hopes by the late, ill-fated Duce.

Ivo was a success with the firm from the beginning. He was intelligent, learned quickly, and everyone adored him. It was impossible not to adore Ivo. He was always smiling, always charming. His friends envied him his wonderful disposition and wondered how he did it. The answer was simple. Ivo kept the dark side of his nature buried. In fact, he was a deeply emotional man, capable of great volatile hatreds, capable of killing.

Ivo's marriage with Simonetta thrived. At first, he had feared that marriage would prove to be a bondage that would strangle his manhood to death, but his fears proved to be unfounded. He simply put himself on an austerity program, reducing the number of his girl friends, and everything went on as before.

Simonetta's father bought them a beautiful home in Olgiata, a large private estate twenty-five kilometers north of Rome, guarded by closed gates and manned by uniformed guards.

Simonetta was a wonderful wife. She loved Ivo and treated him like a king, which was no more than he felt he deserved. There was just one tiny flaw in Simonetta. When she became jealous, she turned into a savage. She had once suspected Ivo of taking a female buyer on a trip to Brazil. He was righteously indignant at the accusation. Before the argument was over, their entire house was a shambles. Not one dish or piece of furniture was left intact, and much of it had been broken over Ivo's head. Simonetta had gone after him with a butcher knife, threatening to kill him and then herself, and it had taken all of Ivo's strength to wrest the knife from her. They had wound up fighting on the floor, and Ivo had finally torn off her clothes and made her forget her anger. But after that incident Ivo became very discreet. He had told the buyer he could not take any more trips with her, and he was careful never to let the faintest breath of suspicion touch him. He knew that he was the luckiest man in the world. Simonetta was young and beautiful and intelligent and rich. They enjoyed the same things and the same people. It was a perfect marriage, and Ivo sometimes found himself wondering, as he transferred a girl from stage two to stage three, and another from stage four to stage five, why he kept on being unfaithful. Then he would shrug philosophically and say to himself, Someone has to make these women happy.

Ivo and Simonetta had been married for three years when Ivo met Donatella Spolini on a business trip to Sicily. It was more of an explosion than a meeting, two planets coming together and colliding. Where Simonetta had the slender, sweet body of a young woman sculpted by Manzù, Donatella had the sensuous, ripe body of a Rubens. Her face was exquisite and her green, smoldering eyes set Ivo aflame. They were in bed one hour after they had met, and Ivo, who had always prided himself on his prowess as a lover, found that he was the pupil and Donatella the teacher. She made him rise to heights he had never achieved before, and her body did things to his that he had never dreamed possible. She was an endless cornucopia of pleasure, and as Ivo lay in bed, his eyes closed, savoring incredible sensations, he knew he would be a fool to let Donatella go.

And so Donatella had become Ivo's mistress. The only condition she imposed was that he had to get rid of all the other women in his life, except his wife. Ivo had happily agreed That had been eight years ago, and in all that time Ivo had never been unfaithful to either his wife or his mistress. Satisfying two hungry women would have been enough to exhaust an ordinary man, but in Ivo's case it was exactly the opposite. When he made love to Simonetta he thought about Donatella and her ripe full body, and he was filled with lust. And when he made love to Donatella, he thought of Simonetta's sweet young breasts and tiny *culo* and he performed like a wild man. No matter which woman he was with, he felt that he was cheating on the other. It added enormously to his pleasure.

Ivo bought Donatella a beautiful apartment in Via Montemignaio, and he was with her every moment that he could manage. He would arrange to be away on a sudden business trip and, instead of leaving, he would spend the time in bed with Donatella. He would stop by to see her on his way to the office, and he would spend his afternoon siestas with her. Once, when Ivo sailed to New York on the *QE 2* with Simonetta, he installed Donatella in a cabin one deck below. They were the five most stimulating days of Ivo's life.

On the evening that Simonetta announced to Ivo that she was pregnant, Ivo was filled with an indescribable joy. A week later Donatella informed Ivo that *she* was pregnant, and Ivo's cup ranneth over. Why, he asked himself, are the gods so good to me? In all humility, Ivo sometimes felt that he did not deserve all the great pleasures that were being bestowed upon him.

In due course Simonetta gave birth to a girl and a week later Donatella gave birth to a boy. What more could any man ask? But the gods were not finished with Ivo. A short time later, Donatella informed Ivo that she was pregnant again, and the following week Simonetta also became pregnant. Nine months later, Donatella gave Ivo another son and Simonetta presented her husband with another daughter. Four months later, both women were pregnant again and this time they gave birth on the same day. Ivo frantically raced from the Salvator

Mundi, where Simonetta was encouched, to the Clinica Santa Chiara where Ivo had taken Donatella. He sped from hospital to hospital, driving on the Raccordo Anulare, waving to the girls sitting in front of their little tents along the sides of the road, under pink umbrellas, waiting for customers. Ivo was driving too fast to see their faces, but he loved them all and wished them well.

Donatella gave birth to another boy and Simonetta to another girl.

Sometimes Ivo wished it had been the other way around. It was ironical that his wife had borne him daughters and his mistress had borne him sons, for he would have liked male heirs to carry on his name. Still, he was a contented man. He had three children with outdoor plumbing, and three children with indoor plumbing. He adored them and he was wonderful to them, remembering their birthdays, their saints' days, and their names. The girls were called Isabella and Benedetta and Camilla. The boys were Francesco and Carlo and Luca.

As the children grew older, life began to get more complicated for Ivo. Including his wife, his mistress and his six children, Ivo had to cope with eight birthdays, eight saints' days, and two of every holiday. He made sure that the children's schools were well separated. The girls were sent to Saint Dominique, the French convent on the Via Cassia, and the boys to Massimo, the Jesuit school in EUR. Ivo met and charmed all their teachers, helped the children with their homework, played with them, fixed their broken toys. It taxed all of Ivo's ingenuity to handle two families and keep them apart, but he managed. He was truly an exemplary father, husband and lover. On Christmas Day he stayed home with Simonetta, Isabella, Benedetta and Camilla. On *Befana*, the sixth of January, Ivo dressed up as the *Befana*, the witch, and handed out presents and *carbone*, the black rock candy prized by children, to Francesco, Carlo and Luca.

Ivo's wife and his mistress were lovely, and his children were bright and beautiful, and he was proud of them all. Life was wonderful.

And then the gods shat in Ivo Palazzi's face.

As in the case of most major disasters, this one struck without any warning.

Ivo had made love to Simonetta that morning before breakfast, and then had gone directly to his office, where he did a profitable morning's work. At one o'clock he told his secretary—male, at Simonetta's insistence—that he would be at a meeting the rest of the afternoon.

Smiling at the thought of the pleasures that lay ahead of him, Ivo circled the construction that blocked the street along the Lungo Tevere, where they had been building a subway for the past seventeen years, crossed the bridge to the Corso Francia, and thirty minutes later was driving into his garage at Via Montemignaio. The instant Ivo opened the door of the apartment, he knew something was terribly wrong. Francesco, Carlo and Luca were clustered around Donatella, sobbing, and as Ivo walked toward Donatella, she looked at him with an expression of such hatred on her face that for a moment Ivo thought he must have entered the wrong apartment.

"*Stronzo!*" she screamed at him.

Ivo looked around him, bewildered. *"Carissima —children—what's wrong? What have I done?"*

Donatella rose to her feet. "Here's what you've done!" She threw a copy of the magazine *Oggi* in his face. "Look at it!"

Bewildered, Ivo reached down and picked up the magazine. Staring out from the cover was a photograph of himself, Simonetta and their three daughters. The caption read: *"Padre di Famiglia."*

Dio! He had forgotten all about it. Months before, the magazine had asked permission to do a story about him and he had foolishly agreed. But Ivo had never dreamed that it would be given this prominence. He looked over at his sobbing mistress and children, and said, "I can explain this . . ."

"Their schoolmates have already explained it," Donatella shrieked. "My children came home crying because everybody at school is calling them bastards!"

"Cara, I—"

"My landlord and the neighbors treated us like we were lepers. We can't hold up our heads anymore. I have to get them out of here."

Ivo stared at her, shocked. "What are you talking about?"

"I'm leaving Rome, and I'm taking my sons with me."

"They're mine too," he shouted. "You can't do it."

"Try to stop me and I'll kill you!"

It was a nightmare. Ivo stood there, watching his three sons and his beloved mistress in hysterics, and he thought, This can't be happening to me.

But Donatella was not finished with him. "Before

we go," she announced, "I want one million dollars. In cash."

It was so ridiculous that Ivo started to laugh. "A million—"

"Either that, or I telephone your wife."

That had happened six months earlier. Donatella had not carried out her threat—not yet—but Ivo knew she would. Each week she had increased the pressure. She would telephone him at his office and say, "I don't care how you get the money. Do it!"

There was only one way that Ivo could possibly obtain such a huge sum. He had to be able to sell the stock in Roffe and Sons. It was Sam Roffe who was blocking the sale, Sam who was jeopardizing Ivo's marriage, his future. He had to be stopped. If one knew the right people, anything could be done.

What hurt Ivo more than anything was that Donatella—his darling, passionate mistress—would not let him touch her. Ivo was permitted to visit the children every day, but the bedroom was off limits.

"After you give me the money," Donatella promised, "then I will let you make love to me."

It was out of desperation that Ivo telephoned Donatella one afternoon and said, "I'm coming right over. The money is arranged."

He would make love to her first and placate her later. It had not worked out that way. He had managed to undress her, and when they were both naked, he had told her the truth. "I don't have the money yet, *cara,* but one day soon—"

It was then that she had attacked him like a wild animal.

* * *

Ivo was thinking of these things now, as he drove away from Donatella's apartment (as he now thought of it) and turned north onto the crowded Via Cassia, toward his home at Olgiata. He glanced at his face in the rearview mirror. The bleeding had lessened, but the scratches were raw-looking and discolored. He looked down at his shirt, stained with blood. How was he going to explain to Simonetta the scratches on his face and his back? For one reckless moment Ivo actually considered telling her the truth, but dismissed the thought as quickly as it came into his head. He might—he just might —have been able to confess to Simonetta that in a moment of mental aberration he had gone to bed with a girl and gotten her pregnant, and he might —he just *might*—have gotten away with a whole skin. But *three children?* Over a period of *three years?* His life would not be worth a five-lire piece. There was no way he could avoid going home now, for they were expecting guests for dinner, and Simonetta would be waiting for him. Ivo was trapped. His marriage was finished. Only San Gennaro, the patron saint of miracles, could help him. Ivo's eye was caught by a sign at the side of the Via Cassia. He suddenly slammed on the brakes, turned off the highway and brought the car to a stop.

Thirty minutes later, Ivo drove through the gates of Olgiata. Ignoring the stares of the guards as they saw his torn-up face and bloodstained shirt, Ivo drove along the winding roads, came to the turn that led to his driveway, and pulled up in front of his house. He parked the car, opened the front door of the house and walked into the living room. Simonetta and Isabella, their eldest daughter, were in the room. A look of shock came over Simonetta's face as she saw her husband.

"Ivo! What happened?"

Ivo smiled awkwardly, trying to ignore the pain it cost, and admitted sheepishly, "I'm afraid I did something stupid, *cara*—"

Simonetta was moving closer, studying the scratches on his face, and Ivo could see her eyes begin to narrow. When she spoke, her voice was frosty. "Who scratched your face?"

"Tiberio," Ivo announced. From behind his back he produced a large, spitting, ugly gray cat that leaped out of his arms and raced off. "I bought it for Isabella, but the damned thing attacked me while I was trying to put it in its case."

"*Povero amore mio!*" Instantly, Simonetta was at his side. "*Angelo mio!* Come upstairs and lie down. I'll get the doctor. I'll get some iodine. I'll—"

"No, no! I'm fine," Ivo said bravely. He winced as she put her arms around him. "Careful! I'm afraid he's clawed my back, too."

"*Amore!* How you must be suffering!"

"No, really," Ivo said. "I feel good." And he meant it.

The front doorbell rang.

"I'll get it," Simonetta said.

"No, I'll get it," Ivo said quickly. "I—I'm expecting some important papers from the office."

He hurried to the front door and opened it.

"Signor Palazzi?"

"*Sì.*"

A messenger, dressed in a gray uniform, handed

him an envelope. Inside was a teletype from Rhys Williams. Ivo read the message rapidly. He stood there for a long, long time.

Then he took a deep breath and went upstairs to get ready for his guests.

CHAPTER
4

Buenos Aires.
Monday, September 7.
Three p.m.

The Buenos Aires autodrome on the dusty outskirts of Argentina's capital city was crammed with fifty thousand spectators who had come to watch the championship classic. It was a 115-lap race over the almost four-mile circuit. The race had been running for nearly five hours, under a hot, punishing sun, and out of a starting field of thirty cars only a handful remained. The crowd was seeing history being made. There had never been such a race before, and perhaps never would be again. All the names that had become legend were on the track this day: Chris Amon from New Zealand, and Brian Redman from Lancashire. There was the Italian Andrea di Adamici, in an Alfa Romeo Tipo 33, and Carlos Maco of Brazil, in a Mach Formula 1. The prize-winning Belgian Jacky Ickx was there, and Sweden's Reine Wisell in a BRM.

The track looked like a rainbow gone mad,

filled with the swirling reds and greens and blacks and whites and golds of the Ferraris and Brabhams and McLaren M19-A's and Lotus Formula 3's.

As lap after grueling lap went by, the giants began to fall. Chris Amon was in fourth place when his throttles jammed open. He sideswiped Brian Redman's Cooper before he brought his own car under control by cutting the ignition, but both cars were finished. Reine Wisell was in first position, with Jacky Ickx close behind the BRM. On the far turn, the BRM gearbox disintegrated and the battery and electrical equipment caught fire. The car started spinning, and Jacky Ickx's Ferrari was caught in the vortex.

The crowd was in a frenzy.

Three cars were outpacing the rest of the field. Jorje Amandaris from Argentina, driving a Surtees; Nils Nilsson from Sweden in a Matra; and a Ferrari 312 B-2, driven by Martel of France. They were driving brilliantly, daring the straight track, challenging the curves, moving up.

Jorje Amandaris was in the lead, and because he was one of them, the Argentinians cheered him madly. Close behind Amandaris was Nils Nilsson, at the wheel of a red-and-white Matra, and behind him the black-and-gold Ferrari, driven by Martel of France.

The French car had gone almost unnoticed until the last five minutes, when it had started gaining on the field. It had reached tenth position, then seventh, then fifth. And was coming on strong. The crowd was watching it now as the French driver started moving up on number two, driven by Nilsson. The three cars were travelling at speeds in excess of 180 miles an hour. That was dangerous enough at carefully contoured racetracks like Brands Hatch or Watkins Glen, but on the cruder Argentine track it was suicide. A red-coated referee stood at the side of the track, holding up a sign: "FIVE LAPS."

The French black-and-gold Ferrari attempted to pass Nilsson's Matra on the outside, and Nilsson inched over, blocking the French car's way. They were lapping a German car on the inside track, moving up on it fast. Now it was opposite Nilsson's car. The French car dropped back and edged over so that it was positioned in the tight space behind the German car and Nilsson's Matra. With a quick burst of acceleration the French driver made for the narrow slot, forcing the two cars out of its way and shooting ahead into the number-two spot. The crowd, which had been holding its breath, roared its approval. It had been a brilliant, dangerous maneuver.

It was Amandaris in the lead now, Martel second and Nilsson in third position, with three laps remaining. Amandaris had seen the move. The French driver is good, Amandaris told himself, but not good enough to beat me. Amandaris intended to win this race. Ahead of him he saw the sign being flashed—"TWO LAPS." The race was almost over, and it was his. Out of the corner of his eye he could see the black-and-gold Ferrari trying to pull up alongside him. He got a glimpse of the driver's goggled, dirt-streaked face, tight and determined. Amandaris gave an inward sigh. He regretted what he was about to do, but he had no choice. Racing was not a game for sportsmen, it was a game for winners.

The two cars were approaching the north end of the oval, where there was a high banking turn, the most dangerous in the track, the scene of a dozen crashes. Amandaris shot another quick look at the French driver of the Ferrari and then tightened his grip on the wheel. As the two cars started to approach the curve, Amandaris imperceptibly lifted his foot from the accelerator, so that the Ferrari began to pull ahead. He saw the driver give him a quick, speculative look. Then the driver was abreast of him, falling into his trap. The crowd was screaming. Jorje Amandaris waited until the black-and-gold Ferrari was fully committed to pass him on the outside. At that moment Amandaris opened his throttles wide and started to move toward the right, cutting off the French driver's path to the straightaway, so that the only choice was to head up the embankment.

Amandaris saw the sudden, dismayed expression on the French driver's face and silently said, *¡Salud!* At that instant the driver of the French car turned the wheel directly into Amandaris' Surtees. Amandaris could not believe it. The Ferrari was on a crash course with him. They were only three feet apart and at that speed Amandaris had to make a split-second decision. *How could anyone have known that the French driver was completely loco?* In a swift, reflex action, Amandaris swung the wheel sharply to the left, trying to avoid the thousand pounds of metal hurtling at him, and braked hard, so that the French car missed him by a fraction of an inch, and shot past him toward the finish line. For a moment Jorje Amandaris' car fishtailed, then went out of control into a spin, flinging itself wildly across the track, rolling over and over until it burst into a tower of red and black flames.

But the crowd's attention was riveted on the French Ferrari, roaring across the finish line to victory. There were wild screams from the spectators as they ran toward the car, surrounding it, cheering. The driver slowly stood up and took off the racing goggles and helmet.

She had wheat-colored hair, cut short, and her face was sculpted with strong, firm features. There was a classic cold beauty about her. Her body was trembling, not with exhaustion, but with excitement, the memory of the moment when she had looked into Jorje Amandaris' eyes as she sent him to his death. Over the loudspeaker the announcer was excitedly yelling, "The winner is Hélène Roffe-Martel, from France, driving a Ferrari."

Two hours later, Hèléne and her husband, Charles, were in their suite in the Ritz Hotel in downtown Buenos Aires, lying on the rug in front of the fireplace, and Hélène was naked on top of him in the classic position of *la Diligence de Lyon,* and Charles was saying, "Oh, Christ! Please don't do that to me! Please!"

And his begging increased her excitement and she began to put on more pressure, hurting him, watching the tears come to his eyes. I'm being punished for no reason, Charles thought. He dreaded to think what Hélène would do to him if she ever found out about the crime he had committed.

* * *

Charles Martel had married Hélène Roffe for her name and for her money. After the ceremony she had kept her name, along with his, and she had kept her money. By the time Charles found out he had made a bad bargain, it was too late.

Charles Martel was a junior attorney in a large Paris law firm when he first met Hélène Roffe. He had been asked to bring some documents into the conference room, where a meeting was taking place. In the room were the four senior partners in the firm and Hélène Roffe. Charles had heard of her. Everyone in Europe had. She was an heiress to the Roffe pharamaceutical fortune. She was wild and unconventional, and the newspapers and magazines adored her. She was a champion skier; flew her own Learjet, had led a mountain-climbing expedition in Nepal, raced cars and horses, and changed men as casually as she changed her wardrobe. Her photograph was constantly appearing in *Paris-Match* and *Jours de France*. She was in the law office now because the firm was handling her divorce. Her fourth or fifth—Charles Martel was not sure which, nor was he interested. The Roffes of the world were out of his reach.

Charles handed the papers to his superior, nervous, not because Hélène Roffe was in the room—he hardly glanced at her—but because of the presence of the four senior partners. They represented Authority, and Charles Martel respected Authority. He was basically a retiring man, content to make a modest living, reside in a little apartment in Passy and tend to his small stamp collection.

Charles Martel was not a brilliant attorney, but he was a competent one, thorough and reliable. He had a stiff *petsec* dignity about him. He was in his early forties and his physical appearance, while not unattractive, was certainly far from prepossessing. Someone had once said that he had the personality of wet sand, and the description was not an unjust one. It was with a good deal of surprise, therefore, that the day after he had met Hélène Roffe, Charles Martel received a summons to go to the office of M. Michel Sachard, the senior partner, where he was told. "Hélène Roffe wishes you to assume personal charge of her divorce case. You will take over at once."

Charles Martel was stunned. He asked. "Why me, Monsieur Sachard?"

Sachard looked him in the eye and replied. "I can't imagine. See that you service her well."

Being in charge of Hélène's divorce action made it necessary for Charles to see her frequently. Too frequently, he felt. She would telephone him and invite him to dinner at her villa in Le Vésinet to discuss the case, and to the opera and to her house in Deauville. Charles kept trying to explain to her that it was a very simple case, that there would be no problem in obtaining the divorce, but Hélène —she insisted that he call her Hélène, to his acute embarrassment—told him she needed his constant reassurance. Later he was to think back on that with bitter amusement.

During the weeks that followed their first meeting, Charles began to suspect that Hélène Roffe was interested in him romantically. He could not believe it. He was a nobody, and she was a member of one of the great families, but Hélène left him in no doubt as to her intentions. "I'm going to marry you, Charles."

He had never thought of getting married. He was not comfortable with women. Besides, he did not love Hélène. He was not even certain he liked her. The fuss and attention that attended her wherever they went discomfited him. He was caught in the limelight of her celebrity and it was a role he was not accustomed to. He was also painfully aware of the contrast between them. Her flamboyance was an irritant to his conservative nature. She set fashion styles and was the epitome of glamour, while he—well, he was a simple, ordinary, middle-aged lawyer. He could not understand what Hélène Roffe saw in him. Nor could anyone else. Because of her well-publicized participation in dangerous sports that were normally the exclusive province of men, there were rumors that Hélène Roffe was an advocate of the women's liberation movement. In fact, she despised the movement, and had only contempt for its concept of equality. She saw no reason why men should be allowed to become the equal of women. Men were handy to have around, when required. They were not particularly intelligent, but they could be taught to fetch and light cigarettes, run errands, open doors and give satisfaction in bed. They made excellent pets, dressed and bathed themselves and were toilet-trained. An amusing species.

Hélène Roffe had had the playboys, the daredevils, the tycoons, the glamour boys. She had never had a Charles Martel. She knew exactly what he was: *Nothing*. A piece of blank clay. And that was precisely the challenge. She intended to take him over, mold him, see what she could make of him. Once Hélène Roffe made up her mind, Charles Martel never had a chance.

They were married in Neuilly and they honeymooned in Monte Carlo, where Charles lost his virginity and his illusions. He had planned on returning to the law firm.

"Don't be a fool," his bride said. "Do you think I want to be married to a law clerk? You'll go into the family business. One day you'll be running it. *We'll* be running it."

Hélène arranged for Charles to work in the Paris branch of Roffe and Sons. He reported to her on everything that went on and she guided him, helped him, gave him suggestions to make. Charles's advancement was rapid. He was soon in charge of the French operation, and a member of the board of directors. Hélène Roffe had changed him from an obscure lawyer to an executive of one of the largest corporations in the world. He should have been ecstatic. He was miserable. From the first moment of their marriage Charles found himself totally dominated by his wife. She chose his tailor, his shoemaker and his shirtmaker. She got him into the exclusive Jockey Club. Hélène treated Charles like a gigolo. His salary went directly to her, and she gave him an embarrassingly small allowance. If Charles needed any extra money, he had to ask Hélène for it. She made him account for every moment of his time, and he was at her constant beck and call. She seemed to enjoy humiliating him. She would telephone him at the office and order him to come home immediately with a jar of massage cream, or something equally stupid. When he arrived, she would be in the bedroom, naked, waiting for him. She was insatiable, an animal. Charles had lived with his mother until he was thirty-two, when she had died of cancer. She had been an invalid for as long as Charles could remember, and he had taken care of her. There had been no time to think about going out with girls or getting married. His mother had been a burden and when she died, Charles thought he would feel a sense of freedom. Instead, he felt a sense of loss. He had no interest in women or sex. He had, in a naive burst of candor, explained his feelings to Hélène when she had first mentioned marriage. "My —libido is not very strong," he had said.

Hélène had smiled. "Poor Charles. Don't worry about sex. I promise you, you'll like it."

He hated it. That only seemed to add to Hélène's pleasure. She would laugh at him for his weakness, and force him to do disgusting things that made Charles feel degraded and sick. The sex act itself was debasing enough. But Hélène was interested in experimenting. Charles never knew what to expect. Once, at the moment he was having an orgasm, she had put crushed ice on his testicles, and another time she had shoved an electric prod up his anus. Charles was terrified of Hélène. She made him feel that she was the male and he was the female. He tried to salvage his pride but, alas, he could find no area in which Hélène was not superior to him. She had a brilliant mind. She knew as much about the law as he did, and much more about business. She spent hour after hour discussing the company with him. She never tired of it. "Think of all that power, Charles! Roffe and Sons can make or break more than half the countries in the world. *I* should be running the company. My great-grandfather founded it. It's part of me."

After one of these outbursts Hélène would be sexually insatiable, and Charles was forced to satisfy her in ways that did not bear thinking about. He came to despise her. His one dream was to get away from her, to escape. But for that he needed money.

One day, over lunch, a friend of his, René Duchamps, told Charles about an opportunity to make a fortune.

"An uncle of mine who owned a large vineyard in Burgundy has just died. The vineyard is going to be put up for sale—ten thousand acres of first-class *Appellation d'origine contrôllée*. I have the inside track," René Duchamps continued, "because it's my family. I don't have enough to swing the deal by myself, but if you came in with me, we could double our money in one year. At least, come and look at it."

Because Charles could not bear to admit to his friend that he was penniless, he went to the rolling red slopes of Burgundy to view the land. He was deeply impressed.

René Duchamps said, "We'll each put in two million francs. In a year we'll each have four million."

Four million francs! It would mean freedom, escape. He could go away to some place where Hélène could never find him.

"I'll think about it," Charles promised his friend.

And he did. Day and night. It was the chance of a lifetime. But *how?* Charles knew that it would be impossible for him to try to borrow money without Hélène immediately learning about it. Everything was in her name, the houses, the paintings, the cars, the jewelry. The jewelry . . . those beautiful, useless ornaments she kept locked up in the safe in the bedroom. Gradually, the idea was born. If he could get hold of her jewelry, a little at a time, he could replace the pieces with copies and borrow money on the real jewelry. After he had made his killing in the vineyard, he would simply return her jewels. And have enough money to disappear forever.

Charles telephoned René Duchamps and said, his heart pounding with excitement, "I've decided to go in with you."

The first part of the plan filled Charles with terror. He had to get into the safe and steal Hélène's jewelry.

The anticipation of the terrible thing he was about to do made Charles so nervous that he was barely able to function. He went through each day like an automaton, neither seeing nor hearing what was happening around him. Every time Charles saw Hélène he began to sweat. His hands would tremble at odd times. Hélène was concerned about him, as she would have been concerned about any pet. She had the doctor examine Charles, but the doctor could find nothing wrong. "He seems a bit tense. A day or two in bed, perhaps."

Hélène looked long at Charles, lying in bed, naked, and smiled, "Thank you, doctor."

The moment the doctor left, Hélène began getting undressed. "I—I'm not feeling very strong." Charles protested.

"I am," Hélène replied.

He had never hated her more.

Charles's opportunity came the following week. Hélène was going to Garmisch-Partenkirchen to ski with some friends. She decided to leave Charles in Paris.

"I want you home every night," Hélène told him. "I'll telephone you."

Charles watched her speed away, at the wheel of her red Jensen, and the moment she was out of sight he hurried to the wall safe. He had watched her open it often, and he knew most of the combination. It took him an hour to figure out the rest of it. With trembling fingers he pulled the safe open. There, in velvet-lined boxes, sparkling like miniature stars, lay his freedom. He had already located a jeweler, one Pierre Richaud, who was a master at duplicating jewelry. Charles had begun a long, nervous explanation about why he wanted the jewels copied, but Richaud said, matter-of-factly, "Monsieur, I am making copies for everyone. No one with any sense wears real jewelry on the streets these days."

Charles gave him one piece at a time to work on, and when the copy was ready, he substituted it for the real piece. He borrowed money on the real jewelry from the Crédit Municipal, the state-owned pawnshop.

The operation took longer than Charles had anticipated. He could only get into the safe when Hélène was out of the house, and there were unforeseen delays in copying the pieces. But finally the day came when Charles was able to say to René Duchamps, "I'll have all the money for you tomorrow."

He had accomplished it. He was half-owner of a great vineyard. And Hélène had not the slightest suspicion of what he had done.

Charles had secretly begun to read up on the growing of vines. And why not? Was he not a vintner now? He learned about the different vines: *cabernet sauvignon* was the principal vine used, but others were planted alongside it: *gros cabernet, merlot, malbec, petit verdot*. The desk drawers of Charles's office were filled with pamphlets on soil and vine pressing. He learned about fermentation and pruning and grafting. And that the worldwide demand for wine kept growing.

He met regularly with his partner. "It's going to be even better than I thought," René told Charles. "Prices for wine are skyrocketing. We should get three hundred thousand francs a *tonneau* for the first pressings."

More than Charles had dreamed! The grapes were red gold. Charles began to buy travel pamphlets on the South Sea Islands and Venezuela and Brazil. The very names had a magic about them. The only problem was that there were few places in the world where Roffe and Sons did not have offices, where Hélène could not find him. And if she found him, she would kill him. He knew that, with an absolute certainty. Unless he killed her first. It was one of his favorite fantasies. He murdered Hélène over and over again, in a thousand delicious ways.

Perversely, Charles now began to enjoy Hélène's abuse. All the time she was forcing him to do unspeakable things to her, he was thinking, I'll be gone soon, you *convasse*. I'll be rich on your money and there's nothing you can do about it.

And she would command, "Faster now," or

"Harder," or "Don't stop!" and he would meekly obey her.

And smile inside.

In wine growing, Charles knew the crucial months were in the spring and summer, for the grapes were picked in September and they had to have a carefully balanced season of sun and rain. Too much sun would burn the flavor, just as too much rain would drown it. The month of June began splendidly. Charles checked the weather in Burgundy once, then twice a day. He was in a fever of impatience, only weeks away from the fulfillment of his dream. He had decided on Montego Bay. Roffe and Sons had no office in Jamaica. It would be easy to lose himself there. He would not go near Round Hill or Ocho Rios, where any of Hélène's friends might see him. He would buy a small house in the hills. Life was cheap on the island. He could afford servants, and fine food, and in his own small way live in luxury.

And so in those first days of June, Charles Martel was a very happy man. His present life was an ignominy, but he was not living in the present: he was living in the future, on a tropical, sun-bathed, wind-caressed island in the Caribbean.

The June weather seemed to get better each day. There was sun, and there was rain. Perfect for the tender little grapes. And as the grapes grew, so did Charles's fortune.

On the fifteenth day of June it began to drizzle in the Burgundy region. Then it began to rain harder. It rained day after day, and week after week, until Charles could no longer bring himself to check the weather reports.

René Duchamps telephoned. "If it stops by the middle of July, the crop can still be saved."

July turned out to be the rainiest month in the history of the French weather bureau. By the first of August, Charles Martel had lost every centime of the money he had stolen. He was filled with a fear such as he had never known.

"We're flying to Argentina next month," Hélène had informed Charles. "I've entered a car race there."

He had watched her speeding round the track in the Ferrari, and he could not help thinking: *If she crashes, I'm free.*

But she was Hélène Roffe-Martel. Life had cast her in the role of a winner, just as it had cast him in the role of a loser.

Winning the race had excited Hélène even more than usual. They had returned to their hotel suite in Buenos Aires, and she had made Charles get undressed and lie on the rug, on his stomach. When he saw what she had in her hand as she straddled him, he said, "Please, no!"

There was a knock on the door.

"Merde!" Hélène said. She waited, silent, but the knocking was repeated.

A voice called, "Señor Martel?"

"Stay here!" Hélène commanded. She got up, whipped a heavy silk robe around her slim, firm body, walked over to the door and pulled it open. A man in a gray messenger's uniform stood there, holding a sealed manila envelope.

"I have a special delivery for Señor and Señora Martel."

She took the envelope and closed the door.

She tore the envelope open and read the message inside, then slowly read it again.

"What is it?" Charles asked.

"Sam Roffe is dead," she said. She was smiling.

CHAPTER

5

London.
Monday, September 7.
Two p.m.

White's Club was situated at the top of St. James's Street, near Piccadilly. Built as a gambling club in the eighteenth century, White's was one of the oldest clubs in England, and the most exclusive. Members put their sons' names in for membership at birth, for there was a thirty-year waiting list.

The facade of White's was the epitome of discretion. The wide bow windows looking out on St. James's Street were meant to accommodate those within rather than to satisfy the curiosity of the outsiders passing by. A short flight of steps led to the entrance but, aside from members and their guests, few people ever got past the door. The rooms in the club were large and impressive, burnished with the dark rich patina of time. The furniture was old and comfortable—leather couches, newspaper racks, priceless antique tables and deep stuffed armchairs that had held the posteriors of half a dozen prime ministers. There was a backgammon room with a large, open fireplace behind a bronze-covered rail, and a formal curved staircase led to the dining room upstairs. The dining room ran across the entire breadth of the house, and contained one huge mahogany table which seated thirty persons, and five side tables. At any luncheon or dinner the room contained some of the most influential men in the world.

Sir Alec Nichols, Member of Parliament, was seated at one of the small corner tables, having lunch with a guest, Jon Swinton. Sir Alec's father had been a baronet, and his father and grandfather before him. They had all belonged to White's. Sir Alec was a thin, pale man in his late forties, with a sensitive, aristocratic face and an engaging smile. He had just motored in from his country estate in Gloucestershire, and was dressed in a tweed sports jacket and slacks, with loafers. His guest wore a pinstripe suit with a loud checked shirt and a red tie, and seemed out of place in this quiet, rich atmosphere.

"They really do you proud here," Jon Swinton said, his mouth full, as he chewed the remains of a large veal chop on his plate.

Sir Alec nodded. "Yes. Things have changed since Voltaire said, 'The British have a hundred religions and only one sauce.'"

Jon Swinton looked up. "Who's Voltaire?"

Sir Alec said, embarrassed, "A—a French chap."

"Oh." Jon Swinton washed his food down with a swallow of wine. He laid down his knife and fork and wiped a napkin across his mouth. "Well, now, Sir Alec. Time for you and I to talk a little business."

Alec Nichols said softly, "I told you two weeks ago I'm working everything out, Mr. Swinton. I need a bit more time."

A waiter walked over to the table, balancing a high stack of wooden cigar boxes. He skillfully set them down on the table.

"Don't mind if I do," Jon Swinton said. He examined the labels on the boxes, whistled in admiration, pulled out several cigars which he put in his breast pocket, then lit one. Neither the waiter nor Sir Alec showed any reaction to this breach of manners. The waiter nodded to Sir Alec, and carried the cigars to another table.

"My employers have been very lenient with you, Sir Alec. Now, I'm afraid, they've got impatient." He picked up the burned match, leaned forward and dropped it into Sir Alec's glass of wine. "Between you and I, they're not nice people when they're upset. You don't want to get them down on you, you know what I mean?"

"I simply don't have the money right now."

Jon Swinton laughed loudly. "Come off it, chum. Your mom was a Roffe, right? You got a hundred-acre farm, a posh town house in Knightsbridge, a Rolls-Royce and a bloody Bentley. You're not exactly on the dole then, are you?"

Sir Alec looked around, pained, and said quietly, "None of them is a liquid asset. I can't—"

Swinton winked and said, "I'll bet that sweet little wife of yours, Vivian, is a liquid asset, eh? She's got a great pair of Bristols."

Sir Alec flushed. Vivian's name on this man's lips was a sacrilege. Alec thought of Vivian as he had left her that morning, still sweetly asleep. They had separate bedrooms, and one of Alec Nichols' great joys was to go into Vivian's room for one of his "visits." Sometimes, when Alec awakened early, he would walk into Vivian's bedroom while she was asleep and simply stare at her. Awake or asleep, she was the most beautiful girl he had ever seen. She slept in the nude, and her soft, curved body would be half exposed as she curled into the sheets. She was blond, with wide, pale-blue eyes and skin like cream. Vivian had been a minor actress when Sir Alec had first met her at a charity ball. He had been enchanted by her looks, but what had drawn him to her was her easy, outgoing personality. She was twenty years younger than Alec, and filled with a zest for living. Where Alec was shy and introverted, Vivian was gregarious and vivacious. Alec had been unable to get her out of his mind, but it had taken him two weeks to summon up nerve enough to telephone her. To his surprise and delight Vivian had accepted his invitation. Alec had taken her to a play at the Old Vic, and then to dinner at the Mirabelle. Vivian lived in a dreary little basement flat in Notting Hill, and when Alec had brought her home, she had said, "Would you like to come in then?" He had stayed the night, and it had changed his whole life. It was the first time that any woman had been able to bring him to a climax. He had never experienced anything like Vivian. She was velvet tongue and trailing golden hair and moist pulsing demanding depths that Alec explored until he was drained. He could become aroused simply thinking about her.

There was something else. She made him laugh, she made him come alive. She poked fun at Alec because he was shy and a bit stodgy, and he adored it. He was with her as often as Vivian would permit it. When Alec took Vivian to a party, she was always the center of attention. Alec was proud of that, but jealous of the young men gathered around her, and he could not help wondering how many of them she had been to bed with.

On the nights when Vivian could not see him because she had another engagement, Alec was frantic with jealousy. He would drive to her flat and park down the block to see what time she came home, and whom she was with. Alec knew that he was behaving like a fool, and yet he could not help himself. He was in the grip of something too strong to break.

He realized that Vivian was wrong for him, that it was out of the question for him to marry her. He was a baronet, a respected Member of Parliament, with a brilliant future. He was part of the Roffe dynasty, on the board of directors of the company. Vivian had no background to help her cope with Alec's world. Her mother and father had been second-rate music-hall artists, playing the provincial circuit. Vivian had had no education except for what she had picked up in the streets, or backstage. Alec knew that she was promiscuous and superficial. She was shrewd but not particularly intelligent. And yet Alec was obsessed with her. He fought it. He tried to stop seeing her, but it was no use. He was happy when he was with her, and he was miserable when he was without her. In the end he proposed to her because he had to, and when Vivian accepted, Sir Alec Nichols was ecstatic.

His new bride moved into the family house, a beautiful old Robert Adam house in Gloucestershire, a Georgian mansion with Delphic columns and a long sweeping driveway. It was set amid the green of a hundred acres of lush farmland, with its own private hunting, and running streams to fish. At the back of the house was a park that had been laid out by "Capability" Brown.

The interior of the house was stunning. The large front hall had a stone floor and walls of painted wood. There were pairs of old lanterns and marble-topped Adam giltwood tables and mahogany chairs. The library had original eighteenth-century built-in bookcases, and a pair of pedestal tables by Henry Holland, and chairs designed by Thomas Hope. The drawing room was a mixture of Hepplewhite and Chippendale, with a Wilton carpet, and a pair of Waterford glass chandeliers. There was a huge dining room that would seat forty guests, and a smoking room. On the second floor were six bedrooms, each with an Adam fireplace, and on the third floor were the servants' quarters.

Six weeks after she had moved into the house, Vivian said, "Let's get out of this place, Alec."

He looked at her, puzzled. "You mean you'd like to go up to London for a few days?"

"I mean I want to *move* back to London."

Alec looked out the window at the emerald-green meadows, where he had played as a child, and at the giant sycamore and oak trees, and he said hesitantly, "Vivian, it's so peaceful here. I—"

And she said, "I know, luv. That's what I can't stand—the fucking peace!"

They moved to London the following week.

Alec had an elegant four-story town house in Wilton Crescent, off Knightsbridge, with a lovely drawing room, a study, a large dining room, and at the back of the house, a picture window that overlooked a grotto, with a waterfall and statues and white benches set amid a beautiful formal garden. Upstairs were a magnificent master suite and four smaller bedrooms.

Vivian and Alec shared the master suite for two weeks, until one morning Vivian said, "I love you, Alec, but you do snore, you know." Alec had not known. "I really must sleep alone, luv. You don't mind, do you?"

Alec minded deeply. He loved the feel of her soft body in bed, warm against him. But deep inside, Alec knew that he did not excite Vivian sexually the way other men excited her. That was why she did not want him in her bed. So now he said, "Of course I understand, darling."

At Alec's insistence, Vivian kept the master suite, and he moved into one of the small guest bedrooms.

In the beginning, Vivian had gone to the House of Commons and sat in the Visitors' Gallery on days when Alec was to speak. He would look up at her and be filled with a deep, ineffable pride. She was undoubtedly the most beautiful woman there. And then came the day when Alec finished his speech and looked up for Vivian's approval, and saw only an empty seat.

Alec blamed himself for the fact that Vivian was restless. His friends were older than Vivian, too conservative for her. He encouraged her to invite her young companions to the house, and brought them together with his friends. The results were disastrous.

Alec kept telling himself that when Vivian had a child, she would settle down and change. But one day, somehow—and Alec could not bear to know how—she picked up a vaginal infection and had to have a hysterectomy. Alec had longed for a son. The news had shattered him, but Vivian was unperturbed.

"Don't worry, luv," she said, smiling. "They took out the nursery, but they left in the playpen."

He looked at her for a long moment, then turned and walked away.

Vivian loved to go on buying sprees. She spent money indiscriminately, recklessly, on clothes and jewelry and cars, and Alec did not have the heart to stop her. He told himself that she had grown up in poverty, hungry for beautiful things. He wanted to buy them for her. Unfortunately, he could not afford it. His salary was consumed by taxes. His fortune lay in his shares of stock in Roffe and Sons but those shares were restricted. He tried to explain that to Vivian but she was not interested. Business discussions bored her. And so Alec let her carry on.

He had first learned of her gambling when Tod Michaels, the owner of Tod's Club, a disreputable gambling place in Soho, had dropped in to see him.

"I have your wife's IOU's here for a thousand pounds, Sir Alec. She had a rotten run at roulette."

Alec had been shocked. He had paid off the IOU's and had had a confrontation with Vivian that evening. "We simply can't afford it," he had told her. "You're spending more than I'm making."

She had been very contrite. "I'm sorry, angel. Baby's been bad."

And she had walked over to him and put her arms around him and pressed her body against his, and he had forgotten his anger.

Alec had spent a memorable night in her bed. He was sure now that there would be no more problems.

Two weeks later Tod Michaels had come to visit Alec again. This time Vivian's IOU's were five thousand pounds. Alec was furious. "Why did you let her have credit?" he demanded.

"She's your wife, Sir Alec," Michaels had replied blandly. "How would it look if we refused her?"

"I'll—I'll have to get the money," Alec had said. "I don't have that much cash at the moment."

"Please! Consider it a loan. Pay it back when you can."

Alec had been greatly relieved. "That's very generous of you, Mr. Michaels."

It was not until a month later that Alec learned that Vivian had gambled away another twenty-five thousand pounds, and that Alec was being charged interest at the rate of 10 percent a week. He was horrified. There was no way he could raise that much cash. There was nothing that he could even sell. The houses, the beautiful antiques, the cars, all belonged to Roffe and Sons. His anger frightened Vivian enough so that she promised not to gamble anymore. But it was too late. Alec found himself in the hands of loan sharks. No matter how much Alec gave them, he could not manage to pay off the debt. It kept mounting each month, instead of getting smaller, and it had been going on for almost a year.

When Tod Michaels' hoodlums first began to press him for the money, Alec had threatened to go to the police commissioner. "I have connections in the highest quarters," Alec had said.

The man had grinned. "I got connections in the lowest."

Now Sir Alec found himself sitting here at White's with this dreadful man, having to contain his pride, and beg for a little more time.

"I've already paid them back more than the money I borrowed. They can't—"

Swinton replied, "That was just on the interest, Sir Alec. You still haven't paid the principal."

"It's extortion," Alec said.

Swinton's eyes darkened. "I'll give the boss your message." He started to rise.

Alec said quickly, "No! Sit down. Please."

Slowly Swinton sat down again. "Don't use words like that," he warned. "The last chap who talked like that had both his knees nailed to the floor."

Alec had read about it. The Kray brothers had invented the punishment for their victims. And the people Alec was dealing with were just as bad, just as ruthless. He could feel the bile rising in his throat. "I didn't mean that," Alec said. "It's just that I— I don't have any more cash."

Swinton flicked the ash from his cigar into Alec's glass of wine, and said, "You have a big bundle of stock in Roffe and Sons, don't you, Alec baby?"

"Yes," Alec replied, "but it's nonsalable and nontransferable. It's no good to anyone unless Roffe and Sons goes public."

Swinton took a puff on his cigar. "And is it going public?"

"That's up to Sam Roffe. I've—I've been trying to persuade him."

"Try harder."

"Tell Mr. Michaels he'll get his money," Alec said. "But please stop hounding me."

Swinton stared. "Hounding you? Why, Sir Alec, you little cocksucker, you'll know when we start hounding you. Your fucking stables will burn down, and you'll be eating roast horsemeat. Then your house will burn. And maybe your wife." He smiled, and Alec wished he had not. "Have you ever eaten cooked pussy?"

Alec had turned pale. "For God's sake—"

Swinton said soothingly, "I'm kidding. Tod Michaels's your friend. And friends help each other, right? We were talking about you at our meeting this morning. And do you know what the boss said? He said, 'Sir Alec's a good sort. If he hasn't got the money, I'm sure he'll think of some other way to take care of us.'"

Alec frowned. "What other way?"

"Well, now, it's not all that hard for a bright chap like you to work out, is it? You're running a big drug company, right? You make things like cocaine, for example. Just between you and I, who'd ever know if you happened to accidentally misplace a few shipments here and there?"

Alec stared at him. "You're insane," he said. "I —I couldn't do that."

"It's amazing what people can do when they have to," Swinton said genially. He rose to his feet. "You either have our money for us, or we'll tell you where to deliver the merchandise."

He ground his cigar out in Alec's butter plate. "Give my regards to Vivian, Sir Alec. Ta."

And Jon Swinton was gone.

Sir Alec sat there alone, unseeing, surrounded

by all the familiar, comfortable things that were so much a part of his past life, that were now threatened. The only alien thing was the obscene wet cigar butt in the plate. How had he ever allowed them to come into his life? He had permitted himself to be maneuvered into a position where he was in the hands of the underworld. And now he knew that they wanted more than money from him. The money was merely the bait with which they had trapped him. They were after his connections with the drug company. They were going to try to force him to work with them. If it became known he was in their power, the Opposition would not hesitate to make capital of it. His own party would probably ask him to resign. It would be done tactfully and quietly. They would probably exert pressure on him to apply for the Chiltern Hundreds, a post that paid a nominal salary of a hundred pounds a year from the Crown. The one barrier to being an M.P. was that you could not be in receipt of pay from the Crown or the Government. So Alec would no longer be allowed to serve in Parliament. The reason could not be kept secret, of course. He would be in disgrace. Unless he could come up with a large sum of money. He had talked to Sam Roffe again and again, asking him to let the company go public, to let the shares of stock be marketed.

"Forget it," Sam had told him. "The minute we let outsiders in, we have a lot of strangers telling us how to run our business. Before you know it, they'll take over the board, and then the company. What's the difference to you, Alec? You have a big salary, an unlimited expense account. You don't *need* the money."

For a moment Alec had been tempted to tell Sam how desperately he needed it. But he knew it would do no good. Sam Roffe was a company man, a man without compassion. If he knew that Alec had in any way compromised Roffe and Sons, he would have dismissed him without a moment's hesitation. No, Sam Roffe was the last person to whom he could turn.

Alec was facing ruin.

The reception porter at White's walked toward Sir Alec's table with a man dressed in a messenger's uniform, carrying a sealed manila envelope.

"Excuse me, Sir Alec," the porter apologized, "but this man insists that he has instructions to deliver something to you personally."

"Thank you," Sir Alec said. The messenger handed him the envelope, and the porter led him back to the door.

Alec sat there a long time before he reached for the envelope and opened it. He read the message through three times, then he slowly crumpled the paper in his fist, and his eyes began to fill with tears.

CHAPTER

6

New York.
Monday, September 7.
Eleven a.m.

The private Boeing 707-320 was making its final approach to Kennedy Airport, gliding out of the stacked-up traffic pattern. It had been a long, tedious flight and Rhys Williams was exhausted, but he had been unable to sleep during the night. He had ridden in this plane too often with Sam Roffe. His presence still filled it.

Elizabeth Roffe was expecting him. Rhys had sent her a cable from Istanbul, merely announcing that he would arrive the following day. He could have broken the news of her father's death over the telephone but she deserved more than that.

The plane was on the ground now, taxiing toward the terminal. Rhys carried very little luggage, and he was quickly ushered through Customs. Outside, the sky was gray and bleak, a foretaste of the winter to come. A limousine was waiting at the side entrance to drive him to Sam Roffe's Long Island estate, where Elizabeth would be waiting.

During the drive Rhys tried to rehearse the words that he would say to her, to try to soften the blow, but the moment Elizabeth opened the front door to greet him, the words flew out of his head. Each time Rhys saw Elizabeth, her beauty caught him by surprise. She had inherited her mother's looks, the same patrician features, midnight-black eyes framed by long heavy lashes. Her skin was white and soft, her hair a shiny black. Her figure was rich and firm. She was wearing an open-necked creamy silk blouse and a pleated gray-flannel skirt and fawn-colored pumps. There was no sign of the awkward little girl Rhys had first met nine years earlier. She had become a woman, intelligent and warm and completely unselfconscious about her beauty. She was smiling at him now, pleased to see him. She took his hand and said, "Come in, Rhys," and led him into the large oak-paneled library. "Did Sam fly in with you?"

There was no way to break it gently. Rhys took a deep breath and said, "Sam had a bad accident, Liz." He watched the color drain from her face. She waited for him to go on. "He was killed."

She stood there frozen. When she finally spoke, Rhys could barely hear her. "What—what happened?"

"We don't have any of the details yet. He was climbing Mont Blanc. A rope broke. He fell into a crevasse."

"Did they find—?"

She closed her eyes for a moment, then opened them.

"A bottomless crevasse."

Her face had turned white. Rhys felt a quick sense of alarm. "Are you all right?"

She smiled brightly, and said, "Of course. I'm fine, thank you. Would you like some tea or something to eat?"

He looked at her in surprise, and started to speak, and then he understood. She was in shock. She was rattling on, making no sense, her eyes unnaturally bright, her smile fixed.

"Sam was such a great athlete," Elizabeth was saying. "You've seen his trophies. He always won, didn't he? Did you know he climbed Mont Blanc before?"

"Liz—"

"Of course you did. You went with him once, didn't you, Rhys?"

Rhys let her talk, anesthetizing herself against the pain, trying to build an armor of words to ward off the moment when she would have to face her own anguish. For an instant, as he listened to her, he was reminded of the vulnerable little girl he had first known, too sensitive and shy to have any protection against brutal reality. She was dangerously wound up now, tense and brittle, and there was a fragility about her that worried Rhys.

"Let me call a doctor," he said. "He can give you something to—"

"Oh, no. I'm really quite all right. If you don't mind, I think I'll lie down for a while. I'm feeling a bit tired."

"Would you like me to stay?"

"Thank you. That won't be necessary."

She walked him to the door, and as he started to get into the car Elizabeth called, "Rhys!"

He turned.

"Thank you for coming."
Jesus Christ.

Long hours after Rhys Williams had gone, Elizabeth Roffe lay in her bed, staring at the ceiling, watching the shifting patterns painted by the pale September sun.

And the pain came. She had not taken a sedative, because she wanted the pain. She owed that to Sam. She would be able to bear it, because she was his daughter. And so she lay there, all day and all night, thinking of nothing, thinking of everything, remembering, feeling. She laughed, and she cried, and she supposed that she was in a state of hysteria. It did not matter. There was no one to hear her. In the middle of the night, she suddenly became ravenously hungry and went down into the kitchen and devoured a large sandwich and then threw it up. She felt no better. Nothing could ease the pain that filled her. She felt as though all her nerve ends were on fire. Her mind kept going back, back over the years with her father. Through her bedroom window she watched the sun rise. Sometime later, one of the servants knocked at the door, and Elizabeth sent her away. Once the phone rang, and her heart leaped and she reached for it, thinking, It's Sam! Then she remembered, and snatched her hand away.

He would never call her again. She would never hear his voice again. She would never see him again.

A bottomless crevasse.

Bottomless.

Elizabeth lay there, letting the past wash over her, remembering it all.

CHAPTER

7

The birth of Elizabeth Rowane Roffe was a double tragedy. The minor tragedy was that Elizabeth's mother died on the delivery table. The major tragedy was that Elizabeth was born a girl.

For nine months, until she emerged from the darkness of her mother's womb, she was the most eagerly awaited child in the world, heir to a colossal empire, the multibillion-dollar giant, Roffe and Sons.

Sam Roffe's wife, Patricia, was a dark-haired woman of surpassing beauty. Many women had tried to marry Sam Roffe, for his position, his prestige, his wealth. Patricia had married him because she had fallen in love with him. It had proved to be the worst of reasons. Sam Roffe had been looking for a business arrangement, and Patricia had suited his requirements ideally. Sam had neither the time nor the temperament to be a family man. There was no room in his life for anything but Roffe and Sons. He was fanatically dedicated to the company, and he expected no less from those around him. Patricia's importance to him lay solely in the contribution she could make to the image of the company. By the time Patricia came to a realization of what kind of marriage she had made, it was too late. Sam gave her a role to play, and she played it beautifully. She was the perfect hostess, the perfect Mrs. Sam Roffe. She received no love from her husband and in time Patricia learned to give none. She served Sam, and was as much an employee of Roffe and Sons as the lowliest secretary. She was on call twenty-four hours a day, ready to fly wherever Sam needed her, capable of entertaining a small company of world leaders or serving a gourmet dinner to a hundred guests, on a day's notice, with crisp, heavily embroidered tablecloths, gleaming Baccarat crystal, heavy Georgian silverware. Patricia was one of Roffe and Sons' unlisted assets. She worked at keeping herself beautiful, and exercised and dieted like a Spartan. Her figure was perfect, and her clothes were designed for her by Norell in New York, Chanel in Paris, Hartnell in London, and young Sybil Connolly in Dublin. The jewelry Patricia wore was created for her by Jean Schlumberger in Bulgaria. Her life was busy and full and joyless and empty. Becoming pregnant had changed all that.

Sam Roffe was the last male heir of the Roffe dynasty, and Patricia knew how desperately he wanted a son. He was depending on her. And now she was the queen mother, busy with the baby within her, the young prince, who would one day inherit the kingdom. When they wheeled Patricia into the delivery room, Sam clasped her hand and said, "Thank you."

She was dead of an embolism thirty minutes later, and the only blessing about Patricia's death was that she died without knowing that she had failed her husband.

Sam Roffe took time off from his grueling schedule to bury his wife, and then turned his attention to the problem of what he should do with his infant daughter.

One week after Elizabeth was born, she was taken home and turned over to a nanny, the beginning of a long series of nannies. During the first five years of her life, Elizabeth saw very little of her father. He was barely more than a blur, a stranger who was always arriving or leaving. He traveled constantly and Elizabeth was a nuisance who had to be carted along, like a piece of extra luggage. One month Elizabeth would find herself living at their Long Island estate, with its bowling alley, tennis court, swimming pool and squash court. A few weeks later, her nanny would pack Elizabeth's clothes and she would be flown to their villa in Biarritz. It had fifty rooms and thirty acres of grounds and Elizabeth kept getting lost.

In addition, Sam Roffe owned a large duplex penthouse apartment on Beekman Place, and a villa on the Costa Smeralda in Sardinia. Elizabeth traveled to all these places, shunted from house to apartment to villa, and grew up amid all the lavish elegance. But always she felt like an outsider who had wandered by mistake into a beautiful birthday party given by unloving strangers.

As Elizabeth grew older, she came to know what it meant to be the daughter of Sam Roffe. Just as her mother had been an emotional victim of the company, so was Elizabeth. If she had no family life, it was because there was no family, only the paid surrogates and the distant figure of the man who had fathered her, who seemed to have no interest in her, only in the company. Patricia had been able to accept her situation, but for the child it was torment. Elizabeth felt unwanted and unloved, and did not know how to cope with her despair, and in the end she blamed herself for being unlovable. She tried desperately to win the affection of her father. When Elizabeth was old enough to go to school, she made things for him in class, childish drawings and watercolor paintings and lopsided ashtrays, and she would guard them fiercely, waiting for him to return from one of his trips, so that she could surprise him, please him, hear him say, *It's beautiful, Elizabeth. You're very talented.*

When he returned, Elizabeth would present her love offering, and her father would glance at it absently and nod, or shake his head. "You'll never be an artist, will you?"

Sometimes Elizabeth would awaken in the middle of the night, and walk down the long winding staircase of the Beekman Place apartment and through the large cavernous hall that led to her father's study. She would step into the empty room as if she were entering a shrine. This was *his* room, where he worked and signed important pieces of paper and ran the world. Elizabeth would walk over to his enormous leather-topped desk and slowly rub her hands across it. Then she would move behind the desk and sit in his leather chair. She felt closer to her father there. It was as though by being where he was, sitting where he sat, she could become a part of him. She would hold imaginary conversations with him, and he would listen, interested and caring as she poured out her problems. One night, as Elizabeth sat at his desk in the dark, the lights in the room suddenly came on. Her father was standing in the doorway. He looked at Elizabeth seated behind his desk, clad in a thin nightgown, and said, "What are you doing here alone in the dark?" And he scooped her up in his arms and carried her upstairs, to her bed; and Elizabeth had lain awake all night, thinking about how her father had held her.

After that, she went downstairs every night and sat in his office waiting for him to come and get her, but it never happened again.

No one discussed Elizabeth's mother with her, but there was a beautiful full-length portrait of Patricia Roffe hanging in the reception hall, and Elizabeth would stare at it by the hour. Then she would turn to her mirror. Ugly. They had put braces on her teeth, and she looked like a gargoyle. No wonder my father isn't interested in me, Elizabeth thought.

Overnight she developed an insatiable appetite, and began to gain weight. For she had arrived at a wonderful truth: if she were fat and ugly, no one would expect her to look like her mother.

When Elizabeth was twelve years old, she attended an exclusive private school on the East Side of Manhattan, in the upper seventies. She would arrive in a chauffeur-driven Rolls-Royce, walk into her classes and sit there, withdrawn and silent, ignoring everyone around her. She never volunteered to answer a question. And when she was called upon, she never seemed to know the answer. Her teachers soon got in the habit of ignoring her. They discussed Elizabeth among themselves and unanimously agreed that she was the most spoiled child they had ever seen. In a confidential year-end report to the headmistress, Elizabeth's homeroom teacher wrote:

* * *

We have been able to make no progress with Elizabeth Roffe. She is aloof from her classmates and refuses to participate in any of the group activities. She has made no friends at school. Her grades are unsatisfactory, but it is difficult to tell if this is because she makes no effort, or because she is unable to handle the assignments. She is arrogant and egotistical. Were it not for the fact that her father is a major benefactor of this school, I would strongly recommend expelling her.

The report was light-years from the reality. The simple truth was that Elizabeth Roffe had no protective shield, no armor against the terrible loneliness that engulfed her. She was filled with such a deep sense of her own unworthiness that she was afraid to make friends, for fear they would discover that she was worthless, unlovable. She was not arrogant, she was almost pathologically shy. She felt that she did not belong in the same world that her father inhabited. She did not belong anywhere. She loathed being driven to school in the Rolls-Royce, because she knew she did not deserve it. In her classes she knew the answers to the questions the teachers asked, but she did not dare to speak out, to call attention to herself. She loved to read, and she would lie awake late at night in her bed, devouring books.

She daydreamed, and oh! what lovely fantasies. She was in Paris with her father, and they were driving through the Bois in a horse-drawn carriage, and he took her to his office, an enormous room something like Saint Patrick's cathedral, and people kept walking in with papers for him to sign, and he would wave them away and say, "Can't you see I'm busy now? I'm talking to my daughter, Elizabeth."

She and her father were skiing in Switzerland, moving down a steep slope side by side, with an icy wind whipping past them, and he suddenly fell and cried out with pain, because his leg was broken, and she said, "Don't worry, Papa! I'll take care of you." And she skied down to the hospital and said, "Quickly, my father's hurt," and a dozen men in white jackets brought him there in a shiny ambulance and she was at his bedside, feeding him (it was probably his arm that was broken, then, not his leg), and her mother walked into the room, alive somehow, and her father said, "I can't see you now, Patricia. Elizabeth and I are talking."

Or they would be in their beautiful villa in Sardinia, and the servants would be away, and Elizabeth would cook dinner for her father. He would eat two helpings of everything and say, "You're a much better cook than your mother was, Elizabeth."

The scenes with her father always ended in the same way. The doorbell would ring and a tall man, who towered over her father, would come in and beg Elizabeth to marry him, and her father would plead with her, "Please, Elizabeth, don't leave me. I need you."

And she would agree to stay.

Of all the homes in which Elizabeth grew up, the villa in Sardinia was her favorite. It was by no means the largest, but it was the most colorful, the friendliest. Sardinia itself delighted Elizabeth. It was a dramatic, rockbound island, some 160 miles southwest of the Italian coast, a stunning panorama of mountains, sea and green farmland. Its enormous volcanic cliffs had been thrown up thousands of years ago from the primal sea, and the shoreline swept in a vast crescent as far as the eye could follow, the Tyrrhenian Sea framing the island in a blue border.

For Elizabeth the island had its own special odors, the smell of sea breezes and forests, the white and yellow *macchia*, the fabled flower that Napoleon had loved. There were the *corbeccola* bushes that grew six feet high and had a red fruit that tasted like strawberries, and the *guarcias*, the giant stone oaks whose bark was exported to the mainland to be used for making cork for wine bottles.

She loved to listen to the singing rocks, the mysterious giant boulders with holes through them. When the winds blew through the holes, the rocks emitted an eerie keening sound, like a dirge of lost souls.

And the winds blew. Elizabeth grew to know them all. The *mistrale* and the *ponente*, the *tramontana* and the *grecate* and the *levante*. Soft winds and fierce winds. And then there was the dreaded scirocco, the warm wind that blew in from the Sahara.

The Roffe villa was on the Costa Smeralda, above Porto Cervo, set high atop a cliff overlooking the sea, secluded by juniper trees and the wild-growing Sardinian olive trees with their bitter fruit. There was a breathtaking view of the harbor far below, and around it, sprinkled over the green hills, a jumble of stucco and stone houses thrown together in a crazy hodgepodge of colors resembling a child's crayon drawing.

The villa was stucco, with huge juniper beans inside. It was built on several levels, with large, comfortable rooms, each with its own fireplace and balcony. The living room and dining room had picture windows that gave a panoramic view of the island. A free-form staircase led to four bedrooms upstairs. The furniture blended perfectly with the surroundings. There were rustic refectory tables and benches, and soft easy chairs. Across the windows were fringed white wool draperies that had been hand-woven on the island, and the floors were laid with colorful *cerasarda* tiles from Sardinia and other tiles from Tuscany. In the bathrooms and bedrooms were native wool carpets, colored with vegetable dyes in the traditional way. The house was ablaze with paintings, a mixture of French Impressionists, Italian masters and Sardo primitives. In the hallway hung portraits of Samuel Roffe and Terenia Roffe, Elizabeth's great-great grandfather and grandmother.

The feature of the house that Elizabeth loved most was the tower room, under the sloping tile roof. It was reached by a narrow staircase from the second floor, and Sam Roffe used it as his study. It contained a large work desk and a comfortable padded swivel chair. The walls were lined with bookcases and maps, most of them pertaining to the Roffe empire. French doors led to a small balcony built over a sheer cliff, and the view from there was heart-stopping.

It was in this house, when she was thirteen years old, that Elizabeth discovered the origins of her family, and for the first time in her life that she felt she belonged, that she was part of something.

* * *

It began the day she found the Book. Elizabeth's father had driven to Olbia, and Elizabeth had wandered upstairs to the tower room. She was not interested in the books on the shelves, for she had long since learned that they were technical volumes on pharmacology and pharmacognosy, and on multinational corporations and international law. Dull and boring. Some of the manuscripts were rare, and these were kept in glass cases. There was a medical volume in Latin called *Circa Instans*, written in the Middle Ages, and another called *De Materia Medica*. It was because Elizabeth was studying Latin and was curious to see one of the old volumes that she opened the glass case to take it out. Behind it, tucked away out of sight, she saw another volume. Elizabeth picked it up. It was thick, bound in red leather, and had no title.

Intrigued, Elizabeth opened it. It was like opening the door to another world. It was a biography of her great-great grandfather, Samuel Roffe, in English, privately printed on vellum. There was no author given, and no date, but Elizabeth was sure that it was more than one hundred years old, for most of the pages were faded, and others were yellowed and flaking with age. But none of this was important. It was the story that mattered, a story that brought life to the portraits hanging on the wall downstairs. Elizabeth had seen the pictures of her great-great grandparents a hundred times: paintings of an old-fashioned man and woman, dressed in unfamiliar clothes. The man was not handsome, but there was great strength and intelligence in his face. He had fair hair, high Slavic cheekbones and keen, bright-blue eyes. The woman was a beauty. Dark hair, a flawless complexion and eyes as black as coal. She wore a white-silk dress with a tabard over the top, and a bodice made of brocade. Two strangers who meant nothing to Elizabeth.

But now, alone in the tower room, as Elizabeth opened the Book and began to read, Samuel and Terenia Roffe became alive. Elizabeth felt as though she had been transported back in time, that she was living in the ghetto of Krakow, in the year 1853, with Samuel and Terenia. As she read deeper and deeper into the Book, she learned that her great-great grandfather Samuel, the founder of Roffe and Sons, was a romantic and an adventurer.

And a murderer.

CHAPTER

8

Samuel Roffe's earliest memory, Elizabeth read, was
of his mother being killed in a pogrom in 1855
when Samuel was five years old. He had been hidden in the cellar of the small wooden house the
Roffes shared with other families in the ghetto of
Krakow. When the rioting was finally over, endless
hours later, and the only sound left was the weeping
of the survivors, Samuel cautiously left his hiding
place and went out into the streets of the ghetto to
look for his mother. It seemed to the young boy
that the whole world was on fire. The entire sky was
red from the blazing wooden buildings that burned
on every side, and clouds of thick black smoke hung
everywhere. Men and women were frantically
searching for their families, or trying to save their
businesses and homes and meager possessions.
Krakow, in the mid-nineteenth century, had a fire
department, but it was forbidden to the Jews. Here
in the ghetto, at the edge of the city, they were
forced to fight the holocaust by hand, with water
drawn from their wells, and scores of people formed
bucket brigades to drown the flames. Samuel saw
death wherever he looked, mutilated bodies of men
and women tossed aside like broken dolls; naked,

raped women and children, bleeding and moaning for help.

Samuel found his mother lying in the street, half conscious, her face covered with blood. The young boy knelt down at her side, his heart pounding wildly. "Mama!"

She opened her eyes and saw him, and tried to speak, and Samuel knew that she was dying. He desperately wanted to save her, but he did not know how, and even as he gently wiped the blood away, it was already too late.

Later, Samuel stood there watching as the burial party carefully dug up the ground under his mother's body: for it was soaked in her blood, and according to the Scriptures, it had to be buried with her so that she could be returned to God whole.

It was at that moment that Samuel made up his mind that he wanted to become a doctor.

The Roffe family shared a three-story narrow wooden house with eight other families. Young Samuel lived in one small room with his father and his aunt Rachel, and in all his life he had never been in a room by himself or slept or eaten alone. He could not remember a single moment when he could not hear the sound of voices, but Samuel did not crave privacy, for he had no idea that it existed. He had always lived in a crowded maze.

Each evening Samuel and his relatives and friends were locked into the ghetto by the gentiles, as the Jews penned up their goats and cows and chickens.

At sundown the massive double wooden gates of the ghetto were closed and locked with a large iron key. At sunrise the gates were opened again, and the Jewish merchants were permitted to go into the city of Krakow to conduct business with the gentiles, but they were required to be back inside the ghetto walls before sunset.

Samuel's father had come from Russia, where he had fled from a pogrom in Kiev, and he had made his way to Krakow, where he had met his bride. Samuel's father was a stooped, gray-haired man, his face worn and wrinkled, a pushcart peddler who hawked his wares of notions and trinkets and utensils through the narrow winding streets of the ghetto. Young Samuel loved to roam the crowded, bustling, cobblestoned streets. He enjoyed the smell of fresh-baked bread mingled with the odors of drying fish and cheeses and ripening fruit and sawdust and leather. He liked to listen to the peddlers singing out their wares, and the housewives bargaining with them in outraged, grieved tones. The variety of goods that the peddlers sold was staggering: linens and laces, ticking and yarn, leather and meats and vegetables and needles and soft soap and plucked whole chickens and candies and buttons and syrups and shoes.

On Samuel's twelfth birthday his father took him into the city of Krakow for the first time. The idea of going through the forbidden gates and seeing Krakow itself, the home of the gentiles, filled the boy with an almost unbearable excitement.

At six o'clock in the morning Samuel, wearing his one good suit, stood in the dark next to his father in front of the huge closed gates to the city, surrounded by a noisy crowd of men with crude, homemade pushcarts, wagons or barrows. The air was cold and raw, and Samuel huddled into his threadbare sheep's-wool coat.

After what seemed hours, a bright-orange sun

peeped over the eastern horizon and there was an expectant stir from the crowd. Moments later, the huge wooden gates began to swing open and the merchants started to pour through them like a stream of industrious ants, heading toward the city.

As they approached the wonderful, terrible city, Samuel's heart began to beat faster. Ahead he could see the fortifications towering over the Vistula. Samuel clung to his father more tightly. He was actually in Krakow, surrounded by the feared goyim, the people who locked them up every night. He stole quick, frightened glances at the faces of the passers-by and he marveled at how different they looked. They did not wear *payves*, earlocks, and *bekeches*, the long black coats, and many of them were clean-shaven. Samuel and his father walked along the Plante toward the Rynek, the crowded marketplace, where they passed the enormous cloth hall, and the twin-towered Church of Saint Mary. Samuel had never seen such magnificence. The new world was filled with wonders. First of all, there was an exciting feeling of freedom and space that left Samuel breathless. The houses on the streets were all set apart, not jumbled together, and most of them had a small garden in front. Surely, Samuel thought, everyone in Krakow must be a millionaire.

Samuel accompanied his father to half a dozen different suppliers, where his father bought goods which he tossed into the cart. When the cart was filled, he and the boy headed back toward the ghetto.

"Can't we stay longer?" Samuel begged.

"No, son. We have to go home."

Samuel did not want to go home. He had been outside the gates for the first time in his life, and he was filled with an elation that was so strong it almost choked him. That people could live like *this*, free to walk wherever they pleased, free to do whatever they wanted . . . Why could he not have been born outside the gate? Instantly, he was ashamed of himself for having such disloyal thoughts.

That night when Samuel went to bed, he lay awake for a long time, thinking about Krakow and the beautiful houses with their flowers and green gardens. He had to find a way to get free. He wanted to talk to someone about the things he felt, but there was no one who would understand him.

Elizabeth put the Book down and sat back, closing her eyes, visualizing Samuel's loneliness, his excitement, his frustration.

It was at that moment that Elizabeth began to identify with him, to feel that she was a part of him, as he was a part of her. His blood ran in her veins. She had a wonderful, heady sense of belonging.

Elizabeth heard the sound of her father's car coming up the driveway, and she quickly put the Book away. She had no further chance to read it during her stay there, but when she returned to New York the Book was hidden at the bottom of her suitcase.

CHAPTER
9

After the warm winter sunshine of Sardinia, New York seemed like Siberia. The streets were filled with snow and slush, and the wind blowing off the East River was frigid; but Elizabeth did not mind. She was living in Poland, in another century, sharing the adventures of her great-great grandfather. Every afternoon after school, Elizabeth would rush up to her room, lock the door and take out the Book. She had thought of discussing it with her father, but she was afraid to, for fear he would take it away from her.

In a wonderful, unexpected way, it was old Samuel who gave Elizabeth encouragement. It seemed to Elizabeth that they were so much alike. Samuel was a loner. He had no one to talk to. Like me, thought Elizabeth. And because they were almost the same age—even though a century apart—she could identify with him.

Samuel wanted to be a doctor.

Only three physicians were allowed to take care of the thousands of people crowded into the unsanitary, epidemic-ridden confines of the ghetto; and of the three, the most prosperous was Dr. Zeno

Wal. His house stood among its poorer neighbors like a castle in the midst of a slum. It was three stories high, and through its windows could be seen freshly washed and starched white-lace curtains and glimpses of shining, polished furniture. Samuel could visualize the doctor inside, treating his patients, helping them, curing them: doing what Samuel longed to do. Surely, if someone like Dr. Wal took an interest in him, Samuel thought, he could help him become a doctor. But as far as Samuel was concerned, Dr. Wal was as inaccessible as any of the gentiles living in the city of Krakow, outside the forbidden wall.

From time to time Samuel would catch glimpses of the great Dr. Zeno Wal walking along the street, engaged in earnest conversation with a colleague. One day, as Samuel was passing the Wal house, the front door opened and the doctor came out with his daughter. She was about Samuel's age, and she was the most beautiful creature Samuel had ever seen. The moment Samuel looked at her, he knew she was going to be his wife. He did not know how he was going to manage that miracle, he only knew that he had to.

Every day after that, Samuel found an excuse to be near her house, hoping to get another glimpse of her.

One afternoon, as Samuel was walking by the Wal house on an errand, he heard piano music coming from inside, and he knew that *she* was playing. He had to see her. Looking around to make sure no one was observing him, Samuel walked to the side of the house. The music was coming from upstairs, directly above his head. Samuel stepped back and studied the wall. There were enough handholds for him to climb it, and without a moment's hesitation he started up. The second floor was higher than he had realized, and before he reached the window he was ten feet above the ground. He looked down and felt a momentary sense of dizziness. The music was louder now, and he felt as if she were playing for him. He grabbed another handhold and pulled himself up to the window. Slowly he raised his head so he could peer over the sill. He found himself looking into an exquisitely furnished parlor. The girl was seated before a gold-and-white piano, playing, and behind her in an armchair, reading a book, was Dr. Wal. Samuel had no eyes for him. He could only stare at the beautiful vision just a few feet away from him. He loved her! He would do something spectacular and daring so that she would fall in love with him. He would— So engrossed was Samuel in his daydream that he loosened his grip and began to fall into space. He let out a cry and saw two startled faces staring at him just before he plunged to the ground.

He woke up on an operating table in Dr. Wal's office, a spacious room outfitted with medical cabinets and an array of surgical equipment. Dr. Wal was holding an awful-smelling piece of cotton under Samuel's nose. Samuel choked and sat up.

"That's better," Dr. Wal said. "I should remove your brain but I doubt if you have one. What were you planning to steal, boy?"

"Nothing," Samuel replied indignantly.

"What's your name?"

"Samuel Roffe."

The doctor's fingers began to probe Samuel's right wrist, and the boy cried out with pain.

"Hm. You have a broken wrist, Samuel Roffe. Maybe we should let the police fix it."

Samuel groaned aloud. He was thinking about what would happen when the police brought him home in disgrace. His aunt Rachel's heart would be broken; his father would kill him. But, even more important, how could he ever hope to win Dr. Wal's daughter now? He was a criminal, a marked man. Samuel felt a sudden, agonizing jerk on his wrist, and he looked up at the doctor in shocked surprise.

"It's all right," Dr. Wal said. "I've set it." He went to work putting a splint on it. "Do you live around here, Samuel Roffe?"

"No, sir."

"Haven't I seen you hanging about?"

"Yes, sir."

"Why?"

Why? If Samuel told him the truth, Dr. Wal would laugh at him.

"I want to become a doctor," Samuel blurted out, unable to contain himself.

Dr. Wal was staring at him in disbelief. *"That's why you climbed the wall of my house like a burglar?"*

Samuel found himself telling his entire story. He told about his mother dying in the streets, and about his father, about his first visit to Krakow and his frustration at being locked inside the ghetto walls at night like an animal. He told how he felt about Dr. Wal's daughter. He told everything, and the doctor listened in silence. Even to Samuel's ears his story sounded ridiculous; and when he was finished, he whispered, "I—I'm sorry."

Dr. Wal looked at him for a long time, and then said, "I'm sorry, too. For you, and for me, and for all of us. Every man is a prisoner, and the greatest irony of all is to be the prisoner of another man."

Samuel looked up at him, puzzled. "I don't understand, sir."

The doctor sighed. "One day you will." He rose to his feet, walked over to his desk, selected a pipe and slowly and methodically filled it. "I'm afraid this is a very bad day for you, Samuel Roffe."

He put a match to the tobacco, blew it out and then turned to the boy. "Not because of your broken wrist. That will heal. But I'm going to have to do something to you that may not heal so quickly." Samuel was watching him, his eyes wide. Dr. Wal walked over to his side, and when he spoke his voice was gentle. "Very few people ever have a dream. You have two dreams. And I'm afraid I am going to have to break both of them."

"I don't—"

"Listen to me carefully, Samuel. You can never be a doctor—not in our world. Only three of us are allowed to practice medicine in the ghetto. There are dozens of skilled doctors here, waiting for one of us to retire or to die, so that they can take our place. There's no chance for you. None. You were born at the wrong time, in the wrong place. Do you understand me, boy?"

Samuel swallowed. "Yes, sir."

The doctor hesitated, then went on. "About your second dream—I'm afraid that one is just as impossible. There is no chance of your ever marrying Terenia."

"Why?" Samuel asked.

Dr. Wal stared at him. "*Why?* For the same reason you can't become a doctor. We live by the rules, by our traditions. My daughter will marry someone of her own class, someone who can afford to keep her in the same style in which she has been raised. She will marry a professional man, a lawyer or a doctor or a rabbi. You—well, you must put her out of your mind."

"But—"

The doctor was ushering him toward the door. "Have someone look at that splint in a few days. See that the bandage is kept clean."

"Yes, sir," Samuel said. "Thank you, Dr. Wal."

Dr. Wal studied the blond, intelligent-looking boy before him. "Good-bye, Samuel Roffe."

Early the next afternoon, Samuel rang the front doorbell of the Wal house. Dr. Wal watched him through the window. He knew that he should send him away.

"Send him in," Dr. Wal said to the maid.

After that, Samuel came to Dr. Wal's house two or three times a week. He ran errands for the doctor, and in exchange Dr. Wal let him watch as he treated patients or worked in his laboratory, concocting medicines. The boy observed and learned and remembered everything. He had a natural talent. Dr. Wal felt a growing sense of guilt, for he knew that in a way he was encouraging Samuel, encouraging him to be something he could never be; and yet he could not bring himself to turn the boy away.

Whether it was by accident or design, Terenia was almost always around when Samuel was there. Occasionally he would get a glimpse of her walking past the laboratory, or leaving the house, and once he bumped into her in the kitchen, and his heart began to pound so hard that he thought he would faint. She studied him for a long moment, a look of speculation in her eyes, then she nodded coolly and was gone. At least she had noticed him! That was the first step. The rest was only a matter of time. There was not the slightest doubt in Samuel's mind. It was fated. Terenia had become a major part of Samuel's dreams about the future. Where once he had dreamed for himself, he now dreamed for the two of them. Somehow he would get them both out of this terrible ghetto, this stinking, overcrowded prison. And he would become a great success. But now his success would not be for him alone, but for both of them.

Even though it was impossible.

Elizabeth fell asleep, reading about old Samuel. In the morning when she awakened, she carefully hid the Book and began to get dressed for school. She could not get Samuel off her mind. How did he marry Terenia? How did he get out of the ghetto? How did he become famous? Elizabeth was consumed by the Book, and she resented the intrusions that tore her away from it and forced her to return to the twentieth century.

One of the classes that Elizabeth had to attend was ballet, and she loathed it. She would stuff herself into her pink tutu, and stare at her image in the mirror and try to tell herself that her figure was voluptuous. But the truth was there for her to see. She was fat. She would never be a ballet dancer.

Shortly after Elizabeth's fourteenth birthday, Mme. Netturova, her dance teacher, announced that in two weeks the class would give its yearly dance recital in the auditorium, and that the students were to invite their parents. Elizabeth was in a state of panic. The mere thought of getting up on a stage in front of an audience filled her with dread. She could not go through with it.

A child was running across a street in front of a car. Elizabeth saw her, raced out and snatched the child from the jaws of death. Unfortunately, ladies and gentlemen, Elizabeth Roffe's toes were crushed by the wheels of the automobile, and she will not be able to dance at the recital this evening.

A careless maid left a bar of soap at the top of the stairs. Elizabeth slipped and fell down the long flight, breaking her hip. Nothing to worry about, the doctor said. It will heal in three weeks.

No such luck. On the day of the performance, Elizabeth was in perfect health, and in a state of hysteria. Again, it was old Samuel who helped her. She remembered how frightened he had been, but he had gone back to face Dr. Wal. She would not do anything to disgrace Samuel. She would face up to her ordeal.

Elizabeth had not even mentioned the recital to her father. In the past she had often asked him to school meetings and parties which parents were requested to attend, but he had always been too busy.

On this evening, as Elizabeth was getting ready to leave for the dance recital, her father returned home. He had been out of town for ten days.

He passed her bedroom, saw her and said, "Good evening, Elizabeth." Then, "You've put on some weight."

She flushed and tried to pull in her stomach. "Yes, Father."

He started to say something, then changed his mind. "How's school coming along?"

"Fine, thank you."

"Any problems?"

"No, Father."

"Good."

It was a dialogue they had had a hundred times over the years, a meaningless litany that seemed to be their only form of communication. How's-school-coming - along-fine-thank-you-any-problems-no-Father-good. Two strangers discussing the weather, neither listening nor caring about the other's opinion. Well, one of us cares, Elizabeth thought.

But this time Sam Roffe stood there, watching his daughter, a thoughtful expression on his face. He was used to dealing with concrete problems and although he sensed that there was a problem here, he had no idea what it was, and if anyone had told him, Sam Roffe's answer would have been, "Don't be a fool. I've given Elizabeth everything."

As her father started to leave, Elizabeth heard herself say, "My—my—ballet class is giving a recital. I'm in it. You don't want to come, do you?"

And even as she said the words, she was filled with a sense of horror. She did not want him there to see her clumsiness. Why had she asked him? But she knew why. Because she was the only girl in the class whose parents would not be in that auditorium. It doesn't matter, anyway, she told herself, because he's going to say no. She shook her head, furious with herself, and turned away. And behind her, incredibly, she heard her father's voice saying, "I'd like that."

The auditorium was crowded with parents, relatives and friends, watching the students dance to the accompaniment of two grand pianos on either side of the stage. Mme. Netturova stood off to one side, counting the beat aloud as the children danced, calling the attention of the parents to herself.

A few of the children were remarkably graceful, and showed signs of real talent. The others went through their performances determined to substitute enthusiasm for ability. The mimeographed program announced three musical excerpts from *Coppélia, Cinderella* and, inevitably, *Swan Lake.* The *pièce de résistance* was to be the solos, when each child would have her moment of glory, alone.

Backstage, Elizabeth was in an agony of apprehension. She kept peering through the side curtain, and each time she saw her father sitting in the second row center, she thought what a fool she had been to ask him. So far during the show, Elizabeth had been able to lose herself in the background, hidden behind the other dancers. But now her solo was coming up. She felt gross in her tutu, like something in a circus. She was certain they would all laugh at her when she came out on the stage— and she had *invited* her father to watch her humiliation! Elizabeth's only consolation was that her solo lasted for only sixty seconds. Mme. Netturova was no fool. It would all be over so quickly that no one would even notice her. All Elizabeth's father had to do was to glance away for a minute, and her number would be finished.

Elizabeth watched the other girls as they danced, one by one, and they seemed to her like Markova, Maximova, Fonteyn. She was startled by a cold hand on her bare arm, and Mme. Netturova hissed, "On your toes, Elizabeth, you're next."

Elizabeth tried to say, "Yes, madame," but her

throat was so dry that no words came out. The two pianists struck up the familiar theme of Elizabeth's solo. She stood there, frozen, incapable of moving, and Mme Netturova was whispering, "Get out there!" and Elizabeth felt a shove against her back, and she was out on the stage, half naked, in front of a hundred hostile strangers. She did not dare look at her father. All she wanted was to get this ordeal over with as quickly as possible and flee. What she had to do was simple, a few pliés and jetés and leaps. She began to execute the steps, keeping time to the music, trying to think herself thin and tall and lithe. As she finished, there was a smattering of polite applause from the audience. Elizabeth looked down at the second row, and there was her father, smiling proudly and applauding—applauding *her*, and something inside Elizabeth snapped. The music had stopped. But Elizabeth kept on dancing, doing pliés and jetés and battements and turns, carried away, transported beyond herself. The confused musicians began to pick up her beat, first one pianist, then the other, trying to keep up with her. Backstage, Mme. Netturova was signaling to Elizabeth wildly, her face filled with fury. But Elizabeth was blissfully unaware of her, transported beyond herself. The only thing that mattered to her was that she was on-stage, dancing for her father.

"I am sure you understand, Mr. Roffe, that this school simply cannot tolerate that type of behavior." Mme. Netturova's voice was trembling with anger. "Your daughter ignored everyone else and took over, as though—as though she were some kind of *star*."

Elizabeth could feel her father turn to look at her, and she was afraid to meet his eyes. She knew that what she had done was unforgivable, but she had been unable to stop herself. For one moment on that stage she had tried to create something beautiful for her father, had tried to impress him, make him notice her, be proud of her. Love her.

Now she heard him say, "You're absolutely right, Madame Netturova. I will see to it that Elizabeth is suitably punished."

Mme. Netturova gave Elizabeth a look of triumph, and said, "Thank you, Mr. Roffe. I will leave it in your hands."

Elizabeth and her father were standing outside the school. He had not said one word to her since leaving Mme. Netturova's office. Elizabeth was trying to compose a speech of apology—but what could she say? How could she ever make her father understand why she had done what she had done? He was a stranger, and she was afraid of him. She had heard him vent his terrible anger on others for making mistakes, or for having disobeyed him. Now she stood there waiting for his wrath to fall upon her.

He turned to her and said, "Elizabeth, why don't we drop in at Rumpelmayer's and get a chocolate soda?"

And Elizabeth burst into tears.

She lay in her bed that night, wide awake, too stimulated to go to sleep. She kept re-playing the evening over and over in her mind. The excitement of it had been almost more than she could bear. Because this was no made-up daydream. It had happened, it was real. She could see herself and her father, seated at the table at Rumpelmayer's, surrounded by the large, colorful stuffed bears and elephants and lions and zebras. Elizabeth had ordered a banana split, which had turned out to be absolutely enormous, and her father had not criticized her. He was talking to her. Not how's-school-coming-along-fine-thank-you-any-problems-no-Father-good. But really *talking*. He told her about his recent trip to Tokyo, and how his host had served chocolate-covered grasshoppers and ants as a special treat for him, and how he had had to eat them in order not to lose face.

When Elizabeth had scooped up the last drop of the ice cream, her father suddenly said, "What made you do it, Liz?"

She knew that everything was going to be spoiled now, that he was going to reprimand her, tell her how disappointed he was in her.

She said, "I wanted to be better than everyone else." She could not bring herself to add, *For you*.

He looked at her for what seemed a long time, and then he laughed. "You certainly surprised the hell out of everybody." There was a note of pride in his voice.

Elizabeth felt the blood rushing to her cheeks, and she said, "You're not angry with me?"

There was a look in his eyes that she had never seen before. "For wanting to be the best? That's what the Roffes are all about." And he reached over and squeezed her hand.

Elizabeth's last thoughts as she drifted off to sleep were: My father likes me, he really likes me. From now on, we'll be together all the time. He'll take me on trips with him. We'll talk about things and we'll become good friends.

* * *

The following afternoon her father's secretary informed her that arrangements had been made to send Elizabeth away to a boarding school in Switzerland.

CHAPTER

10

Elizabeth was enrolled in the International Château Lemand, a girls' school situated in the village of Sainte-Blaise, overlooking the Lake of Neuchâtel. The age of the girls ranged from fourteen to eighteen. It was one of the finest schools in the excellent Swiss educational system.

Elizabeth hated every minute of it.

She felt exiled. She had been sent away from home, and it was like some dire punishment for a crime she had not committed. On that one magic evening she had felt that she was on the verge of something wonderful, discovering her father, and her father discovering her, and their becoming friends. But now he was farther away than ever.

Elizabeth was able to keep track of her father in the newspapers and magazines. There were frequent stories and photographs of him meeting with a prime minister or a president, opening a new pharmaceutical plant in Bombay, mountain climbing, dining with the Shah of Iran. Elizabeth pasted all the stories in a scrapbook which she constantly pored over. She hid it next to the book of Samuel.

Elizabeth remained aloof from the other students. Some of the girls shared rooms with two or three others, but Elizabeth had asked for a room by herself. She wrote long letters to her father, then tore up the ones that revealed her feelings. From time to time she received a note from him, and there were gaily wrapped packages from expensive stores on her birthday, sent by his secretary. Elizabeth missed her father terribly.

She was going to join him at the villa in Sardinia for Christmas, and as the time drew nearer, the waiting became almost unbearable. She was sick with excitement. She made a list of resolutions for herself and carefully wrote them down:

> Do not be a pest.
> Be interesting.
> Do not complain about anything,
>   especially school.
> Do not let him know you are lonely.
> Do not interrupt while he is speaking.
> Be well groomed at all times, even at breakfast.
> Laugh a lot so that he can see how happy you
>   are.

The notes were a prayer, a litany, her offering to the gods. If she did all these things, maybe—maybe—Elizabeth's resolutions merged into fantasies. She would make profound observations about the Third World and the nineteen developing nations, and her father would say, "I didn't know you were so interesting" (rule number two). "You're a very bright girl, Elizabeth." Then he would turn to his secretary and say, "I don't think Elizabeth needs to go back to school. Why don't I keep her here with me?"

A prayer, a litany.

* * *

A company Learjet picked Elizabeth up at Zurich and flew her to the airport at Olbia, where she was met by a limousine. Elizabeth sat in the back of the car, silent, forcing her knees together to keep them from trembling. No matter what happens, she thought fiercely, I won't let him see me cry. He mustn't know how much I've missed him.

The car drove up the long, winding mountain highway that led to the Costa Smeralda, then off onto the small road that wound to the top. This road had always frightened Elizabeth. It was very narrow and steep, with the mountain on one side and a terrifying abyss on the other.

The car pulled up in front of the house, and Elizabeth stepped out and began walking toward the house and then running, her legs carrying her as fast as they could. The front door opened and Margherita, the Sardinian housekeeper, stood there smiling. "Hello, Miss Elizabeth."

"Where's my father?" Elizabeth asked.

"He had to go to Australia on some emergency. But he left a lot of pretty presents for you. It's going to be a lovely Christmas."

CHAPTER
11

Elizabeth had brought the Book with her. She stood in the hallway of the villa, studying the painting of Samuel Roffe, and next to him, Terenia, feeling their presence, as though they had come to life. After a long time Elizabeth turned and climbed up the ladder to the tower room, taking the Book. She spent hours every day in the tower room, reading and rereading, and each time she felt closer to Samuel and Terenia, the century that separated them disappearing...

Over the next few years, Elizabeth read, Samuel spent long hours in Dr. Wal's laboratory, helping him mix ointments and medicines, learning how they worked. And always in the background was Terenia, haunting, beautiful. The very sight of her was enough to keep alive Samuel's dream that one day she would belong to him. Samuel got along well with Dr. Wal, but Terenia's mother was another story. She was a sharp-tongued virago, a snob, and she hated Samuel. He tried to keep out of her way.

Samuel was fascinated by the many drugs that could heal people. A papyrus had been found that listed 811 prescriptions used by the Egyptians in

1550 B.C. Life expectancy at birth then was fifteen years and Samuel could understand why when he read some of the prescriptions: crocodile dung, lizard flesh, bat's blood, camel's spit, lion's liver, toe of a frog, unicorn powder. The Rx sign on every prescription was the ancient prayer to Horae, the Egyptian god of healing. Even the word "chemistry" derived from the ancient name of Egypt, the land of Kahmi, or Chemi. The priest-physicians were called magi, Samuel learned.

The apothecary shops in the ghetto and in Krakow itself were primitive. Most of the bottles and jars were filled with untested and untried medicinal items, some useless, some harmful. Samuel became familiar with them all. There were castor oil, calomel, and rhubarb, iodine compounds and codeine and ipecac. You could purchase panaceas for whooping cough, colic and typhoid fever. Because no sanitary precautions were taken, it was common to find ointments and gargles filled with dead insects, roaches, rat droppings and bits of feathers and furs. The majority of patients who took the remedies died either of their diseases or from the remedies.

Several magazines were printed that were devoted to apothecary news, and Samuel read them all avidly. He discussed his theories with Dr. Wal.

"It stands to reason," Samuel said, his voice ringing with conviction, "that there must be a cure for every disease. Health is natural, disease is unnatural."

"Perhaps," Dr. Wal said, "but most of my patients won't even let me try the new medications on them." He added dryly, "And I think they're wise."

Samuel devoured Dr. Wal's sparse library on pharmacy. And when he had read and reread those books, he felt frustrated by the unanswered questions that lay between the covers.

Samuel was fired by the revolution that was taking place. Some scientists believed that it was possible to counteract the cause of diseases by building up a resistance that would destroy the illness. Dr. Wal tried it once. He took the blood of a patient with diphtheria and injected it into a horse. When the horse died, Dr. Wal gave up his experiments. But young Samuel was sure that Dr. Wal had been on the right track.

"You can't stop now," Samuel said. "I know it will work."

Dr. Wal shook his head. "That's because you're seventeen, Samuel. When you're my age, you won't be as sure of anything. Forget about it."

But Samuel was not convinced. He wanted to continue his experiments, but for that Samuel needed animals, and there were few available except for the stray cats and rats that he was able to catch. No matter how minute the doses that Samuel gave them, they died. They're too small, Samuel thought. I need a larger animal. A horse or a cow or a sheep. But where was he going to find one?

One late afternoon when Samuel arrived home, an ancient horse and cart stood in front of the house. On the side of the cart a crudely lettered sign read: "ROFFE & SON." Samuel stared at it unbelievingly, then raced into the house to find his father. "That—that horse out there," he said. "Where did you get it?"

His father smiled at him proudly. "I made a deal. We can cover more territory with a horse. Maybe in four or five years we can buy another horse. Think of it. We'll have *two* horses."

That was the extent of his father's ambition, owning two broken-down horses pulling carts through the dirty, crowded streets of the Krakow ghetto. It made Samuel want to weep.

That night when everyone was asleep, Samuel went out to the stable and examined the horse, which they had named Ferd. As horses went, this one was without question one of the lowest of the species. She was a very old horse, swaybacked and spavined. It was doubtful whether she could move much faster than Samuel's father. But none of that mattered. What was important was that Samuel now had his laboratory animal. He could do his experiments without having to worry about catching rats and stray cats. Of course, he would have to be careful. His father must never find out what he was doing. Samuel stroked the horse's head. "You're going into the drug business," he informed Ferd.

Samuel improvised his own laboratory, using a corner of the stable in which Ferd was kept.

He grew a culture of diphtheria germs in a dish of rich broth. When the broth turned cloudy, he removed some of it to another container and then weakened it, first by diluting the broth, then by heating it slightly. He filled a hypodermic needle with it and approached Ferd. "Remember what I told you?" Samuel whispered. "Well, this is your big day."

Samuel plunged the contents of the hypodermic into the loose skin of the horse's shoulder, as he had seen Dr. Wal do. Ferd turned to look at him reproachfully, and sprayed him with urine.

Samuel estimated that it would take about seventy-two hours for the culture to develop in Ferd. At the end of that time Samuel would give her a larger dose. Then another. If the antibody theory was right, each dose would build up a stronger blood resistance to the disease. Samuel would have his vaccine. Later, he would have to find a human being to test it on, of course, but that should not be difficult. A victim of the dread disease should be only too happy to try something that might save his life.

For the next two days Samuel spent almost every waking moment with Ferd.

"I've never seen anyone love an animal so much," his father said. "You can't keep away from her, can you?"

Samuel mumbled an inaudible reply. He felt a sense of guilt about what he was doing, but he knew what would happen if he even mentioned it to his father. However, there was no need for his father to know. All Samuel had to do was extract enough blood from Ferd to make up a vial or two of serum, and no one would ever be the wiser.

On the morning of the third and crucial day, Samuel was awakened by the sound of his father's voice from in front of the house. Samuel got out of bed, hurried to the window and looked out. His father was standing in the street with his cart, bellowing at the top of his lungs. There was no sign of Ferd. Samuel threw on some clothes and raced outside.

"*Momser!*" his father was yelling. "Cheater! Liar! Thief!"

Samuel pushed past the crowd that was beginning to gather around his father.

"Where's Ferd?" Samuel demanded.

"I'm glad you asked me," his father moaned.

"She's dead. She died in the streets like a dog."

Samuel's heart sank.

"We're going along as nice as you please. I'm tending to business, not rushing her, you understand, not whipping her, or pushing her like some of the other peddlers I could name. And how does she show her appreciation? She drops dead. When I catch that *gonif* who sold her to me, I'll kill him!"

Samuel turned away, sick at heart. More than Ferd had passed away. Samuel's dreams had died. With Ferd went the escape from the ghetto, the freedom, the beautiful house for Terenia and their children.

But a greater disaster was to befall.

The day after Ferd died, Samuel learned that Dr. Wal and his wife had arranged for Terenia to marry a rabbi. Samuel could not believe it. Terenia belonged to *him!* Samuel raced over to the Wal house. He found Dr. and Mrs. Wal in the parlor. He walked up to them, took a deep breath and announced, "There's been a mistake, Terenia's mistake, Terenia's going to marry *me*."

They stared at him in astonishment.

"I know I'm not good enough for her," Samuel hurried on, "but she won't be happy married to anyone but me. The rabbi's too old for—"

"*Nebbich!* Out! Out!" Terenia's mother was apoplectic.

Sixty seconds later Samuel found himself standing out in the street, forbidden ever to enter the Wal house again.

In the middle of the night Samuel had a long talk with God.

"What do you want from me? If I can't have

Terenia, why did you make me love her? Haven't you any feelings?" He raised his voice in frustration and yelled, "Can you hear me?"

And the others in the crowded little house yelled back, "We can all hear you, Samuel. For God's sake, shut up and let us get some sleep!"

The following afternoon Dr. Wal sent for Samuel. He was ushered into the parlor, where Dr. and Mrs. Wal and Terenia were gathered.

"It seems we have a problem," Dr. Wal began. "Our daughter can be quite a stubborn young lady. For some reason she's taken a fancy to you. I cannot call it love, Samuel, because I don't believe that young girls know what love is. However, she has refused to marry Rabbi Rabinowitz. She thinks she wants to marry you."

Samuel sneaked a glance at Terenia, and she smiled at him and he almost burst with joy. It was short-lived.

Dr. Wal was going on. "You said that you love my daughter."

"Y—y—yes, sir," Samuel stammered. He tried it again, his voice stronger. "Yes, sir."

"Then let me ask you something, Samuel. Would you like Terenia to spend the rest of her life married to a peddler?"

Samuel instantly saw the trap, but there was no way out of it. He looked at Terenia again and said slowly, "No, sir."

"Ah. Then you see the problem. None of us wants Terenia to marry a peddler. And you're a peddler, Samuel."

"I won't always be, Dr. Wal." Samuel's voice was strong and sure.

"And what *will* you be?" Mrs. Wal snapped. "You come from a family of peddlers, you'll remain a family of peddlers. I will not allow my daughter to marry one."

Samuel looked at the three of them, his mind filled with confusion. He had come here with trepidation and despair, had been lifted to the heights of joy, and now he had been plunged into a black abyss again. What did they want from him?

"We've agreed on a compromise," Dr. Wal said. "We're going to give you six months to prove that you're more than just a peddler. If, by the end of that time, you cannot offer Terenia the kind of life she is accustomed to, then she is going to marry Rabbi Rabinowitz."

Samuel stared at him, aghast. "Six months!"

No one could become a success in six months! No one, certainly, who lived in the ghetto of Krakow.

"Do you understand?" Dr. Wal asked.

"Yes, sir." Samuel understood only too well. He felt as if his stomach were filled with lead. He did not need a solution, he needed a miracle. The Wals would only be content with a son-in-law who was a doctor or a rabbi, or who was wealthy. Samuel quickly examined each possibility.

The law forbade him to become a doctor.

A rabbi? One had to start studying for the rabbinate by thirteen, and Samuel was almost eighteen now.

Wealthy? That was out of the question. If he worked twenty-four hours a day peddling his wares in the streets of the ghetto until he was ninety, he would still be a poor man. The Wals had set an impossible task for him. They had seemingly given in to Terenia by allowing her to postpone her marriage to the rabbi, while at the same time setting conditions that they knew would be impossible for Samuel to meet. Terenia was the only one who believed in him. She had confidence that he could find some kind of fame or fortune in six months. She's crazier than I am, Samuel thought in despair.

The six months began, and time flew.. Samuel's days were spent as a peddler, helping his father. But the moment the shadows of the setting sun began to fall on the walls of the ghetto, Samuel would hurry home, gulp down a bite to eat, and then go to work in his laboratory. He made hundreds of batches of serums, and injected rabbits and cats and dogs and birds, and all the animals died. They're too small, Samuel thought desperately. I need a larger animal.

But he had none, and time was racing by.

Twice a week Samuel would go into Krakow to replenish the merchandise that he and his father sold from the cart. He would stand inside the locked gates at dawn, surrounded by the other peddlers, but he neither saw nor heard them. His mind was in another world.

As Samuel stood there one morning, daydreaming, a voice yelled, "You! Jew! Move on!"

Samuel looked up. The gates had been opened and his cart was blocking the way. One of the guards was angrily motioning for Samuel to move. There were always two guards on duty in front of the gate. They wore green uniforms and special insignia and were armed with pistols and heavy clubs. On a chain around his waist one of the guards carried a large key that opened and locked the gates. Alongside the ghetto ran a small river spanned by an old wooden bridge. Across the bridge was the police garrison where the ghetto guards were stationed. More than once, Samuel had witnessed a hapless Jew being dragged across the bridge. It was always a one-way trip. Jews were required to be back inside the ghetto by sundown, and any Jew caught outside the gates after dark was arrested and deported to a labor camp. It was the nightmare of every Jew that he might be caught outside the ghetto after sunset.

Both guards were supposed to remain on duty, patrolling in front of the gates, all night; but it was common knowledge inside the ghetto that after the Jews were locked in, one of the guards would slip away for a night of pleasure in the city. Just before dawn he would return to help his partner open the gates for the new day.

The two guards that were usually stationed there were named Paul and Aram. Paul was a pleasant man with a genial disposition. Aram was an entirely different matter. He was an animal, swarthy and stockily built, with powerful arms and a body like a beer keg. He was a Jew-baiter, and whenever he was on duty, all the Jews outside the gates made sure that they returned early, because nothing delighted Aram more than to lock a Jew out, club him senseless and drag him across the bridge to the dreaded police barracks.

It was Aram now who stood yelling at Samuel to move his cart. He hurriedly went through the gates and headed for the city, and he could feel Aram's eyes boring into his back.

Samuel's six-months grace period quickly dwindled to five months and then to four months, then three.

There was not a day, not an hour, when Samuel was not thinking about a solution to his problem, or feverishly working in his tiny laboratory. He tried to speak to some of the wealthy merchants of the ghetto, but few had time for him, and those who had time offered him useless advice.

"You want to make money? Save your pennies, boy, and one day you'll have enough to buy a fine business like mine."

That was easy enough for them to say—most of them had been born into wealthy homes.

Samuel thought of taking Terenia and running away. But where? At the end of their journey would lie another ghetto, and he would still be a penniless *nebbich*. No, he loved Terenia too much to do that to her. That was the real trap in which he was caught.

Inexorably the clock ran on, and the three months became two, and then one. Samuel's only consolation during that time was that he was allowed to see his beloved Terenia three times a week, chaperoned, of course, and each time Samuel saw her, he loved her more deeply. It was a bittersweet feeling, for the more often he saw her, the closer he was coming to losing her. "You'll find a way," Terenia kept assuring him.

But now there were only three weeks left, and Samuel was no closer to a solution than when he had started.

Late one night Terenia came to see Samuel at the stable. She put her arms around him and said, "Let's run away, Samuel."

He had never loved her so much as he loved her at that moment. She was willing to disgrace herself, give up her mother and father, the wonderful life she lived, for him.

He held her close and said, "We can't. Wherever we went, I'd still be a peddler."

"I don't mind."

Samuel thought of her beautiful home with the spacious rooms and the servants, and he thought of the tiny squalid room he shared with his father and his aunt, and he said, "*I* would mind, Terenia."

And she turned and left.

The following morning Samuel met Isaac, a former schoolmate, walking down the street, leading a horse. It had one eye, suffered from acute colic, was spavined and deaf.

"Morning, Samuel."

"Morning, Isaac. I don't know where you're going with that poor horse, but you'd better hurry. It doesn't look like it's going to last much longer."

"It doesn't have to. I'm taking Lottie to a glue factory."

Samuel eyed the animal with a sudden, quickened interest. "I shouldn't think they'd give you much for her."

"I know. I just want a couple of florins to buy a cart."

Samuel's heart began to pump faster. "I think I can save you a trip. I'll trade you my cart for your horse."

It took less than five minutes to conclude the bargain.

Now all Samuel had to do was build another cart and explain to his father how he had lost the old one, and how he had come into possession of a horse that was on its last legs.

Samuel led Lottie to the barn where he had kept Ferd. On closer examination the horse was an even more discouraging sight. Samuel patted the animal and said, "Don't worry, Lottie, you're going to make medical history."

A few minutes later Samuel was at work on a new serum.

Because of the crowded and unsanitary conditions of the ghetto, epidemics were frequent. The latest plague was a fever that produced a choking cough, swollen glands and a painful death. The doctors did not know what caused it, or how to treat it. Isaac's father came down with the disease. When Samuel heard the news, he hurried over to see Isaac.

"The doctor has been here," the weeping boy told Samuel. "He said there's nothing to be done."

From upstairs they could hear the terrible sounds of a wracking cough that seemed to go on forever.

"I want you to do something for me," Samuel said. "Get me a handkerchief of your father's."

Isaac stared at him. *"What?"*

"One that he's used. And be careful how you handle it. It will be full of germs."

An hour later Samuel was back at the stable, carefully scraping the contents of the handerchief into a dish filled with broth.

He worked all that night and all the next day and the following day, injecting small doses of the substance into the patient Lottie, then larger doses, fighting against time, trying to save the life of Isaac's father.

Trying to save his own life.

* * *

In later years Samuel was never sure whether God was looking out for him or for the old horse, but Lottie survived the gradually increased doses, and Samuel had his first batch of antitoxin. His next task was to persuade Isaac's father to let him use it on him.

As it turned out, it needed no persuasion. When Samuel reached Isaac's house, it was filled with relatives, mourning the dying man upstairs.

"He only has a little time left," Isaac told Samuel. "Can I see him?"

The two boys went upstairs. Isaac's father was in bed, his face flushed with fever. Each racking cough sent his wasted frame into spasms that left him weaker. It was obvious that he was dying.

Samuel took a deep breath and said, "I want to talk to you and your mother."

Neither of them had any confidence in the little glass vial that Samuel had brought, but the alternative was death. They took a chance simply because there was nothing to lose.

Samuel injected Isaac's father with the serum. He waited at the bedside for three hours, and there was no change. The serum had no effect. If anything, the coughing spells seemed more frequent. Finally Samuel left, avoiding Isaac's eyes.

At dawn the next day Samuel had to go into Krakow to buy goods. He was in a fever of impatience to get back to see whether Isaac's father was still alive.

There were large crowds at all the markets, and it seemed to Samuel that it took forever to make his purchases. It was late afternoon by the time his cart was finally filled and he headed back toward the ghetto.

When Samuel was still two miles away from the gates, disaster struck. One of the wheels of the cart broke in half and the merchandise began to spill onto the sidewalk. Samuel was in a terrible dilemma. He had to find another wheel somewhere, and yet he did not dare leave the cart unguarded. A crowd had begun to gather, eyeing the spilled merchandise with avid eyes. Samuel saw a uniformed policeman approaching—a gentile—and he knew that he was lost. They would take everything away from him. The policeman pushed his way through the crowd and turned to the frightened boy. "Your cart needs a new wheel."

"Y—yes, sir."

"Do you know where to find one?"

"No, sir."

The policeman wrote something on a piece of paper. "Go there. Tell him what you need."

Samuel said, "I can't leave the cart."

"Yes, you can," the policeman said. He cast a stern eye over the crowd. "I'll be right here. Hurry!"

Samuel ran all the way. Following the directions on the piece of paper, he found himself in a blacksmith's shop, and when Samuel explained the situation, the blacksmith found a wheel that was the right size for the wagon. Samuel paid for the wheel out of the small bag of money he carried. He had half a dozen guldens left.

He raced back to his cart, rolling the wheel before him. The policeman was still there, and the crowd had dispersed. The merchandise was safe. With the policeman helping him, it took another half hour to get the wheel on and secure it. Once more he started back home. His thoughts were on Isaac's father. Would Samuel find him dead or alive? He did not think he could stand the suspense of not knowing a moment longer.

He was only a mile from the ghetto now. Samuel could see the high walls rising against the sky. And even as he watched, the sun set on the western horizon, and the unfamiliar streets were bathed in darkness. In the excitement of what had happened, Samuel had forgotten about the time. It was past sundown and he was outside the gates! He began to run, pushing the heavy cart ahead of him, his heart pounding until it felt ready to burst. The ghetto gates would be closed. Samuel recalled all the terrible stories he had heard about Jews who were locked out of the ghetto at night. He began running faster. There would probably be only one guard on duty now. If it were Paul, the friendly one, then Samuel might have a chance. If it were Aram—Samuel could not bear to think about it. The darkness was thickening now, closing in on him like a black fog, and a light rain began to fall. Samuel was nearing the ghetto walls, only two blocks away, and suddenly the huge gates loomed into view. They were locked.

Samuel had never seen them closed from the outside before. It was as though life had suddenly been turned inside out, and he shivered with terror. He was shut away from his family, from his world, from everything that was familiar. He slowed down, approaching the gates warily, looking for the guards. They were not in sight. Samuel was filled with a sudden wild hope. The guards had probably been called away on some emergency. Samuel would find a way to open the gates, or to scale the walls without being seen. As he reached the gates, the figure of a guard stepped out of the shadows.

"Keep coming," the guard commanded.

In the darkness Samuel could not see his face. But he recognized the voice. It was Aram.

"Closer. Come here."

Aram was watching Samuel approach, a thin grin on his face. The boy faltered.

"That's it," Aram called encouragingly. "Keep walking."

Slowly, Samuel moved toward the giant, his stomach churning, his head pounding. "Sir," Samuel said. "Please let me explain. I had an accident. My cart—"

Aram reached out with his hamlike fist, grabbed Samuel by the collar and lifted him into the air. "You dumb son-of-a-bitch of a Jew," he crooned softly. "Do you think I care why you're out? You're on the wrong side of the gates! Do you know what's going to happen to you now?"

The boy shook his head in terror.

"Let me tell you," Aram said. "We got a new edict last week. All Jews caught outside the gates after sundown are to be shipped to Silesia. Ten years at hard labor. How do you like that?"

Samuel could not believe it. "But I—I haven't done anything. I—"

With his right hand Aram hit Samuel hard across the mouth, then let him drop heavily to the ground. "Let's go," Aram said.

"Wh—where?" Samuel asked. His voice was choked with terror.

"To the police barracks. In the morning you'll be shipped out with the rest of the scum. Get up."

Samuel lay there, unable to bring his mind into focus. "I—I have to go inside to say good-bye to my family."

Aram grinned. "They won't miss you."

"Please!" Samuel pleaded. "Let me—let me at least send them a message."

The smile died on Aram's face. He stood over Samuel menacingly. When he spoke his voice was soft. "I said get up, Jew shit. If I have to say it once more, I'll kick your balls in for you."

Slowly, Samuel rose to his feet. Aram took his arm with an iron grip and started walking him toward the police barracks. *Ten years of hard labor in Silesia!* No one ever returned from there. He looked up at the man holding his arm, pulling him toward the bridge that led to the barracks.

"Please don't do this," Samuel pleaded. "Let me go."

Aram squeezed his arm tighter, so that the blood seemed to stop flowing. "Keep begging," Aram said. "I love to hear a Jew beg. Have you heard about Silesia? You'll be just in time for the winter. But don't worry, it's nice and warm underground in the mines. And when your lungs get black with coal and you start coughing them up, they'll leave you out in the snow to die."

Ahead of them across the bridge, barely visible in the rain, was the stark building that served as the police barracks.

"Faster!" Aram said.

And suddenly Samuel knew that he could not let anyone do this to him. He thought of Terenia and his family and Isaac's father. No one would take his life from him. Somehow he had to escape, to save himself. They were crossing the narrow bridge now, the river running noisily below, swollen by the winter rains. There were only thirty yards

154

left to go. Whatever was going to be done had to be done now. But how could he escape? Aram had a gun and even without it the enormous guard could have killed him easily. He was almost twice as big as Samuel and much more powerful. They had reached the other side of the bridge now, and the barracks lay just ahead of them.

"Hurry up," Aram growled, pulling Samuel along. "I've got other things to do."

They were so close to the building now that Samuel could hear the laughter of the guards coming from inside. Aram tightened his grip and started to drag the boy across the cobblestoned yard that led to the police station. There were only seconds left. Samuel reached into his pocket with his right hand and felt the bag with the half-dozen guldens in it. His fingers closed around it, and his blood began to course with excitement. Carefully, he pulled the bag out of his pocket with his free hand, loosened the drawstring and dropped the bag. It landed on the stones with a loud tinkle of coins.

Aram stopped suddenly. "What was that?"

"Nothing," Samuel replied quickly.

Aram looked into the boy's eyes and grinned. Holding Samuel tightly, he took a step back, looked down at the ground and saw the open bag of money.

"You won't need money where you're going," Aram said.

He reached down to pick up the sack, and Samuel reached down at the same time. Aram snatched the sack of money away from him. But it was not the sack that Samuel was after. His hand closed on one of the large cobblestones lying on the ground, and as Samuel straightened up, he smashed it into Aram's right eye with all his strength, turning it into a red jelly, and he kept pounding at him, again and again. He watched the guard's nose cave in, and then his mouth, until the face was nothing but a gout of red blood. And still Aram stood there on his feet, like some blind monster. Samuel looked at him sick with fear, unable to hit him again. Then, slowly, the giant body began to collapse. Samuel stared down at the dead guard, unable to believe what he had done. He heard the voices from the barracks and he became suddenly aware of the terrible danger he was in. If they caught him now, they would not send him to Silesia. They would flay him alive and hang him in the town square. The penalty for even *striking* a policeman was death. And Samuel had killed one of them. He must get away quickly. He could try to flee across the border, but then he would be a hunted fugitive for the rest of his life. There had to be another solution. He stared down at the faceless corpse and suddenly he knew what he had to do. He reached down and searched the guard's body until he found the large key that opened the gates. Then, overcoming his revulsion, Samuel grabbed Aram's boots and began pulling the guard toward the riverbank. The dead man seemed to weigh a ton. Samuel kept pulling, spurred by the sounds coming from the barracks. He reached the riverbank. He stopped a moment to regain his breath, then shoved the body over the edge of the steep embankment and watched it roll into the coursing waters below. One hand clung to the sides of the bank for what seemed an eternity, and then the body was slowly washed downstream, out of sight. Samuel stood there, hypnotized, filled with horror at what he had done. He picked up the rock he had used and threw it into the water. He was still in great danger. He turned and ran back across the bridge toward the huge, locked gates of the ghetto. There was no one around. With trembling fingers Samuel placed the giant key into the lock and turned it. He pulled against the great wooden gates. Nothing happened. They were too heavy for him to move. But on *that* night nothing was impossible to Samuel. He was filled with a strength that came from outside and he pulled the huge gates open. He shoved the cart inside, then closed the gates behind him, and ran toward his house, pushing the cart ahead of him. The tenants of the house were gathered in the living room, and when Samuel walked in, they stared at him as if he were a living ghost.

"They let you come back!"

"I—I don't understand," his father stammered. "We thought you—"

Quickly, Samuel explained what had happened, and their looks of concern turned to expressions of terror.

"Oh, my God!" groaned Samuel's father. "They'll murder us all!"

"Not if you listen to me," Samuel said. He explained his plan.

Fifteen minutes later Samuel and his father and two of their neighbors stood at the gates of the ghetto.

"Suppose the other guard comes back?" Samuel's father whispered.

Samuel said, "We have to take that chance. If he's there, I'll take all the blame."

Samuel pushed open the huge gates and slipped outside alone, expecting to be pounced upon at any moment. He put the huge key in the lock and turned it. The gates of the ghetto were now locked from the outside. Samuel tied the key around his waist, and walked a few yards to the left of the gates. A moment later a rope slithered down the wall like a thick snake. Samuel clung to it while on the other side his father and the others began to haul him up. When Samuel reached the top of the wall, he made a noose of one end of the rope, fastened it to a projecting spike and lowered himself to the ground. When he was safely down, he shook the rope loose.

"Oh, my God!" his father was mumbling. "What's going to happen at sunup?"

Samuel looked at him and replied, "We're going to be pounding on the gates, telling them to let us out."

At dawn the ghetto was swarming with uniformed police and soldiers. They had had to locate a special key to open the gates at sunrise for the merchants who were yelling to be let out. Paul, the second guard, had confessed to leaving his post and spending the night in Krakow, and he had been placed under arrest. But that still did not solve the mystery of Aram. Ordinarily the incident of a guard disappearing so close to the ghetto would have been a perfect excuse to start a pogrom. But the police were baffled by the locked gate. Since the Jews were safely locked up on the *inside*, they obviously could not have harmed him. In the end they decided that Aram must have run off with one of his many girl friends. They thought he might have thrown away the heavy, cumbersome key, and they searched for it everywhere, but they could not find it. Nor would they because it was buried deep in the ground, under Samuel's house.

Exhausted physically and emotionally, Samuel had fallen into his bed and was asleep almost instantly. He was awakened by someone yelling and shaking him. Samuel's first thought was: *They've found Aram's body. They've come to get me.*

He opened his eyes. Isaac was standing there in a state of hysteria. "It's stopped," Isaac was screaming. "The coughing's stopped. It's a *bracha!* Come back to the house."

Isaac's father was sitting up in bed. The fever had miraculously disappeared, and the coughing had stopped.

As Samuel walked up to his bedside, the old man said, "I think I could eat some chicken soup," and Samuel began to cry.

In one day he had taken a life and saved a life.

The news about Isaac's father swept through the ghetto. The families of dying men and women besieged the Roffe house, pleading with Samuel for some of his magic serum. It was impossible for him to keep up with the demand. He went to see Dr. Wal. The doctor had heard about what Samuel had done, but was skeptical.

"I'll have to see it with my own eyes," he said. "Make up a batch and I'll try it out on one of my patients."

There were dozens to choose from, and Dr. Wal selected the one he felt was closest to death. Within twenty-four hours the patient was on his way to recovery.

Dr. Wal went to the stable where Samuel had

been working day and night, preparing serum, and said, "It works, Samuel. You've done it. What do you want for your dowry?"

And Samuel looked up at him and replied wearily, "Another horse."

That year, 1868, was the beginning of Roffe and Sons.

Samuel and Terenia were married, and Samuel's dowry was six horses and a small, well-equipped laboratory of his own. Samuel expanded his experiments. He began to distill drugs from herbs, and soon his neighbors began coming to the little laboratory to buy remedies for whatever ills bothered them. They were helped, and Samuel's reputation spread. To those who could not afford to pay, Samuel would say, "Don't worry about it. Take it anyway." And to Terenia, "Medicine is for healing, not for profit."

His business kept increasing, and soon he was able to say to Terenia, "I think it's time to open a small apothecary shop where we can sell ointments and powders and other things besides prescriptions."

The shop was a success from the beginning. The rich men who had refused to help Samuel before came to him now with offers of money.

"We'll be partners," they said. "We'll open a chain of shops."

Samuel discussed it with Terenia. "I'm afraid of partners. It's *our* business. I don't like the idea of strangers owning part of our lives."

Terenia agreed with him.

As the business grew and expanded into additional shops, the offers of money increased. Samuel continued to turn them all down.

When his father-in-law asked him why, Samuel replied, "Never let a friendly fox into your hen house. One day he's going to get hungry."

As the business flourished, so did the marriage of Samuel and Terenia. She bore him five sons—Abraham, Joseph, Anton, Jan and Pitor—and with the birth of each son Samuel opened a new apothecary shop, each one larger than the one before. In the beginning Samuel hired one man to work for him, then two, and soon he had more than two dozen employees.

One day Samuel received a visit from a government official. "We're lifting some of the restrictions on Jews," he told Samuel. "We would like you to open an apothecary shop in Krakow."

And Samuel did. Three years later he had prospered enough to erect his own building in downtown Krakow and to buy Terenia a beautiful house in the city. Samuel had finally achieved his dream of escaping from the ghetto.

But he had dreams far beyond Krakow.

As the boys grew older, Samuel hired tutors for them, and each of the boys learned a different language.

"He's gone crazy," Samuel's mother-in-law said. He's the laughingstock of the neighborhood, teaching Abraham and Jan English, Joseph German, Anton French and Pitor Italian. Who are they going to speak to? No one here speaks any of those barbaric languages. The boys won't even be able to talk to one another!"

Samuel merely smiled and said patiently, "It's part of their education." He knew to whom his sons would be talking.

By the time the boys reached their middle teens,

they had traveled to different countries with their father. On each of his trips Samuel laid the groundwork for his future plans. When Abraham was twenty-one years old, Samuel called the family together and announced, "Abraham is going to America to live."

"America!" Terenia's mother shouted. "It's filled with savages! I will not let you do this to my grandson. The boy is staying here where he will be safe."

Safe. Samuel thought of the pogroms and Aram, and of his mother's murder.

"He's going abroad," Samuel declared. He turned to Abraham. "You'll open a factory in New York and be in charge of the business there."

Abraham said proudly, "Yes, Father."

Samuel turned to Joseph. "On your twenty-first birthday you will go to Berlin." Joseph nodded.

Anton said, "And I will go to France. Paris, I hope."

"Just watch yourself," Samuel growled. "Some of those gentiles are very beautiful."

He turned to Jan. "You will go to England."

Pitor, the youngest son, said eagerly, "And I'm going to Italy, Papa. How soon can I leave?"

Samuel laughed and replied, "Not tonight, Pitor. You'll have to wait until you're twenty-one."

And thus it worked out. Samuel accompanied his sons abroad and helped them establish offices and factories. Within the next seven years, there were branches of the Roffe family in five foreign countries. It was becoming a dynasty, and Samuel had his lawyer set it up so that, while each company was independent, it was at the same time responsible to the parent company.

"No strangers," Samuel kept warning the lawyer. "The stock must never leave the family."

"It won't," the lawyer assured him. "But if your sons can't sell their stock, Samuel, how are they going to get along? I'm sure you'll want them to live in comfort."

Samuel nodded. "We'll arrange for them to live in beautiful homes. They'll have generous salaries and expense accounts, but everything else must go back into the business. If they ever want to sell the stock, it must be unanimous. The majority of the stock will belong to my oldest son, and his heirs. We're going to be big. We're going to be bigger than the Rothschilds."

Over the years Samuel's prophecy became a reality. The business grew and prospered. Though the family was widely scattered, Samuel and Terenia saw to it that they remained as closely knit as possible. Their sons returned home for birthdays and high holidays. Their visits were more than festive occasions, however. The boys would closet themselves with their father and discuss business. They had their own private espionage system. Whenever one son in one country heard about a new drug development, he would dispatch couriers to report it to the others, and they would begin manufacturing it themselves, so that in this way they kept constantly ahead of their competitors.

As the wheel of the century turned, the boys married and had children and gave Samuel grandchildren. Abraham had gone to America on his twenty-first birthday, in the year 1891. He had married an American girl seven years later and in

1905 she gave birth to Samuel's first grandchild, Woodrow, who sired a son named Sam. Joseph had married a German girl, who bore him a son and a daughter. The son in his turn married a girl, who bore a daughter, Anna. Anna married a German, Walther Gassner. In France, Anton had married a French girl, by whom he had two sons. One son committed suicide. The other married and had one daughter, Hélène. She married several times but had no children. Jan, in London, had married an English girl. Their only daughter had married a baronet named Nichols and had a son whom they christened Alec. In Rome, Pitor had married an Italian girl. They had a son and a daughter. When the son, in his turn, married, his wife gave him a daughter, Simonetta, who fell in love with and married a young architect, Ivo Palazzi.

These then were the descendants of Samuel and Terenia Roffe.

Samuel lived long enough to see the winds of change that swept across the world. Marconi created wireless telegraphy and the Wright brothers launched the first aëroplane at Kitty Hawk. The Dreyfus affair captured the headlines and Admiral Peary reached the North Pole. Ford's Model T's were in mass production; there were electric lights and telephones. In medicine, the germs that caused tuberculosis and typhoid and malaria were isolated and tamed.

Roffe and Sons, a little less than half a century after it had been founded, was a multinational behemoth that circled the globe.

Samuel and his broken-down horse, Lottie, had created a dynasty.

* * *

When Elizabeth had finished reading the Book for perhaps the fifth time, she quietly returned it to its place in the glass case. She no longer needed it. She was a part of it, just as it was a part of her.

For the first time in her life, Elizabeth knew who she was, and where she had come from.

CHAPTER

12

It was on her fifteenth birthday in the second term of her first year at school that Elizabeth first met Rhys Williams. He had dropped in at the school to bring Elizabeth a birthday present from her father.

"He wanted to come himself," Rhys explained, "but he couldn't get away." Elizabeth tried to conceal her disappointment but Rhys was quick to see it. There was something forlorn about the young girl, a naked vulnerability, that touched him. On an impulse he said, "Why don't you and I have dinner together?"

It was a terrible idea, Elizabeth thought. She could visualize the two of them walking into a restaurant together: him, incredibly good-looking and suave, and her, all braces and pudge. "Thank you, no," Elizabeth said stiffly. "I—I have some studying to do."

But Rhys Williams refused to accept no for an answer. He thought of the lonely birthdays he had spent by himself. He got permission from the headmistress to take Elizabeth out for dinner. They got into Rhys's car and started heading toward the airport.

"Neuchâtel is the other way," Elizabeth said.

Rhys looked at her and asked innocently, "Who said we were going to Neuchâtel?"

"Where are we going?"

"Maxim's. It's the *only* place to celebrate a fifteenth birthday."

They flew to Paris in a private jet, and had a superb dinner. It began with pâté de foie gras with truffles, lobster bisque, crisp duck à l'orange and Maxim's special salad, and ended with champagne and a birthday cake. Rhys drove Elizabeth down the Champs-Élysées afterward, and they returned to Switzerland late that night.

It was the loveliest evening of Elizabeth's life. Somehow Rhys managed to make her feel interesting, and beautiful, and it was a heady experience. When Rhys dropped Elizabeth off at school, she said, "I don't know how to thank you. I—it's the nicest time I've ever had."

"Thank your father." Rhys grinned. "It was all his idea."

But Elizabeth knew that that was not true.

She decided that Rhys Williams was the most wonderful man she had ever met. And without doubt the most attractive. She got into her bed that night thinking about him. Then she rose and went to the small desk under the window. She took out a piece of paper and a pen, and wrote, "Mrs. Rhys Williams."

She stared at the words for a long time.

Rhys was twenty-four hours late for his date with a glamorous French actress, but he was not concerned. They wound up at Maxim's, and somehow

Rhys could not help thinking that his evening there with Elizabeth had been more interesting.

She would be someone to reckon with, one day.

Elizabeth was never certain who was more responsible for the change that began in her—Samuel or Rhys Williams—but she began to take a new pride in herself. She lost the compulsion to eat constantly, and her body began to slim down. She began to enjoy sports and started to take an interest in school. She made an effort to socialize with the other girls. They could not believe it. They had often invited Elizabeth to their pajama parties, and she had always declined. Unexpectedly, she appeared at a pajama party one night.

The party was being held in a room shared by four girls, and when Elizabeth arrived, the room was crammed with at least two dozen students, all in pajamas or robes. One of the girls looked up in surprise and said, "Look who's here! We were betting you wouldn't come."

"I—I'm here."

The air was filled with the pungent sweet aroma of cigarette smoke. Elizabeth knew that many of the girls smoked marijuana, but she had never tried any. Her hostess, a French girl named Renée Tocar, walked up to Elizabeth, smoking a stubby brown cigarette. She took a deep puff, then held it out to Elizabeth. "You smoke?"

It was more of a statement than a question.

"Of course," Elizabeth lied. She took the cigarette, hesitated a moment, then put it between her lips and inhaled. She could feel her face going green, and her lungs rebelling, but she managed a smile and gasped, "Neat."

The moment Renée turned away, Elizabeth sank down onto a couch. She experienced a dizziness, but in a moment it passed Experimentally she took another puff. She began to feel curiously light-headed. Elizabeth had heard and read about the effects of marijuana. It was supposed to release inhibitions, take you out of yourself. She took another puff, deeper this time, and she began to feel a pleasant floating sensation, as if she were on another planet. She could see the girls in the room and hear them talking, but somehow they were all blurred, and the sounds were muted and far away. The lights seemed very bright, and she closed her eyes. The moment she did, she was floating off into space. It was a lovely feeling. She could watch herself drifting over the roof of the school, up and up, over the snowy Alps into a sea of fluffy white clouds. Someone was calling her name, calling her back to earth. Reluctantly, Elizabeth opened her eyes. Renée was leaning over her, a look of concern on her face.

"Are you all right, Roffe?"

Elizabeth gave her a slow, contented smile, and said fuzzily, "I'm just wonderful." And in her infinite, euphoric state, she confessed, "I've never smoked marijuana before."

Renée was staring at her, "Marijuana? That's a Gauloise."

On the other side of the village of Neuchâtel was a boys' school, and Elizabeth's classmates sneaked away for trysts at every opportunity. The girls talked about the boys constantly. They talked about their bodies and the size of their penises and what they allowed the boys to do to them, and what they did to the boys in turn. At times it seemed to Elizabeth that she was trapped in a school full of raving nymphomaniacs. Sex was an obsession with them. One of the private games at school was *frôlage*. A girl would completely strip, and lie in bed on her back while another girl stroked her from her breasts to her thighs. The payment was a pastry bought in the village. Ten minutes of *frôlage* earned one pastry. By the end of ten minutes the girl usually reached orgasm, but if she had not, the one administering the *frôlage* would continue and earn an additional pastry.

Another favorite sexual *divertissement* was to be found in the bathroom. The school had large, old-fashioned bathtubs, with flexible hand showers that could be removed from the hook on the side of the wall. The girls would sit in a tub, turn on the shower, and then with the warm water gushing out, they would push the head of the shower between their legs and rub it gently back and forth.

Elizabeth indulged in neither *frôlage* nor the shower head, but her sexual urges were beginning to get stronger and stronger. It was at about this time that she made a shattering discovery.

One of Elizabeth's teachers was a small, slim woman named Chantal Harriot. She was in her late twenties, almost a schoolgirl herself. She was attractive-looking, and when she smiled she became beautiful. She was the most sympathetic teacher Elizabeth had, and Elizabeth felt a strong bond with her. Whenever Elizabeth was unhappy, she would go to Mlle. Harriot and tell her her problems. Mlle. Harriot was an understanding listener. She would take Elizabeth's hand and stroke it, and give her soothing advice and a cup of hot chocolate and cookies, and Elizabeth always felt better immediately.

Mlle. Harriot taught French and also taught a class in fashion, in which she emphasized style and harmony of colors, and the proper accessories.

"Remember, girls," she would say, "the smartest clothes in the world will look terrible if you wear the wrong accessories." "Accessories" was Mlle. Harriot's watchword.

Whenever Elizabeth lay in the warm tub, she found that she was thinking of Mlle. Harriot, of the look on her face when they talked together, and of the way Mlle. Harriot caressed her hand, softly and tenderly.

When Elizabeth was in other classes, she would find her mind drifting toward Mlle. Harriot, and she would remember the times that the teacher had put her arms around her, consoling her, and had touched her breasts. At first Elizabeth had believed that the touches were accidental, but they had happened more and more often, and each time Mlle. Harriot would give Elizabeth a soft, questioning look as though waiting for some response. In her mind Elizabeth could see Mlle. Harriot, with her gently swelling breasts, and her long legs, and she would wonder what she looked like naked, in bed. It was then that the full realization stunned Elizabeth.

She was a lesbian.

She was not interested in boys, because she was interested in girls. Not the kind of silly little girls who were her classmates, but someone sensitive and understanding, like Mlle. Harriot. Elizabeth could visualize the two of them in bed together, holding and comforting each other.

Elizabeth had read and heard enough about lesbians to know how difficult life was for them. Society did not approve. Lesbianism was considered a crime against nature. But what was wrong, Elizabeth wondered, in loving someone tenderly and deeply? Did it matter whether it was a man or a woman? Was it not the love itself that was the important thing? Was it better to have a loveless heterosexual marriage than a loving homosexual one?

Elizabeth thought about how horrified her father was going to be when he learned the truth about her. Well, she would just have to face up to it. She would have to readjust her thinking about the future. She could never have a so-called normal life like other girls, with a husband and children. Wherever she went, she would always be an outcast, a rebel, living outside the mainstream of society. She and Mlle. Harriot—Chantal—would find a little apartment somewhere, or perhaps a small house. Elizabeth would decorate it beautifully in soft pastels, with all the proper accessories. There would be graceful French furniture and lovely paintings on the walls. Her father could help—no, she must not expect any help from her father. In all probability he would never even speak to her again.

Elizabeth thought about her wardrobe. She might be a lesbian, but she was determined not to dress like one. No tweeds or slacks, or tailored suits or vulgar mannish hats. They were the lepers' bells of emotionally crippled women. She would try to look as feminine as possible.

Elizabeth decided that she would learn to be a great cook so that she could prepare Mlle. Harriot's —Chantal's—favorite dishes. She visualized the two of them sitting in their apartment, or small house, enjoying a candle-lit dinner that Elizabeth had prepared. First, there would be vichyssoise, followed by a lovely salad, then perhaps shrimp or lobster, or a Chateaubriand, with delicate ices for dessert. After dinner they would sit on the floor before a blazing fire in the hearth, watching the soft snowflakes fall outside. *Snowflakes*. So it would be winter. Elizabeth hastily revised the menu. Instead of a cold vichyssoise she would prepare a nice, hearty onion soup, and perhaps make a fondue. The dessert could be a soufflé. She would have to learn to time it so that it would not fall. *Then* the two of them would sit on the floor before a warming fire, and read poetry to each other. T. S. Eliot, perhaps. Or V. J. Rajadhon.

> Time is the enemy of love,
> The thief that shortens
> All our golden hours.
> I have never understood then
> Why lovers count their happiness
> In days and nights and years,
> While our love can only be measured
> In our joys and sighs and tears.

Ah, yes, Elizabeth could see the long years stretching out before the two of them, and the passage of time would begin to melt into a golden, warm glow.

She would fall asleep.

Elizabeth had been expecting it, and yet when it happened it caught her by surprise. She was awakened one night by the sound of someone entering her room and softly closing the door. Elizabeth's eyes flew open. She could see a shadow moving across the moon-dappled room toward her bed, and a ray of moonlight fell across Mlle. Harriot's—Chantal's face. Elizabeth's heart began to beat wildly.

Chantal whispered, "Elizabeth," and, standing there, slipped off her robe. She was wearing nothing underneath. Elizabeth's mouth went dry. She had thought of this moment so often, and now that it was actually happening, she was in a panic. In truth she was not sure exactly what she was supposed to do, or how. She did not want to make a fool of herself in front of the woman she loved.

"Look at me," Chantal commanded hoarsely. Elizabeth did. She let her eyes roam over the naked body. In the flesh Chantal Harriot was not quite what Elizabeth had envisioned. Her breasts looked a little like puckered apples, and they sagged a bit. She had a tiny potbelly, and her derrière seemed—this was the only word Elizabeth could think of—underslung.

But none of that was important. What mattered was what lay underneath, the soul of the woman, the courage and the daring to be different from everyone else, to defy the whole world and to want to share the rest of her life with Elizabeth.

"Move over, *mon petit ange*," she was whispering.

Elizabeth did as she was told, and the teacher slipped into bed beside her. There was a strong, feral smell about her. She turned toward Elizabeth and put her arms around her, and said, "Oh, *chérie*, I have dreamed of this moment." And she kissed Elizabeth on the lips, forcing her tongue into Elizabeth's mouth, and making quick, groaning noises.

It was without doubt the most unpleasant sensation Elizabeth had ever experienced. She lay there in shock. Chantal's—Mlle. Harriot's—fingers were moving across Elizabeth's body, squeezing her breasts, slowly sliding down her stomach toward her thighs. And all the time her lips were on Elizabeth's, slobbering, like an animal.

This was it. This was the beautiful magic moment. *If we were one, you and I, together we would make a universe to shake the stars and move the heavens.*

Mlle. Harriot's hands were moving downward, caressing Elizabeth's thighs, starting to reach between her legs. Quickly, Elizabeth tried to conjure up the candle-lit dinners and the soufflé and the evenings before the fireplace, and all the wonderful years the two of them would share together; but it was no use. Elizabeth's mind and flesh were repelled; she felt as though her body was being violated.

Mlle. Harriot moaned, "Oh, *chérie,* I want to fuck you."

And all Elizabeth could think of to say was, "There's a problem. One of us has the wrong accessories."

And she began to laugh and cry hysterically, weeping for the beautiful candlelit vision that had died, and laughing because she was a healthy, normal girl who had just learned that she was free.

The next day Elizabeth tried the shower nozzle.

CHAPTER

13

At Easter vacation, in her final year at school, when she was eighteen, Elizabeth went to the villa in Sardinia to spend ten days. She had learned to drive, and for the first time she was free to explore the island on her own. She took long drives along the beaches and visited tiny fishing villages. She swam at the villa, under the warm Mediterranean sun, and at night lay in her bed listening to the mournful sound of the singing rocks, as the wind gently blew through them. She went to a carnival in Tempio, where the entire village dressed up in national costumes. Hidden behind the anonymity of domino masks, the girls invited the boys to dance, and everyone felt free to do things they would not dare do at any other time. A boy might *think* he knew which girl he made love to that night, but the next morning he could not be certain. It was, Elizabeth thought, like an entire village playing *The Guardsman*.

She drove to Punta Murra and watched the Sardos cook small lambs on open fires. The native islanders gave her *seada*, a goat cheese covered in a dough, with hot honey over it. She drank the delicious *selememont*, the local white wine that could be had nowhere else in the world because it was too delicate to travel.

One of Elizabeth's favorite haunts was the Red Lion Inn at Porto Cervo. It was a little pub in a basement, with ten tables for dining, and an old-fashioned bar.

Elizabeth dubbed that vacation the Time of the Boys. They were the sons of the rich, and they came in swarms, inviting Elizabeth to a constant round of swimming and riding parties. It was the first move in the mating rite.

"They're all highly eligible," Elizabeth's father assured her.

To Elizabeth they were all clods. They drank too much, talked too much and pawed her. She was sure they wanted her not for herself, because she might be an intelligent or worthwhile human being, but because she was a Roffe, heiress to the Roffe dynasty. Elizabeth had no idea that she had grown into a beauty, for it was easier to believe the truth of the past than the reflection in her mirror.

The boys wined and dined her and tried to get her into bed. They sensed that Elizabeth was a virgin, and some aberration in the male ego deluded each boy into the conviction that if he could take away Elizabeth's virginity, she would fall madly in love with him and be his slave forever. They refused to give up. No matter where they took Elizabeth, the evenings always ended up the same. "Let's go to bed." And always she politely refused them.

They did not know what to make of her. They knew she was beautiful, so it followed that she must be stupid. It never occurred to them that she was more intelligent than they. Who ever heard of a girl being both beautiful *and* intelligent?

And so Elizabeth went out with the boys to please her father, but they all bored her.

Rhys Williams came to the villa, and Elizabeth was surprised at how excited and pleased she was to see him again. He was even more attractive than she had remembered.

Rhys seemed glad to see her. "What's happened to you?" he asked.

"What do you mean?"

"Have you looked in your mirror lately?"

She blushed. "No."

He turned to Sam. "Unless the boys are all deaf, dumb and blind, I have a feeling Liz isn't going to be with us much longer."

Us! Elizabeth enjoyed hearing him say that. She hung around the two men as much as she dared, serving them drinks, running errands for them, enjoying just looking at Rhys. Sometimes Elizabeth would sit in the background, listening as they discussed business affairs, and she was fascinated. They spoke of mergers and of new factories, and products that had succeeded and others that had failed, and why. They talked about their competitors, and planned strategies and counter-strategies. To Elizabeth it was all heady stuff.

One day when Sam was up in the tower room, working, Rhys invited Elizabeth to lunch. She took him to the Red Lion and watched him shoot darts with the men at the bar. Elizabeth marveled at how much at home Rhys was. He seemed to fit in anywhere. She had heard a Spanish expression that she had never understood, but she did now as she watched Rhys. *He's a man easy in his skin.*

They sat at a small corner table with a red-and-white tablecloth, and had shepherd's pie and ale, and they talked. Rhys asked her about school.

"It's really not too bad," Elizabeth confessed. "I'm learning how little I know."

Rhys smiled. "Very few people get that far. You finish in June, don't you?"

Elizabeth wondered how he had known. "Yes."

"Do you know what you want to do after that?"

It was the question she had been asking herself. "No. Not really."

"Interested in getting married?"

For one quick instant her heart missed a beat. Then she realized that it was a general question. "I haven't found anyone yet." She thought of Mlle. Harriot and the cozy dinners in front of the fireplace and the snow falling, and she laughed aloud.

"Secret?" Rhys asked.

"Secret." She wished she could share it with him, but she did not know him well enough. The truth was, Elizabeth realized, that she did not know Rhys at all. He was a charming, handsome stranger who had once taken pity on her and flown her to Paris for a birthday dinner. She knew that he was brilliant in business and that her father depended on him. But she knew nothing about his personal life, or what he was really like. Watching him, Elizabeth had the feeling that he was a many-layered man, that the emotions he showed were to conceal the emotions he felt, and Elizabeth wondered if anyone really knew him.

It was Rhys Williams who was responsible for Elizabeth's losing her virginity.

The idea of going to bed with a man had become more and more appealing to Elizabeth. Part of it was the strong physical urge that sometimes caught her unaware and gripped her in waves of frustration, an urgent physical ache that would not leave. But there was also a strong curiosity, the need to know what *it* was like. She could not go to bed with just anyone, of course. He had to be someone special, someone she could cherish, someone who would cherish her.

On a Saturday night Elizabeth's father gave a gala at the villa.

"Put on your most beautiful dress," Rhys told Elizabeth. "I want to show you off to everyone."

Thrilled, Elizabeth had taken it for granted that she would be Rhys's date. When Rhys arrived, he had with him a beautiful blond Italian princess. Elizabeth felt so outraged and betrayed that at midnight she left the party and went to bed with a bearded drunken Russian painter named Vassilov.

The entire, brief affair was a disaster. Elizabeth was so nervous and Vassilov was so drunk that it seemed to Elizabeth that there was no beginning, middle or end. The foreplay consisted of Vassilov pulling down his pants and flopping onto the bed. At that point Elizabeth was tempted to flee but she was determined to punish Rhys for his perfidy. She got undressed and crawled into bed. A moment later, with no warning, Vassilov was entering her. It was a strange sensation. It was not unpleasant, but neither did the earth shake. She felt Vassilov's body give a quick shudder, and a moment later he was snoring. Elizabeth lay there filled with self-disgust. It was hard to believe that all the songs and books and poems were about *this*. She thought of Rhys, and she wanted to weep. Quietly, Elizabeth put on her clothes and went home. When the painter telephoned her the next morning, Elizabeth had the housekeeper tell him that she was not in. The following day Elizabeth returned to school.

She flew back in the company jet with her father and Rhys. The plane, which had been built to carry a hundred passengers, had been converted into a luxury ship. It had two large, beautifully decorated bedrooms in the rear, with full bathrooms, a comfortable office, a sitting room amidship, with paintings, and an elaborately equipped galley up front. Elizabeth thought of it as her father's magic carpet.

The two men talked business most of the time. When Rhys was free, he and Elizabeth played a game of chess. She played him to a draw, and when Rhys said, "I'm impressed," Elizabeth blushed with pleasure.

The last few months of school went by swiftly. It was time to begin thinking about her future. Elizabeth thought of Rhys's question, *Do you know what you want to do with your life?* She was not sure yet. But because of old Samuel, Elizabeth had become fascinated by the family business, and knew that she would like to become a part of it. She was not sure what she could do. Perhaps she could start by helping her father. She remembered all the tales of the wonderful hostess her mother had become, how invaluable she had been to Sam. She would try to take her mother's place.

It would be a start.

CHAPTER

14

The Swedish Ambassador's free hand was squeezing Elizabeth's bottom, and she tried to ignore it as they danced around the room, her lips smiling, her eyes expertly scanning the elegantly dressed guests, the orchestra, the liveried servants, the buffet heaped with a variety of exotic dishes and fine wines, and she thought to herself with satisfaction, It's a good party.

They were in the ballroom of the Long Island estate. There were two hundred guests, all of them important to Roffe and Sons. Elizabeth became aware that the Ambassador was pressing his body closer to hers, trying to arouse her. He flicked his tongue in her ear and whispered, "You're a beautiful dancer."

"So are you," Elizabeth said with a smile, and she made a sudden misstep and came down hard on his toe with the sharp heel of her shoe. He gave a cry of pain and Elizabeth exclaimed contritely, "I'm so sorry, Ambassador. Let me get you a drink."

She left him and threaded her way toward the bar, making her way easily through the guests, her eyes moving carefully around the room, checking to see that everything was perfect.

Perfection—that was what her father demanded. Elizabeth had been the hostess for a hundred of Sam's parties now, but she had never learned to relax. Each party was an event, an opening night, with dozens of things that could go wrong. Yet she had never known such happiness. Her girlhood dream of being close to her father, of his wanting her, needing her, had come true. She had learned to adjust to the fact that his needs were impersonal, that her value to him was based on how much she could contribute to the company. That was Sam Roffe's only criterion for judging people. Elizabeth had been able to fill the gap that had existed since her mother's death. She had become her father's hostess. But because Elizabeth was a highly intelligent girl, she had become much more than that. She attended business conferences with Sam, in airplanes and in foreign hotel suites and factories and at embassies and palaces. She watched her father wield his power, deploying the billions of dollars at his command to buy and sell, tear down and build. Roffe and Sons was a vast cornucopia, and Elizabeth watched her father bestow its largesse on its friends, and withhold its bounty from its enemies. It was a fascinating world, filled with interesting people, and Sam Roffe was the master of it all.

As Elizabeth looked around the ballroom now, she saw Sam standing at the bar, chatting with Rhys, a prime minister and a senator from California. Her father saw Elizabeth and waved her over. As Elizabeth moved toward him, she thought of the time, three years earlier, when it had all begun.

Elizabeth had flown home the day of her graduation. She was eighteen. Home, at the moment, had been the apartment at Beekman Place in Manhattan. Rhys had been there with her father. She had somehow known that he would be. She carried pictures of him in the secret places of her thoughts, and whenever she was lonely or depressed or discouraged, she would take them out and warm herself with her memories. In the beginning it had seemed hopeless. A fifteen-year-old schoolgirl and a man of twenty-five. Those ten years might as well have been a hundred. But through some wonderful mathematical alchemy, at eighteen the difference in years was less important. It was as though she were growing older faster than Rhys, trying to catch up to him.

Both men rose as she walked into the library, where they were talking business. Her father said casually, "Elizabeth. Just get in?"

"Yes."

"Ah. So school's finished."

"Yes."

"That's fine."

And that was the extent of her welcome home. Rhys was walking toward her, smiling. He seemed genuinely pleased to see her. "You look wonderful, Liz. How was the graduation? Sam wanted to be there but he couldn't get away."

He was saying all the things her father should have been saying.

Elizabeth was angry with herself for being hurt. It was not that her father did not love her, she told herself, it was just that he was dedicated to a world in which she had no part. He would have taken a son into his world; a daughter was alien to him. She did not fit into the Corporate Plan.

"I'm interrupting." She moved toward the door.

"Wait a minute," Rhys said. He turned to Sam. "Liz has come home just in time. She can help with the party Saturday night."

Sam turned to Elizabeth, studying her objectively, as though newly assessing her. She resembled her mother. She had the same beauty, the same natural elegance. A flicker of interest came into Sam's eyes. It had not occurred to him before that his daughter might be a potential asset to Roffe and Sons. "Do you have a formal dress?"

Elizabeth looked at him in surprise. "I—"

"It doesn't matter. Go buy one. Do you know how to give a party?"

Elizabeth swallowed and said, "Certainly." Wasn't that one of the advantages of going to a Swiss finishing school? They taught you all the social graces. "Of course I know how to give a party."

"Good. I've invited a group from Saudi Arabia. There'll be about—" He turned to Rhys.

Rhys smiled at Elizabeth and said, "Forty. Give or take a few."

"Leave everything to me," Elizabeth said confidently.

The dinner was a complete fiasco.

Elizabeth had told the chef to prepare crab cocktails for the first course, followed by individual cassoulets, served with vintage wines. Unfortunately the cassoulet had pork in it, and the Arabs touched neither shellfish nor pork. Nor did they drink alcoholic beverages. The guests stared at the food, eating nothing. Elizabeth sat at the head of the long table, across the room from her father, frozen with embarrassment, dying inside.

It was Rhys Williams who saved the evening.

He disappeared into the study for a few moments and spoke into the telephone. Then he came back into the dining room and entertained the guests with amusing stories, while the staff began to clear the table.

In what seemed no time at all, a fleet of catering trucks drove up, and as if by magic a variety of dishes began appearing. Couscous and lamb *en brochette* and rice and platters of roast chicken and fish, followed by sweetmeats and cheese and fresh fruits. Everyone enjoyed the food except Elizabeth. She was so upset that she could not swallow a bite. Each time she looked up at Rhys, he was watching her, a conspiratorial look in his eyes. Elizabeth could not have said why, but she was mortified that Rhys should not only witness her shame but save her from it. When the evening finally ended, and the last of the guests had reluctantly departed in the early hours of the morning, Elizabeth and Sam and Rhys were in the drawing room. Rhys was pouring a brandy.

Elizabeth took a deep breath and turned to her father, "I'm sorry about the dinner. If it hadn't been for Rhys—"

"I'm sure you'll do better next time," Sam said flatly.

Sam was right. From that time on, when Elizabeth gave a party, whether it was for four people or for four hundred, she researched the guests, found out their likes and dislikes, what they ate and drank, and what type of entertainment they enjoyed. She kept a catalog with file cards on each person. The guests were flattered to find that their favorite brand of wine or whiskey or cigars had been stocked for them, and that Elizabeth was able to discuss their work knowledgeably.

Rhys attended most of the parties, and he was always with the most beautiful girl there. Elizabeth hated them all. She tried to copy them. If Rhys brought a girl who wore her hair pinned up in the back, Elizabeth did her hair the same way. She tried to dress the way Rhys's girls dressed, to act the way they acted. But none of it seemed to make any impression on Rhys. He did not even seem to notice. Frustrated, Elizabeth decided that she might as well be herself.

On the morning of her twenty-first birthday, when Elizabeth came down to breakfast, Sam said, "Order some theater tickets for tonight. Supper afterward at 'Twenty-one.' "

Elizabeth thought, He remembered, and she was inordinately pleased.

Then her father added, "There'll be twelve of us. We'll be going over the new Bolivian contracts."

She said nothing about her birthday. She received telegrams from a few former schoolmates, but that was it. Until six o'clock that evening, when an enormous bouquet of flowers arrived for her. Elizabeth was sure it was from her father. But the card read: "What a lovely day for a lovely lady." It was signed "Rhys."

Her father left the house at seven o'clock that evening on his way to the theater. He noticed the flowers and said absently, "Got a beau, huh?"

Elizabeth was tempted to say, "They're a birthday present," but what would have been the point? If you had to remind someone you loved that it was your birthday, then it was futile.

She watched her father leave, and wondered what she would do with her evening. Twenty-one had always seemed such an important milestone. It signified growing up, having freedom, becoming a woman. Well, here was the magic day, and she felt no different from the way she had felt last year, or the year before. Why couldn't he have remembered? Would he have remembered if she were his son?

The butler appeared to ask her about dinner. Elizabeth was not hungry. She felt lonely and deserted. She knew she was feeling sorry for herself, but it was more than this uncelebrated birthday she was regretting. It was all the lonely birthdays of the past, the pain of growing up alone, without a mother or a father or anyone to give a damn.

At ten o'clock that night she dressed in a robe, sitting in the living room in the dark, in front of the fireplace, when a voice said, "Happy birthday."

The lights came on and Rhys Williams stood there. He walked over to her and said reprovingly, "This is no way to celebrate. How many times does a girl have a twenty-first birthday?"

"I—I thought you were supposed to be with my father tonight," Elizabeth said, flustered.

"I was. He mentioned that you were staying home alone tonight. Get dressed. We're going to dinner."

Elizabeth shook her head. She refused to accept his pity. "Thank you, Rhys. I—I'm really not hungry."

"I am, and I hate eating alone. I'm giving you five minutes to get into some clothes, or I'm taking you out like that."

They ate at a diner in Long Island, and they had hamburgers and chili and french-fried onions and root beer, and they talked, and Elizabeth thought it was better than the dinner she had had at Maxim's. All of Rhys's attention was focused on her, and she could understand why he was so damned attractive to women. It was not just his looks. It was the fact that he truly liked women, that he enjoyed being with them. He made Elizabeth feel like someone special, that he wanted to be with her more than with anyone else in the world. No wonder, Elizabeth thought, everyone fell in love with him.

Rhys told her a little about his boyhood in Wales, and he made it sound wonderful and adventurous and gay. "I ran away from home," he said, "because there was a hunger in me to see everything and do everything. I wanted to be everyone I saw. *I* wasn't enough for me. Can you understand that?"

Oh, how well she understood it!

"I worked at the parks and the beaches and one summer I had a job taking tourists down the Rhosili in coracles, and—"

"Wait a minute," Elizabeth interrupted. "What's a Rhosili and what's a—a coracle?"

"The Rhosili is a turbulent, swift-flowing river, full of dangerous rapids and currents. Coracles are ancient canoes, made of wooden lathes and waterproof animal skins, that go back to pre-Roman days. You've never seen Wales, have you?" She shook her head. "Ah, you would love it." She knew she would. "There's a waterfall at the Vale of Neath that's one of the beautiful sights of this world. And the lovely places to see: Aber-Eiddi and Caerbwdi and Porthclais and Kilgetty and Llangwm," and the words rolled off his tongue like the lilt of music. "It's a wild, untamed country, full of magical surprises."

"And yet you left Wales."

Rhys smiled at her and said, "It was the hunger in me. I wanted to own the world."

What he did not tell her was that the hunger was still there.

Over the next three years Elizabeth became indispensable to her father. Her job was to make his life comfortable, so that he could concentrate on the thing that was all-important to him: the Business. The details of running his life were left entirely to Elizabeth. She hired and fired servants, opened and closed the various houses as her father's needs required, and entertained for him.

More than that, she became his eyes and ears. After a business meeting Sam would ask Elizabeth her impression of a man, or explain to her why he had acted in a particular fashion. She watched him make decisions that affected the lives of thousands of people and involved hundreds of millions of dollars. She heard heads of state plead with Sam Roffe to open a factory, or beg him not to close one down.

After one of those meetings Elizabeth said, "It's unbelievable. It's—it's as though you're running a country."

Her father laughed and replied, "Roffe and Sons has a larger income than three quarters of the countries in the world."

In her travels with her father Elizabeth became reacquainted with the other members of the Roffe family, her cousins and their husbands or wives.

As a young girl Elizabeth had seen them during holidays when they had come to one of her father's houses, or when she had gone to visit them during brief school vacations.

Simonetta and Ivo Palazzi, in Rome, had always been the most fun to be with. They were open and friendly, and Ivo had always made Elizabeth feel like a woman. He was in charge of the Italian division of Roffe and Sons, and he had done very well. People enjoyed dealing with Ivo. Elizabeth remembered what a classmate had said when she had met him. "You know what I like about your cousin? He has warmth and charmth."

That was Ivo, warmth and charmth.

Then there was Hélène Roffe-Martel, and her husband, Charles, in Paris. Elizabeth had never really understood Hélène, or felt at ease with her. She had always been nice to Elizabeth, but there was a cool reserve that Elizabeth had never been able to break through. Charles was head of the French branch of Roffe and Sons. He was competent, though from what Elizabeth had overheard her father say, he lacked drive. He could follow orders, but he had no initiative. Sam had never replaced him, because the French branch ran very profitably. Elizabeth suspected that Hélène Roffe-Martel had a great deal to do with its success.

Elizabeth liked her German cousin Anna Roffe Gassner, and her husband, Walther. Elizabeth remembered hearing family gossip that Anna Roffe had married beneath her. Walther Gassner was reputed to be a black sheep, a fortune hunter, who had married an unattractive woman years older than himself, for her money. Elizabeth did not think her cousin was unattractive. She had always found Anna to be a shy, sensitive person, withdrawn, and a little frightened by life. Elizabeth had liked Walther on sight. He had the classic good looks of a movie star, but he seemed to be neither arrogant nor phony. He appeared to be genuinely in love with Anna, and Elizabeth did not believe any of the terrible stories she had heard about him.

Of all her cousins, Alec Nichols was Elizabeth's favorite. His mother had been a Roffe, and she had married Sir George Nichols, the third baronet. It was Alec to whom Elizabeth had always turned when she had a problem. Somehow, perhaps because of Alec's sensitivity and gentleness, he had seemed to the young child to be her peer, and she realized now what a great compliment that was to Alec. He had always treated her as an equal, ready to offer whatever aid and advice he could. Elizabeth remembered that once, in a moment of black despair, she had decided to run away from home. She had packed a suitcase and then, on a sudden impulse, had telephoned Alec in London to say good-bye. He had been in the middle of a conference, but he had come to the phone and talked to Elizabeth for more than an hour. When he had finished, Elizabeth had decided to forgive her father and give him another chance. That was Sir Alec Nichols. His wife, Vivian, was something else. Where Alec was generous and thoughtful, Vivian was selfish and thoughtless. She was the most self-centered woman Elizabeth had ever known.

Years ago, when Elizabeth was spending a weekend in their country home in Gloucestershire, she went on a picnic by herself. It had begun to rain, and she had returned to the house early. She had gone in the back door, and as she had started down the hallway, she had heard voices from the study, raised in a quarrel.

"I'm damned tired of playing nursemaid," Vivian was saying. "You can take your precious little cousin and amuse her yourself tonight. I'm going up to London. I have an engagement."

"Surely you can cancel it, Viv. The child is only going to be with us another day, and she——"

"Sorry, Alec. I feel like a good fuck, and I'm getting one tonight."

"For God's sake, Vivian!"

"Oh, shove it up your ass! Don't try to live my life for me."

At that moment, before Elizabeth could move, Vivian had stormed out of the study. She had taken one quick look at Elizabeth's stricken face, and said cheerily, "Back so soon, pet?" And strode upstairs.

Alec had come to the doorway. He had said gently, "Come in, Elizabeth."

Reluctantly she had walked into the study. Alec's face was aflame with embarrassment. Elizabeth had wanted desperately to comfort him, but she did not know how. Alec had walked over to a large refectory table, picked up a pipe, filled it with tobacco and lit it. It had seemed to Elizabeth that he took forever.

"You must understand Vivian."

Elizabeth had replied, "Alec, it's none of my business. I——"

"But in a sense it is. We're all family. I don't want you to think harshly of her."

Elizabeth could not believe it. After the incredible scene she had just heard, Alec was defending his wife.

"Sometimes in a marriage," Alec had continued, "a husband and a wife have different needs." He had paused awkwardly, searching for the right phrase. "I don't want you to blame Vivian because I—I can't fulfill some of those needs. That's not her fault, you see."

Elizabeth had not been able to stop herself. "Does—does she go out with other men often?"

"I'm rather afraid she does."

Elizabeth had been horrified. "Why don't you leave her?"

He had given her his gentle smile. "I can't leave her, dear child. You see, I love her."

The next day Elizabeth had returned to school. From that time on, she had felt closer to Alec than to any of the others.

Of late, Elizabeth had become concerned about her father. He seemed preoccupied and worried about something, but Elizabeth had no idea what it was. When she asked him about it, he replied, "Just a little problem I have to clear up. I'll tell you about it later."

He had become secretive, and Elizabeth no longer had access to his private papers. When he had said to her, "I'm leaving tomorrow for Chamonix to do a little mountain climbing," Elizabeth had been pleased. She knew he needed a rest. He had lost weight and had become pale and drawn-looking.

"I'll make the reservations for you," Elizabeth had said.

"Don't bother. They're already made."

That, too, was unlike him. He had left for

Chamonix the next morning. That was the last time she had seen him. The last time she would ever see him ...

Elizabeth lay there in her darkened bedroom, remembering the past. There was an unreality about her father's death, perhaps because he had been so alive.

He was the last to bear the name of Roffe. Except for her. What would happen to the company now? Her father had held the controlling interest. She wondered to whom he had left the stock.

Elizabeth learned the answer late the next afternoon. Sam's lawyer had appeared at the house. "I brought a copy of your father's will with me. I hate to intrude on your grief at a time like this, but I thought it best that you know at once. You are your father's sole beneficiary. That means that the controlling shares of Roffe and Sons are in your hands."

Elizabeth could not believe it. Surely he did not expect *her* to run the company. "Why?" she asked. "Why me?"

The attorney hesitated, then said, "May I be frank, Miss Roffe? Your father was a comparatively young man. I'm sure he didn't expect to die for many years. In time, I'm confident he would have made another will, designating someone to take over the company. He probably had not made up his mind yet." He strugged. "All that is academic, however. The point is that the control now rests in your hands. You will have to decide what you want to do with it, who you want to give it to." He studied her for a moment, then continued, "There has never before been a woman on the board of directors of Roffe and Sons, but—well, for the moment you're taking your father's place. There's a board meeting in Zurich this Friday. Can you be there?"

Sam would have expected it of her.

And so would old Samuel.

"I'll be there," Elizabeth said.

BOOK
TWO

CHAPTER

15

In the bedroom of a small rented apartment in Rua dos Bombeiros, one of the winding, dangerous back alleys of Alto Estoril, a motion-picture scene was being filmed. There were four people in the room. A cameraman, and on a bed the two actors in the scene, the man in his thirties and a young blond girl with a stunning figure. She wore nothing except a vivid red ribbon tied around her neck. The man was large, with a wrestler's shoulders and a barrel-shaped, incongruously hairless chest. His phallus, even in detumescence, was huge. The fourth person in the room was a spectator, seated in the background, wearing a black broad-brimmed hat and dark glasses.

The cameraman turned to the spectator, questioningly, and the spectator nodded. The cameraman pressed a switch and the camera began to whir. He said to the actors, "All right. Action."

The man knelt over the girl and she took his penis in her mouth until it began to grow hard. The girl took it out and said, "Jesus, that's big!"

"Shove it in her," the cameraman ordered.

The man slid down over the girl and put his penis between her legs.

"Take it easy, honey." She had a high, querulous voice.

"Look as though you're enjoying it."

"How can I? It's the size of a fucking watermelon."

The spectator was leaning forward, watching every move as the man entered her. The girl said, "Oh, my God, that feels wonderful. Just take it slow, baby."

The spectator was breathing harder now, staring at the scene on the bed. This girl was the third, and she was even prettier than the others.

She was writhing from side to side now, making little moaning noises. "Oh, yes," she gasped. "Don't stop!" She grasped the man's hips and began pulling them toward her. The man began to pump harder and faster, in a frantic, pounding motion. Her movements began to quicken, and her nails dug into the man's naked back. "Oh, yes," she moaned. "Yes, yes, yes! I'm coming!"

The cameraman looked toward the spectator, and the spectator nodded, eyes glistening behind the dark glasses.

"Now!" the cameraman called to the man on the bed.

The girl, caught in her own furious frenzy, did not even hear him. As her face filled with a wild ecstasy, and her body began to shudder, the man's huge hands closed around her throat and began to squeeze, closing off the air so that she could not breathe. She stared up at him, bewildered, and then her eyes filled with a sudden, terrified comprehension.

The spectator thought: *This is the moment. Now! Jesus God! Look at her eyes!* They were dilated with terror. She fought to tear away the iron bands around her throat, but it was useless. She was still coming, and the deliciousness of her orgasm and the frantic shudder of her death throes were blending into one.

The spectator's body was soaked with perspiration. The excitement was unbearable. In the middle of life's most exquisite pleasure the girl was dying, her eyes staring into the eyes of death. It was so beautiful.

Suddenly it was over. The spectator sat there, exhausted, shaken with spasms of pleasure, lungs filled with long, deep breaths. The girl had been punished.

The spectator felt like God.

CHAPTER

16

Zurich.
Friday, September 11.
Noon.

The World Headquarters of Roffe and Sons occupied sixty acres along the Sprettenbach on the western outskirts of Zurich. The administration building was a twelve-story modern glass structure, towering over a nest of research buildings, manufacturing plants, experimental laboratories, planning divisions, and railroad spurs. It was the brain center of the far-flung Roffe and Sons empire.

The reception lobby was starkly modern, decorated in green and white, with Danish furniture. A receptionist sat behind a glass desk, and those who were admitted by her into the recesses of the building had to be accompanied by a guide. To the right rear of the lobby was a bank of elevators, with one private express elevator for the use of the company president.

On this morning the private elevator had been

used by the members of the board of directors. They had arrived within the past few hours from various parts of the world by plane, train, helicopter and limousine. They were gathered now in the enormous, high-ceilinged, oak-paneled boardroom; Sir Alec Nichols, Walther Gassner, Ivo Palazzi and Charles Martel. The only nonmember of the board in the room was Rhys Williams.

Refreshments and drinks had been laid out on a sideboard, but no one in the room was interested. They were tense, nervous, each preoccupied with his own thoughts.

Kate Erling, an efficient Swiss woman in her late forties, came into the room. "Miss Roffe's car has arrived."

Her eye swept around the room to make sure that everything was in order: pens, note pads, a silver carafe of water at each place, cigars and cigarettes, ashtrays, matches. Kate Erling had been Sam Roffe's personal secretary for fifteen years. The fact that he was dead was no reason for her to lower his standards, or hers. She nodded, satisfied, and withdrew.

Downstairs, in front of the administration building, Elizabeth Roffe was stepping out of a limousine. She wore a black tailored suit with a white blouse. She had on no makeup. She looked much younger than her twenty-four years, pale and vulnerable.

The press was waiting for her. As she started into the building, she found herself surrounded by television and radio and newspaper reporters, with cameras and microphones.

"I'm from *L'Europeo*, Miss Roffe. Could we have

a statement? Who's going to take over the company now that your father——?"

"Look this way, please, Miss Roffe. Can you give our readers a big smile?"

"Associated Press, Miss Roffe. What about your father's will?"

"New York *Daily News*. Wasn't your father an expert mountain climber? Did they find out how——?"

"*Wall Street Journal*. Can you tell us something about the company's financial——?"

"I'm from the London *Times*. We're planning to do an article on the Roffe——"

Elizabeth was fighting her way into the lobby, escorted by three security guards, pushing through the sea of reporters.

"One more picture, Miss Roffe——"

And Elizabeth was in the elevator, the door closing. She took a deep breath and shuddered. Sam was dead. Why couldn't they leave her alone?

A few moments later, Elizabeth walked into the boardroom. Alec Nichols was the first to greet her. He put his arms around her shyly and said, "I'm so sorry, Elizabeth. It was such a shock to all of us. Vivian and I tried to telephone you but——"

"I know. Thank you, Alec. Thank you for your note."

Ivo Palazzi came up and gave her a kiss on each cheek. "*Cara*, what is there to say? Are you all right?"

"Yes, fine. Thank you, Ivo." She turned. "Hello, Charles."

"Elizabeth, Hélène and I were devastated. If there is anything at all——"

"Thank you."

Walther Gassner walked over to Elizabeth and said awkwardly, "Anna and I wish to express our great sorrow at what has happened to your father."

Elizabeth nodded, her head high. "Thank you, Walther."

She did not want to be here, surrounded by all the reminders of her father. She wanted to flee, to be alone.

Rhys Williams was standing off to one side, watching Elizabeth's face, and he was thinking, If they don't stop, she's going to break down. He deliberately moved through the group, held out his hand and said, "Hello, Liz."

"Hello, Rhys." She had last seen him when he had come to the house to bring her the news of Sam's death. It seemed like years ago. Seconds ago. It had been one week.

Rhys was aware of the effort it was costing Elizabeth to keep her composure. He said, "Now that everyone's here, why don't we begin?" He smiled reassuringly. "This won't take long."

She gave him a grateful smile. The men took their accustomed places at the large rectangular oak table. Rhys led Elizabeth to the head of the table and pulled out a chair for her. My father's chair, Elizabeth thought. Sam sat here, chairing these meetings.

Charles was saying, "Since we do not have a—" He caught himself and turned to Alec. "Why don't you take over?"

Alec glanced around, and the others murmured approval. "Very well."

Alec pressed a button on the table in front of him, and Kate Erling returned, carrying a notebook.

She closed the door behind her and pulled up a straight chair, her notebook and pen poised.

Alec said, "I think that under the circumstances we can dispense with the formalities. All of us have suffered a terrible loss. But"—he looked apologetically at Elizabeth—"the essential thing now is that Roffe and Sons show a strong public face."

"D'accord. We have been taking enough of a hammering in the press lately," Charles growled.

Elizabeth looked over at him and asked, "Why?"

Rhys explained, "The company is facing a lot of unusual problems just now, Liz. We're involved in heavy lawsuits, we're under government investigation, and some of the banks are pressing us. The point is that none of it is good for our image. The public buys pharmaceutical products because they trust the company that makes them. If we lose that trust, we lose our customers."

Ivo said reassuringly, "We have no problems that can't be solved. The important thing is to reorganize the company immediately."

"How?" Elizabeth asked.

Walther replied, "By selling our stock to the public."

Charles added, "In that way we can take care of all our bank loans, and have enough money left—" He let the sentence trail off.

Elizabeth looked at Alec. "Do you agree with that?"

"I think we're all in agreement, Elizabeth."

She leaned back in her chair, thoughtful. Rhys picked up some papers, rose and carried them to Elizabeth. "I've had all the necessary documents prepared. All you have to do is sign."

Elizabeth glanced at the papers lying before her. "If I sign these, what happens?"

Charles spoke up. "We have a dozen international brokerage firms ready to form a consortium to underwrite the stock issue. They will guarantee the sale at a price we mutually agree upon. In an offering as large as this one, there will be several institutional purchases, as well as private ones."

"You mean like banks and insurance companies?" Elizabeth asked.

Charles nodded. "Exactly."

"And they'll put their people on the board of directors?"

"That's usual . . ."

Elizabeth said, "So, in effect, they would control Roffe and Sons."

"We would still remain on the board of directors," Ivo interposed quickly.

Elizabeth turned to Charles. "You said a consortium of stockbrokers is ready to move ahead."

Charles nodded. "Yes."

"Then why haven't they?"

He looked at her, puzzled. "I don't understand."

"If everyone is in agreement that the best thing for the company is to let it get out of the family and into the hands of outsiders, why hasn't it been done before?"

There was an awkward silence. Ivo said, "It has to be by mutual consent, *cara. Everyone* on the board must agree."

"Who didn't agree?" Elizabeth asked.

The silence was longer this time.

Finally Rhys spoke up. "Sam."

And Elizabeth suddenly realized what had disturbed her from the moment she had walked into this room. They had all expressed their condolences and their shock and grief over her father's death, and yet at the same time there had been an atmosphere of charged excitement in the room, a feeling of—strangely, the word that came into her mind was *victory*. They had had the papers all drawn up for her, everything ready. *All you have to do is sign.* But if what they wanted was right, then why had her father objected to it? She asked the question aloud.

"Sam had his own ideas," Walther explained. "Your father could be very stubborn."

Like old Samuel, Elizabeth thought. Never let a friendly fox into your hen house. One day he's going to get hungry. And Sam had not wanted to sell. He must have had good reason.

Ivo was saying, "Believe me, *cara*, it is much better to leave all this to us. You don't understand these things."

Elizabeth said quietly, "I would like to."

"Why bother yourself with this?" Walther objected. "When your stock is sold, you will have an enormous amount of money, more than you'll ever be able to spend. You can go off anywhere you like and enjoy it."

What Walther said made sense. Why *should* she get involved? All she had to do was sign the papers in front of her, and leave.

Charles said impatiently, "Elizabeth, we're simply wasting time. You have no choice."

It was at that instant that Elizabeth knew she did have a choice. Just as her father had had a choice. She could walk away and let them do as they pleased with the company, or she could stay and find out why they were all so eager to sell the stock, why they were pressuring her. For she could feel the pressure. It was so strong it was almost physical. Everyone in that room was *willing* her to sign the papers.

She glanced over at Rhys, wondering what he was thinking. His expression was noncommittal. Elizabeth looked at Kate Erling. She had been Sam's secretary for a long time. Elizabeth wished she could have had a chance to speak to her alone. They were all looking at Elizabeth, waiting for her to agree.

"I'm not going to sign," she said. "Not now."

There was a moment of stunned silence. Then Walther said, "I don't understand, Elizabeth." His face was ashen. "Of course you must! Everything is arranged."

Charles said angrily, "Walther's right. You must sign."

They were all speaking at once, in a confused and angry storm of words that beat at Elizabeth.

"*Why* won't you sign?" Ivo demanded.

She could not say: *Because my father would not sign. Because you're rushing me.* She had a feeling, an instinct that something was wrong, and she was determined to find out what it was. So now she merely said, "I'd like a little more time to think about it."

The men looked at one another.

"How much time, *cara?*" Ivo asked.

"I don't know yet. I'd like to get a better understanding of what's involved here."

Walther exploded. "Damn it, we can't—"

Rhys cut in firmly, "I think Elizabeth is right."

The others turned to look at him. Rhys went on, "She should have a chance to get a clear picture of the problems the company is facing, and then make up her own mind."

They were all digesting what Rhys had said.

"I agree with that," Alec said.

Charles said bitterly, "Gentlemen, it doesn't make any difference whether we agree with it or not. Elizabeth is in control."

Ivo looked at Elizabeth. *"Cara*—we need a decision quickly."

"You'll have it," Elizabeth promised.

They were all watching her, each busy with his own thoughts.

One of them was thinking, Oh, God. *She's going to have to die, too.*

CHAPTER

17

Elizabeth was awed.

She had been here in her father's Zurich head-quarters often, but always as a visitor. The power belonged to him. And now it belonged to her. She looked around the huge office and felt like an imposter. The room had been magnificently deco-rated by Ernst Hohl. At one end stood a Roentgen cabinet with a Millet landscape over it. There was a fireplace, and in front of it a chamois leather couch, a large coffee table and four easy chairs. Around the walls were Renoirs, Chagalls, Klees and two early Courbets. The desk was a solid block of black mahogany. Next to it, on a large console table, was a communications complex—a battery of telephones with direct lines to company headquarters around the world. There were two red phones with scram-blers, an intricate intercom system, a ticker tape machine, and other equipment. Hanging behind the desk was a portrait of old Samuel Roffe.

A private door led to a large dressing room, with cedar closets and lined drawers. Someone had re-moved Sam's clothing, and Elizabeth was grateful. She walked through a tiled bathroom that included a marble bathtub and a stall shower. There were fresh Turkish towels hanging on warming racks. The medicine chest was empty. All the daily paraphernalia of her father's life had been taken away. Kate Erling, probably. Elizabeth idly wondered whether Kate had been in love with Sam.

The executive suite included a large sauna, a fully equipped gymnasium, a barbershop, and a dining room that could seat a hundred people. When foreign guests were being entertained, a little flag representing their country was placed in the floral centerpiece on the table.

In addition, there was Sam's private dining room, tastefully decorated, with muraled walls.

Kate Erling had explained to Elizabeth, "There are two chefs on duty during the day, and one at night. If you are having more than twelve guests for luncheon or dinner, they need two hours' notice."

Now Elizabeth sat at the desk, piled high with papers, memoranda, and statistics and reports, and she did not know where to begin. She thought of her father sitting here, in this chair, behind this desk, and she was suddenly filled with a sense of unbearable loss. Sam had been so able, so brilliant. How she needed him now!

Elizabeth had managed to see Alec for a few moments before he returned to London.

"Take your time," he had advised her. "Don't let anyone pressure you."

So he had sensed her feelings.

"Alec, do you think I should vote to let the company go public?"

He had smiled at her and said awkwardly, "I'm afraid I do, old girl, but then I've got my own ax to grind, haven't I? Our shares are no good to any of us until we can sell them. That's up to you now."

Elizabeth was remembering that conversation as she sat alone in the huge office. The temptation to telephone Alec was overpowering. All she had to say was, "I've changed my mind." And get out. She did not belong here. She felt so inadequate.

She looked at the set of intercom buttons on the console. Opposite one of them was the name RHYS WILLIAMS. Elizabeth debated a moment, then flicked down the switch.

Rhys was seated across from her, watching her. Elizabeth knew exactly what he must be thinking, what they were all thinking. That she had no business being there.

"That was quite a bomb you dropped at the meeting this morning," Rhys said.

"I'm sorry if I upset everyone."

He grinned. " 'Upset' is hardly the word. You put everyone in a state of shock. It was all supposed to have been cut-and-dried. The publicity releases were ready to send out." He studied her a moment. "What made you decide not to sign, Liz?"

How could she explain that it was nothing more than a feeling, an intuition? He would laugh at her. And yet Sam had refused to let Roffe and Sons go public. She had to find out why.

As though reading her thoughts, Rhys said, "Your great-great grandfather set this up as a family business, to keep away outsiders. But it was a small company then. Things have changed. We're running one of the biggest drugstores in the world. Whoever sits in your father's chair has to make all the final decisions. It's one hell of a responsibility."

She looked at him and wondered whether this

217

was Rhys's way of telling her to get out. "Will you help me?"

"You know I will."

She felt a rush of relief and she realized how much she had been counting on him.

"The first thing we'd better do," Rhys said, "is take you on a tour of the plant here. Do you know about the physical structure of this company?"

"Not much."

That was not true. Elizabeth had been in enough meetings with Sam over the past few years to have picked up a good deal of knowledge about the workings of Roffe and Sons. But she wanted to hear it from Rhys's point of view.

"We manufacture much more than drugs, Liz. We make chemicals and perfumes and vitamins and hair sprays and pesticides. We produce cosmetics and bio-electronic instruments. We have a food division, and a division of animal nitrates." Elizabeth was aware of all that, but she let Rhys go on. "We publish magazines for distribution to doctors. We make adhesives, and building protection agents and plastic explosives."

Elizabeth could sense that he was becoming caught up by what he was saying, she could hear the undertone of pride in his voice, and she was oddly reminded of her father.

"Roffe and Sons owns factories and holding companies in over a hundred countries. Every one of them reports to this office." He paused, as though to make sure that she understood the point. "Old Samuel went into business with a horse and a test tube. It's grown to sixty factories around the world, ten research centers and a network of thousands of salesmen and detail men and women." They were the ones, Elizabeth knew, who called on the doctors and hospitals. "Last year, in the United States alone, they spent over fourteen billion dollars on drugs— and we have a healthy share of that market."

And yet Roffe and Sons was in trouble with the banks. Something was wrong.

Rhys took Elizabeth on a tour of the company's headquarters' factory. In actuality, the Zurich division was a dozen factories, with seventy-five buildings on the sixty acres of ground. It was a world in microcosm, completely self-sustaining. They visited the manufacturing plants, the research departments, the toxicology laboratories, the storage plants. Rhys brought Elizabeth to a sound stage, where they made motion pictures for research and for their worldwide advertising and products divisions. "We use more film here," Rhys told Elizabeth, "than the major Hollywood studios."

They went through the molecular biology department, and the liquid center, where fifty giant stainless steel, glass-lined tanks hung suspended from the ceiling, filled with liquids ready to be bottled. They saw the tablet-compression rooms, where powders were formed into tablets, sized, stamped with ROFFE AND SONS, packaged and labeled, without anyone ever touching them. Some of the drugs were ethical products, available only on prescription, others were proprietary items, sold over the counter.

Set apart from the other buildings were several small buildings. These were for the scientists: the analytical chemists, biochemists, organic chemists, parasitologists, pathologists.

"More than three hundred scientists work here," Rhys told Elizabeth. "Most of them are Ph.D.'s.

Would you like to see our hundred-million-dollar room?"

Elizabeth nodded, intrigued.

It was in an isolated brick building, guarded by a uniformed policeman with a gun. Rhys showed his security pass, and he and Elizabeth were permitted to enter a long corridor with a steel door at the end of it. The guard used two keys to open the door, and Elizabeth and Rhys entered. The room contained no windows. It was lined from floor to ceiling with shelves filled with every variety of bottles, jars and tubes.

"Why do they call this the hundred-million-dollar room?" Elizabeth asked.

"Because that's what it cost to furnish it. See all those compounds on the shelves? None of them have names, only numbers. They're the ones that didn't make it. They're the failures."

"But a hundred million—"

"For every new drug that works, there are about a thousand that end up in this room. Some drugs are worked on for as long as ten years, and then abandoned. A single drug can cost five or ten million dollars in research before we find out that it's no good, or that someone else has beaten us to it. We don't throw any of these things away because now and then one of our bright young men will back into a discovery that can make something in this room valuable."

The amounts of money involved were awesome.

"Come on," Rhys said. "I'll show you the Loss Room."

It was in another building, this one unguarded, containing, like the other rooms, only shelves filled with bottles and jars.

"We lose a fortune here too," Rhys said. "But we plan it that way."

"I don't understand."

Rhys walked over to a shelf and picked up a bottle. It was labeled "Botulism." "Do you know how many cases of botulism there were in the United States last year? Twenty-five. But it costs us millions of dollars to keep this drug in stock." He picked up another bottle at random. "This is an antidote for rabies. This room is full of drugs that are cures for rare diseases—snakebites, poisonous plants. We furnish them free to the armed forces and to hospitals, as a public service."

"I like that," Elizabeth said. Old Samuel would have liked it too, she thought.

Rhys took Elizabeth to the capsule rooms, where empty bottles were carried in on a giant conveyor belt. By the time they had crossed the room, the bottles had been sterilized, filled with capsules, labeled, topped with cotton, and sealed. All done by automation.

There was a glassblowing factory, an architectural center to plan new buildings, a real estate division to acquire the land for them. In one building there were scores of writers turning out pamphlets in fifty languages, and printing presses to print them.

Some of the departments reminded Elizabeth of George Orwell's *1984*. The Sterile Rooms were bathed in eerie ultraviolet lights. Adjoining rooms were painted in different colors—white, green or blue—and the workers wore uniforms to match. Each time they entered or left the room, they had to go through a special sterilizing chamber. Blue workers were locked in for the entire day. Before they could eat or rest or go to the toilet, they had to undress, enter a neutral green zone, put on other clothes, and reverse the process when they returned.

"I think you'll find this interesting," Rhys said.

They were walking down the gray corridor of a research building. They reached a door marked "RESTRICTED—DO NOT ENTER." Rhys pushed the door open, and he and Elizabeth walked through. They went through a second door and Elizabeth found herself in a dimly lit room filled with hundreds of cages containing animals. The room was hot and humid, and she felt as if she had suddenly been transported to a jungle. As her eyes grew accustomed to the half-light, she saw that the cages were filled with monkeys and hamsters and cats and white mice. Many of the animals had obscene-looking growths protruding from various parts of their bodies. Some had their heads shaven, and were crowned with electrodes that had been implanted in their brains. Some of the animals were screaming and gibbering, racing around in their cages, while others were comatose and lethargic. The noise and the stench were unbearable. It was like some kind of hell. Elizabeth walked up to a cage that contained a single white kitten. Its brain was exposed, enclosed in a clear plastic covering through which protruded half a dozen wires.

"What—what's going on here?" Elizabeth asked.

A tall, bearded young man making notes in front of a cage explained, "We're testing a new tranquilizer."

"I hope it works," Elizabeth said weakly. "I think I could use it." And she walked out of the room before she could become sick.

Rhys was at her side in the corridor. "Are you all right?"

She took a deep breath. "I—I'm fine. Is all that really necessary?"

Rhys looked at her and replied. "Those experiments save a lot of lives. More than one third of the people born since nineteen fifty are alive only because of modern drugs. Think about that."

Elizabeth thought about it.

It took six full days to tour the key buildings, and when Elizabeth had finished, she was exhausted, her head spinning with the vastness of it. And she realized she was seeing just one Roffe plant. There were dozens of others scattered around the world.

The facts and figures were stunning. "It takes between five and ten years to market a new drug, and out of every two thousand compounds tested, we'll average only three products. . . ."

And ". . . Roffe and Sons has three hundred people working here in quality control alone."

And ". . . Worldwide, Roffe and Sons is responsible for over half a million employees. . . ."

And ". . . our gross income last year was . . ."

Elizabeth listened, trying to digest the incredible figures that Rhys was throwing at her. She had known that the company was large, but "large" was such an anonymous word. Having it actually translated into terms of people and money was staggering.

That night as Elizabeth lay in bed, recalling all the things she had seen and heard, she was filled with an overpowering feeling of inadequacy.

IVO: *Believe me, cara, it is much better to leave all this to us. You don't understand these things.*

ALEC: *I think you should sell but I have an ax to grind.*

WALTHER: *Why bóther yourself with this? You*

can go off anywhere you like and enjoy your money.

They were right, all of them, Elizabeth thought. I'm going to get out and let them do what they like with the company. I do not belong in this position.

The moment she made the decision, she felt a deep sense of relief. She fell asleep almost immediately.

The following day, Friday, was the beginning of a holiday weekend. When Elizabeth arrived at the office, she sent for Rhys to announce her decision.

"Mr. Williams had to fly to Nairobi last night," Kate Erling informed her. "He said to tell you he would be back on Tuesday. Can anyone else help you?"

Elizabeth hesitated. "Put in a call to Sir Alec, please."

"Yes, Miss Roffe." Kate added, a note of hesitation in her voice, "A package for you was delivered this morning by the police department. It contains the personal belongings your father had with him at Chamonix."

The mention of Sam brought back that sharp sense of loss, of grief.

"The police apologized because they could not give it to your messenger. It was already on its way to you."

Elizabeth frowned. "My messenger?"

"The man you sent to Chamonix to pick it up."

"I didn't send anyone to Chamonix." It was obviously some bureaucratic mix-up. "Where is it?"

"I put it in your closet."

There was a Vuitton suitcase, containing Sam's clothes, and a locked attaché case with a key taped to it. Probably company reports. She would let Rhys handle them. Then she remembered that he was away. Well, she decided, she would go away for the weekend too. She looked at the attaché case and thought, Perhaps there's something personal belonging to Sam. I'd better look at it first.

Kate Erling buzzed. "I'm sorry, Miss Roffe. Sir Alec's out of the office."

"Leave a message for him to call me, please. I'll be at the villa in Sardinia. Leave the same message for Mr. Palazzi, Mr. Gassner and Mr. Martel."

She would tell them all that she was leaving, that they could sell the stock, do as they pleased with the company.

She was looking forward to the long weekend. The villa was a retreat, a soothing cocoon, where she could be alone to think about herself and her future. Events had been flung at her so rapidly that she had had no chance to put things into any kind of perspective. Sam's accident—Elizabeth's mind tripped over the word "death"; inheriting the controlling stock of Roffe and Sons; the urgent pressure from the family to let the company go public. And the company itself. The awesome heartbeat of a behemoth whose power spanned the world. It was too much to cope with all at once.

When she flew to Sardinia late that afternoon, Elizabeth had the attaché case with her.

CHAPTER

18

She took a taxi from the airport. There was no one at the villa because it had been closed, and Elizabeth had not told anyone she was coming. She let herself in and walked slowly through the large familiar rooms and it was as if she had never been away. She had not realized how much she had missed this place. It seemed to Elizabeth that the few happy memories of her childhood had been here. It felt strange to be alone in this labyrinth where there had always been half a dozen servants bustling around, cooking, cleaning, polishing. Now there was only herself. And the echoes of the past.

She left Sam's attaché case in the downstairs hallway and carried her suitcase upstairs. With the habit of long years, she started to head for her bedroom in the center of the hallway, then stopped. Her father's room was at the far end. Elizabeth turned and walked toward it. She opened the door slowly, because while her mind understood the reality, some deep, atavistic instinct made her half expect to see Sam there, to hear the sound of his voice.

The room was empty, of course, and nothing had changed since Elizabeth had last seen it. It contained a large double bed, a beautiful highboy, a dressing table, two comfortable overstuffed chairs, and a couch in front of the fireplace. Elizabeth set down her suitcase and walked over to the window. The iron shutters had been closed against the late September sun, and the draperies were drawn. She opened them wide and let the fresh mountain air flow in, soft and cool with the promise of fall. She would sleep in this room.

Elizabeth returned downstairs and went into the library. She sat down in one of the comfortable leather chairs, rubbing her hands along the sides. This was where Rhys always sat when he had a conference with her father.

She thought about Rhys and wished that he were here with her. She remembered the night he had brought her back to school after the dinner in Paris, and how she had gone back to her room and had written "Mrs. Rhys Williams" over and over. On an impulse Elizabeth walked over to the desk, picked up a pen and slowly wrote "Mrs. Rhys Williams." She looked at it and smiled. "I wonder," she mocked herself aloud, "how many other idiots are doing the same thing right now?"

She turned her thoughts away from Rhys, but still he was at the back of her mind, pleasantly comforting. She got up and wandered around the house. She explored the large, old-fashioned kitchen, with its wood-burning stove, and two ovens.

She walked over to the refrigerator and opened it. It was empty. She should have anticipated that, with the house shut down. Because the refrigerator was empty, she became suddenly hungry. She searched the cupboards. There were two small cans of tuna fish, a half-filled jar of Nescafé, and an unopened package of crackers. If she was going to be her for a long weekend, Elizabeth decided, she had better do some planning. Rather than drive into town for every meal, she would shop at one of the little markets in Cala di Volpe and stock enough food for several days. A utility Jeep was always kept in the carport and she wondered if it was still there. She went to the back of the kitchen and through the door that led to the carport, and there was the Jeep. Elizabeth walked back into the kitchen, where, on a board behind the cupboard, were hooks with labeled keys on them. She found the key to the Jeep and returned to the carport. Would there be gasoline in it? She turned the key and pressed the starter. Almost immediately the motor sparked into life. So *that* problem was eliminated. In the morning she would drive into town and pick up whatever groceries she needed.

She went back into the house. As she walked across the tiled floor of the reception hall, she could hear the echo of her footsteps, and it was a hollow, lonely sound. She wished that Alec would call, and even as she was thinking it the telephone rang, startling her. She walked to it and picked it up. "Hello."

"Elizabeth. It's Alec here."

Elizabeth laughed aloud.

"What's so funny?"

"You wouldn't believe me if I told you. Where are you?"

"Down in Gloucester." And Elizabeth felt a sudden, urgent impulse to see him, to tell him her decision about the company. But not over the telephone. "Would you do me a favor, Alec?"

"You know I will."

"Could you fly down here for the weekend? I'd like to discuss something with you."

There was only the slightest hesitation, and then Alec said, "Of course."

Not a word about what engagements he would have to break, how inconvenient it might be. Just "Of course." That was Alec.

Elizabeth forced herself to say, "And bring Vivian."

"I'm afraid she won't be able to come. She's—ah—rather involved in London. I can arrive tomorrow morning. Will that do?"

"Perfect. Let me know what time, and I'll pick you up at the airport."

"It will be simpler if I just take a taxi."

"All right. Thank you, Alec. Very much."

When Elizabeth replaced the receiver, she was feeling infinitely better.

She knew she had made the right decision. She was in this position only because Sam had died before he had had the time to name his successor.

Elizabeth wondered who the next president of Roffe and Sons would be. The board could decide that for themselves. She thought about it from Sam's point of view, and the name that sprang instantly to mind was Rhys Williams. The others were competent in their own areas, but Rhys was the only one who had a working knowledge of the company's complete global operation. He was brilliant and effective. The problem, of course, was that Rhys was not eligible to be president. Because he was not a Roffe, or married to a Roffe, he could not even sit on the board.

Elizabeth walked into the hallway and saw her father's attaché case. She hesitated. There was hardly any point in her going through it now. She could give it to Alec when he arrived in the morning. Still, if there *was* something personal in it . . . She carried it into the library, set it on the desk, untaped the key and opened the little locks on each side. In the center of the case lay a large manila envelope. Elizabeth opened it and removed a sheaf of typewritten papers lying loosely in a cardboard cover labeled:

> MR. SAM ROFFE
> CONFIDENTIAL
> NO COPIES.

It was obviously a report of some kind, but without anyone's name on it so that Elizabeth could not know who had drawn it. She started to skim through the report, then slowed down, then stopped. She could not believe what she was reading. She carried the papers over to an armchair, kicked off her shoes, curled her legs up underneath her and turned to page one again.

This time she read every word, and she was filled with horror.

It was an astonishing document, a confidential report of an investigation into a series of events that had occurred over the past year.

In Chile a chemical plant owned by Roffe and Sons had exploded, sending tons of poisonous materials spouting over a ten-square-mile area. A dozen people had been killed, hundreds more had been taken to hospitals. All the livestock had died, the vegetation was poisoned. The entire region had had to be evacuated. The lawsuits filed against Roffe and Sons had run into hundreds of millions of dollars. But the shocking thing was that the explosion had been deliberate. The report read: "The Chilean government's investigation into the accident was cursory. The official attitude seems to be: the Company is rich, the people are poor, let the Company pay. There is no question in the minds of our investigating staff but that it was an act of sabotage, by a person or persons unknown, using plastic explosives. Because of the antagonistic official attitude here, it will be impossible to prove."

Elizabeth remembered the incident only too well. Newspapers and magazines had been full of horror stories complete with photographs of the victims, and the world's press had attacked Roffe and Sons, accusing it of being careless and indifferent to human suffering. It had damaged the image of the company badly.

The next section of the report dealt with major research projects that Roffe and Sons' scientists had been working on for a number of years. There were four projects listed, each of them of inestimable potential value. Combined, they had cost more than fifty million dollars to develop. In each case a rival pharmaceutical firm had applied for a patent to one of the products, just ahead of Roffe and Sons, using the identical formula. The report continued: "One isolated incident might have been put down as coincidence. In a field where dozens of companies are working in related areas, it is inevitable that several companies might be working on the same type of product. But four such incidents in a period of a few months force us to the conclusion that someone in the employ of Roffe and Sons gave or sold the research material to the competitive firms. Because of the secret nature of the experiments, and the fact that they were conducted in widely separated laboratories under conditions of maximum security, our investigation indicates that the person, or persons, behind this would need to have access to top security clearances. We therefore conclude that whoever is responsible is someone in the highest executive echelon of Roffe and Sons."

There was more.

A large batch of toxic drugs had been mislabeled and shipped. Before they could be recalled there were several deaths, and more bad publicity for the company. No one could learn where the wrong labels had come from.

A deadly toxin had disappeared from a heavily guarded laboratory. Within an hour an unidentified person had leaked the story to the newspapers and started a scare-hunt.

The afternoon shadows had long since lengthened into evening, and the night air had turned chilly. Elizabeth remained totally absorbed in the document she held in her hands. When the study became dark, she switched on a lamp and continued to read, the horror piled on horror.

Not even the dry, terse tone of the report could conceal the drama in it. One thing was clear. Someone was methodically attempting to damage or destroy Roffe and Sons.

Someone in the highest echelon of the company. On the last page was a marginal note in her father's neat, precise handwriting. "Additional pressure on me to let the company go public? Trap the bastard."

She remembered now how worried Sam had been, and his sudden secrecy. He had not known whom to trust.

Elizabeth looked at the front page of the report again. "No COPIES."

Elizabeth was sure the report had been done by an outside investigative agency. So in all probability no one had been aware of this report but Sam. And now herself. The guilty person had no idea he was under suspicion. Had Sam known who he was? Had Sam confronted him before his accident? Elizabeth had no way of knowing. All she knew was that there was a traitor.

Someone in the highest echelon of the company.
No one else would have the opportunity or the ability to carry out so much destruction on so many different levels. Was that why Sam had refused to let the company go public? Was he trying to find the guilty person first? Once the company was sold, it would be impossible to conduct a secret investigation, with every move being reported to a group of strangers.

Elizabeth thought about the board meeting, and how they had urged her to sell. All of them.

Elizabeth suddenly felt very alone in the house. The loud ringing of the telephone made her jump. She walked over to it and picked it up. "Hello?"

"Liz? It's Rhys. I just received your message."

She was glad to hear his voice, but she suddenly remembered why she had called him. To tell him that she was going to sign the papers, let the company be sold. In a few short hours everything had completely changed. Elizabeth glanced out into the hallway, at the portrait of old Samuel. He had founded this company and had fought for it. Elizabeth's father had built it up, helped turn it into a giant, had lived for it, dedicated himself to it.

"Rhys," Elizabeth said, "I'd like to have a board

meeting Tuesday. Two o'clock. Would you please arrange for everyone to be there?"

"Tuesday at two o'clock," Rhys agreed. "Anything else?"

She hesitated. "No. That's all. Thank you."

Elizabeth slowly replaced the receiver. She was going to fight them.

She was high on a mountain with her father, climbing at his side. *Don't look down,* Sam kept saying, and Elizabeth disobeyed, and there was nothing below but thousands of feet of empty space. There was a loud rumble of thunder, and a bolt of lightning came hurtling toward them. It hit Sam's rope and set it on fire, and Sam started falling through space. Elizabeth watched her father's body tumble end over end, and she began to scream, but her screams were drowned out by the roar of the thunder.

Elizabeth awakened suddenly, her nightgown drenched with perspiration, her heart pounding wildly. There was a loud clap of thunder, and she looked toward the window and saw that it was pouring outside. The wind was driving the rain into the bedroom through the open French doors. Quickly, Elizabeth got out of bed, crossed over to the doors and pushed them tightly shut. She looked out at the storm clouds that filled the sky, and at the lightning flashes across the horizon, but she was not seeing them.

She was thinking about her dream.

In the morning the storm had passed over the island, leaving only a light drizzle. Elizabeth hoped that the weather would not delay Alec's arrival.

After reading the report she desperately needed someone to talk to. In the meantime she decided it would be a good idea to put it away in a secure place. There was a safe up in the tower room. She would keep it there. Elizabeth bathed, put on a pair of old slacks and a sweater, and went down into the library to get the report.

It was gone.

CHAPTER

19

The room looked as though a hurricane had swept through it. The storm had blown open the French doors during the night, and the wind and the rain had wreaked havoc, scattering everything before it. A few loose pages of the report lay on the wet rug, but the rest of the pages had obviously been carried away by the wind.

Elizabeth stepped to the French windows and looked out. She could see no papers on the lawn, but the wind could easily have blown them over the cliff. That must have been what happened.

No copies. She must find out the name of the investigator Sam had hired. Perhaps Kate Erling would know. But Elizabeth could not be sure now that Sam had trusted Kate. This had become like a terrible game, where no one could trust anybody. She would have to move very carefully.

Elizabeth suddenly remembered that there was no food in the house. She could shop at Cala di Volpe and be back before Alec arrived. She went to the hall closet and got her raincoat and a scarf for her hair. Later, when the rain let up, she would search the grounds for the missing papers. She went into the kitchen and took the key to the Jeep from the key rack. She walked out the back door that led to the carport.

Elizabeth started the engine and carefully backed the Jeep out of the carport. She turned it around and headed out the private driveway, braking to slow down because of the wet surface. At the bottom of the driveway she turned right, onto the narrow mountain road that led to the little village of Cala di Volpe below. There was no traffic on the road at this hour, but there seldom was, for few houses had been built up this high. Elizabeth glanced down to her left and saw that the sea below had become dark and angry, swollen with the night storm.

She drove slowly, for this part of the road became treacherous. It was narrow, with two lanes that had been cut into the side of the mountain, along a sheer precipice. On the inside lane was the solid rock of the mountain, and on the outside, a drop of hundreds of feet to the sea below. Elizabeth kept as close as she could to the inside lane, braking to fight the momentum of the steep mountain gradient.

The car was approaching a sharp curve. Automatically, Elizabeth put her foot on the brakes to slow the Jeep down.

The brakes were dead.

It took a long moment to register. Elizabeth pressed again, harder, pushing down on the pedal with all her strength, and her heart began to pound as the Jeep kept gathering speed. It took the curve and was moving faster now, racing down the steep mountain road, gaining momentum with each second. She pressed down on the brakes again. They were useless.

Another curve lay ahead. Elizabeth was afraid to

take her eyes off the road to look at the speedometer, but out of the corner of her eye she could see the needle racing upward and she was filled with an icy terror. She reached the curve and skidded around it, much too fast. The back wheels slid toward the edge of the precipice, then the tires found their traction and the Jeep plunged forward again, hurtling down the steep road ahead. There was nothing to stop it now, no barriers, no controls, only the swift roller-coaster ride down, and the deadly, beckoning curves ahead.

Elizabeth's mind raced frantically, seeking some escape. She thought of jumping. She risked a quick look at the speedometer. She was going seventy miles an hour now, and building up speed every moment, trapped between the solid mountain wall on one side and the deadly drop into space on the other. She was going to die. And in an instant revelation, Elizabeth knew that she was being murdered, and that her father had been murdered. Sam had read the report, and he had been killed. As she was going to be killed. And she had no idea who her murderer was, who hated them enough to do this terrible thing. Somehow she could have borne it better if it had been a stranger. But it was someone she knew, someone who knew her. Faces flashed through her mind. Alec . . . Ivo . . . Walther . . . Charles . . . It had to be one of them. *Someone in the highest echelon of the company*

Her death would be listed as an accident, as Sam's had been. Elizabeth was crying now, silently, her tears mixing with the fine mist of rain that was falling, but she was not even aware of it. The Jeep was beginning to skid out of control on the wet surface, and Elizabeth fought to keep the wheels on the road. She knew it was only a matter of seconds before she hurtled over the cliff, into oblivion. Her body became rigid, and her hands were numb from gripping the steering wheel. There was nothing in the universe now but herself, careering down the mountain road, with the roaring wind tugging at her, saying *Come join me*, tearing at the car, trying to push it over the brink of the cliff. The Jeep started into another skid, and Elizabeth fought desperately to straighten it out, remembering what she had been taught. *Steer into the skid, always into the skid,* and the rear wheels straightened out and the car continued racing downhill. Elizabeth stole another quick glance at the speedometer . . . eighty miles an hour. She was catapulting toward a steep hairpin curve ahead, and she knew she was not going to make this one.

Something in her mind seemed to freeze, and it was as if there was a thin veil between her and reality. She heard her father's voice saying, *What are you doing down here alone in the dark?* and he was picking her up and carrying her to bed and she was on stage dancing and turning and turning and turning and she could not stop, and Mme. Netturova was screaming at her (or was it the wind?) and Rhys was there, saying, *How many times does a girl have her twenty-first birthday?* And Elizabeth thought, I'll never see Rhys again, and she screamed his name and the veil disappeared, but the nightmare was still there. The sharp curve was looming closer now, the car speeding toward it like a bullet. She would go over the cliff. *Let it happen quickly,* she prayed silently.

At that moment, to the right, just before the hairpin curve, Elizabeth caught a glimpse of a small firebreak trail that had been cut through the rock, going up the mountainside. She had to make a decision in a split second. She had no idea where the trail led. All she knew was that it went *upward*, that it might slow her momentum, give her a chance. And she took it. At the last instant, as the Jeep reached the trail, Elizabeth swung the wheel hard to the right. The rear wheels started to skid, but the front wheels were on the gravel road and the momentum gave them enough traction to hold. The Jeep was now hurtling upward, and Elizabeth was fighting the wheel, trying to keep the car on the narrow trail. There was a thin line of trees and their branches were slashing at her as she raced by them, tearing at her face and her hands. She looked ahead, and to her horror, she could see the Tyrrhenian Sea below. The path had merely led to the other side of the cliff. There was no safety here at all.

She was getting closer and closer to the brink now, moving too fast to jump from the Jeep. The edge of the cliff was just ahead of her, the sea hundreds of feet below. As the Jeep hurtled toward the edge, it went into a wild skid, and the last thing Elizabeth remembered was a tree looming up in front of her and then an explosion that seemed to fill the universe.

After that the world became still and white and peaceful and silent.

CHAPTER

20

She opened her eyes and she was in a hospital bed and the first thing she saw was Alec Nichols.

"There's nothing in the house for you to eat," she whispered, and started to cry.

Alec's eyes filled with pain, and he put his arms around her and held her close. "Elizabeth!"

And she mumbled, "It's all right, Alec. Everything is fine."

And it was. Every inch of her body felt bruised and beaten, but she was alive, and she could not believe it. She remembered the terror of that drive down the mountain, and her body went cold.

"How long have I been here?" Her voice was weak and hoarse.

"They brought you in two days ago. You've been unconscious since then. The doctor says it was a miracle. According to everybody who saw the scene of the accident, you should be dead. A service crew came across you and rushed you in here. You have a concussion and a hell of a lot of bruises, but, thank the Lord, there's nothing broken." He looked at her, puzzled, and said, "What were you doing up there on that firebreak road?"

Elizabeth told him. She could see the horror on

his face as he lived through the terrible ride with her. He kept repeating, "Oh, my God," over and over. When Elizabeth had finished, Alec was pale. "What a stupid, terrible accident!"

"It wasn't an accident, Alec."

He looked at her, puzzled. "I don't understand."

How could he? He had not read the report. Elizabeth said, "Someone tampered with the brakes."

He shook his head incredulously. "Why would anyone do that?"

"Because—" She could not tell him. Not yet. She trusted Alec more than she trusted anyone else, but she was not ready to talk. Not until she felt stronger, not until she had had time to think.

"I don't know," she said evasively. "I'm just sure someone did."

She watched him and she could read the changing expressions on his face. They went from disbelief to puzzlement to anger.

"Well, we're certainly going to find out." His voice was grim.

He picked up the telephone, and a few minutes later he was talking to the Chief of Police in Olbia. "This is Alec Nichols," he said. "I— Yes, she's fine, thank you. . . . Thank you. I'll tell her. I'm calling about the Jeep she was driving. Could you tell me where it is? . . . Would you keep it there, please? And I'd like you to get hold of a good mechanic. I'll be there in half an hour." He replaced the receiver. "It's in the police garage. I'm going over."

"I'm coming with you."

He looked at her in surprise. "The doctor said you must stay in bed for at least another day or two. You can't—"

"I'm coming with you," she insisted stubbornly.

Forty-five minutes later Elizabeth checked her bruised and swollen body out of the hospital over a doctor's protests, and was on her way to the police garage with Alec Nichols.

Luigi Ferraro, the Chief of Police of Olbia, was a swarthy, middle-aged Sardo, with a large stomach and bandy legs. Next to him was Detective Bruno Campagna, who towered over his chief. Campagna was a muscularly built man in his fifties, with an air of solid competence. He stood next to Elizabeth and Alec, watching a mechanic examine the underside of a Jeep that was raised on a hydraulic hoist. The left front fender and radiator had been smashed, and they were streaked with the sap of the trees they had crashed into. Elizabeth had felt faint at her first sight of the car, and she had had to lean on Alec for support. He looked at her with concern. "Are you sure you're up to this?"

"I feel fine," Elizabeth lied. She felt weak and terribly tired. But she had to see for herself.

The mechanic wiped his hands on a greasy cloth and walked over to the group. "They don't build them like that no more," he said.

Thank God, Elizabeth thought.

"Any other car woulda been in bits and pieces."

"What about the brakes?" Alec asked.

"The brakes? They're in perfect condition."

Elizabeth felt a sudden sense of unreality engulfing her. "What—what do you mean?"

"They're workin' fine. The accident didn't hurt them at all. That's what I meant when I said that they don't build—"

"That's impossible," Elizabeth interrupted. "The brakes weren't working on that Jeep."

245

"Miss Roffe believes that someone tampered with them," Chief Ferraro explained.

The mechanic shook his head. "No, sir." He walked back to the Jeep and pointed to the under-side. "There's only two ways you can *fregare*—" He turned to Elizabeth. "Excuse me, signorina— screw up the brakes on a Jeep. You can either cut the brake links or you can loosen this nut"—he indicated a piece of metal on the underside—"and let the brake fluid run out. You can see for yourself that this link is solid, and I checked the brake drum. It's full."

Chief Ferraro said to Elizabeth soothingly, "I can understand how in your condition it could—"

"Just a moment," Alec interrupted. He turned to the mechanic. "Isn't it possible that those links were cut and then replaced or that someone drained the brake fluid and then filled it again?"

The mechanic shook his head stubbornly. "Mister, those links ain't been touched." He took his rag again and carefully wiped off the oil around the nut that held the brake fluid. "See this nut? If anyone had loosened it, there'd be fresh wrench marks on it. I'll guarantee that no one's touched it in the last six months. There's not a thing wrong with these brakes. I'll show you."

He walked over to the wall and pulled a switch. There was a whirring sound and the hydraulic lift began to lower the Jeep to the floor. They watched as the mechanic got in it, started the engine and backed the Jeep up. When it was touching the back wall, he put the Jeep in first gear and pressed down on the accelerator. The car raced toward Detective Campagna. Elizabeth opened her mouth to scream, and at that instant the Jeep jerked to a stop an inch away from him. The mechanic ignored the look the detective gave him and said, "See? These brakes are perfect."

They were all looking at Elizabeth now, and she knew what they were thinking. But that did not change the terror of that ride down the mountain. She could feel her foot pressing on the brakes, and nothing happening. Yet the police mechanic had proved that they worked. Unless he was in on it. And that meant the Chief of Police probably knew too. I'm becoming paranoiac, Elizabeth thought.

Alec said helplessly, "Elizabeth—"

"When I drove that Jeep, those brakes were not working."

Alec studied her for a moment, then said to the mechanic, "Let's suppose that someone *did* arrange it so that the brakes on this Jeep wouldn't work. How else could it have been done?"

Detective Campagna spoke up. "They could have wet the brake lining."

Elizabeth could feel an excitement stirring in her. "What would happen if they did that?"

Detective Campagna said, "When the brake lining pressed against the drum, it would have no traction."

The mechanic nodded. "He's right. The only thing is—" He turned to Elizabeth. "Were your brakes working when you started driving?"

Elizabeth remembered using the brakes to back out of the carport, and braking again later when she came to the first curves. "Yes," she said, "they were working."

"There's your answer," the mechanic said triumphantly. "Your brakes got wet in the rain."

"Hold on," Alec objected. "Why couldn't some-one have wet them *before* she started?"

"Because," the mechanic said patiently, "if any-one had wet them *before* she started, she wouldn'ta had no brakes at all."

The Chief of Police turned to Elizabeth. "Rain can be dangerous, Miss Roffe. Particularly on these narrow mountain roads. This sort of thing happens all too often."

Alec was watching Elizabeth, not knowing what to do next. She felt like a fool. It *had* been an ac-cident after all. She wanted to get out of here. She looked at the Chief of Police. "I—I'm sorry to have put you to all this trouble."

"*Please*. It is a pleasure. I mean—I am distressed about the circumstances, but it is always a pleasure to be of service. Detective Campagna will drive you back to your villa."

Alec said to her. "If you don't mind my saying so, old girl, you look ghastly. Now, I want you to hop into your bed and stay there for a few days. I'll order some groceries by telephone."

"If I stay in bed, who's going to cook?"

"I am," Alec declared.

That evening he prepared dinner and served it to Elizabeth in bed.

"I'm afraid I'm not a very good cook," he said cheerfully, as he set a tray down in front of Elizabeth.

It was the understatement of the year, Elizabeth thought. Alec was a terrible cook. Every dish was either burned, underdone or oversalted. But she managed to eat, partly because she was starving, and partly because she did not want to hurt Alec's feelings. He sat with her, making cheerful small talk. Not a word about what a fool she had made of herself at the police garage. She loved him for it.

The two of them spent the next few days at the villa, with Elizabeth remaining in bed, and Alec fussing over her, cooking all the meals, reading to her. During that time it seemed to Elizabeth that the telephone never stopped ringing. Ivo and Simonetta called every day to see how she was, and Hélène and Charles, and Walther. Even Vivian called. They all offered to come and stay with her.

"I'm really all right," she told them. "There's no reason for you to come. I'll be returning to Zurich in a few days."

Rhys Williams called. Elizabeth had not realized how much she had missed him until she heard the sound of his voice.

"I hear you decided to give Hélène some competition," he said. But she could hear the concern in his voice.

"Wrong. I only race on mountains, downhill." It was incredible to her that she could joke about it now.

Rhys said, "I'm glad you're all right, Liz."

His tone, as much as his words, warmed her. She wondered if he was with another woman now, and who she was. It would be someone beautiful, of course.

Damn her.

"Did you know you made the headlines?" Rhys asked.

"No."

" 'Heiress narrowly escapes death in car accident. Only a few weeks after her father, the well-known —' You can write the rest of the story yourself."

They spoke on the phone for half an hour, and when Elizabeth hung up she was feeling much better. Rhys seemed so genuinely interested in her, and concerned. She wondered whether he made every woman he knew feel that way about him. It was part of his charm. She remembered how they had celebrated her birthdays together. *Mrs. Rhys Williams.*

Alec walked into the bedroom. He said, "You look like the Cheshire cat."

"Do I?"

Rhys had always been able to make her feel that way. Perhaps, she thought, I should tell Rhys about the confidential report.

Alec had arranged for one of the company planes to fly them back to Zurich.

"I hate to take you back so soon," he said apologetically, "but there are some rather urgent decisions that have to be made."

The flight to Zurich was uneventful. There were reporters at the airport. Elizabeth made a brief statement about her accident, and then Alec had her safely inside the limousine and they were on their way to the company headquarters.

She was in the conference room with all the members of the board, and Rhys, present. The meeting had been going on for the past three hours, and the air was stale with cigar and cigarette smoke. Elizabeth was still shaken from her experience, and she had a pounding headache—*Nothing to be con-*

*cerned about, Miss Roffe. When the concussion
wears off, the headaches will go away.*

She looked around the room, at the tense, angry
faces. "I've decided not to sell," Elizabeth had told
them. They thought she was being arbitrary and
stubborn. If they only knew how close she had
come to giving in. But now it was impossible. Someone in this room was an enemy. If she quit now,
it would be his victory.

They had all tried to convince her, each in his
own fashion.

Alec said reasonably, "Roffe and Sons needs an
experienced president, Elizabeth. Particularly now.
For your own sake, as well as everyone else's, I
would like to see you walk away from this."

Ivo used his charm. "You're a beautiful young
girl, *carissima*. The whole world is yours. Why do
you want to become a slave to something as dull as
business when you could be out, having a wonderful time, traveling—"

"I've traveled," Elizabeth said.

Charles used Gallic logic. "You happen to hold
the controlling stock, through a tragic accident,
but it makes no sense for you to try to run the company. We have serious problems. You will only
make them worse."

Walther spoke bluntly. "The company is in
enough trouble. You have no idea how much
trouble. If you do not sell now, it will be too late."

Elizabeth felt as though she were under siege.
She listened to them all, studying them, evaluating
what they were telling her. Each of them based
his argument on the good of the company—yet one
of them was working to destroy it.

One thing was clear. They all wanted her to get

out, to let them sell their stock, and bring in out-siders to take over Roffe and Sons. Elizabeth knew that the moment she did that, her chances of finding out who was behind this were finished. As long as she stayed here, on the inside, there was the pos-sibility that she could learn who was sabotaging the company. She would stay only as long as she had to. She had not spent the last three years with Sam without learning something about the business. With the help of the experienced staff he had built up, she would continue to carry out her father's policies. The insistence from all the board members that she get out now only made her more stubbornly deter-mined to remain.

She decided it was time to end the meeting.

"I've made my decision," Elizabeth said. "I don't plan to run this company alone. I'm aware of how much I have to learn. I know I can count on all of you to help me. We'll deal with the problems one by one."

She sat at the head of the table, still pale from her accident, looking small and defenseless.

Ivo threw up his hands helplessly. "Can't anyone talk logic into her?"

Rhys turned to Elizabeth and smiled. "I think everyone's going to have to go along with whatever the lady wants to do."

"Thank you, Rhys." Elizabeth looked at the others. "There's one thing more. Since I'm taking my father's place, I think it would be best to make it official."

Charles stared at her. "You mean—you want to become president?"

"In effect," Alec reminded him dryly, "Elizabeth is already president. She's merely showing us the courtesy of letting us handle the situation gracefully."

Charles hesitated, then said, "All right. I move that Elizabeth Roffe be nominated president of Roffe and Sons."

"I second the motion." Walther.

The motion was carried.

It was such a bad time for presidents, he thought sadly. *So many were being assassinated.*

CHAPTER

21

No one was more aware than Elizabeth of the enormous responsibility she had assumed. As long as she was running the company, the jobs of thousands of people depended upon her. She needed help, but she had no idea whom she could trust. Alec and Rhys and Ivo were the ones she most wanted to confide in, but she was not ready yet. It was too soon. She sent for Kate Erling.

"Yes, Miss Roffe?"

Elizabeth hesitated, wondering how to begin. Kate Erling had worked for Elizabeth's father for many years. She would have a sense of the undercurrents that flowed beneath the deceptively calm surface. She would know about the inner workings of the company, about Sam Roffe's feelings, his plans. Kate Erling would make a strong ally.

Elizabeth said, "My father was having some kind of confidential report drawn up for him, Kate. Do you know anything about it?"

Kate Erling frowned in concentration, then shook her head. "He never discussed it with me, Miss Roffe."

Elizabeth tried another approach. "If my father

had wanted a confidential investigation, to whom would he have gone?"

This time the answer was unhesitating. "Our security division."

The last place Sam would have gone. "Thank you," Elizabeth said.

There was no one she could talk to.

There was a current financial report on her desk. Elizabeth read it with growing dismay, and then sent for the company comptroller. His name was Wilton Kraus. He was younger than Elizabeth had expected. Bright, eager, an air of faint superiority. The Wharton School, she decided, or perhaps Harvard.

Elizabeth began without preamble. "How can a company like Roffe and Sons be in financial difficulty?"

Kraus looked at her and shrugged. He was obviously not used to reporting to a woman. He said condescendingly, "Well, putting it in words of one syllable—"

"Let's begin with the fact," Elizabeth said curtly, "that up until two years ago Roffe and Sons had always done its own capital financing."

She watched his expression change, trying to adjust. "Well—yes, ma'am."

"Then why are we so heavily indebted to banks now?"

He swallowed and said, "A few years ago, we went through a period of unusually heavy expansion. Your father and the other members of the board felt that it would be wise to raise that money by borrowing from banks on short-term loans. We have current net commitments to various banks for six hundred and fifty million dollars. Some of those loans are now due."

"Overdue," Elizabeth corrected him.

"Yes, ma'am. Overdue."

"We're paying the prime rate, plus one percent, plus penalty interest. Why haven't we paid off the overdue loans and reduced the principal on the others?"

He was beyond surprise now. "Because of—er —certain unfortunate recent occurrences, the company's cash-flow position is considerably less than we had anticipated. Under ordinary circumstances we would go to the banks and ask for extensions. However, with our current problems, the various litigation settlements, the write-offs in our experimental laboratory, and . . ." His voice trailed off.

Elizabeth sat there, studying him, wondering whose side he was on. She looked down at the balance sheets again, trying to pinpoint where things had gone wrong. The statement showed a sharp decline over the past three quarters, largely because of the heavy lawsuit payoffs listed under the column "Extraordinary Expenses (Nonrecurring)." In her mind's eye she saw the explosion in Chile, the cloud of poisonous chemicals spouting into the air. She could hear the screams of the victims. A dozen people dead. Hundreds more taken to hospitals. And in the end all the human pain and misery had been reduced to money, to Extraordinary Expenses (Nonrecurring).

She looked up at Wilton Kraus. "According to your report, Mr. Kraus, our problems are of a temporary nature. We are Roffe and Sons. We're still a first-class risk for any bank in the world."

It was his turn to study her. His supercilious air was gone, but he was wary now.

"You must realize, Miss Roffe," he began cautiously, "that a drug firm's reputation is as important as its products."

Who had said that to her before? Her father? Alec? She remembered. Rhys.

"Go on."

"Our problems are becoming too well-known. The business world is a jungle. If your competitors suspect that you've been wounded, they move in for the kill." He hesitated, then added, "They're moving in for the kill."

"In other words," Elizabeth replied, "our competitors bank with our bankers, too."

He gave her a brief congratulatory smile. "Exactly. The banks have a limited amount of funds to loan out. If they're convinced that A is a better risk than B—"

"And *do* they think that?"

He ran his fingers through his hair, nervously. "Since your father's death I've had several calls from Herr Julius Badrutt. He heads up the banking consortium we're dealing with."

"What did Herr Badrutt want?" She knew what was coming.

"He wanted to know who was going to be the new president of Roffe and Sons."

"Do you know who the new president is?" Elizabeth asked.

"No ma'am."

"I am." She watched him try to conceal his surprise. "What do you think will happen when Herr Badrutt learns the news?"

"He'll pull the plugs on us," Wilton Kraus blurted out.

"I'll talk to him," Elizabeth said. She leaned back in her chair and smiled. "Would you care for some coffee?"

"Why that's—that's very kind of you. Yes, thank you."

Elizabeth watched him relax. He had sensed that she had been testing him, and he felt that he had passed the test.

"I'd like your advice," Elizabeth said. "If you were in my position, Mr. Kraus, what would you do?"

That faintly patronizing air was back. "Well," he said confidently, "that's very simple. Roffe and Sons has enormous assets. If we sold off a substantial block of stock to the public, we could easily raise more than enough money to satisfy all our bank loans."

She knew now whose side he was on.

CHAPTER

22

Hamburg.
Friday, October 1.
Two a.m.

The wind was blowing from the sea, and the early-morning air was chill and damp. In the Reeperbahn section of Hamburg the streets were crowded with visitors eager to experience the forbidden pleasures of the city of sin. The Reeperbahn catered to all tastes impartially. Drinks, drugs, girls or boys—they were all available at a price.

The garishly lighted hostess bars were on the main street, while the Grosse Freiheit featured the lewd strip shows. The Herbertstrasse, one block away, was for pedestrians only, and both sides of the street were lined with prostitutes sitting in the windows of their flats, displaying their wares through flimsy soiled nightgowns that concealed nothing. The Reeperbahn was a vast market, a human butcher shop, where you could select any piece of meat you could afford to pay for. For the straitlaced there was simple sex, missionary style; for those who enjoyed a bit of variety there was cunnilingus and analingus and sodomy. On the Reeperbahn you could buy a twelve-year-old boy or girl, or get into bed with a mother and daughter. If your tastes ran that way, you could watch a woman being serviced by a Great Dane, or get yourself whipped until you achieved orgasm. You could hire a toothless crone to perform fellatio on you in a busy alley or buy yourself an orgy in an elaborately mirrored bedroom with as many girls or boys as your libido required. The Reeperbahn prided itself on having something for everyone. Younger whores in short skirts and tight-fitting blouses cruised the pavements, propositioning men, women and couples impartially.

The cameraman walked down the street slowly, the target for a dozen girls and brightly rouged boys. He ignored them all until he came to a girl who looked to be no more than eighteen. She had blond hair. She was leaning against a wall, talking to a girl friend. She turned as the man approached, and smiled. "Would you like a party, *liebchen?* My friend and I will show you a good time."

The man studied the girl and said, "Just you."

The other girl shrugged and moved off.

"What's your name?"

"Hildy."

"Would you like to be in the movies, Hildy?" the cameraman asked.

The young girl studied him with cold eyes. *"Herrgott!* You're not going to give me that old Hollywood *Scheiss?"*

He smiled reassuringly. "No, no. This is a genuine offer. It's a porno film. I make them for a friend of mine."

"It will cost you five hundred marks. In advance."

"*Gut.*"

She regretted instantly that she had not asked for more. Well, she would find some way to get a bonus out of him. "What do I have to do?" Hildy asked.

Hildy was nervous.

She lay sprawled out naked on the bed in the small, shabbily furnished apartment, watching the three people in the room, and thinking, There's something wrong here. Her instincts had been sharpened on the streets of Berlin and Munich and Hamburg. She had learned to rely on them. There was something about these people she did not trust. She would have liked to have walked out before it started, but they had already paid her five hundred marks, and promised her another five hundred if she did a good job. She would do a good job. She was a professional and she took pride in her work. She turned to the naked man in bed beside her. He was strong and well built; his body was hairless. What bothered Hildy was his face. He was too old for this sort of film. But it was the spectator who sat quietly at the back of the room who disturbed Hildy the most. The spectator wore a long coat, a large hat and dark glasses. Hildy could not even tell if it was a man or a woman. The vibrations were bad. Hildy fingered the red ribbon tied around her neck, wondering why they had asked her to wear it. The cameraman said, "All right. We're ready now. Action."

The camera began whirring. Hildy had been told what to do. The man was lying on his back. Hildy went to work.

She started with a trip around the world, skillfully

using her tongue and lips on the man's ears and neck, moving down across his chest and stomach and belly, lightly flicking her tongue in quick butterfly strokes against his groin and penis, then each leg, down to his toes, slowly licking each toe, watching his erection begin. She rolled him over on his stomach, and her tongue began to work its way back up his body, moving slowly, expertly, finding all the erotic crevices and sensitive areas and exploring them. The man was fully aroused now, rock-hard.

"Get inside her," the cameraman said. The man rolled her over and was on top of her, forcing her thighs apart, his penis swollen to an enormous tumescence, and as he entered her, Hildy forgot her earlier fears. It felt wonderful.

"Shove it in me, *liebchen!*" she cried.

The man was deep, deep inside her, rocking back and forth, and Hildy started to move with him, her hips writhing in quickening spasms. In the back of the room the spectator was leaning forward, watching every movement. The girl on the bed closed her eyes.

She was spoiling it!"

"Her eyes!" the spectator shouted.

The director called out, *"Öffne die Augen!"*

Startled, Hildy opened her eyes. She watched the man on top of her. He was good. It was the kind of sex she liked. Hard and thrusting. He was moving faster now, and she began to respond to him. Usually she did not have orgasms, except with her girl friend. With customers she always faked it, and they never knew the difference. But the cameraman had warned her that if she did not have an orgasm, she would not be paid the bonus. And so now she relaxed and let herself think about all the beautiful things she was going to buy with the money, and she felt herself beginning to climax.

"*Schneller!*" she cried. "*Schneller!*"

Her body began to shudder. "*Ah, jetzt!*" she screamed. "*Es kommt! Es kommt!*"

The spectator nodded, and the cameraman cried, "Now!"

The man's hands moved up toward the girl's neck. His enormous fingers closed over the windpipe and squeezed. She looked up into his eyes and saw what was there, and she was filled with terror. She tried to scream, but she was unable to breathe. She fought desperately to fight free, her body jerking in great, orgiastic spasms, but he had her pinned down. There was no escape.

The spectator sat there drinking it in, feasting on it, looking into the dying girl's eyes, watching her being punished.

The girl's body shuddered once, and then was still.

CHAPTER

23

Zurich.
Monday, October 4.
Ten a.m.

When Elizabeth arrived at her office, a sealed envelope marked "CONFIDENTIAL," with her name on it, was lying on her desk. She opened it. In it was a report from the chemical laboratory. It was signed "Emil Joeppli." It was full of technical terms, and Elizabeth read it through without understanding it. Then she read it again. And again. Each time more slowly. When finally she had grasped its significance, she said to Kate, "I'll be back in an hour." And she went to find Emil Joeppli.

He was a tall man about thirty-five, with a thin, freckled face, and a scalp that was bald except for a tonsure of bright red hair. He fidgeted uncomfortably, as though unused to having visitors in his little laboratory.

"I read your report," Elizabeth told him. "There's a great deal in it that I don't understand. I wonder if you would mind explaining it to me."

Instantly, Joeppli's nervousness vanished. He leaned forward in his chair, sure and confident, and began to speak rapidly. "I've been experimenting with a method of inhibiting rapid differentiation of the collagens, by using mucopolysaccharides and enzyme blocking techniques. Collagen, of course, is the fundamental protein basis of all connective tissue."

"Of course," Elizabeth said.

She did not even try to understand the technical part of what Joeppli was saying. What Elizabeth did understand was that the project he was working on could retard the aging process. It was a breathtaking concept.

She sat there, silent, listening, thinking about what this could mean in terms of revolutionizing the lives of men and women all over the world. According to Joeppli, there was no reason why everyone should not live to be a hundred, or a hundred and fifty, or even two hundred years old.

"It would not even be necessary to have injections," Joeppli told Elizabeth. "With this formula the ingredients could be taken orally in a pill or a capsule."

The possibilities were staggering. It would mean nothing less than a social revolution. And billions of dollars for Roffe and Sons. They would manufacture it themselves, and license it out to other companies as well. There was no one over fifty years of age who would not take a pill that would keep him or her young. It was difficult for Elizabeth to conceal her excitement.

"How far along are you on this project?"

"As I wrote in my report, I've been doing tests with animals for the last four years. All the recent results have been positive. It's just about ready for testing on human beings." She liked his enthusiasm.

"Who else knows about this?" Elizabeth asked.

"Your father knew. It's a Red Folder project. Top security. That means that I report only to the president of the company and to one member of the board."

Elizabeth suddenly felt chilled. "Which member?"

"Mr. Walther Gassner."

Elizabeth was silent for a moment. "From this time on," she said, "I want you to report directly to me. And only to me."

Joeppli looked at her in surprise. "Yes, Miss Roffe."

"How soon could we have this on the market?"

"If everything goes well, eighteen to twenty-four months from now."

"Fine. If you need anything—money, extra help, equipment—let me know. I want you to move as quickly as possible."

"Yes, ma'am."

Elizabeth rose, and instantly Emil Joeppli jumped to his feet.

"It's a pleasure meeting you." He smiled, and added shyly, "I liked your father."

"Thank you," Elizabeth said. Sam had known about this project. Was that another reason he refused to sell the company?

"At the door Emil Joeppli turned to Elizabeth. "It's going to work on people!"

"Yes," Elizabeth said. "Of course it will."

It had to.

"How is a Red Folder project handled?"

Kate Erling asked, "From the beginning?"

"From the beginning."

"Well. As you know, we have several hundred new products in various experimental stages. They—"

"Who authorizes them?"

"Up to a certain amount of money, the heads of the different departments involved," Kate Erling said.

"What amount of money?"

"Fifty thousand dollars."

"And after that?"

"There must be board approval. Of course, a project does not come into the Red Folder category until it has passed its initial tests."

"You mean until it looks like it has a chance of being successful?" Elizabeth asked.

"That's right."

"How is it protected?"

"If it's an important project, all the work is transferred to one of our high-security laboratories. All the papers are removed from the general files and put into a Red Folder file. Only three people have access to that. The scientist in charge of the project, the president of the company, and one member of the board."

"Who decides who that member will be?" Elizabeth asked.

"Your father selected Walther Gassner."

The moment the words were out of her mouth, Kate realized her mistake.

The two women looked at each other, and Elizabeth said, "Thank you, Kate. That will be all."

Elizabeth had made no mention of Joeppli's project. Yet Kate had known what Elizabeth was talking about. There were two possibilities. Either

Sam had trusted her and told her about Joeppli's project, or she had learned about it on her own. For someone else.

This was too important to allow anything to go wrong. She would check on the security herself. And she had to speak to Walther Gassner. She reached for the telephone, then stopped. There was a better way.

Late that afternoon Elizabeth was on a commercial airliner to Berlin.

Walther Gassner was nervous.

They were seated at a corner booth in the upstairs dining room of the Papillon on the Kurfürstendamm. Whenever Elizabeth had visited Berlin in the past, Walther had always insisted that Elizabeth have dinner at his home, with Anna and him. This time there had been no mention of that. He had suggested instead that they meet at this restaurant. And he had come without Anna.

Walther Gassner still had the clear-cut, boyish, moviestar handsomeness, but the surface gloss had begun to crack. There were lines of tension in his face, and his hands never stopped moving. He seemed to be under some extraordinary tension. When Elizabeth asked about Anna, Walther was vague. "Anna's not feeling well. She couldn't come."

"Is it anything serious?"

"No, no. She'll be fine. She's at home, resting."

"I'll call her and—"

"Better not to disturb her."

It was a puzzling conversation, totally unlike Walther, whom Elizabeth had always found so open and outgoing.

She brought up the subject of Emil Joeppli. "We

need what he's working on very badly," Elizabeth said.

Walther nodded. "It's going to be big."

"I've asked him not to report to you anymore," Elizabeth told him.

Walther's hands suddenly went very still. It was like a shout. He looked at Elizabeth and asked, "Why did you do that?"

"It has nothing to do with you, Walther. I would have done exactly the same thing with any other board member working with him. I simply want to handle this my own way."

He nodded. "I see." But his hands remained motionless on the table. "You have a right, of course." He forced a smile and she could see what it was costing him. "Elizabeth," he said, "Anna has a lot of stock in the company. She can't sell it unless you vote yes. It's—it's very important. I—"

"I'm sorry, Walther, I can't let the stock be sold now."

His hands suddenly began to move again.

CHAPTER

24

Herr Julius Badrutt was a thin, brittle man who resembled a praying mantis in a black suit. He was like a stick figure drawn by a child, with angular arms and legs, and a dry, unfinished face sketched on top of his body. He was seated stiffly at the conference table of the Roffe and Sons boardroom, facing Elizabeth. There were five other bankers with him. They all wore black suits with waistcoats, white shirts and dark ties. They appeared, Elizabeth thought, not so much *dressed* as in uniform. Looking around at the cold, impassive eyes at the table, Elizabeth was filled with a sense of misgiving. Before the meeting had begun, Kate had brought in a tray of coffee and delicious, freshly baked pastries. The men had all declined. Just as they had declined Elizabeth's invitation to come to lunch. She decided it was a bad sign. They were there to get the money that was owed them.

Elizabeth said, "First of all, I wish to thank all of you for coming here today."

There were polite, meaningless murmurs in response.

She took a deep breath. "I asked you here to

discuss an extension on the loans owed to you by Roffe and Sons."

Julius Badrutt shook his head in tiny, jerky movements. "I am sorry, Miss Roffe. We have already informed——"

"I haven't finished," Elizabeth said. She glanced around the room. "If I were you, gentlemen, I would refuse."

They stared at her, then looked at one another in confusion.

Elizabeth continued, "If you were concerned about the loans when my father was running this company—and he was a brilliant businessman— why would you extend them for a woman who is inexperienced in business?"

Julius Badrutt said dryly, "I think you have answered your own question, Miss Roffe. We have no intention of——"

Elizabeth said, "I haven't finished."

They were eyeing her more warily now. She looked at each of them in turn, making sure she had their full attention. They were Swiss bankers, admired, respected and envied by their lesser colleagues in other parts of the financial world. They were leaning forward now, listening carefully, their attitude of impatience and boredom replaced by curiosity.

"You have all known Roffe and Sons for a long time," Elizabeth went on. "I am sure most of you knew my father and, if you did, you must have respected him."

There were nods of agreement from some of the men.

"I imagine," Elizabeth continued, "that you gentlemen must have choked over your morning coffee when you learned that I was taking his place here."

One of the bankers smiled, then laughed aloud, and said, "You are quite right, Miss Roffe. I do not mean to be ungallant, but I think I am speaking for the rest of my colleagues when I say that—what were your words?—we choked over our morning coffee."

Elizabeth smiled ingenuously. "I don't blame you. I'm sure I would have reacted in exactly the same way."

Another banker spoke up. "I am curious, Miss Roffe. Since we are all in agreement about the outcome of this meeting"—he spread his hands expressively—"why are we here?"

"You're here," Elizabeth said, "because in this room are some of the greatest bankers in the world. I can't believe that you became so successful by looking at everything only in terms of dollars and cents. If that were true, then any of your bookkeepers could run your business for you. I am sure that there is much more to banking than that."

"Of course there is," another banker murmured, "but we're businessmen, Miss Roffe, and—"

"And Roffe and Sons is a business. It's a great business. I didn't know how great until I sat behind my father's desk. I had no idea how many lives this company has saved in countries all over the world. Or of the enormous contributions we've made to medicine. Or how many thousands of people depend on this company for their livelihood. If—"

Julius Badrutt interrupted. "That is all very commendable, but we seem to be getting off the point. I understand that it has been suggested to you that if you release the company stock, there will be more than sufficient monies to satisfy our loans."

His first mistake, Elizabeth thought. *I understand that it has been suggested to you.*

The suggestion had been made in the privacy of a board of directors' meeting, where everything was confidential. Someone at that meeting had talked. Someone who was trying to put pressure on her. She intended to find out who, but that would have to come later.

"I want to ask you a question," Elizabeth said. "If your loans are repaid, would it matter to you where the money came from?"

Julius Badrutt studied her, his mind circling the question, looking for a trap. Finally he said, "No. Not as long as we receive the money due us."

Elizabeth leaned forward and said earnestly, "So it doesn't matter whether you're paid from the sale of company stock to outsiders, or from our own financial resources. All of you know that Roffe and Sons isn't going out of business. Not today. Not tomorrow. Not ever. All I'm asking is the courtesy of a little extra time."

Julius Badrutt smacked his dry lips and said, "Believe me, Miss Roffe, we are most sympathetic. We understand the terrible emotional stress you have gone through, but we cannot—"

"Three months," Elizabeth said. "Ninety days. With your getting additional penalty interest, of course."

There was a silence around the table. But it was a negative silence. Elizabeth could see their cold, hostile faces. She decided on one last desperate gamble.

"I—I don't know whether it's proper for me to reveal this," she said with deliberate hesitation, "and I must ask you to keep it confidential." She looked around and saw that she had their interest again. "Roffe and Sons is on the verge of a break-through that's going to revolutionize the entire pharmaceutical industry." She paused to heighten the suspense. "This company is about to reveal a new product that our projections show will *far out-sell every drug available on the market today.*"

She could feel the change in the atmosphere.

It was Julius Badrutt who rose to the bait first. "What—er—type of—?"

Elizabeth shook her head. "I'm sorry, Herr Bad-rutt. Perhaps I've already said too much. I can only tell you that it will be the biggest innovation in the history of this business. It will require a tremendous expansion of our facilities. We'll have to double them, perhaps triple them. Of course, we'll be look-ing for new financing on a large scale."

The bankers were glancing at one another, ex-changing silent signals. The silence was broken by Herr Badrutt. "If we *were* to give you a ninety-day extension, we would naturally expect to act as the prime bankers for Roffe and Sons in all future transactions."

"Naturally."

Another exchange of meaningful looks. It's like a form of jungle drums, Elizabeth thought.

"In the meantime," Herr Badrutt said, "we would have your assurance that at the end of ninety days all your outstanding notes will be met in full?"

"Yes."

Herr Badrutt sat there, staring into space. He looked at Elizabeth, then looked around at the others, and received their silent signals. "For my part, I am willing to agree. I do not think a delay—with penalty interest—will do any harm."

277

One of the other bankers nodded. "If you think we should go along, Julius . . ."

And it was done. Elizabeth leaned back in her chair, trying to conceal the feeling of relief flooding through her. She had gained ninety days.

She would need every minute of that time.

CHAPTER
25

It was like being in the eye of a hurricane.

Everything flowed across Elizabeth's desk from the hundreds of departments at headquarters, from the factories in Zaire, the laboratories in Greenland, the offices in Australia and Thailand, from the four corners of the earth. There were reports on new products, sales, statistical projections, advertising campaigns, experimental programs.

There were decisions to be made on building new factories, selling old ones, acquiring companies, hiring and firing executives. Elizabeth had expert advice on every phase of the business, but all final decisions had to be made by her. As they had once been made by Sam. She was grateful now for the three years she had worked with her father. She knew much more about the company than she had realized, and much less. Its very scope was awesome. Elizabeth had once thought of it as a kingdom, but it was a *series* of kingdoms, run by viceroys, with the president's office as the throne room. Each of her cousins had charge of his own domain, but in addition they supervised other overseas territories, so that they were all traveling constantly.

Elizabeth soon learned that she had a special

problem. She was a woman in a man's world, and she discovered that it made a difference. She had never really believed that men subscribed to the myth of the inferiority of women, but she quickly learned better. No one ever put it into words or acted overtly, but Elizabeth was faced with it every day. It was an attitude born of ancient prejudices and it was inescapable. The men did not like taking orders from a woman. They resented the idea of a woman questioning their judgments, trying to improve on their ideas. The fact that Elizabeth was young and attractive made it worse. They tried to make her feel that she should be at home, in a bed or kitchen, and that she should leave serious business matters to the men.

Elizabeth scheduled meetings with different department heads every day. Not all were hostile. Some were predatory. A beautiful girl sitting behind the president's desk was a challenge to the male ego. Their minds were easy to read: If I can fuck her, I can control her.

Like the grown-up version of the boys in Sardinia.

The men went after the wrong part of Elizabeth. They should have gone after her mind, because in the end that was where she controlled them. They underestimated her intelligence, and that was their mistake.

They miscalculated her capacity to assume authority, and that was another error.

And they misjudged her strength, and that was their greatest mistake. She was a Roffe, with the bloodline of old Samuel and her father in her, and she had their determination and spirit.

While the men around her were trying to use Elizabeth, she used them. She tapped the knowledge and the experience and the insights that they had accumulated, and she made them her own. She let the men talk, and she listened. She asked questions, and she remembered the answers.

She learned.

Every night Elizabeth took home two heavy brief-cases filled with reports to be studied. Sometimes she worked until four in the morning. One evening a newspaper photographer snapped a picture of Elizabeth walking out of the building with a secretary carrying her two briefcases. The photograph appeared in the newspapers the next day. The caption read: "Working Heiress."

Elizabeth had become an international celebrity overnight. The story of a beautiful young girl inheriting a multibillion-dollar corporation and then taking command was irresistible. The press jumped at it. Elizabeth was lovely, intelligent, and down-to-earth, a combination they rarely came across in celebrities. She made herself available to them whenever possible, trying to build up the damaged image of the company, and they appreciated it. When she didn't know the answer to a reporter's question, she was not afraid to pick up a telephone and ask someone. Her cousins flew into Zurich once a week for meetings and Elizabeth spent as much time with them as possible. She saw them together, and one at a time. She talked to them and studied them, searching for a clue as to which one of them had allowed innocent people to die in an explosion, had sold secrets to competitors, and which one of them was trying to destroy Roffe and Sons. One of her cousins.

Ivo Palazzi, with his irresistible warmth and charmth.

Alec Nichols, a correct and proper gentleman, and gentle man, always helpful when Elizabeth needed him.

Charles Martel, a dominated, frightened man. And frightened men could be dangerous when cornered.

Walther Gassner. The All-German boy. Beautiful-looking and friendly on the outside. What was he like on the inside? He had married Anna, an heiress, thirteen years his senior. Had he married for love or money?

When Elizabeth was with them, she watched, and listened, and probed. She mentioned the explosion in Chile and studied their reactions, and she talked about the patents that Roffe had lost to other companies, and she discussed the impending government suits.

She learned nothing. Whoever it was, he was too clever to give himself away. He would have to be trapped. Elizabeth recalled Sam's marginal note on the report. *Trap the bastard.* She would have to find a way.

Elizabeth found herself becoming more and more fascinated by the inside operation of the pharmaceutical business.

Bad news was deliberately spread. If there was a report that a patient had died from a competitor's medication, within half an hour a dozen men were placing telephone calls all around the world. "By the way, did you happen to hear about . . . ?"

Yet on the surface all the companies appeared to be on the best of terms. The heads of some of the large firms held regular informal get-togethers, and Elizabeth was invited to one. She was the only woman present. They talked about their mutual problems.

The president of one of the large companies, a pompous, middle-aged roué, who had been following Elizabeth around all evening, said, "Government restrictions get more unreasonable every God-damned day. If some genius invented aspirin tomorrow, the government would never okay it." He gave Elizabeth a superior smile. "And do you have any idea, little lady, how long we've had aspirin?"

Little lady replied, "Since four hundred B.C., when Hippocrates discovered salicin in the bark of the willow tree."

He stared at her a moment, and the smile died. "Right." He walked away.

The company heads all agreed that one of their biggest problems was the me-too firms, the copycat houses that stole the formulas of successful products, changed the names and rushed them onto the market. It was costing the reputable drug firms hundreds of millions of dollars a year.

In Italy it was not even necessary to steal it.

"Italy is one of the countries that has no patent regulations protecting new drugs," one of the executives told Elizabeth. "For a bribe of a few hundred thousand lire, anyone can buy the formulas and pirate them under another name. We spend millions of dollars on research—they walk off with the profits."

"Is it just Italy?" Elizabeth asked.

"Italy and Spain are the worst. France and West Germany aren't bad. England and the United States are clean."

Elizabeth looked around at all these indignant, moral men and wondered if any of them was involved in the thefts of the patents of Roffe and Sons.

It seemed to Elizabeth that she spent most of her time in airplanes. She kept her passport in the top drawer of her desk. At least once a week there was a frantic call from Cairo or Guatemala or Tokyo, and within a few hours Elizabeth would find herself in a plane with half a dozen members of her staff, to cope with some emergency.

She met factory managers and their families in large cities like Bombay, and at remote outposts like Puerto Vallarta, and gradually Roffe and Sons began to take on a new perspective. It was no longer an impersonal mass of reports and statistics. A report headed "Guatemala" now meant Emil Nunoz and his fat, happy wife and their twelve children; "Copenhagen" was Nils Bjorn and the crippled mother with whom he lived; "Rio de Janeiro" was an evening spent with Alessandro Duval and his exquisite mistress.

Elizabeth kept in regular touch with Emil Joeppli. She always telephoned him on her private line, calling him at his little flat in Aussersihl in the evenings.

She was cautious even over the telephone.

"How are things going?"

"A little slower than I hoped, Miss Roffe."

"Do you need anything?"

"No. Just time. I ran into a little problem but I think it's solved now."

"Good. Call me if you need anything—anything at all."

"I will. Thank you, Miss Roffe."

Elizabeth hung up. She had an urge to push him, to tell him to hurry, for she knew that her time with the banks was running out. She desperately needed what Emil Joeppli was working on, but pressing him was not the answer, and so she kept her impatience to herself. Elizabeth knew that the experiments could not possibly be completed by the time the bank notes were due. But she had a plan. She intended to let Julius Badrutt into the secret, take him into the laboratory and let him see for himself what was happening. The banks would give them all the time they needed.

Elizabeth found herself working with Rhys Williams more and more closely, sometimes late into the night. They often worked alone, just the two of them, having dinner in her private dining room at the office, or at the elegant apartment she had taken. It was a modern condominium in Zurichberg, overlooking the Lake of Zurich, and it was large and airy and bright. Elizabeth was more aware than ever of the strong animal magnetism of Rhys, but if he felt an attraction for her, he was careful not to show it. He was always polite and friendly. *Avuncular* was the word that came into Elizabeth's mind, and somehow it had a pejorative sound. She wanted to lean on him, confide in him, and yet she knew she had to be careful. More than once she had found herself on the verge of telling Rhys about the efforts to sabotage the company, but something held her back. She was not ready to discuss it with anyone yet. Not until she knew more.

Elizabeth was gaining more confidence in herself. At a sales meeting they were discussing a new hair conditioner that was selling badly. Elizabeth had tried it, and she knew that it was superior to similar products on the market.

"We're getting heavy returns from drugstores," one of the sales executives complained. "It's just not catching on. We need more advertising."

"We're already over our advertising budget," Rhys objected. "We'll have to find a different approach."

Elizabeth said, "Take it out of the drugstores."

They all looked at her. "What?"

"It's too available." She turned to Rhys. "I think we should continue the advertising campaign, but sell it only at beauty salons. Make it exclusive, hard to get. That's the image it should have."

Rhys thought for a moment, then nodded and said, "I like it. Let's try it."

It became a big seller overnight.

Afterward, Rhys had complimented her. "You're not just another pretty face," he had said, grinning.

So he *was* beginning to notice!

CHAPTER
26

Alec Nichols was alone in the club sauna when the
door opened and a man walked into the steam-
filled room, wearing a towel around his waist. He
sat down on the wooden bench, next to Alec. "Hot
as a witch's tit in here, ain't it, Sir Alec?"

Alec turned. It was Jon Swinton. "How did you
get in here?"

Swinton winked. "I said you was expectin' me.
He looked into Alec's eyes and asked, "You *was*
expectin' me, wasn't you, Sir Alec?"

"No," Alec replied. "I told you I need more
time."

"You also told us your little cousin was going to
sell the stock, and you'd give us our money."

"She—she changed her mind."

"Ah, then you'd better change it back for her,
hadn't you?"

"I'm trying. It's a question of—"

"It's a question of how much more horseshit we're going to take from you." Jon Swinton was moving closer, forcing Alec to slide along the bench. "We don't want to get rough with you 'cause it's nice to have a good friend like you in Parliament. You know what I mean? But there's a limit." He was leaning against Alec now, and Alec slid farther away from him. "We did you a favor. Now it's time to pay us back. You're gonna get hold of a shipment of drugs for us."

"No! That's impossible," Alec said. "I can't. There's no way—"

Alec suddenly found that he had been crowded to the end of the bench, next to the large metal container filled with hot rocks. "Be careful," Alec said. "I—"

Swinton grabbed hold of Alec's arm and twisted it, forcing it toward the bed of rocks. Alec could feel the hair on his arm begin to singe.

"No!"

The next instant his arm was pressed down onto the rocks, and he screamed with pain and fell to the floor in agony. Swinton was standing over him.

"You find a way. We'll be in touch."

CHAPTER
27

Anna Roffe Gassner did not know how much longer she would be able to stand it.

She had become a prisoner in her own home. Except for the cleaning woman who came in for a few hours once a week, Anna and the children were alone, completely at Walther's mercy. He no longer bothered to conceal his hatred. Anna had been in the children's room as they listened together to one of their favorite records.

> *"Welch ein Singen, Musizieren,*
> *Pfeifen, Zwitschken, Tiriliern . . ."*

Walther had stormed in. "I'm sick of that!" he had yelled.

And he had smashed the record, while the children cowered in terror.

Anna had tried to placate him. "I—I'm sorry,

289

Walther. I—I didn't know you were home. Can I do something for you?"

He had walked up to her, his eyes blazing, and he said, "We're going to get rid of the children, Anna."

In front of them!

He put his hands on her shoulders. "What happens in this house must be our secret." *Our secret. Our secret. Our secret.*

She could feel the words reverberating in her head, and his arms started to crush her until she could not breathe. She fainted.

When Anna woke up, she was lying in her bed. The shades were drawn. She looked at the bedside clock. Six P.M. The house was quiet. Too quiet. Her first thought was of the children, and terror swept through her. She rose from the bed on shaky legs, and stumbled over to the door. It was locked from the outside. She pressed her ear hard against the panel, listening. There should have been the sounds of the children. They should have come up to see her.

If they had been able to. If they were still alive.

Her legs were trembling so hard that she could barely walk to the telephone. She breathed a silent prayer, then picked it up. She heard the familiar dial tone. She hesitated, dreading the thought of what Walther would do to her if he caught her again. Without giving herself a chance to think, Anna began to dial 110. Her hands shook so badly that she dialed a wrong number. And another. She began to sob. There was so little time left. Fighting her growing hysteria, she tried again, willing her fingers to move slowly. She heard a ringing, then miraculously a man's voice said, *"Hier ist de Notruf der Polizei."*

Anna could not find her voice.

"Hier ist der Notruf der Polizei. Kann ich Ihnen helfen?"

"Ja!" It was a high-pitched sob. *"Ja, bitte! Ich bin in grosser Gefahr. Bitte schicken sie jemanden—"*

Walther loomed in front of her, ripping the telephone out of her hand and hurling her against the bed. He slammed down the receiver, breathing hard, tore the cord out of the wall, and turned to Anna.

"The children," she whispered. "What have you done with the children?"

Walther did not answer.

The Central Division of the Berlin Kriminal Polizei was located at 2832 Keithstrasse in a district of ordinary-looking apartment houses and office buildings. The emergency number of the *Delikt am Mensch* department was equipped with an automatic hold system, so that a caller was unable to disconnect until the line had been electronically released by the switchboard. In this way every number calling in could be traced, no matter how brief the conversation. It was a sophisticated piece of equipment of which the department was proud.

Within five minutes of Anna Gassner's telephone call, Detective Paul Lange walked into the office of his chief, Major Wageman, carrying a cassette player.

"I would like you to listen to this." Detective Lange pressed a button. A metallic male voice said,

"Hier ist der Notruf der Polizei. Kann ich Ihnen helfen?"

Then a woman's voice, filled with terror. *"Ja! Ja, bitte! Ich bin in grosser Gefahr. Bitte schicken sie jemanden—"*

There was the sound of a thud, a click, and the line went dead. Major Wageman looked up at Detective Lange. "You've traced the call?"

"We know whose residence it came from," Detective Lange replied carefully.

"Then what's the problem?" Major Wageman demanded impatiently. "Have Central send a car to investigate."

"I wanted your authority first." Detective Lange placed a slip of paper on the desk in front of the major.

"Scheiss!" Major Wageman stared at him. "Are you sure?"

"Yes, Major."

Major Wageman looked down at the slip of paper again. The telephone was listed in the name of Gassner, Walther. Head of the German division of Roffe and Sons, one of the industrial giants of Germany.

There was no need to discuss the implications. Only an idiot could miss them. One wrong move and they would both be walking the streets, looking for a job. Major Wageman thought for a moment and then said, "All right. Check it out. I want you to go there yourself. And walk on fucking eggs. Do you understand?"

"I understand, Major."

The Gassner estate was in Wannsee, an exclusive suburb in southwest Berlin. Detective Lange took the longer Hohenszollerndamm instead of the speedier autobahn, because the traffic was lighter. He went through the Clayalle, past the CIA building, hidden behind half a mile of barbed-wire fences. He passed the American Army Headquarters and turned right on what was once known as Road One, the longest road in Germany, running from East Prussia to the Belgian border. On his right was the Brücke der Einheit, the Bridge of Unity, where the spy Abel had been exchanged for the American U-2 pilot Gary Powers. Detective Lange turned the car off the highway into the wooded hills of Wannsee.

The houses were beautiful, impressive. On Sundays, Detective Lange sometimes took his wife out here, just to look at the outside of the houses and the grounds.

He found the address he was looking for and turned into the long driveway leading to the Gassner estate. The estate represented something more than money: it represented power. The Roffe dynasty was big enough to make governments fall. Major Wageman had been right: he would be very careful.

Detective Lange drove to the front door of the three-story stone house, got out of the car, took off his hat and pressed the doorbell. He waited. There was the heavy hanging silence of a house that has been deserted. He knew that was impossible. He rang again. Nothing but that still, oppressive silence. He was debating whether to go around to the back when the door unexpectedly opened. A woman stood in the doorway. She was middle-aged, plain-looking, wearing a wrinkled dressing gown. Detective Lange took her for the housekeeper. He pulled out his identification. "I'd like to see Mrs. Walther Gassner. Please tell her Detective Lange."

"I am Mrs. Gassner," the woman said.

Detective Lange tried to conceal his surprise. She was totally unlike his image of the lady of this house.

"I—we received a telephone call at police head-quarters a short time ago," he began.

She watched him, her face blank, disinterested. Detective Lange felt that he was handling this badly, but he did not know why. He had a feeling that he was missing something important.

"Did you make that call, Mrs. Gassner?" he asked.

"Yes," she answered. "It was a mistake."

There was a dead, remote quality to her voice that was disturbing. He remembered the shrill, hysteircal voice on the tape recorder half an hour earlier.

"Just for our records, may I ask what kind of mistake?"

Her hesitation was barely perceptible. "There was—I thought that a piece of my jewelry was missing. I found it."

The emergency number was for murder, rape, mayhem. *Walk on fucking eggs.*

"I see." Detective Lange hesitated, wanting to get inside the house, wanting to find out what she was covering up. But there was nothing more he could say or do. "Thank you, Mrs. Gassner. I'm sorry to have troubled you."

He stood there, frustrated, and watched the door close in his face. He slowly got into his car and drove off.

Behind the door Anna turned.

Walther nodded and said softly, "You did very well, Anna. Now we're going back upstairs."

He turned toward the stairway, and Anna pulled out a pair of shears that had been concealed in the folds of her dressing gown and plunged them into his back.

CHAPTER

28

**Rome.
Sunday, November 4.
Noon.**

It was a perfect day, Ivo Palazzi thought, for visiting the Villa d'Este with Simonetta and their three beautiful daughters. As Ivo strolled through the fabled Tivoli Gardens arm in arm with his wife, watching the girls race ahead from fountain to splashing fountain, he idly wondered whether Pirro Ligorio, who had built the park for his patrons, the D'Este family, had ever dreamed how much joy he would one day give to millions of sightseers. The Villa d'Este was a short distance northeast of Rome, nestled high in the Sabine Hills. Ivo had been there often, but it always gave him a feeling of special pleasure to stand at the very top level and look down on the dozens of sparkling fountains below, each one cunningly designed, each one different from the others.

In the past Ivo had taken Donatella and his three sons here. How they had adored it! The thought of them made Ivo sad. He had not seen or talked to Donatella since that horrifying afternoon at the apartment. He still remembered vividly the terrible scratches she had inflicted on him. He knew what remorse she must be going through, and how she must be longing for him. Well, it would do her good to suffer for a while, as he had suffered. In his mind he could hear Donatella's voice, and she was saying, "Come along. This way, boys."

It was so clear it seemed almost real. He could hear her say, "Faster, Francesco!" and Ivo turned and Donatella was in back of him, with their three boys, moving determinedly toward him and Simonetta and the three girls. Ivo's first thought was that Donatella had happened to be here at the Tivoli Gardens by coincidence, but the instant he saw the expression on her face, he knew better. The *putana* was trying to bring his two families together, trying to destroy him! Ivo rose to the occasion like a madman.

He shouted to Simonetta, "There's something I must show you. Quickly, everybody."

And he swept his family down the long winding stone steps toward a lower level, pushing tourists aside, casting frantic glances over his shoulder. Above, Donatella and the boys were moving toward the steps. Ivo knew that if the boys saw him, everything was lost. All it needed was for one of them to shout "Papa!" and he might as well drown himself in the fountains. He hurried Simonetta and the girls along, not giving them a chance to pause, not daring to let them stop for an instant.

"Where are we rushing to?" Simonetta gasped. "What's the hurry?"

"It's a surprise," Ivo said gaily. "You'll see."

He risked another quick glance back. Donatella and the three boys were out of sight for the moment. Ahead was a labyrinth, with one set of stairs leading up and another leading down. Ivo chose the stairs going up.

"Come along," he called to the girls. "Whoever gets to the top first gets a prize!"

"Ivo! I'm exhausted!" Simonetta complained. "Can't we rest a minute?"

He looked at her in shock. *Rest?* That would spoil the surprise. Hurry!"

He took Simonetta's arm and dragged her up the steep steps, his three daughters racing ahead of them. Ivo found himself gasping for breath. It would serve them all right, he thought bitterly, if I have a heart attack and die right here. Goddamn women! You can't trust any of them. How could she do this to me? She adores me. I'll kill the bitch for this.

He could visualize himself strangling Donatella in her bed. She was wearing nothing by a flimsy negligée. He ripped it off and began to mount her, while she screamed for mercy. Ivo could feel himself getting an erection.

"Can we stop now?" Simonetta begged.

"No! We're almost there!"

They had reached the upper level again. Ivo took a hasty look around. Donatella and the boys were nowhere in sight.

"Where are you taking us?" Simonetta demanded.

"You'll see," Ivo said hysterically. "Follow me!" He shoved them toward the exit.

Isabella, the oldest girl, said, "Are we leaving, Papa? We just got here!"

"We're going to a better place," Ivo panted. He

glanced back. Coming into sight, climbing the stairs, were Donatella and the boys.

"Faster, girls!"

A moment later Ivo and one of his families were outside the gates of the Villa d'Este, racing toward their car on the large square.

"I've never seen you like this," Simonetta gasped.

"I've never been like this," Ivo said truthfully. He had the motor going before the car doors were closed, and he raced out of the parking lot like the devil was pursuing him.

"Ivo!"

He patted Simonetta's hand. "I want everybody to relax now. As a special treat I'm—I'm taking you to lunch at the Hassler."

They sat at a picture window overlooking the Spanish Steps, with Saint Peter's looming gloriously in the distance.

Simonetta and the children had a marvelous time. The food was delicious. Ivo could have been eating cardboard. His hands were trembling so badly that he could hardly hold his knife and fork. I can't stand much more of this, he thought. I'm not going to let her ruin my life.

For he had no doubt now that that was exactly what Donatella intended to do. *Il giuoco è stato fatto*. The game was up. Unless he could find a way to give Donatella the money she was demanding.

He had to get it. It did not matter how.

CHAPTER
29

Paris.
Monday, November 5.
Six p.m.

The instant Charles Martel arrived home he knew he was in trouble. Hélène was waiting for him, and with her was Pierre Richaud, the jeweler who had made the replicas of her stolen jewelry. Charles stood in the doorway, in shock.

"Come in, Charles," Hélène said. There was an undercurrent in her voice that terrified him. "I believe that you and M. Richaud know each other."

Charles stared, knowing that whatever he said would hang him. The jeweler was studying the floor in embarrassment, obviously ill at ease.

"Sit down, Charles." It was a command. Charles sat down.

Hélène said, "What you're facing, *mon cher mari,* is a criminal charge of grand theft. You have been stealing my jewelry and replacing the pieces with clumsy imitation paste, made by M. Richaud."

To his horror Charles found himself wetting his

pants, a thing he had not done since he was a small boy. He blushed. He wished desperately that he could leave the room for a moment to clean himself. No, he wanted to flee and never return.

Hélène knew everything. It did not matter how she had found him out. There would be no escape and no mercy. It was terrifying enough that Hélène had discovered he had been stealing from her. Wait until she learned his motive! Wait until she found out that he had been planning to use the money to run away from her! Hell was going to have a new meaning. No one knew Hélène as Charles did. She was *une sauvage*, capable of anything. She would destroy him, without a moment's thought, turn him into a *clochard*, one of those sad bums who sleep on the streets of Paris in rags. His life had suddenly turned into an *emmerdement*, a shower of shit.

"Did you really think you could get away with anything so stupid!" Hélène was asking.

Charles remained miserably silent. He could feel his pants getting wetter, but he did not dare look down.

"I have persuaded M. Richaud to give me all the facts."

Persuaded. Charles dreaded to think how.

"I have photostatic copies of the receipts for the money you stole from me. I can put you in prison for the next twenty years." She paused, and added, "If I choose to."

Her words only served to increase Charles's panic. Experience had taught him that a generous Hélène was a dangerous Hélène. Charles was afraid to meet her glance. He wondered what it was she would demand from him. Something monstrous.

Hélène turned to Pierre Richaud. "You will say nothing of this to anyone until I have made up my mind what I wish to do."

"Of course, Mme. Roffe-Martel, of course, of course." The man was babbling. He looked hopefully toward the door. "May I—?"

Hélène nodded, and Pierre Richaud scurried out.

Hélène watched him go, then swung around to study her husband. She could smell his fear. And something else. Urine. She smiled. Charles had pissed himself out of fear. She had taught him well. Hélène was pleased with Charles. It was a very satisfying marriage. She had broken Charles, then made him her creature. The innovations he had brought to Roffe and Sons were brilliant, for they had all come from Hélène. She ruled a small part of Roffe and Sons through her husband, but now it was not enough. She was a Roffe. She was wealthy in her own right; her earlier marriages had made her even wealthier. But it was not money she was interested in. It was the control of the company. She had planned to use her stock to acquire more stock, to buy up the interest of the others. She had already discussed it with them. They were willing to go along with her, to form a minority group. First, Sam had stood in the way of her plan, and now Elizabeth. But Hélène had no intention of allowing Elizabeth or anyone else to keep her from getting what she wanted. Charles was going to get it for her. If anything went wrong, he would be her scapegoat.

Now, of course, he must be punished for his *petite révolte*. She watched his face and said, "No one steals from me, Charles. No one. You're finished. Unless I decide to save you."

He sat there, silent, wishing her dead, terrified of her. She walked over to where he sat, her thighs brushing against his face.

She said, "Would you like me to save you, Charles?"

"Yes," he said hoarsely. She was stepping out of her skirt, her eyes vicious, and he thought, *Oh, my God! Not now!*

"Then listen to me. Roffe and Sons is my company. I want the controlling interest."

He looked up at her miserably and said, "You know Elizabeth won't sell."

Hélène slipped out of her blouse and pants. She stood there, animal naked, her body lean and magnificent, her nipples hard. "Then you must do something about her. Or spend the next twenty years of your life in prison. Don't worry. I'll tell you what you will do. But first, come here, Charles."

CHAPTER

30

The following morning, at ten o'clock, Elizabeth's private phone rang. It was Emil Joeppli. She had given him the number so that no one would be aware of their conversations. "I wonder if I could see you," he said. He sounded excited.

"I'll be there in fifteen minutes."

Kate Erling looked up in surprise as Elizabeth came out of her office wearing a coat. "You have an appointment at—"

"Cancel everything for the next hour," Elizabeth said, and walked out.

In the Development Building an armed guard examined Elizabeth's pass. "Last door to the left, Miss Roffe."

Elizabeth found Joeppli alone in his laboratory. He greeted her with enthusiasm.

"I finished the final tests last night. It works. The enzymes completely inhibit the aging process. Look."

He led her to a cage holding four young rabbits, alert and filled with restless vitality. Next to it was another cage containing four more rabbits, quieter, more mature.

"This is the five hundredth generation to receive the enzyme," Joeppli said.

Elizabeth stood in front of the cage. "They look healthy."

Joeppli smiled. *"That's* part of the control group." He pointed to the cage on the left. *"Those* are the senior citizens."

Elizabeth stared at the energetic rabbits, frisking around in the cage like newborn bunnies, and she could not believe it.

"They'll outlive the others by at least three to one," Joeppli told her.

When you applied that ratio to human beings, the implications were staggering. She could barely contain her excitement.

"When—when will you be ready to start testing it on people?"

"I'm getting my final notes together. After that, another three or four weeks at the most."

"Emil, don't discuss this with anyone," Elizabeth warned.

Emil Joeppli nodded. "I won't, Miss Roffe. I'm working alone. I'm being very careful."

The entire afternoon had been taken up with a board meeting, and it had gone well. Walther had not appeared. Charles had again brought up the subject of selling the stock, but Elizabeth had firmly vetoed it. After that, Ivo had been his charming self, as had Alec. Charles seemed unusually tense. Elizabeth wished she knew why.

She invited them all to stay in Zurich and have dinner with her. As casually as possible, Elizabeth brought up the problems that had been mentioned in the report, watching for a reaction of some kind, but she could detect no sign of nervousness or guilt. And everyone who could have been involved, except for Walther, was seated at that table.

Rhys had not attended the meeting or the dinner. "I have some urgent business to take care of," he had said, and Elizabeth had wondered if it was a girl. Elizabeth was aware that whenever Rhys stayed late at night to work with her, he had had to cancel a date. Once, when he had been unable to reach the girl in time, she had appeared at the office. She was a stunning redhead, with a figure that made Elizabeth feel like a boy. The girl had been furious at being stood up, and she had not bothered to hide her displeasure. Rhys had escorted her to the elevator and returned.

"Sorry about that," he had said.

Elizabeth could not help herself. "She's charming," she said sweetly. "What does she do?"

"She's a brain surgeon," Rhys had replied earnestly, and Elizabeth had laughed. The following day Elizabeth had learned that the girl *was* a brain surgeon.

There were others, and Elizabeth found herself resenting all of them. She wished that she understood Rhys better. She knew the gregarious and public Rhys Williams; she wanted to meet the private Rhys Williams, the self he kept hidden. More than once, Elizabeth had thought, Rhys should be running this company instead of taking orders from me. I wonder how he really feels about it?

That evening after dinner, when the members of the board had dispersed to catch trains and planes back to their homes, Rhys walked into Elizabeth's office where she was working with Kate. "Thought I ought to give you a hand," Rhys said lightly.

No explanation of where he had been. Why should there be? Elizabeth thought. He doesn't have to account to me.

They all set to work and the time flew. Elizabeth watched Rhys now, bent over some papers, rapidly scanning them, his eyes quick and alert. He had found several flaws in some important contracts, that the attorneys had missed. Now Rhys straightened up, stretched and glanced at his watch.

"Oops! It's after midnight. I'm afraid I have an appointment. I'll come in early tomorrow and finish checking these agreements."

Elizabeth wondered if his appointment was with the brain surgeon or with one of his other— She stopped herself. What Rhys Williams did with his private life was his own business.

"I'm sorry," Elizabeth said. "I didn't realize it was so late. You run along. Kate and I will finish reading these papers."

Rhys nodded. "See you in the morning. Good night, Kate."

"Good night, Mr. Williams."

Elizabeth watched Rhys leave, then forced her mind back to the contracts. But a moment later her thoughts were on Rhys again. She had been eager to tell him about the progress that Emil Joeppli was making on the new drug, to share it with him, yet she had held back. Soon, she told herself.

By one o'clock in the morning, they were finished.

Kate Erling said, "Will there by anything else, Miss Roffe?"

"No, I think that's all. Thank you, Kate. Come in late tomorrow."

Elizabeth stood up, and realized how stiff her body felt from sitting so long.

"Thank you. I'll have everything typed up for you tomorrow afternoon."

"That will be fine."

Elizabeth got her coat and purse, waited for Kate, and they walked to the door. They went out into the corridor together and headed toward the private express elevator that stood there, door open, waiting. The two of them stepped inside the elevator. As Elizabeth reached for the lobby button, they heard the sudden ringing of the telephone from the office.

"I'll answer it, Miss Roffe," Kate Erling said. "You go on ahead." She stepped out of the car.

Downstairs the night guard on duty in the lobby looked up at the elevator control board as a red light at the top of the board flashed on and began descending. It was the signal light for the private elevator. That meant Miss Roffe was on her way down. Her chauffeur was sitting in a chair in a corner, drowsing over a newspaper.

"The boss is coming," the guard said.

The chauffeur stretched, and started lazily to his feet.

An alarm bell suddenly shattered the peace of the lobby. The guard's eyes flashed to the control board. The red light was moving in a quick plunging pattern, gathering speed, marking the descent of the elevator.

It was out of control.

"Oh, Jesus!" the guard mumbled.

He hurried to the board, jerked open a panel and

pulled the emergency switch to activate the safety brake. The red light continued its downward plunge. The chauffeur had hurried over to the control panel. He saw the look on the guard's face.

"What's going—?"

"Get away!" the guard yelled. "It's going to crash!"

They ran from the bank of elevators toward the farthest wall. The lobby was beginning to vibrate with the speed of the runaway car inside the shaft, and the guard thought, *Don't let her be in it,* and as the plunging elevator shot past the lobby, he heard the terrified screams from inside.

An instant later, there was a loud roar, and the building shuddered as though it had been hit by an earthquake.

CHAPTER
31

Chief Inspector Otto Schmied of the Zurich Kriminal Polizei was seated at his desk, eyes closed, taking deep yoga breaths, trying to calm himself, trying to control the fury that filled him.

In police procedure there were rules that were so basic, so obvious, that no one had thought it even necessary to put them in the police manual. They were simply taken for granted, like eating, or sleeping, or breathing. For example, when an accident-related fatality occurred, the first thing the investigating detective did—the *very* first thing a detective did, the simple, obvious, you-don't-have-to-draw-it-on-a-fucking-blackboard thing he did—was to visit the scene of the accident. Nothing could be more elementary than that. Yet staring up at Chief Inspector Otto Schmied from his desk was a report from Detective Max Hornung that violated every element of police procedure. I should have expected it, the inspector told himself bitterly. Why am I even surprised?

Detective Hornung was Inspector Schmied's albatross, his bête noire, his—Inspector Schmied was an ardent admirer of Melville—his Moby Dick. The inspector took another deep breath and slowly exhaled. Then, only slightly less agitated, he picked up Detective Hornung's report and read it again from the beginning.

BRANDTOUR OFFIZIER REPORT

Wednesday, November 7

TIME:	1:15 A.M.
SUBJECT:	Report from central switchboard of accident at Roffe and Sons administration building at Eichenbahn factory
TYPE OF ACCIDENT:	Unknown
CAUSE OF ACCIDENT:	Unknown
NUMBER OF INJURED OR DECEASED:	Unknown
TIME:	1:27 A.M.
SUBJECT:	Second message from central switchboard re accident at Roffe and Sons
TYPE OF ACCIDENT:	Elevator crash
CAUSE OF ACCIDENT:	Unknown
NUMBER OF INJURED OR DECEASED:	One female, deceased

I began an immediate investigation. By 1:35 A.M. I obtained the name of the superintendent of the Roffe and Sons administration building and from him got the name of the chief architect of the building.

2:30 A.M. I located the chief architect. He

was celebrating his birthday at La Puce. He gave me the name of the company that had installed the elevators in the building, Rudolf Schatz, A. G.

At 3:15 A.M. I telephoned Mr. Rudolf Schatz at his home and requested him to immediately locate the plans for the elevators. I also requested the master budget sheets along with preliminary estimates, final estimates and final costs; I also requested a complete inventory of all mechanical and electrical materials used.

At this point Inspector Schmied could feel a familiar twitch starting in his right cheek. He took several deep breaths and read on.

6:15 A.M. The requested documents were delivered to me here at police headquarters by Mr. Schatz's wife. After an examination of the preliminary budget and final costs I was satisfied that:

    a) no inferior materials were substituted in building the elevators;

    b) because of the reputation of the builders, inferior workmanship could be ruled out as a cause of the crash;

    c) the safety measures built into the elevators were adequate;

    d) my conclusion therefore was that the cause of the crash was not an accident.
    [Signed] *Max Hornung, CID*

N.B. Since my phone calls took place during the course of the night and early morn-

ing, it is possible that you may receive
one or two complaints from some of the
people I might have awakened.

Inspector Schmied savagely slammed the report
down on his desk. "It is possible!" "Might have
awakened!" The chief inspector had been under attack the entire morning by half of the officials of the
Swiss government. What did he think he was running—a gestapo? How dare he awaken the president
of a respectable building corporation and order him
to deliver documents in the middle of the night?
How dare he impugn the integrity of a reputable
firm like Rudolf Schatz? And on and on and on.

But the thing that was so stunning—that was so
incredible—was that Detective Max Hornung had
not even *appeared* at the scene of the accident until
fourteen hours after it was reported! By the time he
arrived the victim had been removed, identified and
autopsied. Half a dozen other detectives had examined the scene of the accident, had questioned wit-
nesses and had filed their reports.

When Chief Inspector Schmied finished rereading
Detective Max Hornung's report, he summoned him
to his office.

The very sight of Detective Max Hornung was
anathema to the chief inspector. Max Hornung was
a dumpy, wistful-looking man, egg-bald, with a face
that had been put together by an absentminded
prankster. His head was too large, his ears were too
small, and his mouth was a raisin stuck in the middle
of a pudding face. Detective Max Hornung was six
inches too short to meet the rigid standards of the
Zurich Kriminal Polizei, fifteen pounds too light,

and hopelessly nearsighted. To top it all off, he was arrogant. All the men on the force felt unanimously about Detective Hornung: they hated him.

"Why don't you fire him?" the chief inspector's wife had asked, and he had almost struck her.

The reason that Max Hornung was on the Zurich detective force was that he had single-handedly contributed more to the Swiss national income than all the chocolate and watch factories combined. Max Hornung was an accountant, a mathematical genius with an encyclopedic knowledge of fiscal matters, an instinct for the chicanery of man, and a patience that would have made Job weep with envy. Max had been a clerk in the Betrug Abteilung, the department set up to investigate financial frauds, irregularities in stock sales and banking transactions, and the ebb and flow of currency in and out of Switzerland. It was Max Hornung who had brought the smuggling of illegal money into Switzerland to a standstill, who had ferreted out billions of dollars' worth of ingenious but illicit financial schemes, and who had put half a dozen of the world's most respected business leaders in prison. No matter how cunningly assets were concealed, mingled, remingled, sent to the Seychelles to be laundered, transferred and retransferred through a complex series of dummy corporations, in the end Max Hornung would ferret out the truth. In short, he had made himself the terror of the Swiss financial community.

Above all things that they held sacred and dear, the Swiss valued their privacy. With Max Hornung on the loose, there was no privacy.

Max's salary as a financial watchdog was meager.

He had been offered bribes of a million francs in numbered bank accounts, a chalet at Cortina d'Ampezzo, a yacht, and in half a dozen instances beautiful, nubile women. In each case the bribe had been rejected and the authorities promptly notified. Max Hornung cared nothing for money. He could have become a millionaire simply by applying his financial skills to the stock market, but the idea never even occurred to him. Max Hornung was interested in but one thing: catching those who strayed from the path of financial probity. Ah, yes, there was one other wish that consumed Max Hornung, and in the end it proved to be a blessing to the business community. For reasons which no one could fathom, Max Hornung wanted to be a police detective. He envisioned himself as a kind of Sherlock Holmes or Maigret, patiently following a labyrinth of clues, relentlessly stalking the criminal to his lair. When one of Switzerland's leading financiers accidentally learned of Max Hornung's ambitions to be a sleuth, he immediately got together with a few powerful friends, and within forty-eight hours Max Hornung was offered a job on the Zurich police force as a detective. Max could not believe his good fortune. He accepted with alacrity, and the entire business community breathed a collective sigh of relief and resumed its arcane activities.

Chief Inspector Schmied had not even been consulted about the matter. He had received a telephone call from the most powerful political leader in Switzerland, had been given his instructions, and there the matter had ended. Or, to be more accurate, there it had begun. For the chief inspector, it was the beginning of a Gethsemane that showed no sign of ending. He had honestly tried to get over his resentment at having a detective—an inexperienced and unqualified one at that—forced upon him. He assumed that there had to be some strong political motivation for such an unheard-of move. Very well, he was determined to cooperate, confident that he could handle the situation easily. His confidence was shaken the moment Max Hornung reported to him. The detective's appearance was ridiculous enough. But what stunned Inspector Schmied as he looked at this lump of humanity was the man's attitude of superiority. He exuded an air that said: Max Hornung is here—now you can all relax and stop worrying.

Inspector Schmied's thoughts of any easy cooperation vanished. Instead he devised another approach. He tried to sweep Max Hornung under the rug, as it were, by transferring him from department to department, assigning him unimportant jobs. Max worked in the Kriminal-Tech Abteilung, the fingerprint-and-identification division, and the Fahndungsabteilung, the division for stolen property and missing persons. But always Max Hornung kept returning, like a bad centime.

There was a rule that every detective had to work as *Brandtour Offizier,* on the night emergency desk, one week out of every twelve. Without fail, each time Max was on duty, something important would occur, and while Inspector Schmied's other detectives ran around trying to track down clues, Max would solve the case. It was infuriating.

He knew absolutely nothing about police procedure, criminology, forensics, ballistics, or criminal psychology—all the things that the other detectives were experienced in—and yet he kept solving cases that baffled everyone else. Chief Inspector Schmied came to the conclusion that Max Hornung was the luckiest man who ever lived.

In reality, luck had nothing to do with it. Detective Max Hornung solved criminal cases in exactly the same way that accountant Max Hornung had exposed a hundred ingenious schemes to defraud banks and the government. Max Hornung had a single-track mind, and it was a very narrow-gauge track at that. All he needed was one loose thread, one tiny piece that did not fit into the rest of the fabric, and once he had that he would begin to unravel it, until somebody's brilliant, foolproof scheme fell apart at the seams.

The fact that Max had a photographic memory drove his colleagues crazy. Max could instantly recall anything he had ever heard, read or seen.

Another mark against him, if indeed one was needed, was that his expense accounts were an embarrassment to the entire detective squadron. The first time he had turned in an expense sheet, the *Oberleutnant* had summoned him to his office and said genially, "You've obviously made a mistake in your figures here, Max."

The equivalent of informing Capablanca that he had sacrificed his queen through stupidity.

Max blinked. "A mistake in my figures?"

"Yes. Several, in fact." The *Oberleutnant* pointed to the paper in front of him. "Transportation across town, eighty centimes. Return, eighty centimes." He looked up and said, "The maximum taxi fare would be thirty-four francs each way."

"Yes, sir. That's why I used the bus."

The *Oberleutnant* stared at him. "A *bus?*"

None of the detectives was required to ride buses while on a case. It was unheard of. The only reply he could think of was "Well, it's—it's not necessary. I mean—we naturally don't encourage spendthrifts in this department, Hornung, but we do have a decent expense budget. Another thing. You were out in the field on this case for three days. You forgot to include meals."

"No, Herr Oberleutnant. I only take coffee in the morning and I prepare my own lunches and carry a lunch pail. My dinners are listed there."

And so they were. Three dinners, total: sixteen francs. He must have eaten at the Salvation Army kitchen.

The *Oberleutnant* said coldly, "Detective Hornung, this department existed for a hundred years before you joined it, and it will exist for a hundred years after you leave it. There are certain traditions that we observe here." He shoved the expense account back to Max. "You must think about your colleagues, you know. Now take this, revise it, and return it."

"Yes, Herr Oberleutnant. I—I'm sorry if I did it incorrectly."

A generous wave of the hand. "Quite all right. After all, you're new here."

Thirty minutes later Detective Max Hornung turned in his revised account. He had decreased his expenses by another 3 percent.

Now, on this day in November, Chief Inspector Schmied was holding Detective Max Hornung's report in his hand while the author of the report stood before him. Detective Hornung was wearing a bright-blue suit, brown shoes and white socks. In spite of his resolves, and the calming yoga breathing exercises, Inspector Schmied found himself yelling. "You were in charge here when that report came in. It was *your* job to investigate the accident and you arrived on the scene *fourteen hours later!* The whole fucking New Zealand police force could have been flown here and been back home in that time."

"Oh, no, sir. The flying time from New Zealand to Zurich by jet is—"

"Oh, shut up!"

Chief Inspector Schmied ran his hands through his thick, rapidly graying hair, trying to think what to say to this man. You could not insult him, you could not reason with him. He was an idiot, shot with luck.

Chief Inspector Schmied barked, "I will not tolerate incompetence in my department, Hornung. When the other detectives came on duty and saw the report, they immediately went to the scene to inspect the accident. They called an ambulance, had the body taken to the morgue, identified it—" He knew he was talking too fast again, and he forced himself to calm down. "In short, Hornung, they did everything a good detective is supposed to do. While you were sitting in your office waking up half of the most important men in Switzerland, in the middle of the night."

"I thought—"

"Don't! I've been on the phone apologizing the whole damned morning because of you."

"I had to find out—"

"Oh, get out of here Hornung!"

"Yes, sir. Is it all right if I attend the funeral? It's this morning."

"Yes! Go!"

"Thank you, sir. I—"

"Just go!"

It was thirty minutes before Chief Inspector Schmied was breathing normally again.

CHAPTER
32

The funeral parlor at Sihlfeld was crowded. It was an ornate, old-fashioned building of stone and marble, with preparation rooms and a crematorium. Inside the large chapel two dozen executives and employees of Roffe and Sons occupied the front row of seats. Toward the rear were the friends, the community representatives and the press. Detective Hornung was seated in the last row, thinking that death was illogical. Man reached his prime and then, when he had the most to give, the most to live for, he died. It was inefficient.

The casket was mahogany and covered with flowers. More waste, Detective Hornung thought. The casket had been ordered sealed. Max could understand why. The minister was speaking in a doomsday voice, ". . . death in the midst of life, born in sin, ashes to ashes." Max Hornung paid little attention. He was studying those in the chapel.

"The Lord giveth, and the Lord taketh away," and people were beginning to stand and head for the exit. The services were over.

Max stood near the door, and as a man and a woman approached him, he stepped in front of the woman and said, "Miss Elizabeth Roffe? I wonder if I might have a word with you?"

Detective Max Hornung was seated with Elizabeth Roffe and Rhys Williams in a booth at a *Konditorei* across from the funeral parlor. Through the window they could see the coffin being loaded into a gray hearse. Elizabeth looked away. Her eyes were haunted.

"What's this all about?" Rhys demanded. "Miss Roffe has already given her statement to the police."

Detective Max Hornung said, "Mr. Williams, isn't it? There are just a few little details I want to check out."

"Can't they wait? Miss Roffe has been through a very trying—"

Elizabeth put her hand on Rhys's. "It's all right. If I can be of any help—" She turned to Max. "What would you like to know, Detective Hornung?"

Max stared at Elizabeth, and for the first time in his life he was at loss for words. Women were as foreign to Max as creatures from an alien planet. They were illogical and unpredictable, subject to emotional reactions rather than rational ones. They did not compute. Max had few sexual stirrings, for he was mind-oriented, but he could appreciate the precise logic of sex. It was the mechanical construction of moving parts fitting together into a coordinated, functioning whole that excited him. That, for Max, was the poetry of loving. The sheer dynamics of it. Max felt that the poets had all missed the point. Emotions were imprecise and untidy, a waste of energy that could not move the smallest grain of sand one inch, while logic could move the world. What was puzzling Max now was that he felt comfortable with Elizabeth. It made him uneasy. No woman had ever affected him that way before. She did not seem to think he was an ugly, ridiculous little man, the way other women did. He forced himself to look away from her eyes so that he could concentrate.

"Were you in the habit of working late at night, Miss Roffe?"

"Very often," Elizabeth said. "Yes."

"How late?"

"It varied. Sometimes until ten. Sometimes until midnight, or after."

"So it was a kind of pattern? That is, people around you would have known about it?"

She was studying him, puzzled. "I suppose so."

"On the night the elevator crashed, you and Mr. Williams and Kate Erling were all working late?"

"Yes."

"But you didn't leave together?"

Rhys said, "I left early. I had an engagement."

Max regarded him a moment, then turned back to Elizabeth. "How long after Mr. Williams left did you leave?"

"I think it was about an hour."

"Did you and Kate Erling leave together?"

"Yes. We got our coats and went out into the hall." Elizabeth's voice faltered. "The—the elevator was there, waiting for us."

The special express elevator.

"What happened then?"

"We both got in. The telephone in the office rang. Kate—Miss Erling—said, 'I'll get it,' and she started to get out. But I was expecting an overseas call I had placed earlier, so I told her I would answer it." Elizabeth stopped, her eyes suddenly brimming with tears. "I got out of the elevator. She asked if she should wait, and I said, 'No, go ahead.' She pressed the lobby button. I started back to the office, and as I was opening the door, I heard—I heard the screaming, then—" She was unable to go on.

Rhys turned to Max Hornung, his face clouded with anger. "That's enough. Will you tell us what this is all about?"

It was about murder, Max thought. Someone had tried to kill Elizabeth Roffe. Max sat there concentrating, recalling everything he had learned in the past forty-eight hours about Roffe and Sons. It was a deeply plagued company, forced to pay astronomical damages in lawsuits, swamped by bad publicity, losing customers, owing enormous sums of money to banks that had grown impatient. A company ripe for a change. Its president, Sam Roffe, who had held the controlling vote, had died. An expert mountain climber who had been killed in a climbing accident. The controlling stock had gone to his daughter, Elizabeth, who had almost died in a Jeep accident in Sardinia, and had narrowly missed being killed in an elevator that had passed a recent inspection. Someone was playing deadly games.

Detective Max Hornung should have been a happy man. He had found a loose thread. But now he had met Elizabeth Roffe, and she was no longer simply a name, an equation in a mathematical puzzle. There was something very special about her. Max felt an urge to shield her, to protect her.

Rhys said, "I asked what this—"

Max looked at him and said vaguely, "Er—police procedure, Mr. Williams. Just routine." He rose. "Excuse me."

He had some urgent work to do.

CHAPTER

33

Chief Inspector Schmied had had a full morning. There had been a political demonstration in front of Iberia Air Lines, three men detained for questioning. A fire of suspicious origin at a paper factory in Brunau. It was being investigated. A girl had been raped in Platzspitz Park. A smash-and-grab job at Guebelin and another at Grima, next to the Baur-au-Lac. And if that weren't enough, Detective Max Hornung was back, filled with some kind of nonsensical theory. Chief Inspector Schmied found himself starting to hyperventilate again.

"The elevator cable drum was cracked," Max was saying. "When it collapsed, all the safety controls went out. Someone——"

"I saw the reports, Hornung. Normal wear and tear."

"No, Chief Inspector. I examined the specifications for the cable drum. It should have lasted another five or six years."

Chief Inspector Schmied felt the tic in his cheek. "What are you trying to say?"

"Someone tampered with the elevator."

Not, I think someone tampered with the elevator, or, In my opinion someone tampered with the ele-

329

vator. Oh, no! Someone tampered with the elevator.

"Why would they do that?"

"That's what I would like to find out."

"You want to go back to Roffe and Sons?"

Detective Max Hornung looked at Inspector Schmied in genuine surpose. "No, sir. I want to go to Chamonix."

The town of Chamonix lies forty miles southeast of Geneva, 3,400 feet above sea level in the French department of Haute-Savoie, between the Mont Blanc massif and the Aiguille Rouge range, with one of the most breathtaking vistas in the world.

Detective Max Hornung was completely unaware of the scenery as he debouched from the train at the Chamonix station, carrying a battered cardboard suitcase. He waved a taxi away and headed on foot for the local police station, a small building situated on the main square in the center of town. Max entered, feeling instantly at home, reveling in the warm camaraderie that he shared with the fraternity of policemen all over the world. He was one of *them.*

The French sergeant behind the desk looked up and asked, *"On vous pourrait aider?"*

"Oui." Max beamed. And he started to talk. Max approached all foreign languages in the same fashion: he slashed his way through the impenetrable thicket of irregular verbs and tenses and participles, using his tongue like a machete. As he spoke, the expression on the desk sergeant's face changed from puzzlement to disbelief. It had taken the French people hundreds of years to develop their tongues and soft palates and larynxes to form the glorious music that was the French language. And now this

man standing before him was somehow managing to turn it into a series of horrible, incomprehensible noises.

The desk sergeant could bear no more. He interrupted. "What—what are you trying to *say?*".

Max replied, "What do you mean? I'm speaking French."

The desk sergeant leaned forward and asked with unabashed curiosity, "Are you speaking it *now?*"

The fool doesn't even speak his own language, Max thought. He pulled out his warrant card and handed it to the sergeant. The sergeant read it through twice, looked up to study Max, and then read it again. It was impossible to believe that the man standing before him was a detective.

Reluctantly he handed the identification back to Max. "What can I do for you?"

"I'm investigating a climbing accident that happened here two months ago. The victim's name was Sam Roffe."

The sergeant nodded. "Yes, I remember."

"I would like to talk to someone who can give me some information about what happened."

"That would be the mountain-rescue organization. It is called the Société Chamoniarde de Secours en Montagne. You will find it in Place du Mont Blanc. The telephone number is five-three-one-six eight-nine. Or they might have some information at the clinic. That's in Rue du Valais. The telephone number there is five-three-zero-one-eight-two. Here. I'll write all this down for you." He reached for a pen.

"That won't be necessary," Max said. "Société Chamoniarde de Secours en Montagne, Place du Mont Blanc, five-three-one-six-eight-nine. Or the clinic in Rue du Valais, five-three-zero-one-eight-two."

The sergeant was still staring, long after Max had disappeared through the door.

The Société Chamoniarde de Secours was in the charge of a dark, athletic-looking young man seated behind a battered pine desk. He looked up as Max walked in, and his instant thought was that he hoped this odd-looking visitor did not plan to climb a mountain.

"Can I help you?"

"Detective Max Hornung." He showed his warrant card.

"What can I do for you, Detective Hornung?"

"I am investigating the death of a man named Sam Roffe," Max said.

The man behind the desk sighed. "Ah, yes. I liked Mr. Roffe very much. It was an unfortunate accident."

"Did you see it happen?"

A shake of the head. "No. I took my rescue team up as soon as we received their distress signal, but there was nothing we could do. Mr. Roffe's body had fallen into a crevasse. It will never be found."

"How did it happen?"

"There were four climbers in the party. The guide and Mr. Roffe were last. As I understand it, they were traversing an icy moraine. Mr. Roffe slipped and fell."

"Wasn't he wearing a harness?"

"Of course. His rope broke."

"Does a thing like that happen often?"

"Only once." He smiled at his little joke, then saw the detective's look and added quickly, "Experienced climbers always check their equipment thoroughly, but accidents still happen."

Max stood there a moment, thinking. "I'd like to speak to the guide."

"Mr. Roffe's regular guide didn't make the climb that day."

Max blinked, "Oh? Why not?"

"As I recall, he was ill. Another guide took his place."

"Do you have his name?"

"If you'll wait a minute, I can look it up for you."

The man disappeared into an inner office. In a few minutes he returned with a slip of paper in his hand. "The guide's name was Hans Bergmann."

"Where can I find him?"

"He's not a local." He consulted the piece of paper. "He comes from a village called Lesgets. It's about sixty kilometers from here."

Before Max left Chamonix, he stopped at the desk of the Kleine Scheidegg hotel and talked to the room clerk. "Were you on duty when Mr. Roffe was staying here?"

"Yes," the clerk said. "The accident was a terrible thing, terrible."

"Mr. Roffe was alone here?"

The clerk shook his head. "No. He had a friend with him."

Max stared. "A friend?"

"Yes. Mr. Roffe made the reservation for both of them."

"Could you give me the name of his friend?"

"Certainly," the clerk said. He pulled out a large ledger from beneath the desk and began to turn back the pages. He stopped, ran his fingers down a page and said, "Ah, here we are . . ."

* * *

It took almost three hours for Max to drive to Lesgets in a Volkswagen, the cheapest rental car he could find, and he almost passed through it. It was not even a village. The place consisted of a few shops, a small Alpine lodge, and a general store with a single gas pump in front of it.

Max parked in front of the lodge and walked in.

There were half a dozen men seated in front of an open fireplace, talking. The conversation trailed off as Max entered.

"Excuse me," he said, "I'm looking for Herr Hans Bergmann."

"Who?"

"Hans Bergmann. The guide. He comes from this village."

An elderly man with a face that was a weather map of his years spat into the fireplace and said. "Somebody's been kidding you, mister. I was born in Lesgets. I never heard of any Hans Bergmann."

CHAPTER

34

It was the first day that Elizabeth had gone to the office since the death of Kate Erling a week earlier. Elizabeth entered the downstairs lobby with trepidation, responding mechanically to the greetings of the doorman and guards. At the far end of the lobby she saw workmen replacing the smashed elevator car. She thought about Kate Erling, and Elizabeth could visualize the terror she must have felt as she plunged twelve interminable stories to her death. She knew that she could never ride in that elevator again.

When she walked into her office, her mail had already been opened by Henriette, the second secretary, and neatly placed on her desk. Elizabeth went through it quickly, initialing some memos, writing questions on others, or marking them for various department heads. At the bottom of the pile was a large sealed envelope marked "Elizabeth Roffe—Personal." Elizabeth took a letter opener and slit the envelope across the top. She reached in and took out an 8-by-10 photograph. It was a close-up of a mongoloid child, its bulging eyes staring out of its encephalic head. Attached to the picture was a note printed in crayon: "THIS IS MY BEAUTI-

FUL SON JOHN. YOUR DRUGS DID THIS TO HIM. I AM GOING TO KILL YOU."

Elizabeth dropped the note and the picture, and found that her hands were trembling. Henriette walked in with a handful of papers.

"These are ready to be signed, Miss——" She saw the look on Elizabeth's face. "Is something wrong?"

Elizabeth said, "Please—ask Mr. Williams to come in here." Her eyes went back to the picture on her desk.

Roffe and Sons could not be responsible for anything so dreadful.

"It was our fault," Rhys said. "A shipment of drugs was mislabeled. We managed to recall most of it, but——" He raised his hands expressively.

"How long ago did this happen?"

"Almost four years ago."

"How many people were affected?"

"About a hundred." He saw the expression on her face and added quickly, "They received compensation. They weren't all like this, Liz. Look, we're damned careful here. We take every safety precaution we can devise, but people are human. Mistakes are sometimes made."

Elizabeth sat staring at the picture of the child. "It's horrible."

"They shouldn't have shown you the letter." Rhys ran his fingers through his thick black hair and said, "This is a hell of a time to bring it up, but we have a few other problems more important than this."

She wondered what could be more important. "Yes?"

"The FDA just gave a decision against us on our

aerosol sprays. There's going to be a complete ban on aerosols within two years."

"How will that affect us?"

"It's going to hurt us badly. It means we'll have to close down half a dozen factories around the world and lose one of our most profitable divisions."

Elizabeth thought about Emil Joeppli and the culture he was working on, but she said nothing. "What else?"

"Have you seen the morning papers?"

"No."

"A government minister's wife in Belgium, Mme. van den Logh, took some Benexan."

"That's one of our drugs?"

"Yes. It's an antihistamine. It's contraindicated for anyone with essential hypertension. Our label carries a clear warning. She ignored it."

Elizabeth felt her body beginning to tense. "What happened to her?"

Rhys said, "She's in a coma. She may not live. The newspaper stories mention that it's our product. Cancellations on orders are pouring in from all over the world. The FDA notified us that it's starting an investigation, but that will take at least a year. Until they finish, we can keep selling the drug."

Elizabeth said, "I want it taken off the market."

"There's no reason to do that. It's a damned effective drug for—"

"Have any other people been hurt by it?"

"Hundreds of thousands of people have been helped by it." Rhys tone was cool. "It's one of our most effective—"

"You haven't answered my question."

"A few isolated cases, I suppose, yes. But—"

"I want it taken off the market. Now."

He sat there, fighting his anger, then he said, "Right. Would you like to know what that will cost the company?"

"No," Elizabeth said.

Rhys nodded. "So far you've only heard the good news. The bad news is that the bankers want a meeting with you. Now. They're calling in their loans."

Elizabeth sat in her office alone, thinking about the mongoloid child, and about the woman who lay in a coma because of a drug that Roffe and Sons had sold her. Elizabeth was well aware that these kinds of tragedies involved other pharmaceutical firms as well as Roffe and Sons. There were almost daily stories in the newspapers about similar cases, but they had not touched her as this had. She felt responsible. She was determined to have a talk with the department heads who were in charge of safety measures to see if they could not be improved.

This is my beautiful son John.

Mme. van den Logh is in a coma. She may not live.

The bankers want a meeting with you. Now. They've decided to call in their loans.

She felt choked, as though everything was beginning to close in on her at once. For the first time Elizabeth wondered if she was going to be able to cope. The burdens were too heavy, and they were piling up too fast. She swung around in her chair, to look up at the portrait of old Samuel hanging on the wall. He looked so competent, so sure. But she knew about his doubts and uncertainties, and his black despairs. Yet he had come through. She would survive somehow, too. She was a Roffe.

She noticed that the portrait was askew. Probably as a result of the elevator crash. Elizabeth got up to straighten it. As she tilted the picture, the hook holding it gave way, and the painting crashed to the floor. Elizabeth did not even look at it. She was staring at the place where the painting had hung. Taped to the wall was a tiny microphone.

It was 4 A.M., and Emil Joeppli was working late again. It had become a habit of his recently. Even though Elizabeth Roffe had not given him a specific deadline, Joeppli knew how important this project was to the company and he was pushing to get it finished as quickly as possible. He had heard disturbing rumors about Roffe and Sons lately. He wanted to do everything he could to help the company. It had been good to him. It gave him a handsome salary and complete freedom. He had liked Sam Roffe, and he liked his daughter too. Elizabeth Roffe would never know, but these late hours were Joeppli's gift to her. He was hunched over his small desk, checking out the results of his last experiment. They were even better than he had anticipated. He sat there, deep in concentration, unaware of the fetid smell of the caged animals in the laboratory or the cloying humidity of the room or the lateness of the hour. The door opened, and the guard on the graveyard shift, Sepp Nolan, walked in. Nolan hated this shift. There was something eerie about the deserted experimental laboratories at night. The smell of the caged animals made him ill. Nolan wondered whether all the animals they had killed here had souls and came back to haunt these corridors. I ought to put in for spook pay, he thought. Everyone in the building had long since gone home. Except for this fucking mad scientist with his cages full of rabbits and cats and hamsters.

"How long you gonna be, Doc?" Nolan asked.

Joeppli looked up, aware of Nolan for the first time. "What?"

"If you're gonna be here awhile, I can bring you back a sandwich or something. I'm gonna run over to the commissary for a quick bite."

Joeppli said, "Just coffee, please." He turned back to his charts.

Nolan said, "I'll lock the outside door behind me when I leave the building. Be right back."

Joeppli did not even hear him.

Ten minutes later the door to the laboratory opened, and a voice said, "You're working late, Emil."

Joeppli looked up, startled. When he saw who it was, he got to his feet, flustered, and said, "Yes, sir." He felt flattered that this man had dropped in to see him.

"The Fountain of Youth project, top secret, eh?"

Emil hesitated. Miss Roffe had said no one was supposed to know about it. But, of course, that did not include his visitor. It was this man who had brought him into the company. So Emil Joeppli smiled and said, "Yes, sir. Top secret."

"Good. Let's keep it that way. How is it going?"

"Wonderfully, sir."

The visitor wandered over to one of the rabbit cages. Emil Joeppli followed him. "Is there anything I can explain to you?"

The man smiled. "No. I'm pretty familiar with it, Emil." As the visitor started to turn away, he brushed against an empty feeding dish on the ledge and it fell to the floor. "Sorry."

"Don't worry about it, sir. I'll get it." Emil Joeppli reached down to pick it up and the back of his head seemed to explode in a shower of red, and the last thing he saw was the floor racing up to meet him.

The insistent ringing of the telephone awakened Elizabeth. She sat up in bed, heavy with sleep, and looked at the digital clock on the little table. Five A.M. She fumbled the telephone off the hook. A frantic voice said, "Miss Roffe? This is the security guard at the plant. There's been an explosion at one of the laboratories. It was completely destroyed."

Instantly she was wide-awake. "Was anybody hurt?"

"Yes, ma'am. One of the scientists was burned to death."

He did not have to tell Elizabeth the name.

CHAPTER

35

Detective Max Hornung was thinking. The detective bureau was filled with the noise of typewriters clattering, voices raised in argument, telephones ringing, but Hornung saw and heard nothing of these things. He had the single-minded concentration of a computer. He was thinking about the charter of Roffe and Sons, as old Samuel had set it up, keeping control within the family. Ingenious, Max thought. And dangerous. It reminded him of the tontine, the Italian insurance plan devised by the banker Lorenzo Tonti in 1695. Every member of the tontine put in an equal amount of money, and as each member died, the survivors inherited his share. It provided a powerful motive to eliminate the other members. Like Roffe and Sons. It was too much of a temptation to let people inherit stock worth millions, and then tell them they could not sell it unless everyone agreed.

Max had learned that Sam Roffe had not agreed. He was dead. Elizabeth Roffe had not agreed. She had narrowly escaped death twice. Too many accidents. Detective Max Hornung did not believe in accidents. He went to see Chief Inspector Schmied.

The chief inspector listened to Max Hornung's

report on Sam Roffe's climbing accident and growled, "So there's been a mix-up about the name of a guide. That hardly constitutes a case for murder, Hornung. Not in *my* department, it doesn't."

The little detective said patiently, "I think there's more to it. Roffe and Sons is having big internal problems. Perhaps someone thought that getting rid of Sam Roffe would solve them."

Chief Inspector Schmied sat back and eyed Detective Hornung. He was certain that there was nothing to his theories. But the idea of having Detective Max Hornung out of sight for a while filled Chief Inspector Schmied with a deep pleasure. His absence would be a boost to the morale of the entire department. And there was something else to consider: The people Max Hornung wanted to investigate. No less than the powerful Roffe family. Ordinarily, Schmied would have ordered Max Hornung to keep a million miles away from them. If Detective Hornung irritated them—and how could he not!—they had enough power to have him thrown off the force. And no one could blame Chief Inspector Schmied. Hadn't the little detective been forced on him? And so he said to Max Hornung, "The case is yours. Take your time."

"Thank you," Max said happily.

As Max was walking through the corridor toward his office, he ran into the coroner, "Hornung! Can I borrow your memory for a minute?"

Max blinked. "I beg your pardon?"

"The river patrol has just fished a girl out of the river. Will you take a look at her?"

Max swallowed and said, "If you wish."

This was not a part of the job that Max enjoyed, but he felt that it was his duty.

She lay in the impersonal metal drawer in the chill of the morgue. She had blond hair and was in her late teens or early twenties. Her body was bloated from the water, and naked, except for a red ribbon knotted around her neck.

"There are signs of sexual intercourse just before death. She was strangled and then dumped into the river," the coroner said. "There's no water in her lungs. We can't get any fingerprints on her. Ever seen her before?"

Detective Max Hornung looked down at the girl's face and said, "No."

He left to catch his bus to the airport.

CHAPTER
36

When Detective Max Hornung landed at the Costa Smeralda airport in Sardinia, he rented the cheapest car available, a Fiat 500, and drove into Olbia. Unlike the rest of Sardinia, Olbia was an industrial city, and the outskirts were an ugly sprawl of mills and factories, a city dump and a giant graveyard of once-beautiful automobiles, now useless old hulks, good only for scrap. Every city in the world had its automobile junkyards, Max thought. Monuments to civilization.

Max reached the center of town and drove up in front of a building with a sign that read: "QUESTURA DI SASSARI COMMISSARIATO DI POLIZIA OLBIA." The moment Max entered, he felt that familiar sense of identity, of belonging. He showed his warrant card to the desk sergeant, and a few minutes later he was ushered into the office of the Chief of Police, Luigi Ferraro. Ferraro rose to his feet, a welcoming smile on his face. It died as he saw his visitor. There was something about Max that did not spell "detective."

"Could I see your identification?" Chief Ferraro asked politely.

"Certainly," Max said. He pulled out his warrant card and Chief Ferraro examined both sides of it carefully, then returned it. His immediate conclusion was that Switzerland must be very hard up for detectives. He took a seat behind his desk and said, "What can I do for you?"

Max started to explain, in fluent Italian. The problem was that it took Chief Ferraro some moments to figure out what language Max was speaking. When he realized what it was supposed to be, he held up a horrified hand and said, *"Basta!* Do you speak English?"

"Of course," Max replied.

"Then I beg of you! Let us speak in English."

When Max was through talking, Chief Ferraro said, "You are mistaken, signore. I can tell you that you are wasting your time. My mechanics have already examined the Jeep. Everyone is agreed that it was an accident."

Max nodded, unperturbed. "*I* haven't looked at it."

Chief Ferraro said, "Very well. It is in a public garage now, up for sale. I will have one of my men take you there. Would you like to see the scene of the accident?"

Max blinked and said, "What for?"

Detective Bruno Campagna was elected as Max's escort. "We've already checked it out. It was an accident," Campagna said.

"No," Max replied.

The Jeep was in a corner of the garage, its front still dented and splashed with dried green sap.

"I haven't had time to work on it yet," the mechanic explained.

Max walked around the Jeep, examining it. "How were the brakes tampered with?" he asked.

The mechanic said, *"Gesù!* You, too?" A note of

irritation crept into his voice. "I been a mechanic for twenty-five years, signore. I examined this Jeep myself. The last time anyone touched these brakes was when this car left the factory."

"Someone tampered with them," Max said.

"How?" The mechanic was spluttering.

"I don't know yet, but I will," Max assured him confidently. He took a last look at the Jeep, then turned and walked out of the garage.

Chief of Police Luigi Ferraro looked at Detective Bruno Campagna and demanded, "What did you *do* with him?"

"I didn't do anything. I took him to the garage, he made an ass of himself with the mechanic, then he said he wanted to go for a stroll by himself."

"Incredible!"

Max was standing on the shore, staring out at the emerald Tyrrhenian waters, seeing nothing. He was concentrating, his mind busily putting pieces together. It was like working a giant jigsaw puzzle. Everything always went neatly into place when you knew where it fitted. The Jeep was a small but important part of the puzzle. Its brakes had been examined by expert mechanics. Max had no reason to doubt either their honesty or competence. He therefore accepted the fact that the brakes of the Jeep had not been tampered with. Because Elizabeth had been driving the Jeep and someone wanted her dead, he also accepted the fact that they *had* been tampered with. There was no way it could have been done. Yet someone had done it. Max was up against someone clever. It made things more interesting.

Max stepped out onto the sandy beach, sat down

on a large rock, closed his eyes and began to concentrate again, focusing on the pieces, shifting, dissecting, rearranging the bits of the puzzle.

Twenty minutes later the last piece clicked into place. Max's eyes flew open and he thought admiringly, Bravo! I must meet the man who thought of this.

After that, Detective Max Hornung had two stops to make, the first just outside Olbia and the second in the mountains. He caught the late afternoon plane back to Zurich.

Economy class.

CHAPTER

37

The head of the security forces of Roffe and Sons said to Elizabeth, "It all happened too fast, Miss Roffe. There was nothing we could do. By the time the fire-fighting equipment got into action, the whole laboratory was gone."

They had found the remains of Emil Joeppli's charred body. There was no way of knowing whether his formula had been removed from the laboratory before the explosion.

Elizabeth asked, "The Development Building was under twenty-four-hour guard, was it not?"

"Yes, ma'am. We—"

"How long have you been in charge of our security department?"

"Five years. I—"

"You're fired."

He started to say something in protest, then changed his mind. "Yes, ma'am."

"How many men are there on your staff?"

"Sixty-five."

Sixty-five! And they could not save Emil Joeppli. "I'm giving them twenty-four hours' notice," Elizabeth said. "I want them all out of here."

He looked at her a moment. "Miss Roffe, do you think you're being fair?"

She thought of Emil Joeppli, and the priceless formula that had been stolen, and of the bug that had been planted in her office that she had ground under the heel of her shoe.

"Get out," Elizabeth said.

She filled every minute that morning, trying to wipe out the vision of the charred body of Emil Joeppli and his laboratory full of burned animals. She tried not to think about what the loss of that formula was going to cost the company. There was a chance a rival company might patent it and there was nothing Elizabeth could do about it. It *was* a jungle. When your competitors thought you were weak, they moved in for the kill. But this wasn't a competitor doing this. This was a friend. A deadly friend.

Elizabeth arranged for a professional security force to take over immediately. She would feel safer with strangers around her.

She phoned the Hôpital Internationale in Brussels to check on the condition of Mme van den Logh, the wife of the Belgian minister. They reported that she was still in a coma. They did not know whether she would live.

Elizabeth was thinking about Emil Joeppli and the mongoloid child and the minister's wife when Rhys walked in. He looked at her face and said gently, "As bad as that?"

She nodded, miserable.

Rhys walked over to her and studied her. She looked tired, drained. He wondered how much more she could stand. He took her hands in his and asked gently, "Is there anything I can do to help?"

Everything, Elizabeth thought. She needed Rhys desperately. She needed his strength and his help and his love. Their eyes met and she was ready to go into his arms, to tell him everything that had happened, that was happening.

Rhys said, "There's nothing new on Mme. van den Logh?"

And the moment had passed.

"No," Elizabeth said.

He asked, "Have you had any calls yet on the *Wall Street Journal* story?"

"What story?"

"You haven't seen it?"

"No."

Rhys sent to his office for a copy. The article enumerated all the recent troubles of Roffe and Sons, but the major theme of the story was that the company needed someone experienced to run it. Elizabeth put the newspaper down. "How much damage will this do?"

Rhys shrugged. "The damage has already been done. They're just reporting it. We're beginning to lose a lot of our markets. We—"

The intercom buzzed. Elizabeth pressed the switch. "Yes?"

"Herr Julius Badrutt is on line two, Miss Roffe. He says it's urgent."

Elizabeth looked up at Rhys. She had been postponing the meeting with the bankers. "Put him on." She picked up the phone. "Good morning, Herr Badrutt."

"Good morning." Over the phone, his voice sounded dry and brittle. "Are you free this afternoon?"

"Well, I'm—"

"Fine. Will four o'clock be satisfactory?"

Elizabeth hesitated. "Yes. Four o'clock."

There was a dry, rustling sound over the phone and Elizabeth realized that Herr Badrutt was clearing his throat. "I was sorry to hear about Mr. Joeppli," he said.

Joeppli's name had not been mentioned in the newspaper accounts of the explosion.

She hung up slowly, and found that Rhys was watching her.

"The sharks smell blood," Rhys said.

The afternoon was filled with phone calls. Alec telephoned "Elizabeth did you see the story in the newspaper this morning?"

"Yes," Elizabeth said. "*The Wall Street Journal* was exaggerating."

There was a pause, and then Alec said, "I'm not talking about *The Wall Street Journal*. The *Financial Times* has a headline story on Roffe and Sons. It's not good. My phones haven't stopped ringing. We're getting heavy cancellations. What are we going to do?"

"I'll get back to you, Alec," Elizabeth promised.

Ivo called. "*Carissima*, I think you'd better prepare yourself for a shock."

I'm prepared, Elizabeth thought wryly. "What is it?"

Ivo said, "An Italian minister was arrested a few hours ago for accepting bribes."

Elizabeth had a sudden feeling of what was coming. "Go on."

There was a note of apology in Ivo's voice. "It wasn't our fault," Ivo said. "He got greedy and he was careless. They caught him at the airport, trying to smuggle money out of Italy. They've traced the money to us."

Even though Elizabeth was prepared for it, she still felt a shock of disbelief. "Why were we bribing him?"

Ivo said matter-of-factly, "So that we could do business in Italy. It's a way of life here. Our crime was not in bribing the minister, *cara*—it was in getting caught."

She sat back in her chair, her head beginning to pound.

"What happens now?"

"I would suggest that we meet with the company attorneys as quickly as possible," Ivo said. "Don't worry. Only the poor go to jail in Italy."

Charles called from Paris, his voice frantic with worry. The French press was full of Roffe & Sons. Charles urged Elizabeth to sell the company while it still had a reputation.

"Our customers are losing faith," Charles said. "Without that, there is no company."

Elizabeth thought about the phone calls, the bankers, her cousins, the press. Too much was happening too quickly. Someone was making it happen. She *had* to find out who.

The name was still in Elizabeth's private telephone book. Maria Martinelli. It brought back long-ago memories of the tall, leggy Italian girl who had been a classmate of Elizabeth's in Switzerland. They had corresponded from time to time. Maria had become a model and she had written to Elizabeth that she was engaged to marry an Italian newspaper publisher in Milan. It took Elizabeth fifteen minutes to reach Maria. When the social amenities had been disposed of, Elizabeth said into the phone, "Are you still engaged to that newspaper publisher?"

"Of course. The minute Tony gets his divorce, we're going to be married."

"I want you to do me a favor, Maria."

"Name it."

Less than one hour later Maria Martinelli called back. "I got that information you wanted. The banker who was caught trying to smuggle money out of Italy was set up. Tony says a man tipped off the border police."

"Was he able to find out the name of the man?"

"Ivo Palazzi."

Detective Max Hornung had made an interesting discovery. He had learned that not only was the explosion at the Roffe and Sons laboratory set deliberately, but that it had been caused by an explosive called Rylar X, made exclusively for the military, and not available to anyone else. What intrigued Max was that Rylar X was manufactured at one of the factories of Roffe and Sons. It took Max only one telephone call to learn which one.

The factory outside Paris.

At exactly 4 P.M. Herr Julius Badrutt lowered his angular figure into a chair and said without preamble, "As much as we would like to accommodate you, Miss Roffe, I am afraid our responsibility toward our stockholders must take precedence."

It was the kind of statement, Elizabeth thought, that bankers made to widows and orphans before they foreclosed their mortgages. But this time she was ready for Herr Badrutt.

". . . My board of directors has therefore instructed me to inform you that our bank is calling in the notes on Roffe and Sons immediately."

"I was told I had ninety days," Elizabeth said.

"Unfortunately, we feel that the circumstances have changed for the worse. I should also inform you that the other banks you are dealing with have reached the same decision."

With the banks refusing to help her, there would be no way to keep the company private.

"I'm sorry to bring you such bad news, Miss Roffe, but I felt that I should tell you personally."

"You know, of course, that Roffe and Sons is still a very strong and healthy company."

Herr Julius Badrutt nodded his head, once. "Of course. It's a great company."

"Yet you won't give us more time."

Herr Badrutt looked at her for a moment, then said, "The bank thinks your problems are manageable, Miss Roffe. But . . ." He hesitated.

"But you don't think there's anyone to manage them?"

"I'm afraid that is correct." He started to rise.

"What if someone else were president of Roffe and Sons?" Elizabeth asked.

He shook his head. "We have discussed that possibility. We don't feel that any of the present members of the board have the overall ability to cope with—"

She said, "I was thinking of Rhys Williams."

CHAPTER

38

Constable Thomas Hiller of the Thames Marine Police Division was in terrible shape. He was sleepy, hungry, horny and wet; and he could not decide which was the greatest of his miseries.

He was sleepy because his fiancée, Flo, had kept him awake all night, fighting; he was hungry because by the time she was through screaming at him, he was late for duty, and he had had no time to pick up a bite; he was horny because she had refused to let him touch her; and he was wet because the thirty-foot police boat on which he was traveling had been built for service, not comfort, and a rising wind was driving the rain into the small wheelhouse where he stood. On days like this there was bloody little to see and even bloody less to do. The Thames Division covered fifty-four miles of river from Dartford Creek to Staines Bridge, and ordinarily Constable Hiller enjoyed patrol duty. But not when he was in this shape. Damn all women! He thought about Flo in bed, naked as a pouter pigeon, her large tits waving up and down as she yelled at him. He glanced at his watch. Another half hour and this miserable tour would be finished. The boat had turned and was headed back toward Waterloo Pier. His only problem now was deciding what to do first: sleep, eat, or jump in the kip with Flo. Maybe all three at once, he thought. He rubbed his eyes to force the sleep out of them, and turned to look at the muddy, swollen river pimpled by the rain.

It seemed to loom out of nowhere. It looked like a large white fish floating belly up, and Constable Hiller's first thought was: If we haul it aboard, we're going to stink of it. It was about ten yards to starboard and the boat was moving away from it. If he opened his mouth, the bloody fish was going to delay his getting off duty. They would have to stop and grapple it, and either pull it over the side or tow it in. Whichever they did would delay his getting to Flo. Well, he didn't *have* to report it. What if he had not seen it? What if——? They were moving farther away.

Constable Hiller called out, "Sergeant, there's a floating fish twenty degrees off starboard. Looks like a big shark."

The hundred-horsepower diesel engine suddenly changed rhythm, and the boat began to slow. Sergeant Gaskins stepped to his side. "Where is it?" he asked.

The dim shape was gone now, buried in the rain. "It was over there."

Sergeant Gaskins hesitated. He too was anxious to get home. His impulse was to ignore the damned fish.

"Was it big enough to menace navigation?" he asked.

Constable Hiller fought with himself and lost. "Yes," he said.

And so the patrol boat turned and slowly headed toward where the object had last been seen. It materialized again unexpectedly, almost under the bow, and they both stood there, staring down at it. It was the body of a young blond girl.

She was naked, except for a red ribbon tied around her swollen neck.

CHAPTER
39

At the moment when Constable Hiller and Sergeant Gaskins were fishing the body of the murdered girl out of the Thames, ten miles on the other side of London, Detective Max Hornung was entering the gray-and-white marble lobby of New Scotland Yard. Just walking through the storied portals gave him a sense of pride. They were all part of the same great fraternity. He enjoyed the fact that the Yard's cable address was HANDCUFFS. Max was very fond of the English. His only problem concerned their ability to communicate with him. The English spoke their native language so strangely.

The policeman behind the reception desk asked, "Can I help you, sir?"

Max turned. "I have an appointment with Inspector Davidson."

"Name, sir?"

Max said, slowly and distinctly, "Inspector Davidson."

The guard looked at him with interest. "Your name is Inspector Davidson?"

"My name is *not* Inspector Davidson. My name is Max Hornung."

The policeman behind the desk said apologetically, "Excuse me, sir, but do you speak any English?"

Five minutes later Max was seated in the office of Inspector Davidson, a large, middle-aged man with a florid face and uneven yellow teeth. Typically British-looking, Max thought happily.

"Over the phone you said you were interested in information on Sir Alec Nichols as a possible suspect in a murder case."

"He's one of half a dozen."

Inspector Davidson stared at him. "His wanted toes are frozen?"

Max sighed. He repeated what he had just said, slowly and carefully.

"Ah." The inspector thought for a moment. "Tell you what I'll do. I'll turn you over to C-Four Criminal Records Department. If they have nothing on him, we'll try C-Eleven and C-Thirteen—Criminal Intelligence."

Sir Alec Nichols' name was not listed in any of the files. But Max knew where he could get the information he wanted.

Earlier that morning Max had phoned a number of executives who worked in the City, the financial center of London.

Their reactions were identical. When Max announced his name, they were filled with trepidation, for everyone doing business in the City had *something* to hide, and Max Hornung's reputation as a financial avenging angel was international. The moment that Max informed them that he was seeking information about someone else, they fell over themselves to cooperate with him.

Max spent two days visiting banks and finance

companies, credit rating organizations and vital statistics offices. He was not interested in talking to the people at those places: he was interested in talking to their computers.

Max was a genius with computers. He would sit before the console board and play the machines like a virtuoso. It did not matter what language the computer had been taught, for Max spoke all of them. He talked to digital computers and low-level and high-level language computers. He was at ease with FORTRAN and FORTRAN IV, the giant IBM 370's and the PDP 10's and 11's and ALGOL 68.

He was at home with COBOL, programmed for business, and BASIC, used by the police, and the high speed APL, which conversed solely in charts and graphs. Max talked to LISP and APT, and PL-1. He held conversations in the binary code, and questioned the arithmetic units and the CPV units, and the high-speed printer answered his questions at the rate of eleven hundred lines a minute. The giant computers had spent their lives sucking up information like insatiable pumps, storing it, analyzing it, remembering it, and now they were spewing it out in Max's ear, whispering their secrets to him in their secluded air-conditioned crypts.

Nothing was sacred, nothing was safe. Privacy in today's civilization was a delusion, a myth. Every citizen was exposed, his deepest secrets laid bare, waiting to be read. People were on record if they had a Social Security number, an insurance policy, a driver's license or a bank account. They were listed if they had paid taxes or drawn unemployment insurance or welfare funds. Their names were stored in computers if they were covered by a medical plan, had made mortgage payments on a home, owned an automobile or bicycle or had a savings or checking account. The computers knew their names if they had been in a hospital, or in the military service, had a fishing or hunting license, had applied for a passport, or telephone, or electricity, or if they had been married or divorced or born.

If one knew where to look, and if one was patient, all the facts were available.

Max Hornung and the computers had a wonderful rapport. They did not laugh at Max's accent, or the way he looked, or acted or dressed. To the computers Max was a giant. They respected his intelligence, admired him, loved him. They happily gave up their secrets to him, sharing their delicious gossip about the fools that mortals made of themselves. It was like old friends chatting.

"Let's talk about Sir Alec Nichols," Max said.

The computers began. They gave Max a mathematical sketch of Sir Alec, drawn in digits and binary codes and charts. In two hours Max had a composite picture of the man, a financial identi-kit.

Copies of bank receipts and canceled checks and bills were all laid out before him. The first puzzling item that caught Max's eye was a series of checks for large amounts, all made out to "Bearer," cashed by Sir Alec Nichols. Where had the money gone? Max looked to see if it had been reported as a business or personal expense, or as a tax deduction. Negative. He went back over the lists of expenditures again: a check to White's Club, a meat-market bill, unpaid . . . an evening gown from John Bates . . . the Guinea . . . a dentist's bill, unpaid . . . Annabelle's . . . one challis robe from Saint Laurent in Paris . . . a bill from the White Elephant, unpaid . . . a rates bill . . . John Wyndham, the hairdresser, unpaid . . . four dresses from Yves Saint Laurent. Rive Gauche . . . household salaries . . .

Max asked a question of the computer at the Vehicle Licensing Center.

Affirmative. Sir Alec owns a Bentley and a Morris.

Something was missing. There was no mechanic's bill.

Max had the computers search their memories. In seven years no such bill existed.

Did we forget something? the computers asked.
No, Max replied, *you didn t forget.*

Sir Alec did not use a mechanic He repaired his own cars. A man with that mechanical ability would have no trouble causing an elevator, or a Jeep, to crash. Max Hornung pored over the arcane figures that his friends set before him, with the eagerness of an Egyptologist translating a set of newly discovered hieroglyphics. He found further mysteries. Sir Alec was spending a great deal more than his income.

Another loose thread.

Max's friends in the City had connections in many quarters. Within two days Max learned that Sir Alec had been borrowing money from Tod Michaels, the owner of a club in Soho.

Max turned to the police computers and asked questions. They listened, and they replied. *Yes, we have Tod Michaels for you. Has been charged with several crimes, but never convicted. Suspected of being involved in blackmail, dope, prostitution and loan-sharking.*

Max went down to Soho and asked more questions. He found out that Sir Alec Nichols did not gamble. But his wife did.

When Max was finished, there was no doubt in

his mind that Sir Alec Nichols was being black-mailed. He had unpaid bills, he needed money fast. He had stock that would be worth millions, if he could sell it. Sam Roffe had stood in his way, and now Elizabeth Roffe.

Sir Alec Nichols had a motive for murder.

Max checked out Rhys Williams. The machines tried, but the information proved too sketchy.

The computers informed Max that Rhys Williams was male, born in Wales, thirty-four years of age, unmarried. An executive of Roffe and Sons. Salary eighty thousand dollars a year, plus bonuses. A London savings account with a balance of twenty-five thousand pounds, a checking account with an average balance of eight hundred pounds. A safety-deposit box in Zurich, contents unknown. All major charge accounts and credit cards. Many of the items purchased with them were for women. Rhys Williams had no criminal record. He had been employed at Roffe and Sons for nine years.

Not enough, Max thought. Not nearly enough. It was as though Rhys Williams was hiding behind the computers. Max remembered how protective the man had been when Max had questioned Elizabeth, after Kate Erling's funeral. Whom had he been protecting Elizabeth Roffe? Or himself?

At six o'clock that evening Max booked himself on an Alitalia economy flight to Rome.

CHAPTER

40

Ivo Palazzi had spent almost ten years carefully and skillfully building an intricate double life that not even his closest associates had penetrated.

It took Max Hornung and his computer friends in Rome less than twenty-four hours. Max held discussions with the computer at the Anagrafe Building, where vital statistics and city-administration data were kept, and he visited the computers at SID, and went to call on the bank computers. They all welcomed Max.

Tell me about Ivo Palazzi, Max said.

Happily, they replied.

The conversations began.

A grocery bill from Amici . . . a beauty salon bill from Sergio in the Via Condoitti . . . one blue suit from Angelo . . . flowers from Carducci . . . two evening dresses from Irene Galitzine . . . shoes from Gucci . . . a Pucci purse . . . utility bills . . .

Max kept reading the print-outs, examining, analyzing, smelling. Something smelled wrong. There were tuition fees for six children.

Have you made an error? Max asked.

Sorry. What type of error?

The computers at Anagrafe told me that Ivo

Palazzi is registered as the father of three children. Do you verify six tuition fees?

We do.

You show Ivo Palazzi's address as being in Olgiata?

That is correct.

But he is paying for an apartment in Via Montemignaio?

Yes.

Are there two Ivo Palazzis?

No. One man. Two families. Three daughters by his wife. Three sons by Donatella Spolini.

Before Max was through, he knew the tastes of Ivo's mistress, her age, the name of her hairdresser, and the names of Ivo's illegitimate children. He knew that Simonetta was a blonde, and Donatella a brunette. He knew what size dresses and bras and shoes each wore and how much they cost.

Among the expenses several interesting items caught Max's eye. The amounts were small, but they stood out like beacons. There was a receipted check for a lathe, a plane and a saw. Ivo Palazzi liked to work with his hands. Max thought about the fact that an architect would probably know something about elevators.

Ivo Palazzi applied for a large bank loan recently, the computers informed Max.

Did he receive it?

No. The bank asked him to have his wife cosign. He withdrew the request.

Thank you.

Max took a bus to the Polizia Scientifica center at EUR, where the giant computer was kept in a large round room.

Does Ivo Palazzi have a criminal record? Max asked.

Affirmative. Ivo Palazzi was convicted on an assault-and-battery charge at age twenty-three. His victim went to the hospital. Palazzi went to jail for two months.

Anything else?

Ivo Palazzi keeps a mistress at Via Montemignaio.

Thank you. I know.

There are several police reports of complaints from neighbors.

What sort of complaints?

Disturbing the peace. Fighting, yelling. One night she smashed all the dishes. Is that important?

Very, Max said. *Thank you.*

So Ivo Palazzi had a temper. And Donatella Spolini had a temper. Had something happened between her and Ivo? Was she threatening to expose him? Was that why he had suddenly gone to the bank for a large loan? How far would a man like Ivo Palazzi go to protect his marriage, his family, his way of life?

There was one final item that caught the little detective's attention. A large payment had been made to Ivo Palazzi by the financial section of the Italian security police. It was a reward, a percentage of the money found on the banker whom Ivo had turned in. If Ivo Palazzi was that desperate for money, what else would he do for it?

Max bade farewell to his computers and caught a noon flight to Paris on Air France.

CHAPTER

41

The taxi fare from Charles de Gaulle Airport to the Notre Dame area is seventy francs, not including a tip. The fare by city bus Number 351, to the same area, is seven and a half francs, no tip required. Detective Max Hornung took the bus. He checked into the inexpensive Hôtel Meublé and began making phone calls.

He talked to the people who held in their hands the secrets of the citizens of France. The French were normally more suspicious than even the Swiss, but they were eager to cooperate with Max Hornung. There were two reasons. The first was that Max Hornung was a virtuoso in his field, greatly admired, and it was an honor to cooperate with such a man. The second was that they were terrified of him. There were no secrets from Max. The odd-looking little man with the funny accent stripped everyone naked. "Certainly," they told Max. "You're welcome to use our computers. Everything to be kept confidential, of course."

"Of course."

Max dropped in at the Inspecteurs des Finances, the Crédit Lyonnais, and the Assurance Nationale and chatted with the tax computers. He visited the computers at the *gendarmerie* at Rosny-sous-Bois and the ones at the Préfecture of Police at Île de la Cité.

They started off with the light, easy gossip of old friends. *Who are Charles and Hélène Roffe-Martel?* Max asked.

Charles and Hélène Roffe-Martel, residence Rue François Premier 5, Vésinet, married May 24, 1970, at the Mairie in Neuilly, children none, Hélène three times divorced, maiden name Roffe, bank account at the Crédit Lyonnais in Avenue Montaigne in name of Hélène Roffe-Martel, average balance in excess of twenty thousand francs.

Expenditures?

With pleasure. A bill from Librairie Marceau for books . . . a dental bill for root-canal work for Charles Martel . . . hospital bills for Charles Martel . . . doctor's bill for examination of Charles Martel.

Do you have result of diagnosis?

Can you wait? I will have to speak to another computer.

Yes, please. Max waited.

The machine containing the doctor's report began to speak. *I have the diagnosis.*

Go ahead.

A nervous condition.

Anything else?

Severe bruises and contusions on thighs and buttocks.

Any explanation?

None given.

Go on, please.

A bill for a pair of men's shoes from Pinet . . . one hat from Rose Valois . . . foie gras from Fauchon

. . . Carita beauty salon . . . Maxim's, dinner party for eight . . . flat silver from Christofle . . . a man's robe from Sulka . . . Max stopped the computer. Something was bothering him. Something about the bills. He realized what it was. Every purchase had been signed by Mme. Roffe-Martel. The bill for men's clothes, the restaurant bills—all the accounts were in her name. Interesting.

And then the first loose thread.

A company named Belle Paix had purchased a land tax stamp. One of the owners of Belle Paix was named Charles Dessain. Charles Dessain's Social Security number was the same as Charles Martel's. Concealment.

Tell me about Belle Paix, Max said.

Belle Paix is owned by René Duchamps and Charles Dessain, also known as Charles Martel.

What does Belle Paix do?

It owns a vineyard.

How much is the company capitalized at?

Four million francs.

Where did Charles Martel get his share of the money?

From Chez ma Tante.

The house of your aunt?

Sorry. A French slang expression. The proper name is Crédit Municipal.

Is the vineyard profitable?

No. It failed.

Max needed more. He kept talking to his friends, probing, cajoling, demanding. It was the insurance computer that confided to Max that there was a warning on file of a possible insurance fraud. Max felt something delicious stir within him.

Tell me about it, he said.

And they talked, like two women gossiping back and forth over the Monday wash.

When Max was through he went to see a jeweler named Pierre Richaud.

In thirty minutes Max knew to a franc how much of Hélène Roffe-Martel's jewelry had been duplicated. It came to just over two million francs, the amount Charles Martel had invested in the vineyard. So Charles Dessain-Martel had been desperate enough to steal his wife's jewelry.

What other acts of desperation had he committed?

There was one other entry that interested Max. It might be of little significance, but Max methodically filed it away in his mind. It was a bill for the purchase of one pair of mountain-climbing boots. It gave Max pause, because mountain climbing did not fit in with his image of Charles Martel-Dessain, a man who was so dominated by his wife that he was allowed no charge accounts of his own, had no bank account in his name, and was forced to steal in order to make an investment.

No, Max could not visualize Charles Martel challenging a mountain. Max went back to his computers.

The bill you showed me yesterday from Timwear Sports Shop. I would like to see an itemized statement, please.

Certainly.

It flashed on the screen before him. There was the bill for the boots. Size *36A*. A woman's size. It was Hélène Roffe-Martel who was the mountain climber.

Sam Roffe had been killed on a mountain.

CHAPTER

42

Rue Armengaud was a quiet Paris street lined with one- and two-story private residences, each with its sloping guttered roof. Towering above its neighbors was Number 26, an eight-story modern structure of glass, steel and stone, the headquarters of Interpol, the clearinghouse for information in international criminal activities.

Detective Max Hornung was talking to a computer in the huge, air-conditioned basement room when one of the staff members walked in and said, "They're running a snuff film upstairs. Want to see it?"

Max looked up and said, "I don't know. What is a snuff film?"

"Come take a look."

Two dozen men and women were seated in the large screening room on the third floor of the building. There were members of the Interpol staff, police inspectors from the Sûreté, plainclothes detectives and a scattering of uniformed policemen.

Standing at the front of the room next to a blank screen, René Almedin, an assistant to the secretary of Interpol, was speaking. Max entered and found a seat in the back row.

René Almedin was saying, ". . . for the last several years we have been hearing increasing rumors of snuff films, pornographic films in which at the end of the sexual act the victim is murdered on camera. There has never been proof that such films actually existed. The reason, of course, is obvious. These films would not have been made for the public. They would have been made to be shown privately to wealthy individuals who got their pleasure in twisted, sadistic ways." René Almedin carefully removed his glasses. "As I have said, everything has been rumor and speculation. That has now changed, however. In a moment you are going to see footage from an actual snuff film." There was an expectant stir from the audience. "Two days ago, a male pedestrian carrying an attaché case was struck down in a hit-and-run accident in Passy. The man died on the way to the hospital. He is still unidentified. The Sûreté found this reel of film in his attaché case and turned it over to the laboratory, where it was developed." He gave a signal and the lights began to dim. The film began.

The blond girl could not have been more than eighteen. There was something unreal about watching that young face and budding woman's body performing fellatio, analingus and a variety of other sexual acts with the large hairless man in bed with her. The camera moved in to a close-up to show his enormous penis driving into her body, then pulled back to show her face. Max Hornung had never seen her face before. But he had seen something else that was familiar. His eyes were fixed on the ribbon that the girl was wearing around her neck. It triggered a memory. A red ribbon. Where? Slowly, the girl on the screen began to build to a peak, and as she started to climax, the man's fingers went around her throat and began to squeeze. The look on the girl's face changed from ecstasy to horror. She fought wildly to escape, but his hands pressed tighter, until at the final moment of orgasm the girl died. The camera moved in for a close-up of her face. The film ended. The lights suddenly came on in the room. Max remembered.

The girl who had been fished out of the river in Zurich.

At Interpol headquarters in Paris, replies from urgent inquiry cables were beginning to arrive from all over Europe. Six similar murders had taken place —in Zurich, London, Rome, Portugal, Hamburg and Paris.

René Almedin said to Max, "The descriptions match exactly. The victims were all blond, female, young; they were strangled during sexual inter- course and their bodies were nude except for a red ribbon around their necks. We're dealing with a mass murderer. Someone who has a passport, and is either affluent enough to travel extensively on his own or is on an expense account."

A man in plain clothes walked into the office and said, "We ran into some good luck. The raw stock of the film is manufactured by a small outfit in Brussels. This particular batch had a color-balance problem, which makes it easy for them to identify. We're get- ting a list of the customers they sold it to."

Max said, "I would like to see that list when you have it."

"Of course," René Almedin said. He studied the little detective. Max Hornung looked like no de- tective he had ever seen. And yet it was Max

Hornung who had tied the snuff murders together.

"We owe you a debt of gratitude," Almedin said.

Max Hornung looked at him and blinked. "What for?" he asked.

CHAPTER
43

Alec Nichols had not wanted to attend the banquet, but he had not wished Elizabeth to go alone. They were both scheduled to speak. The banquet was in Glasgow, a city Alec hated. A car was outside the hotel, waiting to take them to the airport as soon as they could decently make their excuses. He had already given his speech but his mind had been elsewhere. He was tense and nervous, and his stomach was upset. Some fool had had the bad judgment to serve haggis. Alec had barely tasted it. Elizabeth was seated next to him. "Are you all right, Alec?"

"Fine." He patted her hand reassuringly.

The speeches were almost finished when a waiter came up to Alec and whispered, "Excuse me, sir. There's a trunk call for you. You can take it in the office."

Alec followed the waiter out of the large dining room into the small office behind the reception desk. He picked up the telephone. "Hello?"

Swinton's voice said, "This is your last warning!" The line went dead.

CHAPTER

44

The last city on Detective Max Hornung's agenda was Berlin.

His friends the computers were waiting for him. Max spoke to the exclusive Nixdorf computer, to which one had access only with a specially punched card. He talked to the great computers at Allianz and Schuffa and to the ones at the Bundeskrimalamt at Wiesbaden, the collection point for all criminal activity in Germany.

What can we do for you? they asked.

Tell me about Walther Gassner.

And they told him. When they were through telling Max Hornung their secrets, Walther Gassner's life was spread out before Max in beautiful mathematical symbols. Max could see the man as clearly as if he were looking at a photograph of him. He knew his taste in clothes, wines, food, hotels. A handsome young ski instructor who had lived off women and had married an heiress much older than himself.

There was one item that Max found curious: a cancled check made out to a Dr. Heissen, for two hundred marks. On the check was written "For consultation." What kind of consultation? The check had been cashed at the Dresdner Bank in Dusseldorf. Fifteen minutes later Max was speaking to the branch manager of the bank. Yes, of course the branch manager knew Dr. Heissen. He was a valued client of the bank.

What kind of doctor was he?

A psychiatrist.

When Max had hung up, he sat back, his eyes closed, thinking. A loose thread. He picked up the telephone and placed a call to Dr. Heissen in Dusseldorf.

An officious receptionist told Max that the doctor could not be disturbed. When Max insisted, Dr. Heissen got on the telephone and rudely informed Max that he never revealed any information about his patients, and that he would certainly not dream of discussing such matters over the telephone. He hung up on the detective.

Max went back to the computers. *Tell me about Dr. Heissen,* he said.

Three hours later Max was speaking to Dr. Heissen on the telephone again.

"I told you before," the doctor snapped, "that if you want any information about any of my patients, you will have to come to my office with a court order."

"It is inconvenient for me to come to Dusseldorf just now," the detective explained.

"That's your problem. Anything else? I'm a busy man."

"I know you are. I have in front of me your income tax reports for the past five years."

"So?"

Max said, "Doctor, I don't want to make trouble for you. But you are illegally concealing twenty-five percent of your income. If you prefer, I can just forward your files to the German income tax authorities and tell them where to look. They could start with your safe-deposit box in Munich, or your numbered bank account in Basel."

There was a long silence, and then the doctor's voice asked, "Who did you say you were?"

"Detective Max Hornung of the Swiss Kriminal Polizei."

There was another pause. The doctor said politely, "And what is it exactly you wish to know?"

Max told him.

Once Dr. Heissen began talking, there was no stopping him. Yes, of course he remembered Walther Gassner. The man had barged in without an appointment and had insisted on seeing him. He had refused to give his name. He had used the pretext that he wanted to discuss the problems of a friend.

"Of course, that alerted me instantly," Dr. Heissen confided to Mox. "It is a classic syndrome of people unwilling or afraid to face their problems."

"What *was* the problem?" Max asked.

"He said his friend was schizophrenic and homicidal, and would probably kill someone unless he could be stopped. He asked if there was some kind of treatment that could help. He said he could not bear to have his friend locked away in an insane asylum."

"What did you tell him?"

"I told him that first, of course, I would have to examine his *friend*, that some types of mental illness could be helped with modern drugs and other psychiatric and therapeutic treatments, and that other types were incurable. I also mentioned that in a case such as he described, treatment might be necessary for an extended period of time."

"What happened then?" Max asked.

"Nothing. That was really all. I never saw the man again. I would like to have helped him. He was very distraught. His coming to me was obviously a cry for help. It is similar to a killer who writes on the wall of his victim's apartment, 'Stop me before I kill again!' "

There was one thing still puzzling Max. "Doctor, you said he wouldn't give you his name, and yet he gave you a check and signed it."

Dr. Heissen explained, "He had forgotten to bring any money with him. He was very upset about that. In the end he had to write the check. That's how I happened to learn his name. Is there anything else you need to know, sir?"

"No."

Something was disturbing Max, a loose thread dangling tantalizingly out of reach. It would come to him—meanwhile, he had finished with the computers. The rest was up to him now.

When Max returned to Zurich the following morning, he found a teletype on his desk from Interpol. It contained a list of customers who had purchased the batch of raw stock used to make the snuff murder film.

There were eight names on the list.

Among them was Roffe and Sons.

Chief Inspector Schmied was listening to Detective Max Hornung make his report. There was no doubt about it. The lucky little detective had stumbled onto another big case.

"It's one of five people," Max was saying. "They all have a motive and they had the opportunity. They were all in Zurich for a board meeting the day the elevator crashed. Any one of them could have been in Sardinia at the time of the Jeep accident."

Chief Inspector Schmied frowned. "You said there were five suspects. Aside from Elizabeth Roffe, there are only four members of the board. Who's your other suspect?"

Max blinked and said patiently, "The man who was in Chamonix with Sam Roffe, when he was murdered. Rhys Williams."

CHAPTER

45

Mrs. Rhys Williams.

Elizabeth could not believe it. The whole thing had an air of unreality. It was something out of a blissful girlhood dream. Elizabeth remembered how she had written in her exercise book, over and over, *Mrs. Rhys Williams, Mrs. Rhys Williams.* She glanced down now at the wedding ring on her finger.

Rhys said, "What are you grinning about?" He was seated in an easy chair across from her in the luxurious Boeing 707-320. They were thirty-five thousand feet somewhere above the Atlantic ocean, dining on Iranian caviar and drinking chilled Don Perignon, and it was such a cliché of *La Dolce Vita* that Elizabeth had to laugh aloud.

Rhys smiled. "Something I said?"

Elizabeth shook her head. She looked at him and marveled at how attractive he was. Her husband. "I'm just happy."

He would never know how happy. How could she tell him how much this marriage meant to her? He would not understand, because to Rhys it was not a marriage, it was a business proposition. But she loved Rhys. It seemed to Elizabeth that she had always loved him. She wanted to spend the rest of her life with him, have his children, belong to him, have him belong to her. Elizabeth looked over at Rhys again and thought wryly, But first I have to solve one small problem. I have to find a way to make him fall in love with me.

Elizabeth had proposed to Rhys the day of her meeting with Julius Badrutt. After the banker had left, Elizabeth had carefully brushed her hair, walked into Rhy's office, taken a deep breath and said, "Rhys—would you marry me?"

She had seen the look of surprise on his face, and before he could speak, she had gone hurriedly on, trying to sound efficient and cool. "It would be a purely business arrangement. The banks are willing to extend our loans if you take over as president of Roffe and Sons. The only way you can do that"—to Elizabeth's horror her voice had cracked—"is to marry a member of the family, and I—I seem to be the only one available."

She felt her face flush. She could not look at him.

"It wouldn't be a real marriage, of course," Elizabeth had said, "in the sense that—I mean—you'd be free to—to come and go as you pleased."

He had watched her, not helping her. Elizabeth wished he would say something. Anything.

"Rhys—"

"Sorry. You took me by surprise." He had smiled. "It isn't every day a man gets proposed to by a beautiful girl."

He was smiling, trying to get out of this without hurting her feelings. *I'm sorry, Elizabeth, but*—

"You have a deal," Rhys said.

And Elizabeth had suddenly felt as though a heavy burden had been lifted from her. She had not realized until that moment how important this had been. She had bought time now to learn who the enemy was. Together she and Rhys could stop all the terrible things that had been happening. There was one thing she had to make clear to him.

"You will be president of the company," she had said, "but the voting control of the stock will remain in my hands."

Rhys had frowned. "If I'm running the company—"

"You will be," Elizabeth had assured him.

"But the controlling stock—"

"Stays in my name. I want to make sure that it can't be sold."

"I see."

She could sense his disapproval. She had wanted to tell him that she had reached a decision. She had decided that the company should go public, that the members of the board should be able to sell their shares. With Rhys as president, Elizabeth would no longer have any fears about strangers coming in and taking over. Rhys would be strong enough to handle them. But Elizabeth could not let that happen until she found out who was trying to destroy the company. She had wanted desperately to tell Rhys all these things, but she knew that now was not the time, and so all she said was "Other than that, you'll have complete control."

Rhys had stood there, silently studying her for what seemed a long time. When he spoke, he said, "When would you like to get married?"

"As soon as possible."

Except for Anna and Walther, who was home, ill, they all came to Zurich for the wedding. Alec and

Vivian, Hélène and Charles, Simonetta and Ivo. They seemed delighted for Elizabeth, and their pleasure made her feel like a fraud. She had not made a marriage, she had made a business deal.

Alec hugged her and said, "You know I wish you everything wonderful."

"I know, Alec. Thank you."

Ivo waxed ecstatic. *"Carissima, tanti auguri e figli maschi.* 'To find riches is a beggar's dream, but to find love is the dream of kings.'"

Elizabeth smiled. "Who said that?"

"I did," Ivo declared. "I hope Rhys appreciates what a lucky man he is."

"I keep telling him," she said lightly.

Hélène took Elizabeth aside. "You are full of surprises, *ma chère.* I had no idea that you and Rhys were interested in each other."

"It happened suddenly."

Hélène studied her with cool, calculating eyes. "Yes. I'm sure it did." And she walked away.

After the ceremony there was a wedding reception at the Baur-au-Lac. On the surface it was gay and festive, but Elizabeth felt the undercurrents. There was something evil in the room, a malediction, but she could not tell from whom it was coming. All she knew was that someone in the room hated her. She could feel it, deep down inside her, yet when she looked around, all she saw were smiles and friendly faces. Charles raising his glass in a toast to her . . . Elizabeth had received a report on the laboratory explosion. *The explosive was manufactured by your factory outside Paris.*

Ivo, a happy grin on his face . . . *The banker who was caught trying to smuggle money out of Italy was*

*set up. A man tipped off the border police. Ivo
Palazzi.*

Alec? Walther? Which? Elizabeth wondered.

The following morning a board meeting was held,
and Rhys Williams was unanimously elected president and chief operating officer of Roffe and Sons.
Charles raised the question that was on everyone's
mind. "Now that you are running the company, are
we going to be allowed to sell our stock?"

Elizabeth could feel the sudden tension in the
room.

"The controlling stock is still in Elizabeth's hands,"
Rhys informed them. "It's her decision."

Every head turned toward Elizabeth.

"We're not selling," she announced.

When Elizabeth and Rhys were alone, he said,
"How would you like to honeymoon in Rio?"

Elizabeth looked at him, and her heart soared. He
added matter-of-factly, "Our manager there is threatening to quit. We can't afford to lose him. I was planning to fly there tomorrow to straighten things out.
It would look a bit strange if I went without my
bride."

Elizabeth nodded and said, "Yes, of course."
You're a fool, she told herself. *This was your idea.
It's an arrangement, not a marriage. You have no
right to expect anything from Rhys.* And still, a
small voice, deep inside her, said, *Who knows what
can happen? . . .*

When they got off the plane at the Galeão airport,
the air was surprisingly warm, and Elizabeth realized
that in Rio it was summer. A Mercedes 600 was

waiting for them. The chauffeur was a thin, dark-skinned man in his late twenties. When they got into the car, Rhys asked the driver, "Where's Luis?"

"Luis is sick, Mr. Williams. I'll be driving you and Mrs. Williams."

"Tell Luis I hope he'll be better soon."

The driver studied them in the rearview mirror and said, "I will."

Half an hour later they were driving along the esplanade, over the colorful tiles of the broad avenue along the Copacabana Beach. They pulled up in front of the modern Princessa Sugarloaf Hotel and a moment later, their luggage was being attended to. They were ushered into an enormous suite with four bedrooms, a beautiful living room, a kitchen, and a huge terrace overlooking the bay. The suite had been stocked with flowers in silver vases, champagne, whiskey, and boxes of chocolates. The manager himself had escorted them to their suite.

"If there is anything at all we can do for you—anything—I am personally at your service twenty-four hours a day." And he bowed himself out.

"They're certainly friendly," Elizabeth said.

Rhys laughed and replied, "They should be. You own this hotel."

Elizabeth felt herself color. "Oh. I—I didn't know."

"Hungry?"

"I—No, thank you," Elizabeth replied.

"Some wine?"

"Yes, thank you."

In her own ears her voice sounded stilted and unnatural. She was not certain how she was supposed to behave, or what to expect from Rhys. He had suddenly become a stranger, and she felt terribly conscious of the fact that they were alone in the honeymoon suite of a hotel, that it was getting late, and that it would soon be time for bed.

She watched Rhys as he deftly opened a bottle of champagne. He did everything so smoothly, with the easy assurance of a man who knows exactly what he wants and how to get it. What did he want?

Rhys carried a glass of champagne to Elizabeth and raised his own glass in a toast. "To beginnings," he said.

"To beginnings," Elizabeth echoed. *And happy endings,* she added silently.

They drank.

We should smash our glasses into a fireplace. Elizabeth thought, to celebrate. She gulped down the rest of her champagne.

They were in Rio on their honeymoon, and she wanted Rhys. Not just for now, but forever.

The phone rang. Rhys picked it up and spoke into it briefly. When he finished he hung up and said to Elizabeth, "It's late. Why don't you get ready for bed?"

It seemed to Elizabeth that the word "bed" hung heavily in the air.

"Right," she said weakly. She turned and went into the bedroom where the bellboys had put their luggage. There was a large double bed in the center of the room. A maid had unpacked their suitcases and prepared the bed. On one side was a sheer silk nightgown of Elizabeth's, and on the other side a pair of men's blue pajamas. She hesitated a moment, then began to undress. When she was naked, she walked into the large mirrored dressing room and carefully removed her makeup. She wrapped a Turkish towel around her head, went into the bathroom and showered, slowly lathering her body and feeling the warm soapy water running between her breasts and down her belly and thighs, like warm wet fingers.

All the time she was trying not to think about Rhys, and she could think of nothing else. She thought of his arms around her and his body on hers. Had she married Rhys to help save the company, or was she using the company as an excuse because she wanted him? She no longer knew. Her desire had turned into one burning, all-consuming need. It was as though the fifteen-year-old child had been waiting for him all these years without being aware of it, and the need had turned into a hunger. She stepped out of the shower, dried herself with a soft warmed towel, put on the sheer silk nightgown, let her hair fall loose and free and climbed into bed. She lay there waiting, thinking about what was going to happen, wondering what he would be like, and she found that her heart was beginning to pound faster. She heard a sound and looked up. Rhys was standing in the doorway. He was fully dressed.

"I'll be going out now," he said.

Elizabeth sat up. "Where—where are you going?"

"It's a business problem I have to take care of." And he was gone.

Elizabeth lay awake all that night, tossing and turning, filled with conflicting emotions, telling herself how grateful she was that Rhys had kept to their agreement, feeling like a fool for what she had been anticipating, furious with him for rejecting her.

It was dawn when Elizabeth heard Rhys return. His footsteps moved toward the bedroom, and Elizabeth closed her eyes, pretending to be asleep. She could hear Rhys's breathing as he came over to the bed. He stood there, watching her for a long time. Then he turned and walked into the other room.

A few minutes later Elizabeth was asleep.

In the late morning they had breakfast on the terrace. Rhys was pleasant and chatty, telling her what the city was like at Carnival time But he volunteered no information about where he had spent the night, and Elizabeth did not ask One waiter took their order for breakfast. Elizabeth noticed that it was a different waiter who served it. She thought no more about it, nor about the maids who were constantly in and out of the suite.

Elizabeth and Rhys were at the Roffe and Sons factory on the outskirts of Rio, seated in the office of the plant manager, Señor Tumas, a middle-aged, frog-faced man who perspired copiously.

He was addressing Rhys. "You must understand how it is. Roffe and Sons is dearer to me than my own life. It is my family. When I leave here, it will be like leaving home. A part of my heart will be torn out. More than anything in the world, I want to stay here." He stopped to wipe his brow. "But I have a better offer from another company, and I have my wife and children and mother-in-law to think of. You understand?"

Rhys was leaning back in his chair, his legs casually stretched out before him. "Of course, Roberto. I know how much this company means to you. You have spent many years here. Still, a man has to think of his family."

"Thank you," Roberto said gratefully. "I knew I could count on you, Rhys."

"What about your contract with us?"

Tumas shrugged. "A piece of paper. We will tear it up, no? What good is a contract if a man is unhappy in his heart?"

Rhys nodded. "That's why we flew down here, Roberto—to make you happy in your heart."

Tumas sighed. "Ah, if only it were not too late. But I have already agreed to go to work for this other company."

"Do they know you're going to prison?" Rhys asked conversationally.

Tumas gasped at him. "Prison?"

Rhys said, "The United States government has ordered every company doing business overseas to turn in a list of all foreign bribes they've paid over the past ten years. Unfortunately, you're heavily involved in that, Roberto. You've broken a few laws here. We had planned to protect you—as a faithful member of the family—but if you're not with us, there's no longer any reason to, is there?"

All the color had drained from Roberto's face. "But—but it was for the company that I did it," he protested. "I was only following orders."

Rhys nodded sympathetically. "Of course. You can explain that to the government at your trial." He rose to his feet and said to Elizabeth, "We'd better be starting back."

"Wait a minute," Roberto yelled. "You can't walk out and leave me like this."

Rhys said, "I think you're confused. *You're* the one who's leaving."

Tumas was mopping his brow again, his lips twitching uncontrollably. He walked over to the window and looked out. A heavy silence hung over the room. Finally, without turning, he said, "If I stay with the company—will I be protected?"

"All the way," Rhys assured him.

They were in the Mercedes, the thin dark chauffeur at the wheel, driving back to the city. "You blackmailed him," Elizabeth declared.

Rhys nodded. "We couldn't afford to lose him. He was going over to a competitor. He knows too much about our business. He would have sold us out."

Elizabeth looked at Rhys and thought, I have so much to learn about him.

That evening they went to Mirander for dinner, and Rhys was charming and amusing and impersonal. Elizabeth felt as though he were hiding behind a facade of words, putting up a verbal smoke screen to conceal his feelings. When they finished dinner, it was after midnight. Elizabeth wanted to be alone with Rhys. She had hoped they would return to the hotel. Instead he said, "I'm going to show you some of the night life in Rio."

They made the rounds of nightclubs, and everyone seemed to know Rhys. Wherever they went, he was the center of attenion, charming everyone. They were invited to join couples at other tables, and groups of people joined **them** at their table. Elizabeth and Rhys were never alone for a moment. It seemed to Elizabeth that it was intentional, that Rhys was deliberately putting a wall of people beween them. They had been friends before, and now they were—what? Elizabeth only knew that there was some unseen barrier between them. What was he afraid of and why?

At the fourth nightclub, where they had joined a table with half a dozen of Rhys's friends, Elizabeth decided she had had enough. She broke into the conversation between Rhys and a lovely-looking Spanish girl. "I haven't had a chance to dance with my husband. I'm sure you'll excuse us."

Rhys looked at her in quick surprise, then rose to his feet. "I'm afraid I've been neglecting my bride," he said lightly to the others. He took Elizabeth's arm and led her out to the dance floor. She was holding herself stiffly, and he looked at her face and said, "You're angry."

He was right, but it was an anger directed at herself. She had made the rules, and was upset now because Rhys would not break them. But it was more than that, of course. It was not knowing how Rhys felt. Was he sticking to their agreement because of a sense of honor, or because he was simply not interested in her? She had to know.

Rhys said, "Sorry about all these people, Liz, but they're in the business, and in one way or another they can be helpful to us."

So he was aware of her feelings. She could feel his arms around her, his body against hers. She thought, It feels right. Everything about Rhys was right for her. They belonged together. She knew it. But did he know how much she wanted him? Elizabeth's pride would not let her tell him. And yet he must feel something. She closed her eyes and pressed closer to him. Time had stopped and there was nothing but the two of them and the soft music and the magic of this moment. She could have gone on dancing forever in Rhys's arms. She relaxed and gave herself up to him completely and she began to feel his male hardness pressing against her thighs. She opened her eyes and looked up at him and there was something in his eyes she had never seen there before, an urgency, a wanting, that was a reflection of her own.

When he spoke, his voice was hoarse. He said, "Let's go back to the hotel."

And she could not speak.

When he helped her on with her wrap, his fingers burned her skin. They sat apart in the back of the limousine, afraid to touch. Elizabeth felt as if she were on fire. It seemed to her that it took an eternity for them to reach their suite. She did not think she could wait another moment. As the door closed, they came together in a wonderful wild hunger that swept through both of them. She was in his arms and there was a ferocity in him that she had never known. He picked her up and carried her into the bedroom. They could not get their clothes off quickly enough. We're like eager children, Elizabeth thought, and she wondered why it had taken Rhys all this time. But it did not matter now. Nothing mattered except their nakedness and the wonderful feel of his body against hers. They were in bed, exploring each other, and Elizabeth gently pulled away from his embrace and started kissing him, her tongue moving down his lean, taut body, embracing him with her lips, feeling his velvet hardness inside her mouth. His hands were on her hips, turning her on her side, and his mouth was running down between her thighs, parting them to his tongue and thrusting into the sweetness there, and when neither of them could bear it an instant longer, he moved on top of her and slowly slid inside her, thrusting deep and making gently circling motions and she began to move to his rhythm, their rhythm, the rhythm of the universe, and everything began to move faster and faster, spinning out of control, until there was a vast ecstatic explosion and the earth became still and peaceful again.

They lay there, holding each other close, and Elizabeth thought joyfully, *Mrs. Rhys Williams.*

CHAPTER
46

"Excuse me, Mrs. Williams," Henriette's voice said on the intercom, "there's a Detective Hornung here to see you. He says it's urgent."

Elizabeth turned to look up at Rhys, puzzled. They had just returned from Rio to Zurich the evening before, and they had only been in the office a few minutes. Rhys shrugged. "Tell her to send the man in. Let's find out what's so important."

A few moments later the three of them were seated in Elizabeth's office. "What did you want to see me about?" Elizabeth asked.

Max Hornung had no small talk. He said, "Someone is trying to murder you." As he watched the color drain from Elizabeth's face, Max was genuinely distressed, wondering if there might have been a more tactful way he could have phrased it.

Rhys Williams said, "What the hell are you talking about?"

Max continued to address himself to Elizabeth. "There have already been two attempts on your life. There will probably be more."

Elizabeth stammered, "I—you must be mistaken."

"No, ma'am. That elevator crash was meant to kill you."

She stared at him in silence, her dark eyes filled with bewilderment, and some other emotion buried deeper, that Max could not define. "So was the Jeep."

Elizabeth found her voice again. "You're wrong. That was an accident. There was nothing the matter with the Jeep. The police in Sardinia examined it."

"No."

"I saw them," Elizabeth insisted.

"No, ma'am. You saw them examine *a* Jeep. It wasn't yours."

They were both staring at him now.

Max went on, "Your Jeep was never in that garage. I found it in an auto junkyard at Olbia. The bolt that sealed the master cylinder had been loosened, and the brake fluid had run out. That's why you had no brakes. The left front fender was still bashed in and there were green markings on it from the sap of the trees you ran into. The lab checked it out. It matches."

The nightmare was back. Elizabeth felt it sweep through her, as though the floodgates of her hidden fears had suddenly opened, and she was filled again with the terror of that ride down the mountains.

Rhys was saying, "I don't understand. How could anyone—?"

Max turned to look at Rhys. "All Jeeps look alike. That's what they were counting on. When she crashed instead of going off the mountain, they had to improvise. They couldn't let anyone examine that Jeep because it had to look like an accident. They had expected it to be at the bottom of the sea. They probably would have finished her off there, but a maintenance crew came along, found her and took her to the hospital. They got hold of another Jeep, smashed it up a little and made the switch before the police came."

Rhys said, "You keep saying 'they.' "

"Whoever was behind it had help."

"Who—who would want to kill me?" Elizabeth asked.

"The same person who killed your father."

She had a sudden feeling of unreality, as if none of this was happening. It was all a nightmare that would go away.

"Your father was murdered," Max went on. "He was set up with a phony guide who killed him. Your father didn't go to Chamonix alone. There was someone with him."

When Elizabeth spoke, her voice was a hollow whisper. "Who?"

Max looked at Rhys and said, "Your husband."

The words echoed in her ears. They seemed to come from far away, fading in and out, and she wondered if she was losing her mind.

"Liz," Rhys said, "I wasn't there with Sam when he was killed."

"You were in Chamonix with him, Mr. Williams," Max insisted.

"That's true." Rhys was talking to Elizabeth now. "I left before Sam went on his climb."

She turned to look at him. "Why didn't you tell me?"

He hesitated a moment, then seemed to make a decision. "It's something I couldn't discuss with anyone. For the past year someone has been sabotaging Roffe and Sons. It was done very cleverly, so that it seemed to be a series of accidents. But I began to see a pattern. I went to Sam with it, and we decided to hire an outside agency to investigate."

Elizabeth knew then what was coming, and she was simultaneously filled with a deep sense of relief and a feeling of guilt. Rhys had known about the report all along. She should have trusted him enough to tell him about it, instead of keeping her fears to herself.

Rhys turned to Max Hornung, "Sam Roffe got a report that confirmed my suspicions. He asked me to go up to Chamonix to discuss it with him. I went. We decided to keep it just between the two of us until we could find out who was responsible for what was happening." When he continued, there was a note of bitterness in his voice. "Obviously, it wasn't kept quiet enough. Sam was killed because someone knew we were getting on to him. The report is missing."

"I had it," Elizabeth said. Rhys looked at her in surprise. "It was with Sam's personal effects." She said to Max, "The report indicates that it was someone on the board of Roffe and Sons, but they all have stock in the company. Why would they want to destroy it?"

Max explained, "They're not trying to destroy it, Mrs. Williams. They're trying to cause enough trouble to make the banks nervous enough to start calling in their loans. They wanted to force your father to sell the stock and go public. Whoever is behind this hasn't gotten what he wanted yet. Your life is still in danger."

"Then you've got to give her police protection," Rhys demanded.

Max blinked and said tonelessly, "I wouldn't worry about that, Mr. Williams. She hasn't been out of our sight since she married you."

CHAPTER
47

**Berlin.
Monday, December 1.
Ten a.m.**

The pain was unbearable and he had lived with it for four weeks.

The doctor had left some pills for him, but Walther Gassner was afraid to take them. He had to stay constantly alert to see that Anna did not try to kill him again, or to escape.

"You should get right to a hospital," the doctor had told him. "You've lost a good deal of blood——"

"No!" That was the last thing Walther wanted. Stab wounds were reported to the police. Walther had sent for the company doctor because he knew he would not report it. Walther could not afford to have the police snooping around. Not now. The doctor had silently stitched up the gaping wound, his eyes filled with curiosity. When he had finished, he had asked, "Would you like me to send a nurse to the house, Mr. Gassner?"

"No. My——my wife will take care of me."

That had been a month ago. Walther had telephoned his secretary and told her that he had had an accident and would be staying home.

He thought about that terrible moment when Anna had tried to kill him with the shears. He had turned just in time to catch the blade in his shoulder instead of through the heart. He had almost fainted from the pain and shock, but he had retained consciousness long enough to drag Anna to her bedroom and lock her in. And all the while she was screaming, "What have you done with the children? What have you done with the children? . . ."

Since then Walther had kept her in the bedroom. He prepared all her meals. He would take a tray up to Anna's room, unlock the door and enter. She would be huddled in a corner, cringing from him, and she would whisper, "What have you done with the children?"

Sometimes he would open the bedroom door and find her with her ear pressed against the wall, listening for the sounds of their son and daughter. The house was silent now, except for the two of them. Walther knew there was very little time left. His thoughts were interrupted by a faint noise. He listened. And then he heard it again. *Someone was moving around in the hallway upstairs. There was not supposed to be anyone in the house. He had locked all the doors himself.*

Upstairs, Frau Mendler was dusting. She was a dayworker, and this was only her second time in this house. She did not like it. When she had worked here on Wednesday the week before, Herr Gassner had followed her around as though expecting her to steal something. When she had tried to go upstairs to clean, he had angrily stopped her, given her her wages and sent her away. There was something about his manner that frightened her.

Today he was nowhere in sight, *Gott sei Dank*. Frau Mendler had let herself in with the key she had taken the week before, and she had gone upstairs. The house was unnaturally silent, and she decided that no one was at home. She had cleaned one bedroom and had found some loose change lying around, and a gold pillbox. She started down the hallway toward the next bedroom and tried to open the door. It was locked. Strange. She wondered if they kept something valuable inside. She turned the handle again, and a woman's voice from behind the door whispered, "Who is it?"

Frau Mendler jerked her hand away from the knob, startled.

"Who is it? Who's out there?"

"Frau Mendler, the cleaning lady. Do you want me to do your bedroom?"

"You can't. I'm locked in." The voice was louder now, filled with hysteria. "Help me! Please! Call the police. Tell them my husband has killed our children. He's going to kill me. Hurry! Get away from here before he—"

A hand spun Frau Mendler around and she found herself staring up into the face of Herr Gassner. He looked as pale as death.

"What are you sneaking around here for?" he demanded. He was holding her arm, hurting it.

"I—I'm not sneaking," she said. "Today is my day to clean. The agency—"

"I told the agency I didn't want anyone here. I—" He stopped. Had he telephoned the agency? He had meant to, but he was in such pain that he could no longer remember. Frau Mendler looked into his eyes and she was terrified by what she saw there.

"They never told me," she said.

He stood still, listening for sounds from behind the locked door. Silence.

He turned to Frau Mendler. "Get out of here. Don't come back."

She could not leave the house fast enough. He had not paid her, but she had the gold pillbox and the coins she had found on the dresser. She felt sorry for the poor woman behind the door. She wished she could help her, but she could not afford to get involved. She had a police record.

In Zurich, Detective Max Hornung was reading a teletype from Interpol headquarters in Paris.

INVOICE NUMBER ON SNUFF FILM RAW STOCK USED FOR ROFFE AND SONS GENERAL EXECUTIVE ACCOUNT. PURCHASING AGENT NO LONGER WITH COMPANY. TRYING TO TRACE. WILL KEEP YOU INFORMED. END MESSAGE.

In Paris the police were fishing a nude body out of the Seine. She was a blonde in her late teens. She wore a red ribbon around her neck.

In Zurich, Elizabeth Williams had been placed under twenty-four-hour police protection.

CHAPTER

48

The white light flashed, signaling a call on Rhys's private line. Fewer than half a dozen people had the number. He picked up the telephone. "Hello."

"Good morning, darling." There was no mistaking the husky, distinctive voice.

"You shouldn't be calling me."

She laughed. "You never used to worry about things like that. Don't tell me that Elizabeth has tamed you already."

"What do you want?" Rhys asked.

"I want to see you this afternoon."

"That's impossible."

"Don't make me cross, Rhys. Shall I come to Zurich or—?"

"No. I can't see you here." He hesitated. "I'll come there."

"That's better. Our usual place, *chéri.*"

And Hélène Roffe-Martel hung up.

Rhys replaced the receiver slowly and sat thinking. As far as he was concerned, he had had a brief physical affair with an exciting woman, and it had been finished for some time. But Hélène was not a woman who let go easily. She was bored with Charles, and she wanted Rhys. "You and I would make a perfect team," she had said, and Hélène Roffe-Martel could be very determined. And very dangerous. Rhys decided the trip to Paris was necessary. He had to make her understand once and for all that there could be nothing further between them.

A few moments later he walked into Elizabeth's office, and her eyes brightened. She put her arms around him and whispered, "I've been thinking about you. Let's go home and play hooky this afternoon."

He grinned. "You're becoming a sex maniac."

She held him closer. "I know. Isn't it lovely?"

"I'm afraid I have to fly to Paris this afternoon, Liz."

She tried to conceal her disappointment. "Shall I come with you?"

"No point. It's just a minor business problem. I'll be back tonight. We'll have a late supper."

When Rhys walked into the familiar small hotel on the Left Bank, Hélène was already there, seated in the dining room, waiting for him. Rhys had never known her to be late. She was organized and efficient, extraordinarily beautiful, intelligent, a wonderful lover; and yet something was missing. Hélène was a woman without compassion. There was a ruthlessness about her, a killer's instinct. Rhys had seen others hurt by it. He had no intention of becoming one of her victims. He sat down at the table.

She said, "You're looking well, darling. Marriage agrees with you. Is Elizabeth taking good care of you in bed?"

He smiled to take the sting out of his words. "That's none of your business."

Hélène leaned forward and took one of his hands, "Ah, but it is, *chéri*. It is *our* business."

She began stroking his hand, and he thought of her in bed. A tiger, wild, skilled and insatiable. He withdrew his hand.

Hélène's eyes chilled. She said, "Tell me, Rhys. How does it feel to be president of Roffe and Sons?"

He had almost forgotten how ambitious she was, how greedy. He remembered the long conversations they had once had. She was obsessed by the idea of taking control of the company. *You and I, Rhys. If Sam were out of the way, we could run it.*

Even in the midst of their lovemaking: *It's my company, darling. Samuel Roffe's blood is in me. It's mine. I want it. Fuck me, Rhys.*

Power was Hélène's aphrodisiac. And danger. "What did you want to see me about?" Rhys asked.

"I think it's time you and I made some plans."

"I don't know what you're talking about."

She said maliciously, "I know you too well, darling. You're as ambitious as I am. Why did you serve as Sam's shadow all those years when you had dozens of offers to run other companies? Because you knew that one day you would be running Roffe and Sons."

"I stayed because I liked Sam."

She grinned. "Of course, *chéri*. And now you've married his charming little daughter." She took a thin black cigar from her purse and lit it with a platinum lighter. "Charles tells me that Elizabeth has arranged to keep control of the stock and that she refuses to sell."

"That's right, Hélène."

"It's occurred to you, of course, that if she had an accident, you would inherit her estate."

Rhys stared at her for a long time.

CHAPTER
49

In his home in Olgiata, Ivo Palazzi was casually looking out the window of his living room when he saw a terrifying sight. Coming up the driveway were Donatella and their three sons. Simonetta was upstairs, taking a nap. Ivo hurried out the front door and went to meet his second family. He was filled with such rage that he could have killed. He had been so wonderful to this woman, so kind, so loving, and now she was deliberately trying to destroy his career, his marriage, his life. He watched Donatella get out of the Lancia Flavia he had so generously given her. Ivo thought she had never looked more beautiful. The boys climbed out of the car, and were hugging and kissing him. Oh, how Ivo loved them. Oh, how he hoped that Simonetta would not wake up from her nap!

"I came to see your wife," Donatella said stiffly. She turned to the boys. "Come on, boys."

"No!" Ivo commanded.

"How are you going to stop me? If I don't see her today, I'll see her tomorrow."

Ivo was cornered. There was no way out. Yet he knew that he could not let her or anyone else ruin everything he had worked so hard for. Ivo thought of himself as a decent man, and he hated what he must do. Not just for himself, but for Simonetta and Donatella and all his children.

"You will have your money," Ivo promised. "Give me five days."

Donatella looked into his eyes. "Five days," she said.

In London, Sir Alec Nichols was taking part in a floor debate in the House of Commons. He had been chosen to make a major policy speech dealing with the crucial subject of the labor strikes that were crippling the British economy. But it was difficult for him to concentrate. He was thinking about the series of telephone calls he had received over the past few weeks. They had managed to find him wherever he was, at his club, at his barber, restaurants, business meetings. And each time Alec had hung up on them. He knew that what they were asking was only the beginning. Once they controlled him, they would find a way to take over his stock, they would own a piece of a gigantic pharmaceutical company that manufactured drugs of every description. He could not let that happen. They had begun telephoning him four and five times a day until his nerves were stretched to the breaking point. What worried Alec now was that on this day he had *not* heard from them. He had expected a call at breakfast, and then again when he had lunched at White's. But there were no calls and somehow he could not shake off the feeling that the silence was more ominous than the threats. He tried to push these thoughts away now as he addressed the House.

"No man has been a stauncher friend of labor than I. Our labor force is what makes our country great. Workers feed our mills, turn the wheels in our factories. They are the true elite of this country, the backbone that makes England stand tall and strong among nations." He paused. "However, there comes a time in the fortunes of every nation when certain sacrifices must be made . . ."

He spoke by rote. He was wondering whether he had frightened them off by calling their bluff. After all, they were just small-time hoodlums. He was Sir Alec Nichols, Baronet, M.P. What could they do to him? In all probability he would not hear from them again. From now on they would leave him in peace. Sir Alec finished his speech amid vociferous applause from the back benches.

He was on his way out when an attendant came up to him and said, "I have a message for you, Sir Alec."

Alec turned. "Yes?"

"You're to go home as quickly as possible. There has been an accident."

They were carrying Vivian into the ambulance when Alec arrived at the house. The doctor was at her side. Alec slammed the car against the curb and was out running before it had stopped. He took one look at Vivian's white unconscious face and turned to the doctor. "What happened?"

The doctor said helplessly, "I don't know, Sir Alec. I received an anonymous call that there had been an accident. When I got here, I found Lady Nichols on the floor of her bedroom. Her—her kneecaps had been hammered to the floor with spikes."

Alec closed his eyes, fighting off the spasm of nausea that gripped him. He could feel the bile rising in his throat.

"We'll do everything we can, of course, but I think you had better be prepared. It's unlikely that she'll ever walk again."

Alec felt as though he could not breathe. He started toward the ambulance.

"She's under heavy sedation," the doctor said. "I don't think she'll recognize you."

Alec did not even hear him. He climbed into the ambulance and sat in a jump seat, staring down at his wife, obvious to the back doors being closed, the sound of the siren, and the ambulance beginning to move. He took Vivian's cold hands in his. Her eyes opened. "Alec." Her voice was a slurred whisper.

Alec's eyes filled with tears. "Oh, my darling, my darling . . ."

"Two men . . . wore masks . . . they held me down . . . broke my legs. . . . I'll never be able to dance again . . . I'm going to be a cripple, Alec. . . . Will you still want me?"

He buried his head in her shoulder and wept. They were tears of despair and agony, and yet there was something else, something he hardly dared admit to himself. He felt a sense of relief. If Vivian were crippled, he would be able to take care of her, she could never leave him for anyone else.

But Alec knew that this was not over. They were not finished with him. This was only their warning. The only way he would ever get rid of them was to give them what they wanted.

Quickly.

CHAPTER

50

It was exactly noon when the call came through the switchboard at the Kriminal Polizei headquarters in Zurich. It was routed through to Chief Inspector Schmied's office, and when the chief inspector had finished talking, he went to find Detective Max Hornung.

"It's all over," he told Max. "The Roffe case has been solved. They've found the killer. Get out to the airport. You've just got time to catch your plane."

Max blinked at him. "Where am I going?"

"To Berlin."

Chief Inspector Schmied telephoned Elizabeth Williams. "I am calling to bring you some good news," he said. "You will no longer need a bodyguard. The murderer has been caught."

Elizabeth found herself gripping the telephone. At long last she was going to learn the name of her faceless enemy. "Who is it?" she asked.

"Walther Gassner."

They were speeding along the autobahn, heading for Wannsee. Max was in the back seat, next to Major Wageman, and two detectives sat in front. They had met Max at Tempelhof Airport, and Major Wageman had briefed Max on the situation as they drove. "The house is surrounded, but we have to be careful how we move in. He's holding his wife hostage."

Max asked, "How did you get on to Walther Gassner?"

"Through you. That's why I thought you would like to be here."

Max was puzzled. "Through me?"

"You told me about the psychiatrist he visited. On a hunch, I sent out Gassner's description to other psychiatrists and found out that he had gone to half a dozen of them, looking for help. Each time he used a different name, then ran away. He knew how ill he was. His wife had phoned us for help a couple of months ago, but when one of our men went out to investigate, she sent him away." They were turning off the autobahn now, only a few minutes from the house. "This morning we received a call from a cleaning woman, a Frau Mendler. She told us she was working at the Gassner house on Monday and that she talked to Mrs. Gassner through the locked door of her bedroom. Mrs. Gassner told her that her husband had killed their two children and was going to kill her."

Max blinked. "This happened on *Monday?* And the woman didn't call you until this morning?"

"Frau Mendler has a long police record. She was

afraid to come to us. Last night she told her boy-friend what had happened, and this morning they decided to call us."

They had reached the Wannsee. The car pulled up a block away from the entrance to the Gassner estate, behind an unmarked sedan. A man got out of the sedan and hurried toward Major Wageman and Max. "He's still inside the house, Major. I have men all around the grounds."

"Do you know if the woman is still alive?"

The man hesitated. "No, sir. All the blinds are drawn."

"All right. Let's make it fast and quiet. Get every-one in place. Five minutes."

The man hurried off. Major Wageman reached into the car and pulled out a small walkie-talkie. He began rapidly to issue orders. Max was not listening. He was thinking of something that Major Wageman had said to him a few minutes ago. Something that made no sense. But there was no time to ask him about it now. Men were starting to move toward the house, using trees and shrubs as cover. Major Wage-man turned to Max. "Coming, Hornung?"

It seemed to Max that there was an army of men infiltrating the garden. Some of them were supplied with telescopic rifles and armored vests; others car-ried snubnosed tear gas rifles. The operation was carried out with mathematical precision. At a signal from Captain Wageman, tear gas grenades were simultaneously hurled through the downstairs and upstairs windows of the house and at the same instant the front and rear doors were smashed in by men wearing gas masks. Behind them came more detectives with drawn guns.

When Max and Major Wageman ran through the

open front door, the hallway was filled with acrid smoke, but it was rapidly being dispersed by the open windows and doors. Two detectives were bringing Walther Gassner into the hallway in handcuffs. He was wearing a robe and pajamas and he was unshaven and his face looked gaunt and his eyes swollen.

Max stared at him, seeing him for the first time in person. Somehow he seemed unreal to Max. It was the *other* Walther Gassner who was real, the man in the computer, whose life had been spelled out in digits. Which was the shadow and which was the substance?

Major Wageman said, "You're under arrest, Herr Gassner. Where is your wife?"

Walther Gassner said hoarsely, "She's not here. She's gone! I—"

Upstairs there was the sound of a door being forced open, and a moment later a detective called down, "I've found her. She was locked in her room."

The detective appeared on the staircase, supporting a trembling Anna Gassner. Her hair was stringy and her face was streaked and blotchy, and she was sobbing.

"Oh, thank God," she said. "Thank God you've come!"

Gently the detective led her downstairs toward the group standing in the enormous reception hall. When Anna Gassner looked up and saw her husband, she began to scream.

"It's all right, Frau Gassner," Major Wageman said soothingly. "He can't harm you anymore."

"My children," she cried. "He killed my children!"

Max was watching Walther Gassner's face. He was

staring at his wife with an expression of utter hopelessness. He looked broken and lifeless.

"Anna," he whispered. "Oh, Anna."

Major Wageman said, "You have the right to remain silent or to ask for a lawyer. For your own sake I hope you will cooperate with us."

Walther was not listening. "Why did you have to call them, Anna?" he pleaded. "Why? Weren't we happy together?"

"The children are dead," Anna Gassner shrieked. "They're dead."

Major Wageman looked at Walther Gassner and asked, "Is that true?"

Walther nodded, and his eyes looked old and defeated. "Yes . . . They're dead."

"Murderer! Murderer!" his wife was shrieking.

Major Wageman said, "We would like you to show us the bodies. Will you do that?"

Walther Gassner was crying now, the tears rolling down his cheeks. He could not speak.

Major Wageman said, "Where are they?"

It was Max who answered. "The children are buried in Saint Paul's graveyard."

Everyone in the room turned to stare at him. "They died at birth five years ago." Max explained.

"Murderer!" Anna Gassner screamed at her husband.

And they turned and saw the madness blazing out of her eyes.

CHAPTER
51

The cold winter night had fallen, snuffing out the brief twilight. It had begun to snow, a soft, wind-blown powder that dusted the city. In the administration building of Roffe and Sons, the lights of the deserted offices glowed against the darkness like pale yellow moons.

In her office Elizabeth was alone, working late, waiting for Rhys to return from Geneva, where he had gone for a meeting. She wished that he would hurry. Everyone had long since left the building. Elizabeth felt restless, unable to concentrate. She could not get Walther and Anna out of her mind. She remembered Walther as she had first met him, boyish and handsome and madly in love with Anna. Or pretending to be. It was so hard to believe that Walther was responsible for all those terrible acts. Elizabeth's heart went out to Anna. Elizabeth had ried several times to telephone her, but there had

425

been no answer. She would fly to Berlin, to give her whatever comfort she could. The telephone rang, startling her. She picked it up. It was Alec on the other end of the line, and Elizabeth was pleased to hear his voice.

"You've heard about Walther?" Alec asked.

"Yes. It's horrible. I can't believe it."

"Don't, Elizabeth."

She thought she had misunderstood him. "What?"

"Don't believe it. Walther's not guilty."

"The police said—"

"They've made a mistake. Walther was the first person Sam and I checked out. We cleared him. He's not the one we were looking for."

Elizabeth stared at the phone, filled with a sense of confusion. *He's not the one we were looking for.* She said, "I—I don't understand what you're saying."

Alec replied hesitantly, "It's awkward doing this over a telephone, Elizabeth, but I haven't had an opportunity to speak to you alone."

"Speak to me about what?" Elizabeth asked.

"For the past year," Alec said, "someone has been sabotaging the company. There was an explosion in one of our South American factories, patents have been stolen, dangerous drugs have been mislabeled. There isn't time to go into it all now. I went to Sam and suggested that we engage an outside investigating agency to try to find out who was behind it. We agreed not to discuss it with anyone else."

It was as though the earth had suddenly stopped and time was frozen. A dizzying feeling of *déjà vu* swept through Elizabeth. Alec's words were coming through the telephone, but it was Rhys's voice she was hearing. Rhys saying, *Someone has been sabotaging Roffe and Sons. It was done very cleverly, so that it seemed to be a series of accidents. But I began to see a pattern. I went to Sam with it and we decided to hire an outside agency to investigate.*

Alec's voice was going on. "They finished their report and Sam took it with him to Chamonix. We discussed it over the telephone."

Elizabeth could hear Rhys's voice saying, *Sam asked me to come up to Chamonix to discuss it with him. . . . We decided to keep it just between the two of us until we could find out who was responsible for what was happening.*

Elizabeth was suddenly finding it hard to breathe. When she spoke, she tried to make her voice sound normal. "Alec, who—who else knew about the report beside you and Sam?"

"No one. That was the whole point. According to Sam, the report showed that whoever was guilty had to be someone high up in the company."

The highest echelon. And Rhys had not mentioned being in Chamonix until the detective had brought it up.

She asked slowly, the words dragged out of her, "Could Sam have told Rhys about it?"

"No. Why?"

There was only one way Rhys could have known what was in the report. He had stolen it. There was only one reason he could have gone to Chamonix. To kill Sam. Elizabeth did not hear the rest of what Alec was saying. The roaring in her ears drowned out his words. She dropped the receiver, her head spinning, fighting off the horror that was starting to engulf her. Her mind was a series of chaotic, jumbled images. At the time she had had the Jeep accident, she had left a message for Rhys that she would be in Sardinia. The night of the elevator crash, Rhys had not been at the board meeting, but he had appeared later when she and Kate were alone. *Thought I ought to give you a hand.* And soon afterward he had left the building. *Or had he?* Her body was trembling now. It had to be some terrible mistake. Not Rhys. *No!* It was a scream in her mind.

Elizabeth rose from the desk and on unsteady legs walked through the connecting door to Rhys's office. The room was dark. She turned on the lights and stood looking around uncertainly, not sure what she expected to find. She was not searching for evidence of Rhys's guilt, she was looking for evidence of his innocence. It was unbearable to think that the man she loved, the man who had held her in his arms and made love to her, could be a cold-blooded murderer.

There was an engagement book on Rhys's desk. Elizabeth opened it, turning the pages back to September, to the holiday weekend of the Jeep accident. Nairobi was marked on his calendar. She would need to check his passport to see if he had gone there. She started to look through Rhys's desk for the passport, feeling guilty, knowing that somehow there had to be an innocent explanation.

The bottom drawer of Rhys's desk was locked. Elizabeth hesitated. She knew she had no right to break into it. Somehow it was a violation of faith, the crossing of a forbidden boundary, from which there could be no return. Rhys would know that she had done this and she would have to tell him why. And yet Elizabeth had to know. She picked up a letter opener from the desk and broke the lock, splintering the wood.

In the drawer were stacks of notes and memoranda. She lifted them out. There was an envelope addressed to Rhys Williams in a woman's handwriting. It was postmarked a few days earlier, from Paris. Elizabeth hesitated a moment, then opened it. The letter was from Hélène. It began, *"Chéri,* I tried to reach you by phone. It is urgent that we meet again soon to make our plans. . . ."* Elizabeth did not finish reading the letter.

She was staring at the stolen report in the drawer.

MR. SAM ROFFE
CONFIDENTIAL
NO COPIES

She felt the room begin to spin and she clutched the edge of the desk for support. She stood there forever, eyes closed, waiting for the dizziness to pass. Her killer had a face now. It was the face of her husband.

The silence was broken by the insistent ringing of a distant telephone. It took Elizabeth a long time to realize where the sound was coming from. Slowly she walked back to her office. She picked up the telephone.

It was the attendant in the lobby, his voice cheerful. "Just checkin' that you're still there, Mrs. Williams. Mr. Williams is on his way up to you."

To stage another accident.

Her life was all that stood between Rhys and the control of Roffe and Sons. She could not face him, could not pretend that nothing was wrong. The moment he saw her, he would know. She had to escape. In a blind panic, Elizabeth grabbed her purse and coat and started out of the office. She stopped. She had forgotten somehing. Her passport! She had to get far away from Rhys, someplace where he could not find her. She hurried back to her desk, found the passport and ran out into the corridor, her heart pounding as though it would burst. The indicator on the private elevator was swinging upward.

Eight ... nine ... ten ...

Elizabeth began racing down the stairs, running for her life.

CHAPTER
52

There was a ferryboat that ran between Civitavecchia and Sardinia, carrying passengers and automobiles. Elizabeth drove aboard in a rental car, lost among a dozen other cars. Airports kept records, but the huge boat was anonymous. Elizabeth was one of a hundred passengers crossing over to the island of Sardinia for a holiday. She was sure she could not have been followed, and yet she was filled with an unreasoning fear. Rhys had gone too far to let anything stop him now. She was the only one who could expose him. He would have to get rid of her.

When Elizabeth had fled from the building, she had had no idea where she was going. She knew only that she must get out of Zurich and hide somewhere, that she would not be safe until Rhys was caught. *Sardinia*. It was the first place she thought of. She had rented a small car and had stopped at a phone booth along the auto route to Italy and had tried to call Alec. He was out. She left a message for him to call her in Sardinia. Unable to reach Detective Max Hornung, she left the same message for him.

She would be at the villa in Sardinia. But this time she would not be alone. The police would be there to protect her.

When the ferryboat landed in Olbia, Elizabeth found that it would not be necessary to go to the police. They were waiting for her in the person of Bruno Campagna, the detective she had met with Chief of Police Ferraro. It had been Campagna who had taken her to look at the Jeep following the accident. The detective hurried over to Elizabeth's car and said, "We were beginning to get very worried about you, Mrs. Williams."

Elizabeth looked at him, surprised.

"We received a call from the Swiss police," Campagna explained, "asking us to keep an eye out for you. We've been covering all the boats and airports."

Elizabeth was filled with a feeling of gratitude. Max Hornung! He had gotten her message. Detective Campagna looked at her tired, drawn face. "Would you like me to drive?"

"Please," Elizabeth said gratefully.

She slid over to the passenger seat, and the tall detective got behind the wheel. "Where would you rather wait—the police station or your villa?"

"The villa, if someone could stay with me. I'd— I'd rather not be there alone."

Campagna nodded reassuringly. "Don't worry. We have orders to keep you well guarded. I'll stay there with you tonight, and we'll have a radio car stationed at the driveway leading to your place. No one will be able to get near you."

His confidence was enough to let Elizabeth relax. Detective Campagna drove swiftly and expertly, winding through the little streets of Olbia, heading up the mountain road that led to the Costa Smeralda. Every place they passed reminded her of Rhys.

Elizabeth asked, "Has there been any—any news of my husband?"

Detective Campagna gave her a quick, compassionate glance, then turned his eyes back to the road. "He's on the run, but he won't get far. They expect to have him in custody by morning."

Elizabeth knew that she should feel a sense of relief, and instead the words brought a terrible, aching pain. It was Rhys they were talking about, Rhys who was being hunted like some animal. He had placed her in this terrible nightmare, and now he was caught up in his own nightmare, fighting for his life, as he had made her fight for hers. And how she had trusted him! How she had believed in his kindness and his gentleness and his love! She shuddered. Detective Campagna asked her, "Are you cold?"

"No. I'm fine." She felt feverish. A warm wind seemed to be whistling through the car, setting her nerves on edge. At first she thought it was her imagination until Detective Campagna said, "I'm afraid we're in for a scirocco. It's going to be a busy night."

Elizabeth understood what he meant. The scirocco could drive people and animals crazy. The wind blew in from the Sahara, hot and dry and grainy with sand, with a macabre keening sound that had an eerie, unbalancing effect on the nerves. The crime rate always went up during a scirocco, and the judges treated criminals leniently.

An hour later, out of the dark, the villa loomed ahead of them. Detective Campagna turned into the driveway, drove into the empty carport and turned off the engine. He walked around to the side of the car and opened Elizabeth's door. "I'd like you to stay right behind me, Mrs. Williams," he said. "Just in case."

"All right," Elizabeth replied.

They moved toward the front door of the darkened

villa. Detective Campagna said, "I'm sure he's not here but we won't take any chances. May I have your key?"

Elizabeth handed him the key. He gently edged her to one side of the door, inserted the key and opened the door, his other hand hovering near his gun. He reached inside and flicked on the light switch, and the hallway was suddenly flooded with brilliant light.

"I'd like you to show me the house," Detective Campagna said. "Make sure we cover every room. Okay?"

"Yes."

They started walking through the house, and everywhere they went the huge detective turned the lights on. He looked in all the closets and corners and checked to make sure the windows and doors were locked There was no one else in the house When they returned to the living room downstairs, Detective Campagna said, "If you don't mind, I'd like to call headquarters."

"Of course," Elizabeth said. She led him into the study.

He picked up the telephone and dialed. A moment later he said, "Detective Campagna. We're at the villa. I'll camp here for the night You can send a cruiser up to park at the foot of the driveway." He listened a moment, then said into the phone, "She's fine. Just a little tired. I'll check in later." He replaced the receiver.

Elizabeth sank into a chair. She was feeling tense and nervous, but she knew that it was going to be worse tomorrow Much worse. She would be safe but Rhys would be either dead or in prison. Somehow, in spite of everything he had done, she could not bear the thought of that.

Detective Campagna was studying her, a look of concern on his face. "I could use a cup of coffee," he said. "How about you?"

She nodded. "I'll make some." She started to rise.

"You stay where you are, Mrs. Williams. My wife says I make the best coffee in the world."

Elizabeth managed a smile. "Thank you." She sank back gratefully. She had not realized how emotionally drained she felt. For the first time now, Elizabeth admitted to herself that even during the telephone conversation with Alec she had felt that there might be some mistake, some explanation, that Rhys must be innocent. Even while she was fleeing, she had held on to the thought that he could not have done all those terrible things, that he could not have killed her father and then made love to her and tried to kill her. It would take a monster to do those things. And so she had kept that tiny ember of hope flickering in her. It had died when Detective Campagna had said, *He's on the run, but he won't get far. They expect to have him in custody by morning.*

She could not bear to think about it anymore, but she could think of nothing else. How long had Rhys been planning to take over the company? Probably from the moment he had met that impressionable fifteen-year-old girl, alone and lonely in a Swiss boarding school. That was when he must have first decided how he was going to outwit Sam—through his daughter. How easy it had been for him. The dinner at Maxim's and the long friendly talks during the years, and the charm—oh, the incredible charm! He had been patient. He had waited until she had become a woman, and the greatest irony of all was that Rhys did not even have to woo her. She had wooed *him*. How he must have laughed at her. He and Hélène Elizabeth wondered whether they were in it together, and she wondered where Rhys was now, and whether the police would kill him when they caught him. She began to weep uncontrollably.

"Mrs. Williams . . ." Detective Campagna was standing over her, holding out a cup of coffee.

"Drink this," he said "You'll feel better."

"I—I'm sorry," Elizabeth apologized. "I don't usually carry on this way."

He said to her gently, "I think you're doing *molto bene*."

Elizabeth took a sip of the hot coffee. He had put something in it. She looked up at him, and he grinned. "I decided a shot of Scotch wouldn't do you any harm."

He sat down across from her in a companionable silence. She was grateful for his company. She could never have stayed here alone. Not until she knew what had happened to Rhys, not until she knew whether he was dead or alive. She finished her coffee.

Detective Campagna looked at his watch. "The patrol car should be here any minute. There'll be two men in it on guard duty all night. I'll stay downstairs. I suggest you go up to bed now and try to get some sleep."

Elizabeth shivered. "I couldn't sleep." But even as she said it, her body was filled with an enormous lassitude. The long drive and the tremendous strain she had been under for so long were finally taking their toll.

"Maybe I'll just lie down for a bit," she said. She found it difficult to get the words out.

* * *

Elizabeth lay in her bed, fighting against sleep. Somehow it did not seem fair that she should be asleep while Rhys was being hunted. She visualized him being shot down on some cold dark street and she shuddered. She tried to keep her eyes open, but they were heavy weights, and the instant they closed she began to feel herself sinking down, down, into a soft cushion of nothingness.

Sometime later she was awakened by the screams.

CHAPTER

53

Elizabeth sat up in bed, her heart beating wildly, not knowing what it was that had awakened her. Then she heard it again. An eerie, high-pitched scream that seemed to come from right outside her window, the sound of someone in the agony of death. Elizabeth arose and stumbled over to the window and looked out into the night. It was a landscape by Daumier, lit by a chill winter moon. The trees were black and stark, their branches whipped by a wild wind. In the distance, far below, the sea was a boiling caldron.

The scream came again. And again. And Elizabeth realized what it was. The singing rocks. The sirocco had risen in intensity and was blowing through them, making that terrible keening sound, over and over. And it became Rhys's voice she was hearing, crying out for her, begging her to help him. She could not stand it. She covered her ears with her hands, but the sound would not go away.

Elizabeth started toward the bedroom door, and she was surprised at how weak she was. Her mind was hazy with exhaustion. She walked out into the hallway and started down the stairs. She felt dazed, as though she had been drugged. She tried to call out to Detective Campagna, but her voice was a hoarse croak. She kept descending the long flight of stairs, fighting to keep her balance. She called aloud, "Detective Campagna."

There was no answer. Elizabeth stumbled into the living room. He was not there. She moved from room to room, holding on to furniture to keep from falling down.

Detective Campagna was not in the house.

She was alone.

Elizabeth stood in the hallway, her mind confused, trying to force herself to think. The detective had stepped outside to talk to the policemen in the patrol car. Of course that was it. She walked to the front door and opened it and looked outside.

No one was there. Only the black night and the screaming wind. With a growing feeling of fear, Elizabeth turned and made her way back to the study. She would call the police station and find out what had happened. She picked up the telephone, and the line was dead.

It was at that instant that all the lights went out.

CHAPTER
54

In London, at Westminster Hospital, Vivian Nichols regained consciousness as she was being wheeled out of the operating room, down the long bleak corridor. The operation had taken eight hours. In spite of everything the skilled surgeons had been able to do, she would never walk again. She woke in agonizing pain, whispering Alec's name over and over. She needed him, she needed to have him at her side, to have him promise that he would still love her.

The hospital staff was unable to locate Alec.

In Zurich, in the communications room of the Kriminal Polizei, an Interpol message was received from Australia. The former film purchasing agent for Roffe and Sons had been located in Sydney. He had died of a heart attack three days earlier. His ashes were being shipped home. Interpol had been unable to obtain any information regarding the purchase of the film. They were awaiting further instructions.

In Berlin, Walther Gassner was seated in the discreet waiting room of an exclusive private sanatorium in a pleasant suburb outside the city. He had been there, motionless for almost ten hours. From time to time a nurse or an attendant would stop by to speak to him and offer him something to eat or drink. Walther paid no attention to them. He was waiting for his Anna.

It would be a long wait.

In Olgiata, Simonetta Palazzi was listening to a woman's voice on the telephone. "My name is Donatella Spolini," the voice said. "We've never met, Mrs. Palazzi, but we have a great deal in common. I suggest we meet for luncheon at the Bolognese in the Piazza del Popolo. Shall we say one o'clock tomorrow?"

Simonetta had a conflicting appointment at the beauty parlor the next day, but she adored mysteries. "I'll be there," she said. "How will I know you?"

"I'll have my three sons with me."

In her villa in Le Vésinet, Hélène Roffe-Martel was reading a note she had found waiting for her on the mantelpiece in the drawing room. It was from Charles. He had left her, run away. "You will never see me again," the note said. "Don't try to find me." Hélène tore the note into small pieces. She would see him again. She would find him.

In Rome, Max Hornung was at Leonardo da Vinci Airport. For the past two hours he had been trying to get a message through to Sardinia, but because of the storm all communications were down. Max went back to the flight operations office to talk to the airport manager again. "You've *got* to get me on a plane to Sardinia," Max said. "Believe me, it's a matter of life and death."

The airport manager said, "I believe you, signore,

but there is nothing I can do about it. Sardinia is shut up tight. The airports are closed. Even the boats have stopped running. Nothing is going in or out of that island until the scirocco is over."

"When will that be?" Max asked.

The airport manager turned to study the large weather map on the wall. "It looks like it's good for at least another twelve hours."

Elizabeth Williams would not be alive in twelve hours.

CHAPTER
55

The dark was hostile, filled with invisible enemies waiting to strike at her. And Elizabeth realized now that she was completely at their mercy Detective Campagna had brought her here to be murdered. He was Rhys's man. Elizabeth remembered Max Hornung explaining about switching the Jeeps. *Whoever did it had help. Someone who knew the island.* How convincing Detective Campagna had been. *We've been covering all the boats and airports.* Because Rhys had known she would come here to hide. *Where would you like to wait—at the police station or your villa?* Detective Campagna had had no intention of letting her go to the police. It had not been headquarters he had phoned. It had been Rhys. *We're at the villa.*

Elizabeth knew she had to flee, but she no longer had the strength. She was fighting to keep her eyes open, and her arms and legs felt heavy. She suddenly realized why. He had drugged her coffee. Elizabeth turned and made her way into the dark kitchen. She opened a cabinet and fumbled around until she found what she wanted. She took down a bottle of vinegar and splashed some into a glass with water and forced herself to drink it. Immediately she began to retch into the sink. In a few minutes she felt a little better, but she was still weak. Her brain refused to function. It was as if all the circuits inside her had already closed down, were preparing for the darkness of death.

"No," she told herself fiercely. "You're not going to die like that. You're going to fight. They're going to have to kill you." She raised her voice and said, "Rhys, come and kill me," but her voice was barely a whisper. She turned and headed for the hallway, feeling her way by instinct. She stopped under the portrait of old Samuel, while outside the moaning, alien wind tore against the house, screaming at her, taunting her, warning her. She stood there in the blackness, alone, facing a choice of terrors. She could go outside, into the unknown, and try to escape from Rhys, or she could stay here and try to fight him. But how?

Her mind was trying to tell her something but she was still dazed by the drug. She could not concentrate. Something about an accident.

She remembered then and said aloud. "He has to make it look like an accident."

You must stop him, Elizabeth. Had Samuel spoken? Or was it in her mind?

"I can't. It's too late." Her eyes were closing, and her face was pressed against the coolness of the portrait. It would be so wonderful to go to sleep. But there was something she had to do. She tried to remember what it was, but it kept slipping away.

Don't let it look like an accident. Make it look like murder. Then the company will never belong to him.

Elizabeth knew what she had to do. She walked into the study. She stood there a moment, then

446

reached for a table lamp and hurled it against a mirror. She could hear them both smash. She lifted a small chair and pounded it against the wall until the chair began to splinter. She moved over to the bookcase and began ripping pages out of the books, scattering them around the room. She tore the useless telephone cord out of the wall. Let Rhys explain this to the police, she thought. Do not go gentle into that good night. Well, she would not go gentle. They would have to take her by force.

A sudden gale swept through the room, swirling the papers through the air, then died away. It took Elizabeth a moment to realize what had happened. She was no longer alone in the house.

At Leonardo da Vinci Airport, near the *merci* area where freight was handled, Detective Max Hornung was watching a helicopter land. By the time the pilot had his door open Max was at his side. "Can you fly me to Sardinia?" he asked.

The pilot stared at him. "What's going on? I just flew somebody there. There's a bad storm blowing."

"Will you take me?"

"It'll cost you triple."

Max did not even hesitate. He climbed into the helicopter. As they took off, Max turned to the pilot and asked, "Who was the passenger you took to Sardinia?"

"His name was Williams."

The dark was Elizabeth's ally now, concealing her from her killer. It was too late to get away. She had to try to find a place to hide somewhere in the house. She went upstairs, putting distance between herself and Rhys. At the top of the stairs she hesitated, then turned toward Sam's bedroom. Something leaped at her out of the dark, and she started to scream, but it was only the shadow of a wind-whipped tree through the window. Her heart was pounding so hard that she was sure that Rhys would be able to hear it downstairs.

Delay him, her mind said. *But how?* Her head felt heavy. Everything was fuzzy. Think! she told herself. What would old Samuel have done? She walked to the bedroom at the end of the hall, took the key from the inside and locked the door from the outside. Then she locked the other doors and they were the doors of the gates of the ghetto in Krakow, and Elizabeth was not sure why she was doing it, and then she remembered that she had killed Aram and that they must not catch her. She saw the beam of a flashlight below, starting to move up the stairs, and her heart leaped. Rhys was coming for her. Elizabeth began to climb the tower stairs, and halfway up, her knees began to buckle. She slid to the floor and crawled the rest of the way on her hands and knees. She reached the top of the stairs and dragged herself upright. She opened the door to the tower room and went in. *The door*, Samuel said. *Lock the door*.

Elizabeth locked the door, but she knew that that would not keep Rhys out. At least, she thought, he will have to break it down. More violence to explain. Her death was going to look like murder. She pushed furniture against the door, moving slowly, as though the darkness were a heavy sea dragging her down. She pushed a table against the door, then an armchair and another table, working like an automaton, fighting for time, building her pitiable fortress against death. From the floor below she heard a crash and a moment later another and then a third. Rhys was breaking down the bedroom doors, looking for her. Signs of an attack, a trail for the police to follow. She had tricked him, as he had tricked her. Yet something was vaguely bothering her. If Rhys had to make her death look like an accident, why was he breaking down doors? She moved to the French doors and looked outside, listening to the mad wind singing a dirge to her. Beyond the balcony there was a sheer drop to the sea below. There was no escape from this room. This was where Rhys would have to come to get her. Elizabeth felt around for a weapon, but there was nothing that could help her.

She waited in the dark for her killer.

What was Rhys waiting for? Why didn't he break the door down and get it over with? *Break the door down.* Something was wrong. Even if he took her body away from here and disposed of it somewhere else, Rhys would still not be able to explain the violence of the house, the smashed mirror, the broken doors. Elizabeth tried to put herself into Rhys's mind, to figure out what plan he could have that would explain all those things without the police suspecting him of her death. There was only one way.

And even as Elizabeth thought of it, she could smell the smoke.

CHAPTER
56

From the helicopter Max could see the coast of Sardinia, thickly blanketed by a cloud of swirling red dust. The pilot shouted above the din of the rotor blades, "It's gotten worse. I don't know if I can land."

"You've got to!" Max yelled. "Head for Porto Cervo."

The pilot turned to look at Max. "That's at the top of a fucking mountain."

"I know," Max said. "Can you do it?"

"Our chances are about seventy–thirty."

"Which way?"

"Against."

The smoke was seeping in under the door, coming up from below through the floorboards, and a new sound had been added to the shrieking of the wind. The roar of flames. Elizabeth knew now, she had the answer, but it was too late to save her life. She was trapped here. Of course it did not matter whether doors and mirrors and furniture had been smashed, because in a few minutes nothing would be left of this house or of her. Everything would be ruined by the fire, as the laboratory and Emil Joeppli had been destroyed, and Rhys would have an alibi in some other place, so that he could not be blamed. He had beaten her. He had beaten them all.

The smoke was beginning to billow into the room now—yellow, acrid fumes that made Elizabeth choke. She could see the edges of flame start to lick at the cracks of the door, and she began to feel the heat.

It was her anger that gave Elizabeth the strength to move.

Through the blinding haze of smoke she felt her way toward the French doors. She pushed them open and stepped onto the balcony. The instant the doors opened, the flames from the hallway leaped into the room, licking at the walls. Elizabeth stood on the balcony, gratefully gulping in deep breaths of fresh air as the wind tore at her clothes. She looked down. The balcony protruded from the side of the building, a tiny island hanging over an abyss. There was no hope, no escape.

Unless . . . Elizabeth looked up at the sloping slate roof above her head. If there was some way for her to reach the roof and get to the other side of the house that was not burning yet, she might get away. She stretched her arms as high as she could, but the eave of the roof was beyond her reach. The flames were beginning to move closer now, enveloping the room. There was one slender chance. Elizabeth took it. She forced herself to go back into the blazing, smoke-filled room, choking from the acrid fumes. She grabbed the chair behind her father's desk and dragged it onto the balcony. Fighting to keep her balance, she positioned the chair and stood on top of it. Her fingers could reach the roof now, but they could not find a grip. She fumbled blindly, vainly, searching to get a purchase.

Inside, the flames had reached the curtains and were dancing all around the room, attacking the books and the carpet and the furniture, moving toward the balcony. Elizabeth's fingers suddenly found a grip on a protruding slate. Her arms were leaden; she was not sure she could hold on. She started to pull herself up, and the chair began to slip away from her. With her last remaining strength she pulled herself up and held on. She was climbing the walls of the ghetto now, fighting for her life. She kept pulling and straining and suddenly she found herself lying on the sloping roof, gasping for breath. She forced herself to move, inching her way upward, pressing her body hard against the steep pitch of the roof, aware that one slip would hurtle her into the black abyss below. She reached the peak of the roof and paused to catch her breath and take her bearings. The balcony she had just escaped from was blazing. There could be no turning back.

Looking down on the far side of the house, Elizabeth could see the balcony of one of the guest bedrooms. There were no flames there yet. But Elizabeth did not know whether she would be able to reach it. The roof slanted sharply downward, the slates were loose, the wind was pulling madly at her. If she slipped, there would be nothing to stop her fall. She stayed where she was, frozen, afraid to try it. And then, like a sudden miracle, a figure appeared on the guest balcony, and it was Alec, and he was looking up and calling out calmly, "You can make it, old girl. Nice and easy."

And Elizabeth's heart soared within her.

"Take it slow," Alec counseled. "One step at a time. It's a piece of cake."

And Elizabeth began to let herself move toward

him, carefully, sliding down inch by inch, not letting go of one slate until she had found a firm grip on another. It seemed to take forever. And all the while she heard Alec's encouraging voice, urging her on. She was almost there now, sliding toward the balcony. A slate loosened, and she started to fall.

"Hold on!" Alec called.

Elizabeth found another hold, grabbing it fiercely. She had reached the edge of the roof now, with nothing below her but endless space. She would have to drop down onto the balcony where Alec stood waiting. If she missed . . .

Alec was looking up at her, his face filled with quiet confidence. "Don't look down," he said. "Close your eyes, and let yourself go. I'll catch you."

She tried. She took a deep breath, and then another. She knew she had to let go and yet she could not bring herself to do it. Her fingers were frozen to the tiles.

"Now!" Alec called, and Elizabeth let herself drop and she was falling into space, and suddenly she was caught in Alec's arms as he pulled her to safety. She closed her eyes in relief.

"Well done," Alec said.

And she felt the muzzle of the gun against her head.

CHAPTER

57

The helicopter pilot was flying as low as he dared over the island, skimming the treetops, trying to avoid the punishing winds. Even at that altitude the air was filled with turbulence. In the distance ahead the pilot saw the mountain peak of Porto Cervo. Max saw it at the same moment. "There it is!" Max shouted. "I can see the villa." And then he saw something else that made his heart jump. "It's on fire!"

On the balcony Elizabeth heard the sound of the approaching helicopter over the wind, and she looked up. Alec paid no attention. He was watching Elizabeth, his eyes filled with pain. "It was for Vivian. I had to do it for Vivian. You see that, don't you? They have to find you in the fire."

Elizabeth was not listening. She could only think, *It wasn't Rhys. It wasn't Rhys.* All the time it had been Alec. Alec had killed her father and had tried to kill her. He had stolen the report and then tried to frame Rhys with it. He had terrified her into running away from Rhys because Alec had known that she would come here.

The helicopter had disappeared from sight now, beyond some nearby trees.

Alec said, "Close your eyes, Elizabeth."

She said fiercely, "No!"

And Rhys's voice suddenly called, "Drop the gun, Alec!"

They both looked down, and on the lawn below, in the light of the flickering flames, they saw Rhys and Chief of Police Luigi Ferraro and half a dozen detectives, armed with rifles.

"It's finished, Alec," Rhys shouted. "Let her go."

One of the detectives with a telescopic rifle said, "I can't shoot at him unless she moves out of the way."

Move, Rhys prayed. *Move!*

From behind the trees across the lawn Max Hornung came hurrying up to Rhys. He stopped as he saw the tableau above. Rhys said, "I got your message. I was too late."

They were both staring up at the two figures on the balcony, puppets, backlit by the rising flames coming from the far side of the villa. The wind was whipping the house into a gigantic torch, lighting the surrounding mountains, turning the night into an inferno, a blazing Valhalla.

Elizabeth turned and looked into Alec's face, and it was a mask of death, his eyes unseeing. He moved away from her toward the balcony door.

On the ground the detective said, "I've got him," and raised his rifle. He fired once. Alec staggered, then disappeared through the door into the house.

One moment there were two figures on the balcony, and then only one.

Elizabeth screamed, "Rhys!"

But he was already racing toward her.

Everything after that happened in a quick, confused kaleidoscope of motion. Rhys was picking her up and carrying her down to safety and she clung tightly to him and could not hold him close enough.

She was lying on the grass, with her eyes closed, and Rhys was holding her in his arms, saying, "I love you, Liz. I love you, my darling."

She listened to his voice washing over her, caressing her. She could not speak. She looked into his eyes and saw all the love and anguish, and there was so much she wanted to tell him. She was filled with guilt for all of her terrible suspicions. She would spend the rest of her life making it up to him.

She was too weary to think about it now, too weary to think about any of it. It was as though it had all happened to someone else in some other place, at some other time.

The only important thing was that she and Rhys were together. She felt his strong arms holding her close, forever, and it was enough.

and lly sank down beside her. He rubbed at his

CHAPTER
58

It was like stepping into a blazing corner of hell. The smoke was getting thicker, filling the room with dancing chimeras that kept vanishing. The fire leaped down at Alec, fondling his hair, and the crackle of the flames became Vivian's voice calling to him in an irresistible siren song.

In a sudden flare of brightness, he saw her. She was stretched out on the bed, her beautiful body naked except for the scarlet ribbon tied around her neck, the same red ribbon she had worn the first time he had made love to her. She called his name again, her voice filled with longing. And this time she wanted *him*, not the others. He moved closer, and she whispered, "You're the only one I ever loved."

And Alec believed it. He had had to punish her because of the things she had done. But he had been clever—he had made those others pay for her sins. The terrible things he had done had been for her. As he moved toward her, Vivian whispered again, "You're the only one I ever loved, Alec," and he knew that it was true.

She was holding out her beckoning arms to him, and he sank down beside her. He embraced her, and they became one. He was inside her, and he *was* her. And this time he was able to satisfy her. And he felt such pleasure that it became an exquisite pain beyond bearing. He could feel the heat from her body consuming him, and even as he watched in wonder, the ribbon around Vivian's neck turned into a vivid tongue of flame caressing him, licking at him. In the next instant, a blazing beam from the ceiling crashed on top of him in a fiery pyre.

Alec died as the others had. In ecstasy.

SIDNEY SHELDON

At the age of twenty-five, Sidney Sheldon had three hit musicals running simultaneously on Broadway. A producer and director as well as a writer, Mr. Sheldon has won an Oscar and a Tony for his work in motion pictures and the Broadway theater. His first novel, *The Naked Face*, was nominated for an Edgar and was acclaimed by *The New York Times* as the "best first mystery novel of the year." His following books, *The Other Side of Midnight* and *The Stranger in the Mirror*, have become international best sellers and have been read by over thirty million people.

There's an epidemic with 27 million victims. And no visible symptoms.

It's an epidemic of people who can't read.

Believe it or not, 27 million Americans are functionally illiterate, about one adult in five.

The solution to this problem is you...when you join the fight against illiteracy. So call the Coalition for Literacy at toll-free **1-800-228-8813** and volunteer.

Volunteer Against Illiteracy. The only degree you need is a degree of caring.

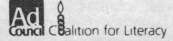

Ad Council   Coalition for Literacy

Warner Books is proud to be an active supporter of the Coalition for Literacy.